THE WORLD'S CLASSICS

RUDYARD KIPLING

Mrs Bathurst
and Other Stories

Selected with an Introduction by
JOHN BAYLEY

Edited and annotated by
LISA LEWIS

Oxford   New York
OXFORD UNIVERSITY PRESS
1991

Oxford University Press, Walton Street, Oxford OX2 6DP

Oxford New York Toronto
Delhi Bombay Calcutta Madras Karachi
Petaling Jaya Singapore Hong Kong Tokyo
Nairobi Dar es Salaam Cape Town
Melbourne Auckland

and associated companies in
Berlin Ibadan

Oxford is a trade mark of Oxford University Press

General Preface, Select Bibliography, Chronology
© *Andrew Rutherford 1987*

Introduction © *John Bayley 1991*
Explanatory Notes © *Lisa Lewis 1991*

First published by Oxford University Press as a World's Classics
paperback 1991

British Library Cataloguing in Publication Data
Kipling, Rudyard 1865–1936
Mrs. Bathurst: and other stories. - (The World's classics).
I. Title II. Bayley, John 1925– III. Lewis, Lisa IV. Series
823.912 [F]
ISBN 0–19–282217–9

Library of Congress Cataloging-in-Publication Data
Kipling, Rudyard, 1865–1936.
Mrs Bathurst and other stories / Rudyard Kipling; selected with an introduction by John
Bayley; edited and annotated by Lisa Lewis.
p. cm. — (The World's classics)
Includes bibliographical references.
I. Bayley, John, 1925– . II. Lewis, Lisa. III. Title. IV. Series.
PR4852 1991 823'.8—dc20 90–40117
ISBN 0–19–282217–9

Typeset by Pentacor plc.
Printed in Great Britain by
BPCC Hazell Books Ltd.
Aylesbury, Bucks

CONTENTS

MRS BATHURST AND OTHER STORIES

GENERAL PREFACE

RUDYARD KIPLING (1865–1936) was for the last decade of the nineteenth century and at least the first two decades of the twentieth the most popular writer in English, in both verse and prose, throughout the English-speaking world. Widely regarded as the greatest living English poet and story-teller, winner of the Nobel Prize for Literature, recipient of honorary degrees from the Universities of Oxford, Cambridge, Edinburgh, Durham, McGill, Strasbourg, and the Sorbonne, he also enjoyed popular acclaim that extended far beyond academic and literary circles.

He stood, it can be argued, in a special relation to the age in which he lived. He was primarily an artist, with his individual vision and techniques, but his was also a profoundly representative consciousness. He seems to give expression to a whole phase of national experience, symbolizing in appropriate forms (as Lascelles Abercrombie said the epic poet must do) the 'sense of the significance of life he [felt] acting as the unconscious metaphysic of the time'.[1] He is in important ways a spokesman for his age, with its sense of imperial destiny, its fascinated contemplation of the unfamiliar world of soldiering, its confidence in engineering and technology, its respect for craftsmanship, and its dedication to Carlyle's gospel of work. That age is one about which many Britons—and to a lesser extent Americans and West Europeans—now feel an exaggerated sense of guilt; and insofar as Kipling was its spokesman, he has become our scapegoat. Hence, in part at least, the tendency in recent decades to dismiss him so contemptuously, so unthinkingly, and so mistakenly. Whereas if we approach him more historically, less hysterically, we shall find in this very relation to his age a cultural phenomenon of absorbing interest.

Here, after all, we have the last English author to appeal to readers of all social classes and all cultural groups, from lowbrow to highbrow; and the last poet to command a mass audience. He was an author who could speak directly to the man in the street, or for that matter in the barrack-room or

[1] Cited in E. M. W. Tillyard, *The Epic Strain in the English Novel*, 1958, p. 15.

factory, more effectively than any left-wing writer of the 'thirties or the present day, but who spoke just as directly and effectively to literary men like Edmund Gosse and Andrew Lang; to academics like David Masson, George Saintsbury, and Charles Eliot Norton; to the professional and service classes (officers and other ranks alike) who took him to their hearts; and to creative writers of the stature of Henry James, who had some important reservations to record, but who declared in 1892 that 'Kipling strikes me personally as the most complete man of genius (as distinct from fine intelligence) that I have ever known', and who wrote an enthusiastic introduction to *Mine Own People* in which he stressed Kipling's remarkable appeal to the sophisticated critic as well as to the common reader.[2]

An innovator and a virtuoso in the art of the short story, Kipling does more than any of his predecessors to establish it as a major genre. But within it he moves confidently between the poles of sophisticated simplicity (in his earliest tales) and the complex, closely organized, elliptical and symbolic mode of his later works which reveal him as an unexpected contributor to modernism.

He is a writer who extends the range of English literature in both subject-matter and technique. He plunges readers into new realms of imaginative experience which then become part of our shared inheritance. His anthropological but warmly human interest in mankind in all its varieties produces, for example, sensitive, sympathetic vignettes of Indian life and character which culminate in *Kim*. His sociolinguistic experiments with proletarian speech as an artistic medium in *Barrack-Room Ballads* and his rendering of the life of private soldiers in all their unregenerate humanity gave a new dimension to war literature. His portrayal of Anglo-Indian life ranges from cynical triviality in some of the *Plain Tales from the Hills* to the stoical nobility of the best things in *Life's Handicap* and *The Day's Work*. Indeed Mrs Hauksbee's Simla, Mulvaney's barrack-rooms, Dravot and Carnehan's search for a kingdom in KaWristan, Holden's illicit, star-crossed love, Stalky's apprenticeship, Kim's Grand Trunk Road, 'William' 's famine

---

[2] See *Kipling: The Critical Heritage*, ed. Roger Lancelyn Green, London, 1971, pp. 159-60. *Mine own People*, published in New York in 1891, was a collection of stories nearly all of which were to be subsumed in *Life's Handicap* later that year.

relief expedition, and the Maltese Cat's game at Umballa, establish the vanished world of Empire for us (as they established the unknown world of Empire for an earlier generation), in all its pettiness and grandeur, its variety and energy, its miseries, its hardships, and its heroism.

In a completely different vein Kipling's genius for the animal fable as a means of inculcating human truths opens up a whole new world of joyous imagining in the two *Jungle Books*. In another vein again are the stories in which he records his delighted discovery of the English countryside, its people and traditions, after he had settled at Bateman's in Sussex: England, he told Rider Haggard in 1902, 'is the most wonderful foreign land I have ever been in'[3]; and he made it peculiarly his own. Its past gripped his imagination as strongly as its present, and the two books of Puck stories show what Eliot describes as 'the development of the imperial . . . into the historical imagination.'[4] In another vein again he figures as the bard of engineering and technology. From the standpoint of world history, two of Britain's most important areas of activity in the nineteenth century were those of industrialism and imperialism, both of which had been neglected by literature prior to Kipling's advent. There is a substantial body of work on the Condition of England Question and the socio-economic effects of the Industrial Revolution; but there is comparatively little imaginative response in literature (as opposed to painting) to the extraordinary inventive energy, the dynamic creative power, which manifests itself in (say) the work of engineers like Telford, Rennie, Brunel, and the brothers Stephenson—men who revolutionized communications within Britain by their road, rail and harbour systems, producing in the process masterpieces of industrial art, and who went on to revolutionize ocean travel as well. Such achievements are acknowledged on a sub-literary level by Samuel Smiles in his best-selling *Lives of the Engineers* (1861–2). They are acknowledged also by Carlyle, who celebrates the positive as well as denouncing the malign aspects of the transition from the feudal to the industrial world, insisting as he does that the true modern epic must be technological, not military: 'For we are to bethink us that the Epic

3 *Rudyard Kipling to Rider Haggard*, ed. Morton Cohen, London, 1965, p. 51.
4 T. S. Eliot, *On Poetry and Poets*, London, 1957, p. 247.

verily is not *Arms and the Man*, but *Tools and the Man*,—an
infinitely wider kind of Epic.'[5] That epic has never been written
in its entirety, but Kipling came nearest to achieving its aims
in verses like 'McAndrew's Hymn' (*The Seven Seas*) and stories
like 'The Ship that Found Herself' and 'Bread upon the
Waters' (*The Day's Work*) in which he shows imaginative
sympathy with the machines themselves as well as sympathy
with the men who serve them. He comes nearer, indeed, than
any other author to fulfilling Wordsworth's prophecy that

If the labours of men of Science should ever create any material
revolution, direct or indirect, in our condition, and in the impressions
which we habitually receive, the Poet will sleep then no more than at
present, but he will be ready to follow the steps of the Man of Science,
not only in those general indirect effects, but he will be at his side,
carrying sensation into the midst of the objects of the Science
itself.[6]

This is one aspect of Kipling's commitment to the world of
work, which, as C. S. Lewis observes, 'imaginative literature
in the eighteenth and nineteenth centuries had [with a few
exceptions] quietly omitted, or at least thrust into the background', though it occupies most of the waking hours of most
men:

And this did not merely mean that certain technical aspects of life were
unrepresented. A whole range of strong sentiments and emotions—for
many men, the strongest of all—went with them. . . . It was Kipling
who first reclaimed for literature this enormous territory.[7]

He repudiates the unspoken assumption of most novelists
that the really interesting part of life takes place outside working
hours: men at work or talking about their work are among his
favourite subjects. The qualities men show in their work, and
the achievements that result from it (bridges built, ships sal-
vaged, pictures painted, famines relieved) are the very stuff of
much of Kipling's fiction. Yet there also runs through his *œuvre*,
like a figure in the carpet, a darker, more pessimistic vision of
the impermanence, the transience—but not the worthless-
ness—of all achievement. This underlies his delighted engage-

5 *Past and Present* (1843), Book iv, ch.1. Cf. ibid., Book iii, ch. 5.
6 *Lyrical Ballads*, ed. R. L. Brett and A. R. Jones, London, 1963, pp. 253-4.
7 'Kipling's World', *Literature and Life: Addresses to the English Association*, London,
1948, pp. 59-60.

ment with contemporary reality and gives a deeper resonance
to his finest work, in which human endeavour is celebrated
none the less because it must ultimately yield to death and
mutability.

ANDREW RUTHERFORD

INTRODUCTION

KIPLING wrote both poems and stories. That much is obvious, but if we take a closer look at what it implies the odder does the fact become. In terms of literary genius practising a given form Kipling's achievement is very rare. Pushkin, Russia's great primary creator and poet, wrote poems and stories and novels too, in each case exploring what a particular form seemed best for. So, in his own way, did Sir Walter Scott. Such multifold creativity seems characteristic of the years after the Romantic Revival, when impulse and spontaneity expressed themselves as their urge required.

Kipling had his 'Daemon' as he called it: the spirit which he said took over when he wrote. In his personal memoir, *Something of Myself*, he uses a nautical metaphor—'as one hung in the wind, waiting'—for the time the writer sat at his desk and the inner afflatus did not come. It is not unlike Coleridge's image of the Aeolian lyre, waiting for the divine breezes to play upon it. Kipling very definitely had his romantic side and his vision of the artist, not only craftsman and spokesman for his tribe but inspired from within to preach to them as well.

In the last decades of the nineteenth century, at the height of Britain's imperial expansion and power, how was this best to be done? The novel was the great nineteenth-century form—Balzac, Dickens, George Eliot, Tolstoy—but by the 1870s and 1880s its great achievement already seemed to have gone by. In any case, something in Kipling knew, must have known—perhaps it was the Daemon?—that he was not cut out to be a novelist. He was to try several times to become one in his own fashion, but always seemed to lack the inner will to complete the form on its own massive terms, as Henry James and Conrad would set themselves to do.

No, he was a poet and a story-teller, and this combination was in one sense a romantic legacy, something which had come naturally to Wordsworth and to Keats (one of Kipling's later stories 'Wireless', was to be an ingenious gloss on 'The Eve of St Agnes') as well as to Tennyson and Browning. Reading Browning at school was a revelation to Kipling. He adored the way the poet created story situations, dramatic monologues of men and women. He refers to him several times in his own school stories, *Stalky & Co.*, and in *Something of Myself*. He was fascinated by the way in which Browning seized a moment of time which revealed a whole way of life or of thought, an instant history of habit, or manners, or expectation. This could and would be done by the Daemon, either in verse or in prose. Portraying the individual as a type in a historical or social organism was something that had been done, in their own spacious and leisurely way, by Scott and Balzac, but now it was to be carried out by Kipling with dazzling swiftness, for maximum impact on the reader.

Many examples could be given of his excitement at the process. Beetle, who is the young Kipling in *Stalky & Co.*, is thrilled by Browning's lightning reference, in the poem that begins 'What's become of Waring', to the assassination by his generals of Tsar Paul of Russia; how they move towards him over the pavement glowing with inlaid marbles, 'serpentine and syenite', unobtrusively removing their silk sashes to strangle their master. Kipling's genius feeds on the colour and the detail, and on Browning's casually knowledgeable comment that a scarf is better for the job than a steel chain, because it leaves no trace on the dead man. Kipling with his natural taste for violence, the taste of many eager, clever, and curious boys, would have avidly noted that.

Browning may draw conclusions and point morals but he often leaves the facts to speak for themselves. Further emphasizing and dramatizing the technique in his own way, Kipling too seeks to stun and enlighten the reader through the facts; but the very stress he lays on them, and the force with which he draws them to our attention, indicate the lesson about life and society he wishes to drive home. Once we *realize* what things are like—how a soldier feels in battle, how a civil servant feels about his work, a farmer about his hedges, a galley-slave about his oar—we shall see and feel more clearly how the fabric of human relation and organization must be maintained.

This was Kipling's tactic and aim in everything he wrote, and it is an impressive one. It makes him the great writer he is. But it is also one source of his unpopularity, and of the dislike which many sensible and discerning people have felt for him over the years. Kipling is in a sense his own worst enemy. The very skill and vividness with which he operates, in the brief span of story or poem, may cause his reader to feel that he is being conned, that this brilliance is all sleight of hand. Of course from one point of view it is, and must be; but Kipling's character and method gives him no time—the time that a novelist would have—to correct the impression or qualify the verdict. The good sense, the sanity, the very deep and earnest belief which underlie Kipling's stories, are sometimes hidden by the brilliance of the surface effect, which itself can create a false impression.

What it is really like to be there—to understand how the people felt who were there—and to show this in a few mesmeric words and paragraphs . . . Yes, it is clear the method has its dangers. The paradox of too much 'reality' is that it can produce its opposite: the result can be in its own way quite unreal. This double effect, as it were, is well known to Kipling addicts, who find themselves simultaneously mesmerized by the vividness of the tale—its overwhelming authenticity of place, people, culture—and at the same time projected into a world which is entirely Kipling's, and thus quite unlike any other place, real or imagined. Critics of the Structuralist school who have taken an interest in his stories have done so, I suspect, for this reason: it justifies their emphasis on 'textuality' and 'literariness', their argument that a work of literature creates its own world out of literary devices.

In practice Kipling's readers, and those who enjoy his art the most, have no difficulty in reconciling his own special kind of literariness with recognition of the factual and social truth in what he tells them. As with many really good authors we have to learn how to read him, a complex and intensely rewarding process. The paradox in his art is what we come to look out for, to savour and to admire. Here is one instance of it. In an analysis of English prose style, Herbert Read took exception to the opening sentences of one of Kipling's Indian stories, 'Love-o'-Women'. A sergeant with the British army in India has just shot a corporal who has been making love to his wife. Kipling as narrator then arrives on the scene.

The horror, the confusion, and the separation of the murderer from his comrades were all over before I came. There remained only on the barrack square the blood of man calling from the ground. The hot sun had dried it to a dusky goldbeater-skin film, cracked lozenge-wise by the heat; and as the wind rose, each lozenge, rising a little, curled up at the edges as if it were a dumb tongue.

Herbert Read very pertinently asks if anyone saw, or could have seen, those dumb tongues made by the dried blood. The answer is probably no, but that does not matter. What does matter is the extraordinary way in which Kipling has fused a mesmerically visual detail with a Bible injunction known to all; and thrust both into his totally realized setting: the heat of India, the strain, the boredom, the killing routine which the soldiers have to operate in these conditions. These are home truths the reader takes in unknowingly, but they are only taken in so completely because of the way in which Kipling sets up the scene, and the way his descriptive images pitchfork the reader into the midst of it.

A memorable although a less good tale than 'Love-o'-Women' works in a similar way. The setting of 'At the End of the Passage' is an Indian construction camp in the hot weather, where four British government servants, an engineer, a doctor, an administrator, and a political agent, meet from time to time to exchange news and play cards. Again what matters is the awful claustrophobia of the life, the loneliness, the crushing burden of work and heat. These things Kipling makes fully known to us. But he also throws in, as it were, an Edgar Allan Poe type horror motif: the thing which can be seen in the eye of a dead man, one of the four, who has died in a terror of nightmare and insomnia. The terror is real, and Kipling makes it so, adding the purely literary artifice from the genre of ghost story in order to clinch the deal with his reader.

The reader does not always receive the message so involuntarily of course. One of the finest of the Indian tales is about Kipling's 'Soldiers Three', Mulvaney, Ortheris, and Learoyd. In 'On Greenhow Hill' an artful framework is set up, in which the three lie all day in the Himalayan pines to get a shot at a deserter from an Indian regiment. They speculate about his reasons for deserting, and Learoyd tells the tale of the love affair which caused him to enlist in the army. Well and good. But Kipling cannot persuade us that the three would talk and reminisce as they do, in spite of his clever contriving of dialect and accent, in the use of which he became more unobtrusively expert the more stories he wrote. Mulvaney is emphatically not a stage Irishman, but he begins here to sound like one ('Fwhy is ut?' said Mulvaney . . . 'In the name of God, fwhy is ut?') when he is expounding on behalf of Kipling views about the bad treatment of the British soldier by ignorant civilians and starchy Low Church folk back home. The story is a remarkable mixture of the wonderfully true (Learoyd's comment on the recruiting sergeant's advice to forget his sweetheart—'I've been forgetting her ever since') and the palpably false or at least contrived: the men's coming together on the Indian hill and the set-up for the shooting of the deserter. But Kipling makes us feel his art decrees that we cannot have one without the other, that the two somehow work hand in hand and increase each other's kind of effectiveness.

A judicious combination of the fantastic and the factual is the oldest recipe for tale-telling. In our day it has been re-christened 'Magic Realism' and practised successfully by many writers, some South American, like García Márquez of *A Hundred Years of Solitude*. They learnt from Kipling as from Hemingway, and Hemingway himself learnt much from Kipling. Another who acknowledged the debt was the French writer Albert Camus, whose famous story 'The Outsider' has a great deal of Kipling magic and obsession in it, recast in the Existentialist mould. A later story, 'The Growing Stone', a re-enactment of the road to Calvary in modern Brazil, is obviously close to Kipling's own later investigations and allegories on a religious theme, of which 'The Manner of Men', in this selection, is an example. Camus is both more insistent and more portentous than Kipling. But there was a time when Kipling was held in much greater respect by intellectuals, particularly in France and Italy, than he has ever been in his own country.

I have mentioned 'On Greenhow Hill', one of the finest of Kipling's earlier stories, as characteristic of his method; and of foreshadowing the way he deepens and complicates that method in later tales such as 'Mrs Bathurst' and 'Mary Postgate'. A reader may get the impression that Kipling became almost slyly aware, as a technician, of the way the method functions; and that he deliberately exaggerates in such stories the relation of fact to fantasy. Certainly the later tales can be very enigmatic indeed, fascinatingly so: and they have provoked a great deal of critical speculation. Was Mrs Bathurst herself the second tramp who is found incinerated in the forest at the end of the tale?—how could she have been? Did Mary Postgate really find a wounded German airman at the end of the garden shrubbery, or was it—and were her subsequent actions—all an illusion fed by bereavement, frustrated love, and hatred for the Germans? There is no answer of course, and Kipling does not intend there should be; for what matters is the power of the stories in conveying what it means to *be* Mary Postgate in her place and time, or in 'Mrs Bathurst', what it means to be a wanderer over all the seas of the world in the Royal Navy, perhaps making contact briefly and irrevocably with a widow in a little New Zealand town, a passion and a haunting which crops up again beside South African sand-dunes, or on a railway platform at Paddington.

Kipling deliberately provokes the question: where's the truth hiding in this? and he does this for the story to show the quieter, less obtrusive truth which lies under the mesmeric and compelling surface effect. As he says in a poem about a story-teller, his embroideries and djinns may make 'a miraculous weaving | But the cool and perspicuous eye overbore unbelieving'. The point is the story, and after the story the impression it has left. As he tells us in *Something of Myself* he used to go through his manuscript with pen and indian ink, blacking things out, so that nothing remained that would give things away. The compulsion of his detail, however copious and arresting, depends upon omission. The catalogue of the dead young nephew's possessions, in 'Mary Postgate', is so exhaustive in its pathos that it almost makes the reader weep; but it serves to convince him, too, of the reality of Mary's delusion, and of the improbable appearance of the wounded German airman. Within the compulsive framework of the story Kipling can 'overbear unbelieving' in his character and his reader alike, and relates the two more closely in so doing.

In an earlier story from *Many Inventions* (1893) Kipling sets out to present the past through a bank clerk who recalls previous incarnations as a galley slave and as a Viking explorer. The atmosphere of the tale is not entirely serious, as if Kipling were well aware of his own impudence in presenting his own imagination of the past as the total recall of a man who had actually been there. The secret is a detail which the reader instantly recognizes as 'true', because it comes within the field of his own experience, and which is then ingeniously blended with other details wholly made up. Introducing his selection of Kipling's poems, T. S. Eliot expressed admiration for these 'true' details ('Can't you imagine', says the clerk, 'the sunlight just squeezing through between the handle and the hole and wobbling about as the ship moves') and for the way in which Kipling 'invents' them. He was to pursue the same tactic in the stories which make up *Puck of Pook's Hill* and *Rewards and Fairies*, inventing characters who can speak with the negligence of total authenticity about the era they belong to.

The method has been perfected in 'The Manner of Men', from Kipling's last collection, *Limits and Renewals* (1932).

Her cinnabar-tinted topsail, nicking the hot blue horizon, showed she was a Spanish wheat-boat hours before she reached Marseilles mole. There, her mainsail brailed itself, a spritsail broke out forward, and a handy driver aft; and she threaded her way through the shipping to her berth at the quay as quietly as a veiled woman slips through a bazaar.

Bemused by the sheer virtuosity of this opening, the reader must pick up what he can from the talk between the three sailors of the story, and although Kipling is very cunning in introducing touches about St Paul's journey, it is far less easy to follow what happens than it is with 'On Greenhow Hill', where the three soldiers seem to be talking more for the reader's benefit than their own. But the figure of Paul comes over all the more impressively from the way the story is told, with the extra ambiguity—typical of Kipling's later manner—that Paul's confidence that God will save the lives of crew and passengers is fortunately underpinned by the skill and experience of the Tyrian shipmaster. The dialogue in 'Mrs Bathurst' is even more obscure, and more suggestive, because the speakers themselves do not understand just what situation it is that they are dealing with.

Mrs Bathurst is indeed one of the stories most argued about by Kipling's critics, and I have not the space to discuss their many and ingenious explanations of its puzzle. Is the puzzle perhaps the point?—that is to say, does the effectiveness of the story lie in suggestion and atmosphere rather than in a complex solution? Like the false teeth in the waistcoat-pocket, Mrs Bathurst is never shown to us: she exists only in other minds, and in the fates of the other characters. But the heroine whom we never meet is certainly one of the most haunting Kipling ever created.

That Kipling is capable of great and moving simplicity, as well as complication, is shown by such a story as 'The Gardener'. There is no question here of the cunning build-up which lies behind the factual prose of 'Mary Postgate'. But the same powerful emergence of theme takes place, as if involuntarily, and hinting again at Kipling's Daemon working in the background. The terrible cemeteries of Flanders, with their miles of raw headstones and new plants, seem in secret but natural collusion with the shifts and hypocrisies of conventional existence. To both the image of the gardener comes as one of healing and silent sanity, although it is typical of Kipling's tendency to overdo things—he can even overdo understatement—that the gardener should regard Helen Turrell 'with infinite compassion', a phrase which in revision should have been given the indian ink treatment. And yet it makes no difference to the story's power to move.

There is overkill again in 'They'—the perfect house, the perfect motor, the perfect ghosts—but the story is again deeply moving, centring on the detail of 'the little brushing kiss' in the centre of the narrator's palm as it hangs down behind his chair. The ghost in 'The Wish House' is truly frightening, although the theme of great and self-sacrificing love in that story perhaps does not entirely convince. It is too overt: whereas in 'The Gardener' and 'They' the theme creeps gradually and naturally out of the tale's hypnotic grip upon us. The same can hardly be said of 'Dayspring Mishandled', the culmination of the many tales in which Kipling gave its head to his native passion for elaborate revenges and practical jokes. Overkill here is itself

the secret source of jest, for instead of the hilarious denouement
aimed at by the practical joker when his trap is sprung, the story
ends on an empty note, a bitter and mysterious anti-climax.
What is Manallace's motive in perjuring himself 'explicitly' to
Lady Castorley? Can he not bear to abandon his life's work,
even though the motive for exposure has gone? As in 'Mrs
Bathurst' the unsolved puzzle is the story's point, or at least its
dynamic. Its hidden subject is not so much the profitlessness
of revenge as the ultimate sadness of a life gone wrong, a
sadness summed up in the inspired, pseudo-Chaucerian poetry
of the title.

There has been much speculation among academic critics
about 'Dayspring Mishandled', as about 'Mrs Bathurst' and
the other puzzle stories. Certainly Kipling lodges clues, but his
intent may be that we should find and be fascinated by them,
rather than that they contain a solution. 'Dayspring Mishandled' is indeed a joke, although a joke of a different kind
from the 'hilarious' one in the earlier story called 'The Village
that Voted the Earth was Flat'; but it may be a joke both at the
expense of the reader and of the author too. Like Castorley,
the good reader is both credulous and curious: he invites the
working on him of the elaborate trick of art. That fascinated
Kipling too; and in addition he appears to have known all about
the elaborate forgery of the Piltdown Skull, whose 'discovery',
not far from where he lived in Sussex, had excited and misled
all the scientists. Manallace has much of Kipling in him, for
Kipling too took great pleasure in the kind of inspiration that
comes from imitation, as it appears among other things in his
admirable versions of Horace's Odes. 'Regulus' is a tribute to
Horace and to his undiminished appeal, even amongst the
barbarian young; as 'The Janeites' is a testimony to the novelist's power of engrossing and cheering the common reader,
even in the most trying circumstances.

There is certainly a kind of slyness in what Kipling writes of
Manallace. 'Given written or verbal outlines of a plot, he was
useless; but, with half a dozen pictures round which to write
his tale, he could astonish.' That is a highly accurate self-de-
scription. It reminds us, too, of the joke against himself which
is lurking in that early tale, 'The Finest Story in the World', in
which the writer exults in having tapped in the young clerk who

can remember his past lives a source for 'material to make my tale sure—so sure that the world would hail it an impudent and vamped fiction'. All that Charlie the bank clerk can and does provide are 'pictures', immensely vivid details round which to write a tale that never gets written, rather as Kipling never got around to writing the longer work he refers to rather wistfully in *Something of Myself*, using the metaphor of a fine, soundly-timbered ship he had never managed to build. Even in that memoir he plays tricks on the reader, referring in the last sentence to the Imperial air route to India and Australia which came into existence 'before my death'. The reader hardly takes that in at first, but when he does it is with a slight shock. Kipling is writing as if posthumously: the book will not appear until after his death, and even then will reveal no secrets about him. As he put it straightforwardly in his poem 'The Appeal', 'Seek not to question other than | The books I leave behind'.

That we can do. But, as with all true art, we can never explain them completely. Kipling's ultimate tactic is to flourish his devices before us and let us, as it were, run after them, rather as the toreadors run after the wise bull in his story 'The Bull that Thought'. Something in him—the Daemon perhaps—seems well aware that what he writes is a show-off, to fascinate, excite, and mislead. Kipling's tales, the later ones more especially, are a singular case—perhaps a unique one—of didactic art concealing its grave and healing simplicity by a tremendous show of cleverness. All the apparatus, all the bad taste and brutality even, are in a queer way a form of reticence. The parallel with Browning is again instructive. Henry James was deeply intrigued by what he felt to be the two Brownings: the anonymous, inexplicable poet, and the bustling, talkative, all too comprehensible man. Something rather the same occurs with Kipling, and with our sense of him. He has no reticence in the sense that Conrad, or Proust, or James himself, have it. Theirs is the reticence of a novelist, who has his big book to get behind. Kipling, without space, length, or weight, does the opposite. He rushes about gesticulating. Not for nothing did he admire General Booth of the Salvation Army, as we learn from *Something of Myself*, for saying that he would play a tambourine with his toes if it would draw one soul to the Lord. And clearly he came to feel the same kind of admiration for St

Paul, whom he presents in the poem at the end of 'The Manner of Men' as praying at his execution to be restored to himself, ceasing to be 'all things to all men'. Like General Booth, or St Paul, the artist gives vent to anything that will help his art, even baring his soul, or seeming to.

One wonders if Kipling knew that his Baldwin nephew called 'Mary Postgate' 'the wickedest story in the world', and if so what he would have felt about that. His admirers and apologists often point out that it is a dramatic tale, like a dramatic monologue; that it explores a certain kind of person, a female nature, and shows what a horrible effect war can have on her. That won't quite do. There is no doubt that Kipling himself is involved in the tale to the hilt: otherwise it would not have the impact that it has. If it were a *conte cruel*, in French style, it would be really distasteful, but Kipling is letting his own wickedness out, in a manner that will ultimately indicate to the reader how wicked wickedness is. As James's Prince remarks to his wife in *The Golden Bowl*, 'Everything is dark, Cara, in the heart of man'. We don't know what we are capable of until we have done it, or thought it, or wished it. Kipling and his readers are in the same boat here, which makes the story so uncomfortable. T. S. Eliot remarked that his mind didn't like to examine Kipling's too closely: but saying that in fact implies a furtive look already taken into the dark of both minds—Kipling's and his own. So art *can* do its work and convey its message.

But what is the message here? In one sense it is made very explicit in the brief poem which follows the story, and seems to act as commentary and conclusion. It is a shocking little poem, more shocking than the story even, and it has a 'voice' in it, not Kipling's voice, at least not by intention, but that of the English people, who have begun, for the first time in their history, to hate their enemies for the barbarous things they have done.

> Their voices were even and low,
> Their eyes were level and straight.
> There was neither sign nor show,
> When the English began to hate.

The explosive little poem certainly imitates that demeanour very convincingly. Kipling seems to be easing himself in it, as the art of the story would not let him do as he wrote it. Even after more than seventy years the sense of proximity, to him and to the events suggested here, is frightening.

Edmund Wilson called the poems which succeed the stories 'a tasteless device'. It can certainly be a jarring one. But it can give us a look into the way Kipling's powers work. The poem at the end of 'The Gardener' is like a cry of anguish, and deeply moving: that at the end of 'Mary Postgate' seems to breathe intense hatred through compressed lips. Whether this is Kipling or his Daemon there is no doubt of the feelings involved. The stories, by contrast, are models of quietude and restraint. Kipling had been reading Jane Austen to his family, as some relief from the war news, and the art in 'Mary Postgate' is clearly modelled on hers. The value of contrast is obvious, but even more striking is the alternation between what the story implies and what the poem says. There are moments in Kipling, as A. O. J. Cockshut so well puts it in his introduction to the World's Classics edition of *Life's Handicap*, when 'his cleverness, his simplicity and his feeling are at one'. But there are also moments when each is the more striking, more impressive, more unnerving even, by contrast with the others; and this is true of many of the best among his later tales.

NOTE ON THE TEXT

THE text of the stories, with two exceptions, is taken from the Uniform Edition in which they were first collected in the United Kingdom. The first exception is 'Proofs of Holy Writ'; this was written too late for inclusion in *Limits and Renewals*, the last of the general collections to be published. 'Proofs' appears in book form only in *Uncollected Prose*, vols. xxx and xxiii respectively of the posthumous Sussex and Burwash editions, the text that has been used for it here. ' "Teem": a Treasure-Hunter', first published in the month of Kipling's death, was collected in *Thy Servant a Dog and other Dog Stories* (Library Edition), as well as in Sussex/Burwash *Uncollected Prose*. There are no textual variants of this story in *Strand Magazine*, Doubleday's US copyright edition, the Library or Sussex/Burwash.

All the stories had their original publication in magazines; particulars of these will be found in the Explanatory Notes. Important textual changes have also been noted. A few misprints and minor slips in the collected texts have been silently corrected, as most of them were in the Sussex/Burwash version, the corrections being carried over to subsequent reprints in the Library and Centenary editions.

The assistance of Dr Gillian Sheehan, MB and Group Captain P. H. T. Lewis, RAF (Retd.) in the compilation of the notes is gratefully acknowledged. Thanks are also due to Mr G. H. Newsom, QC and the Librarian of the Commercial Union Assurance Co. Ltd., who helped on points of law and insurance history; to Professor Peter Parsons and Dr R. B. Rutherford of Christ Church, Oxford, who with Dr Bruce Barker-Benfield of the Department of Western Manuscripts, Bodleian Library, together decoded Kipling's 'monkish hymn'; and to Mr G. L'E. Turner of the Museum of the History of Science, Oxford, who answered a query about early microscopes. *The Reader's Guide* (see Select Bibliography) has been a useful source, especially Rear-Admiral P. W. Brock's notes on 'Mrs Bathurst' and Roger Lancelyn Green's on 'Regulus'.

None of these experts is responsible for any slips that may have been made in compiling notes from the information they provided.

SELECT BIBLIOGRAPHY

THE standard bibliography is J. McG. Stewart's *Rudyard Kipling: A Bibliographical Catalogue*, ed. A. W. Yeats (1959). Reference may also be made to two earlier works: Flora V. Livingston's *Bibliography of the Works of Rudyard Kipling* (1927) with its *Supplement* (1938), and Lloyd H. Chandler's *Summary of the Work of Rudyard Kipling, Including Items ascribed to Him* (1930). We still await a bibliography which will take account of the findings of modern scholarship over the last quarter-century.

The official biography, authorized by Kipling's daughter Elsie, is Charles Carrington's *Rudyard Kipling: His Life and Work* (1955; 3rd edn., revised, 1978). Other full-scale biographies are Lord Birkenhead's *Rudyard Kipling* (1978) and Angus Wilson's *The Strange Ride of Rudyard Kipling* (1977). Briefer, copiously illustrated surveys are provided by Martin Fido's *Rudyard Kipling* (1974) and Kingsley Amis's *Rudyard Kipling and his World* (1975), which combine biography and criticism, as do the contributions to *Rudyard Kipling: the man, his work and his world* (also illustrated), ed. John Gross (1972). Information on particular periods of his life is also to be found in such works as A. W. Baldwin, *The Macdonald Sisters* (1960); Alice Macdonald Fleming (*née* Kipling), 'Some Childhood Memories of Rudyard Kipling' and 'More Childhood Memories of Rudyard Kipling', *Chambers Journal*, 8th series, vol. 8 (1939); L. C. Dunsterville, *Stalky's Reminiscences* (1928); G. C. Beresford, *Schooldays with Kipling* (1936); E. Kay Robinson, 'Kipling in India', *McClure's Magazine*, vol. 7 (1896); Edmonia Hill, 'The Young Kipling', *Atlantic Monthly*, vol. 157 (1936); *Kipling's Japan*, ed. Hugh Cortazzi and George Webb (1988); H. C. Rice, *Rudyard Kipling in New England* (1936); Frederic Van de Water, *Rudyard Kipling's Vermont Feud* (1937); Julian Ralph, *War's Brighter Side* (1901); Angela Thirkell, *Three Houses* (1931); *Rudyard Kipling to Rider Haggard: The Record of a Friendship*, ed. Morton Cohen (1965); and *'O Beloved Kids': Rudyard Kipling's Letters to his Children*, ed. Elliot L. Gilbert (1983). Useful background on the India he knew is provided by 'Philip Woodruff' (Philip Mason) in *The Men Who Ruled India* (1954), and by Pat Barr and Ray Desmond in their illustrated *Simla: A Hill Station in British India* (1978). Kipling's own autobiography, *Something of Myself* (1937), is idiosyncratic but indispensable.

The early reception of Kipling's work is usefully documented in *Kipling: The Critical Heritage*, ed. Roger Lancelyn Green (1971). Richard Le Gallienne's *Rudyard Kipling: A Criticism* (1900), Cyril

Falls's *Rudyard Kipling: A Critical Study* (1915), André Chevrillon's *Three Studies in English Literature* (1923) and *Rudyard Kipling* (1936), Edward Shanks's *Rudyard Kipling: A Study in Literature and Political Ideas* (1940), and Hilton Brown's *Rudyard Kipling: A New Appreciation* (1945) were all serious attempts at reassessment; while Ann M. Weygandt's study of *Kipling's Reading and Its Influence on His Poetry* (1939), and (in more old-fashioned vein) Ralph Durand's *Handbook to the Poetry of Rudyard Kipling* (1914) remain useful pieces of scholarship.

T. S. Eliot's introduction to *A Choice of Kipling's Verse* (1941; see *On Poetry and Poets*, 1957) began a period of more sophisticated reappraisal. There are influential essays by Edmund Wilson (1941; see *The Wound and the Bow*), George Orwell (1942; see his *Critical Essays*, 1946), Lionel Trilling (1943; see *The Liberal Imagination*, 1951), W. H. Auden (1943; see *New Republic*, vol. 109), and C. S. Lewis (1948; see *They Asked for a Paper*, 1962). These were followed by a series of important book-length studies which include J. M. S. Tompkins, *The Art of Rudyard Kipling* (1959); C. A. Bodelsen, *Aspects of Kipling's Art* (1964); Roger Lancelyn Green, *Kipling and the Children* (1965); Louis L. Cornell, *Kipling in India* (1966); and Bonamy Dobrée, *Rudyard Kipling: Realist and Fabulist* (1967), which follows on from his earlier studies in *The Lamp and the Lute* (1929) and *Rudyard Kipling* (1951). There were also two major collections of critical essays: *Kipling's Mind and Art*, ed. Andrew Rutherford (1964), with essays by W. L. Renwick, Edmund Wilson, George Orwell, Lionel Trilling, Noel Annan, George Shepperson, Alan Sandison, the editor himself, Mark Kinkead-Weekes, J. H. Fenwick, and W. W. Robson; and *Kipling and the Critics*, ed. Elliot L. Gilbert (1965), with essays, parodies, etc. by Andrew Lang, Oscar Wilde, Henry James, Robert Buchanan, Max Beerbohm, Bonamy Dobrée, Boris Ford, George Orwell, Lionel Trilling, C. S. Lewis, T. S. Eliot, J. M. S. Tompkins, Randall Jarrell, Steven Marcus, and the editor himself. Nirad C. Chaudhuri's essay on *Kim* as 'The Finest Story about India—in English' (1957) is reprinted in John Gross's collection (see above); and Andrew Rutherford's lecture 'Some Aspects of Kipling's Verse' (1965) appears in the *Proceedings of the British Academy* for that year.

Other recent studies devoted in whole or in part to Kipling include Richard Faber, *The Vision and the Need: Late Victorian Imperialist Aims* (1966); T. R. Henn, *Kipling* (1967); Alan Sandison, *The Wheel of Empire* (1967); Herbert L. Sussman, *Victorians and the Machine: The Literary Response to Technology* (1968); P. J. Keating, *The Working Classes in Victorian Fiction* (1971); Elliot L. Gilbert, *The Good Kipling: Studies in the Short Story* (1972); Jeffrey Meyers, *Fiction and the Colonial Experience* (1972); Shamsul Islam, *Kipling's 'Law'* (1975); J. S. Bratton,

The Victorian Popular Ballad (1975); Philip Mason, *Kipling: The Glass, The Shadow and The Fire* (1975); John Bayley, *The Uses of Division* (1976); M. Van Wyk Smith, *Drummer Hodge: The Poetry of the Anglo-Boer War 1899–1902* (1978); Stephen Prickett, *Victorian Fantasy* (1979); Martin Green, *Dreams of Adventure, Deeds of Empire* (1980); J. A. McClure, *Kipling and Conrad* (1981); R. F. Moss, *Rudyard Kipling and the Fiction of Adolescence* (1982); S. S. Azfar Husain, *The Indianness of Rudyard Kipling: A Study in Stylistics* (1983); Norman Page, *A Kipling Companion* (1984); and B. J. Moore-Gilbert, *Kipling and 'Orientalism'* (1986). *The Readers' Guide to Rudyard Kipling's Work*, ed. R. E. Harbord (8 vols., privately printed, 1961–72) is an eccentric compilation, packed with useful information but by no means free from blunders and inaccuracy. Two important additions to the available corpus of Kipling's writings are *Kipling's India: Uncollected Sketches*, ed. Thomas Pinney (1986); and *Early Verse by Rudyard Kipling 1879–89: Unpublished, Uncollected and Rarely Collected Poems*, ed. Andrew Rutherford (1986). As this volume goes to press the first two volumes of Pinney's forthcoming edition of Kipling's letters are eagerly awaited.

A CHRONOLOGY OF KIPLING'S LIFE AND WORKS

THE dates given here for Kipling's works are those of first authorized publication in volume form, whether this was in India, America, or England. (The dates of subsequent editions are not listed.) It should be noted that individual poems and stories collected in these volumes had in many cases appeared in newspapers or magazines of earlier dates. For full details see James McG. Stewart, *Rudyard Kipling: A Bibliographical Catalogue*, ed. A. W. Yeats, Toronto, 1959; but see also the editors' notes in this World's Classics series.

1865   Rudyard Kipling born at Bombay on 30 December, son of John Lockwood Kipling and Alice Kipling (*née* Macdonald).

1871   In December Rudyard and his sister Alice Macdonald Kipling ('Trix'), who was born in 1868, are left in the charge of Captain and Mrs Holloway at Lorne Lodge, Southsea ('The House of Desolation'), while their parents return to India.

1877   Alice Kipling returns from India in March/April and removes the children from Lorne Lodge, though Trix returns there subsequently.

1878   Kipling is admitted in January to the United Services College at Westward Ho! in Devon. First visit to France with his father that summer. (Many visits later in his life.)

1880   Meets and falls in love with Florence Garrard, a fellow-boarder of Trix's at Southsea and prototype of Maisie in *The Light that Failed*.

1881   Appointed editor of the *United Services College Chronicle*. *Schoolboy Lyrics* privately printed by his parents in Lahore, for limited circulation.

1882   Leaves school at end of summer term. Sails for India on 20 September; arrives Bombay on 18 October. Takes up post as assistant editor of the *Civil and Military Gazette* in Lahore in the Punjab, where his father is now Principal of the Mayo College of Art and Curator of the Lahore Museum. Annual leaves from 1883 to 1888 are spent at Simla, except in 1884 when the family goes to Dalhousie.

1884   *Echoes* (by Rudyard and Trix, who has now rejoined the family in Lahore).

1885   *Quartette* (a Christmas Annual by Rudyard, Trix, and their parents).

1886   *Departmental Ditties.*

1887   Transferred in the autumn to the staff of the *Pioneer*, the *Civil and Military Gazette*'s sister-paper, in Allahabad in the North-West Provinces. As special correspondent in Rajputana he writes the articles later collected as 'Letters of Marque' in *From Sea to Sea*. Becomes friendly with Professor and Mrs Hill, and shares their bungalow.

1888   *Plain Tales from the Hills.* Takes on the additional responsibility of writing for the *Week's News*, a new publication sponsored by the *Pioneer*.

1888–9   *Soldiers Three*; *The Story of the Gadsbys*; *In Black and White*; *Under the Deodars*; *The Phantom Rickshaw*; *Wee Willie Winkie*.

1889   Leaves India on 9 March; travels to San Francisco with Professor and Mrs Hill via Rangoon, Singapore, Hong Kong, and Japan. Crosses the United States on his own, writing the articles later collected in *From Sea to Sea*. Falls in love with Mrs Hill's sister Caroline Taylor. Reaches Liverpool in October, and makes his début in the London literary world.

1890   Enjoys literary success, but suffers breakdown. Visits Italy. *The Light that Failed.*

1891   Visits South Africa, Australia, New Zealand, and (for the last time) India. Returns to England on hearing of the death of his American friend Wolcott Balestier. *Life's Handicap.*

1892   Marries Wolcott's sister Caroline Starr Balestier ('Carrie') in January. (The bride is given away by Henry James.) Their world tour is cut short by the loss of his savings in the collapse of the Oriental Banking Company. They establish their home at Brattleboro in Vermont, on the Balestier family estate. Daughter Josephine born in December. *The Naulahka* (written in collaboration with Wolcott Balestier). *Barrack-Room Ballads.*

1893   *Many Inventions.*

1894   *The Jungle Book.*

1895   *The Second Jungle Book.*

1896   Second daughter Elsie born in February. Quarrel with brother-in-law Beatty Balestier and subsequent court case end their stay in Brattleboro. Return to England (Torquay). *The Seven Seas.*

1897   Settles at Rottingdean in Sussex. Son John born in August. *Captains Courageous*.

1898   The first of many winters at Cape Town. Meets Sir Alfred Milner and Cecil Rhodes who becomes a close friend. Visits Rhodesia. *The Day's Work*.

1899   Disastrous visit to the United States. Nearly dies of pneumonia in New York. Death of Josephine. Never returns to USA. *Stalky and Co.*; *From Sea to Sea*.

1900   Helps for a time with army newspaper *The Friend* in South Africa during Boer War. Observes minor action at Kari Siding.

1901   *Kim*.

1902   Settles at 'Bateman's' at Burwash in Sussex. *Just So Stories*.

1903   *The Five Nations*.

1904   *Traffics and Discoveries*.

1906   *Puck of Pook's Hill*.

1907   Nobel Prize for Literature. Visit to Canada. *Collected Verse*.

1909   *Actions and Reactions*; *Abaft the Funnel*.

1910   *Rewards and Fairies*. Death of Kipling's mother.

1911   Death of Kipling's father.

1913   Visit to Egypt. *Songs from Books*.

1914–18 Visits to the Front and to the Fleet. *The New Army in Training*, *France at War*, *Sea Warfare*, and other war pamphlets.

1915   John Kipling reported missing on his first day in action with the Irish Guards in the Battle of Loos on 27 September. His body was never found.

1917   *A Diversity of Creatures*. Kipling becomes a member of the Imperial War Graves Commission.

1919   *The Years Between*; *Rudyard Kipling's Verse: Inclusive Edition*.

1920   *Letters of Travel*.

1923   *The Irish Guards in the Great War*; *Land and Sea Tales for Scouts and Guides*.

1924   Daughter Elsie marries Captain George Bambridge, MC.

1926   *Debits and Credits*.

1927   Voyage to Brazil.

1928   *A Book of Words*.

1930   *Thy Servant a Dog*. Visit to the West Indies.

Mrs Bathurst
and Other Stories

MRS BATHURST *

FROM LYDEN'S 'IRENIUS'*

ACT III. SC. ii.

GOW.—Had it been your Prince instead of a groom caught in this noose there's not an astrologer of the city—

PRINCE.—Sacked! Sacked! We were a city yesterday.

GOW.—So be it, but I was not governor. Not an astrologer, but would ha' sworn he'd foreseen it at the last versary* of Venus, when Vulcan caught her with Mars in the house of stinking Capricorn. But since 'tis Jack of the Straw that hangs, the forgetful stars had it not on their tablets.

PRINCE.—Another life! Were there any left to die? How did the poor fool come by it?

GOW.—*Simpliciter* thus. She that damned him to death knew not that she did it, or would have died ere she had done it. For she loved him. He that hangs him does so in obedience to the Duke, and asks no more than 'Where is the rope?' The Duke, very exactly he hath told us, works God's will, in which holy employ he's not to be questioned. We have then left upon this finger, only Jack whose soul now plucks the left sleeve of Destiny in Hell to overtake why she clapped him up like a fly on a sunny wall. Whuff! Soh!

PRINCE.—Your cloak, Ferdinand. I'll sleep now.

FERDINAND.—Sleep, then . . . He too, loved his life?

GOW.—He was born of woman . . . but at the end threw life from him, like your Prince, for a little sleep . . . 'Have I any look of a King?' said he, clanking his chain—'to be so baited on all sides by Fortune, that I must e'en die now to live with myself one day longer.' I left him railing at Fortune and woman's love.

FERDINAND.—Ah, woman's love!

    (*Aside*) Who knows not Fortune, glutted on easy thrones,
    Stealing from feasts as rare to coneycatch,*
    Privily in the hedgerows for a clown

With that same cruel-lustful hand and eye,
Those nails and wedges, that one hammer and lead,
And the very gerb * of long-stored lightnings loosed
Yesterday 'gainst some King.

Mrs Bathurst

THE day that I chose to visit HMS *Peridot* in Simon's Bay* was the day that the Admiral had chosen to send her up the coast. She was just steaming out to sea as my train came in, and since the rest of the Fleet were either coaling or busy at the rifle-ranges a thousand feet up the hill, I found myself stranded, lunchless, on the sea-front with no hope of return to Cape Town before 5 p.m. At this crisis I had the luck to come across my friend Inspector Hooper, Cape Government Railways, in command of an engine and a brake-van chalked for repair.

'If you get something to eat,' he said, 'I'll run you down to Glengariff siding till the goods comes along. It's cooler there than here, you see.'

I got food and drink from the Greeks* who sell all things at a price, and the engine trotted us a couple of miles up the line to a bay of drifted sand and a plank-platform half buried in sand not a hundred yards from the edge of the surf. Moulded dunes, whiter than any snow, rolled far inland up a brown and purple valley of splintered rocks and dry scrub. A crowd of Malays hauled at a net beside two blue and green boats on the beach; a picnic-party danced and shouted barefoot where a tiny river trickled across the flat, and a circle of dry hills, whose feet were set in sands of silver, locked us in against a seven-coloured sea. At either horn of the bay the railway line cut just above high-water mark, ran round a shoulder of piled rocks, and disappeared.

'You see there's always a breeze here,' said Hooper, opening the door as the engine left us in the siding on the sand, and the strong south-easter buffeting under Elsie's Peak dusted sand into our tickey beer. Presently he sat down to a file full of spiked documents. He had returned from a long trip up-country, where he had been reporting on damaged rolling-stock, as far away as Rhodesia. The weight of the bland wind on my eyelids; the song of it under the car roof, and high up among the rocks; the drift of fine grains chasing each other musically ashore; the

tramp of the surf; the voices of the picnickers;* the rustle of
Hooper's file, and the presence of the assured sun, joined with
the beer to cast me into magical slumber. The hills of False Bay
were just dissolving into those of fairyland when I heard
footsteps on the sand outside, and the clink of our couplings.

'Stop that!' snapped Hooper, without raising his head from
his work. 'It's those dirty little Malay boys, you see: they're
always playing with the trucks. . . .'

'Don't be hard on 'em. The railway's a general refuge in
Africa,' I replied.

''Tis—up-country at any rate. That reminds me,' he felt in
his waistcoat-pocket,* 'I've got a curiosity for you from Wankies—beyond Bulawayo. It's more of a souvenir perhaps than—
—'

'The old hotel's inhabited,' cried a voice. 'White men, from
the language. Marines to the front! Come on, Pritch. Here's
your Belmont. Wha—i—i!'

The last word dragged like a rope as Mr Pyecroft ran round
to the open door, and stood looking up into my face. Behind
him an enormous Sergeant of Marines trailed a stalk of dried
seaweed, and dusted the sand nervously from his fingers.

'What are you doing here?' I asked. 'I thought the *Hierophant*
was down the coast?'

'We came in last Tuesday—from Tristan d'Acunha—for
overhaul, and we shall be in dockyard 'ands for two months,
with boiler-seatings.'*

'Come and sit down.' Hooper put away the file.

'This is Mr Hooper of the Railway,' I exclaimed, as Pyecroft
turned to haul up the black-moustached sergeant.

'This is Sergeant Pritchard, of the *Agaric*, an old shipmate,'
said he. 'We were strollin' on the beach.' The monster blushed
and nodded. He filled up one side of the van when he sat down.

'And this is my friend, Mr Pyecroft,' I added to Hooper,
already busy with the extra beer which my prophetic soul had
bought from the Greeks.

'*Moi aussi*,' quoth Pyecroft, and drew out beneath his coat a
labelled quart bottle.

'Why, it's Bass!' cried Hooper.

'It was Pritchard,' said Pyecroft. 'They can't resist him.'

'That's not so,' said Pritchard mildly.

'Not *verbatim** per'aps, but the look in the eye came to the same thing.'

'Where was it?' I demanded.

'Just on beyond here—at Kalk Bay. She was slappin' a rug in a back verandah. Pritch 'adn't more than brought his batteries to bear, before she stepped indoors an' sent it flyin' over the wall.'

Pyecroft patted the warm bottle.

'It was all a mistake,' said Pritchard. 'I shouldn't wonder if she mistook me for Maclean. We're about of a size.'

I had heard householders of Muizenburg, St James's, and Kalk Bay complain of the difficulty of keeping beer or good servants at the seaside, and I began to see the reason. None the less, it was excellent Bass, and I too drank to the health of that large-minded maid.

'It's the uniform that fetches 'em, an' they fetch it,' said Pyecroft. 'My simple navy blue is respectable, but not fascinatin'. Now Pritch in 'is Number One rig is always "purr Mary, on the terrace"—*ex officio** as you might say.'

'She took me for Maclean, I tell you,' Pritchard insisted. 'Why—why—to listen to him you wouldn't think that only yesterday——'

'Pritch,' said Pyecroft, 'be warned in time. If we begin tellin' what we know about each other we'll be turned out of the pub. Not to mention aggravated desertion on several occasions——'

'Never anything more than absence without leaf—I defy you to prove it,' said the Sergeant hotly. 'An' if it comes to that, how about Vancouver in '87?'

'How about it? Who pulled bow in the gig going ashore? Who told Boy Niven . . .?'

'Surely you were court-martialled for that?' I said. The story of Boy Niven who lured seven or eight able-bodied seamen and marines into the woods of British Columbia used to be a legend of the Fleet.

'Yes, we were court-martialled to rights,' said Pritchard, 'but we should have been tried for murder if Boy Niven 'adn't been unusually tough. He told us he had an uncle 'oo'd give us land to farm. 'E said he was born at the back o' Vancouver Island, and *all* the time the beggar was a balmy Barnado* Orphan!'

'*But* we believed him,' said Pyecroft. 'I did—you did—
Paterson did—an' 'oo was the Marine that married the
cocoanut-woman afterwards—him with the mouth?'

'Oh, Jones, Spit-Kid Jones. I 'aven't thought of 'im in years,'
said Pritchard. 'Yes, Spit-Kid believed it, an' George Anstey
and Moon. We were very young an' very curious.'

'*But* lovin' an' trustful to a degree,' said Pyecroft.

''Remember when 'e told us to walk in single file for fear o'
bears? 'Remember, Pye, when 'e 'opped about in that bog full
o' ferns an' sniffed an' said 'e could smell the smoke of 'is
uncle's farm? An' *all* the time it was a dirty little outlyin'
uninhabited island. We walked round it in a day, an' come back
to our boat lyin' on the beach. A whole day Boy Niven kept us
walkin' in circles lookin' for 'is uncle's farm! He said his uncle
was compelled by the law of the land to give us a farm!'*

'Don't get hot, Pritch. We believed,' said Pyecroft.

'He'd been readin' books. He only did it to get a run ashore
an' have himself talked of. A day an' a night—eight of us—
followin' Boy Niven round an uninhabited island in the Vancouver archipelago! Then the picket came for us an' a nice pack
o' idiots we looked!'

'What did you get for it?' Hooper asked.

'Heavy thunder with continuous lightning for two hours.
Thereafter sleet-squalls, a confused sea, and cold, unfriendly
weather till conclusion o' cruise,' said Pyecroft. 'It was only
what we expected, but what we felt—an' I assure you, Mr
Hooper, even a sailor-man has a heart to break—was bein' told
that we able seamen an' promisin' marines 'ad misled Boy
Niven. Yes, we poor back-to-the-landers was supposed to 'ave
misled him! He rounded on us, o' course, an' got off easy.'

'Excep' for what we gave him in the steerin'-flat* when we
came out o' cells. 'Eard anything of 'im lately, Pye?'

'Signal Boatswain in the Channel Fleet, I believe—Mr L. L.
Niven is.'

'An' Anstey died o' fever in Benin,' Pritchard mused. 'What
come to Moon? Spit-Kid we know about.'

'Moon—Moon! Now where did I last . . .? Oh yes, when I
was in the *Palladium*. I met Quigley at Buncrana* Station. He
told me Moon 'ad run when the *Astrild* sloop was cruising
among the South Seas three years back. He always showed

signs o' bein' a Mormonastic* beggar. Yes, he slipped off
quietly an' they 'adn't time to chase 'im round the islands even
if the navigatin' officer 'ad been equal to the job.'

'Wasn't he?' said Hooper.

'Not so. Accordin' to Quigley the *Astrild* spent half her
commission rompin' up the beach like a she-turtle, an' the
other half hatching turtles' eggs on the top o' numerous reefs.
When she was docked at Sydney her copper* looked like Aunt
Maria's washing on the line—an' her 'mid-ship frames was
sprung. The commander swore the dockyard 'ad done it
haulin' the pore thing on to the slips. They *do* do strange things
at sea, Mr Hooper.'

'Ah! I'm not a taxpayer,' said Hooper, and opened a fresh
bottle. The Sergeant seemed to be one who had a difficulty in
dropping subjects.

'How it all comes back, don't it?' he said. 'Why, Moon must
'ave 'ad sixteen years' service before he ran.'

'It takes 'em at all ages. Look at—you know,' said Pyecroft.

'Who?' I asked.

'A service man within eighteen months of his pension is the
party you're thinkin' of,' said Pritchard. 'A warrant 'oo's name
begins with a V., isn't it?'

'But, in a way o' puttin' it, we can't say that he actually did
desert,' Pyecroft suggested.

'Oh no,' said Pritchard. 'It was only permanent absence
up-country without leaf. That was all.'

'Up-country?' said Hooper. 'Did they circulate his description?'

'What for?' said Pritchard, most impolitely.

'Because deserters are like columns in the war. They don't
move away from the line, you see. I've known a chap caught at
Salisbury that way tryin' to get to Nyassa. They tell me, but o'
course I don't know, that they don't ask questions on the
Nyassa Lake Flotilla up there. I've heard of a P. and O.*
quartermaster in full command of an armed launch there.'

'Do you think Click 'ud ha' gone up that way?' Pritchard
asked.

'There's no saying. He was sent up to Bloemfontein to take
over some Navy ammunition* left in the fort. We know he took
it over and saw it into the trucks. Then there was no more

Click—then or thereafter. Four months ago it transpired, and thus the *casus belli** stands at present,' said Pyecroft.

'What were his marks?' said Hooper again.

'Does the Railway get a reward for returnin' 'em, then?' said Pritchard.

'If I did d'you suppose I'd talk about it?' Hooper retorted angrily.

'You seemed so very interested,' said Pritchard with equal crispness.

'Why was he called Click?' I asked, to tide over an uneasy little break in the conversation. The two men were staring at each other very fixedly.

'Because of an ammunition hoist carryin' away,' said Pyecroft. 'And it carried away four of 'is teeth—on the lower port side, wasn't it, Pritch? The substitutes which he bought weren't screwed home, in a manner o' sayin'. When he talked fast they used to lift a little on the bed-plate. 'Ence, "Click."* They called 'im a superior man, which is what we'd call a long, black-'aired, genteelly speakin', 'alf-bred beggar on the lower deck.'

'Four false teeth in the lower left jaw,' said Hooper, his hand in his waistcoat-pocket. 'What tattoo marks?'

'Look here,' began Pritchard, half rising. 'I'm sure we're very grateful to you as a gentleman for your 'orspitality, but per'aps we may 'ave made an error in——'

I looked at Pyecroft for aid—Hooper was crimsoning rapidly.

'If the fat marine now occupying the foc'sle will kindly bring 'is *status quo** to an anchor yet once more, we may be able to talk like gentlemen—not to say friends,' said Pyecroft. 'He regards you, Mr Hooper, as a emissary of the Law.'

'I only wish to observe that when a gentleman exibits such a peculiar, or I should rather say, such a *bloomin*' curiosity in identification marks as our friend here——'

'Mr Pritchard,' I interposed, 'I'll take all the responsibility for Mr Hooper.'

'An' *you*'ll apologize all round,' said Pyecroft. 'You're a rude little man, Pritch.'

'But how was I——' he began, wavering.

'I don't know an' I don't care. Apologize!'

The giant looked round bewildered and took our little hands into his vast grip, one by one.

'I was wrong,' he said meekly as a sheep. 'My suspicions was unfounded. Mr Hooper, I apologize.'

'You did quite right to look out for your own end o' the line,' said Hooper. 'I'd ha' done the same with a gentleman I didn't know, you see. If you don't mind I'd like to hear a little more o' your Mr Vickery. It's safe with me, you see.'

'Why did Vickery run?' I began, but Pyecroft's smile made me turn my question to 'Who was she?'

'She kep' a little hotel at Hauraki—near Auckland,' said Pyecroft.

'By Gawd!' roared Pritchard, slapping his hand on his leg. 'Not Mrs Bathurst!'

Pyecroft nodded slowly, and the Sergeant called all the powers of darkness to witness his bewilderment.

'So far as I could get at it, Mrs B. was the lady in question.'

'But Click was married,' cried Pritchard.

'An' 'ad a fifteen-year-old daughter. 'E's shown me her photograph. Settin' that aside, so to say, 'ave you ever found these little things make much difference? Because I haven't.'

'Good Lord Alive an' Watchin'! . . . Mrs Bathurst. . . .' Then with another roar: 'You can say what you please, Pye, but you don't make me believe it was any of 'er fault. She wasn't *that*!'

'If I was going to say what I please, I'd begin by callin' you a silly ox an' work up to the higher pressures at leisure. I'm trying to say solely what transpired. M'rover, for once you're right. It wasn't her fault.'

'You couldn't 'aven't made me believe it if it 'ad been,' was the answer.

Such faith in a Sergeant of Marines interested me greatly. 'Never mind about that,' I cried. 'Tell me what she was like.'

'She was a widow,' said Pyecroft. 'Left so very young and never re-spliced. She kep' a little hotel for warrants and non-coms close to Auckland, an' she always wore black silk, and 'er neck——'

'You ask what she was like,' Pritchard broke in. 'Let me give you an instance. I was at Auckland first in '97, at the end o' the *Marroquin's* commission,* an' as I'd been promoted I went up with the others. She used to look after us all, an' she never lost by it—not a penny! "Pay me now," she'd say, "or settle later. I know you won't let me suffer. Send the money from home if you like." Why, gentlemen all, I tell you I've seen that lady take her own gold watch an' chain off her neck in the bar an' pass it to a bosun 'oo'd come ashore without 'is ticker an' 'ad to catch the last boat. "I don't know your name," she said, "but when you've done with it, you'll find plenty that know me on the front. Send it back by one o' them." And it was worth thirty pounds if it was worth 'arf-a-crown. The little gold watch, Pye, with the blue monogram at the back. But, as I was sayin', in those days she kep' a beer that agreed with me—Slits* it was called. One way an' another I must 'ave punished a good few bottles of it while we was in the bay—comin' ashore every night or so. Chaffin' across the bar like, once when we were alone, "Mrs B.," I said, "when next I call I want you to remember that this is my particular—just as you're my particular." (She'd let you go *that* far!) "Just as you're my particular," I said. "Oh, thank you, Sergeant Pritchard," she says, an' put 'er hand up to the curl be'ind 'er ear. Remember that way she had, Pye?'

'I think so,' said the sailor.

'Yes, "Thank you, Sergeant Pritchard," she says. "The least I can do is to mark it for you in case you change your mind. There's no great demand for it in the Fleet," she says, "but to make sure I'll put it at the back o' the shelf," an' she snipped off a piece of her hair ribbon with that old dolphin cigar-cutter on the bar—remember it, Pye?—an' she tied a bow round what was left—just four bottles. That was '97—no, '96. In '98 I was in the *Resilient*—China station—full commission. In Nineteen One, mark you, I was in the *Carthusian*, back in Auckland Bay again. Of course I went up to Mrs B.'s with the rest of us to see how things were goin'. They were the same as ever. (Remember the big tree on the pavement by the side-bar, Pye?) I never said anythin' in special (there was too many of us talkin' to her), but she saw me at once.'

'That wasn't difficult?' I ventured.

'Ah, but wait. I was comin' up to the bar, when, "Ada," she says to her niece, "get me Sergeant Pritchard's particular," and, gentlemen all, I tell you before I could shake 'ands with the lady, there were those four bottles o' Slits, with 'er 'air ribbon in a bow round each o' their necks, set down in front o' me, an' as she drew the cork she looked at me under her eyebrows in that blindish way she had o' lookin', an', "Sergeant Pritchard," she says, "I do 'ope you 'aven't changed your mind about your particulars." That's the kind o' woman she was— after five years!'

'I don't *see* her yet somehow,' said Hooper, but with sympathy.

'She—she never scrupled to feed a lame duck or set 'er foot on a scorpion *at any time of 'er life,' Pritchard added valiantly.

'That don't help me either. My mother's like that for one.'

The giant heaved inside his uniform and rolled his eyes at the car-roof. Said Pyecroft suddenly:—

'How many women have you been intimate with all over the world, Pritch?'

Pritchard blushed plum colour to the short hairs of his seventeen-inch neck.

''Undreds,' said Pyecroft. 'So've I. How many of 'em can you remember in your own mind, settin' aside the first—an' per'aps the last—*and one more*?'

'Few, wonderful few, now I tax myself,' said Sergeant Pritchard relievedly.

'An' how many times might you 'ave been at Auckland?'

'One—two,' he began—'why, I can't make it more than three times in ten years. But I can remember every time that I ever saw Mrs B.'

'So can I—an' I've only been to Auckland twice—how she stood an' what she was sayin' an' what she looked like. That's the secret. 'Tisn't beauty, so to speak, nor good talk necessarily. It's just It. Some women'll stay in a man's memory if they once walk down a street, but most of 'em you can live with a month on end, an' next commission you'd be put to it to certify whether they talked in their sleep or not, as one might say.'

'Ah!' said Hooper. 'That's more the idea. I've known just two women of that nature.'

'An' it was no fault o' theirs?' asked Pritchard.

'None whatever. I know *that*!'

'An' if a man gets struck with that kind o' woman, Mr Hooper?' Pritchard went on.

'He goes crazy—or just saves himself,' was the slow answer.

'You've hit it,' said the Sergeant. 'You've seen an' known somethin' in the course o' your life, Mr Hooper. I'm lookin' at you!' He set down his bottle.

'And how often had Vickery seen her?' I asked.

'That's the dark an' bloody mystery,' Pyecroft answered. 'I'd never come across him till I come out in the *Hierophant* just now, an' there wasn't any one in the ship who knew much about him. You see, he was what you call a superior man. 'E spoke to me once or twice about Auckland and Mrs B. on the voyage out. I called that to mind subsequently. There must 'ave been a good deal between 'em, to my way o' thinkin'. Mind you, I'm only giving you my *résumé* of it all, because all I know is second-hand so to speak, or rather I should say more than second-'and.'

'How?' said Hooper peremptorily. 'You must have seen it or heard it.'

'Ye-es,' said Pyecroft. 'I used to think seein' and hearin' was the only regulation aids to ascertainin' facts, but as we get older we get more accommodatin'. The cylinders work easier, I suppose. . . . Were you in Cape Town last December when Phyllis's Circus* came?'

'No—up-country,' said Hooper, a little nettled at the change of venue.

'I ask because they had a new turn of a scientific nature called "Home and Friends for a Tickey." '*

'Oh, you mean the cinematograph—the pictures of prize-fights and steamers. I've seen 'em up-country.'

'Biograph or cinematograph was what I was alludin' to. London Bridge with the omnibuses—a troopship goin' to the war—marines on parade at Portsmouth, an' the Plymouth Express arrivin' at Paddin'ton.'

'Seen 'em all. Seen 'em all,' said Hooper impatiently.

'We *Hierophants* came in just before Christmas week an' leaf was easy.'

'I think a man gets fed up with Cape Town quicker than anywhere else on the station. Why, even Durban's more like Nature. We was there for Christmas,' Pritchard put in.

'Not bein' a devotee of Indian *peeris*,* as our Doctor said to the Pusser, I can't exactly say. Phyllis's was good enough after musketry practice at Mozambique. I couldn't get off the first two or three nights on account of what you might call an imbroglio with our Torpedo Lieutenant in the submerged flat, * where some pride of the West country had sugared up a gyroscope; but I remember Vickery went ashore with our Carpenter Rigdon—old Crocus we called him. As a general rule Crocus never left 'is ship unless an' until he was 'oisted out with a winch, but *when* 'e went 'e would return noddin' like a lily gemmed with dew. We smothered him down below that night, but the things 'e said about Vickery as a fittin' playmate for a Warrant Officer of 'is cubic capacity, before we got him quiet, was what I should call pointed.'

'I've been with Crocus—in the *Redoubtable*,' said the Sergeant. 'He's a character if there is one.'

'Next night I went into Cape Town with Dawson and Pratt; but just at the door of the Circus I came across Vickery. "Oh!" he says, "you're the man I'm looking for. Come and sit next me. This way to the shillin' places!" I went astern at once, protestin' because tickey seats better suited my so-called finances. "Come on," says Vickery, "I'm payin'." Naturally I abandoned Pratt and Dawson in anticipation o' drinks to match the seats. "No," he says, when this was 'inted—"not now. Not now. As many as you please afterwards, but I want you sober for the occasion." I caught 'is face under a lamp just then, an' the appearance of it quite cured me of my thirsts. Don't mistake. It didn't frighten me. It made me anxious. I can't tell you what it was like, but that was the effect which it 'ad on me. If you want to know, it reminded me of those things in bottles in those herbalistic shops at Plymouth—preserved in spirits of wine. White an' crumply things—previous to birth as you might say.'

'You 'ave a beastial mind, Pye,' said the Sergeant, relighting his pipe.

'Perhaps. We were in the front row, an' "Home an' Friends" came on early. Vickery touched me on the knee when the number went up. "If you see anything that strikes you," he says, "drop me a hint"; then he went on clicking. We saw London Bridge an' so forth an' so on, an' it was most interestin'. I'd never seen it before. You 'eard a little dynamo like buzzin', but the pictures were the real thing—alive an' movin'.'

'I've seen 'em,' said Hooper. 'Of course they are taken from the very thing itself—you see.'

'Then the Western Mail came in to Paddin'ton on the big magic lantern sheet. First we saw the platform empty an' the porters standin' by. Then the engine come in, head on, an' the women in the front row jumped: she headed so straight. Then the doors opened and the passengers came out and the porters got the luggage—just like life. Only—only when any one came down too far towards us that was watchin', they walked right out o' the picture, so to speak. I was 'ighly interested, I can tell you. So were all of us. I watched an old man with a rug 'oo'd dropped a book an' was tryin' to pick it up, when quite slowly, from be'ind two porters—carryin' a little reticule an' lookin' from side to side—comes out Mrs Bathurst. There was no mistakin' the walk in a hundred thousand. She come forward—right forward—she looked out straight at us with that blindish look which Pritch alluded to. She walked on and on till she melted out of the picture—like—like a shadow jumpin' over a candle, an' as she went I 'eard Dawson in the tickey seats be'ind sing out: "Christ! there's Mrs B.!" '

Hooper swallowed his spittle and leaned forward intently.

'Vickery touched me on the knee again. He was clickin' his four false teeth with his jaw down like an enteric at the last kick. "Are you sure?" says he. "Sure," I says, "didn't you 'ear Dawson give tongue? Why, it's the woman herself." "I was sure before," he says, "but I brought you to make sure. Will you come again with me tomorrow?"

' "Willingly," I says, "it's like meetin' old friends."

' "Yes," he says, openin' his watch, "very like. It will be four-and-twenty hours less four minutes before I see her again. Come and have a drink," he says. "It may amuse you, but it's no sort of earthly use to me." He went out shaking his head an' stumblin' over people's feet as if he was drunk already. I anticipated a swift drink an' a speedy return, because I wanted to see the performin' elephants. Instead o' which Vickery began to navigate the town at the rate o' knots, lookin' in at a bar every three minutes approximate Greenwich time. I'm not a drinkin' man, though there are those present'—he cocked his unforgetable eye at me—'who may have seen me more or less imbued with the fragrant spirit. * None the less when I drink I like to do it at anchor an' not at an average speed of eighteen knots on the measured mile. There's a tank as you might say at the back o' that big hotel up the hill—what do they call it?'

'The Molteno Reservoir,' I suggested, and Hooper nodded.

'That was his limit o' drift. We walked there an' we come down through the Gardens—there was a South-Easter blowin'—an' we finished up by the Docks. Then we bore up the road to Salt River, and wherever there was a pub Vickery put in sweatin'. He didn't look at what he drunk—he didn't look at the change. He walked an' he drunk an' he perspired in rivers. I understood why old Crocus 'ad come back in the condition 'e did, because Vickery an' I 'ad two an' a half hours o' this gipsy manœuvre, an' when we got back to the station there wasn't a dry atom on or in me.'

'Did he say anything?' Pritchard asked.

'The sum total of 'is conversation from 7.45 p.m. till 11.15 p.m. was "Let's have another." Thus the mornin' an' the evenin' were the first day, as Scripture says.*... To abbreviate a lengthy narrative, I went into Cape Town for five consecutive nights with Master Vickery, and in that time I must 'ave logged about fifty knots over the ground an' taken in two gallon o' all the worst spirits south the Equator. The evolution never varied. Two shilling seats for us two; five minutes o' the pictures, an' perhaps forty-five seconds o' Mrs B. walking down towards us with that blindish look in her eyes an' the reticule in her hand. Then out walk—and drink till train time.'

'What did you think?' said Hooper, his hand fingering his waistcoat-pocket.*

'Several things,' said Pyecroft. 'To tell you the truth, I aren't quite done thinkin' about it yet. Mad? The man was a dumb lunatic—must 'ave been for months—years p'raps. I know somethin' o' maniacs, as every man in the Service must. I've been shipmates with a mad skipper—an' a lunatic Number One, but never both together I thank 'Eaven. I could give you the names o' three captains now 'oo ought to be in an asylum, but you don't find me interferin' with the mentally afflicted till they begin to lay about 'em with rammers an' winch-handles. Only once I crept up a little into the wind towards Master Vickery. "I wonder what she's doin' in England," I says. "Don't it seem to you she's lookin' for somebody?" That was in the

Gardens again, with the South-Easter blowin' as we were makin' our desperate round. "She's lookin' for me," he says, stoppin' dead under a lamp an' clickin'. When he wasn't drinkin', in which case all 'is teeth clicked on the glass, 'e was clickin' 'is four false teeth like a Marconi ticker. "Yes! lookin' for me," he said, an' he went on very softly an' as you might say affectionately. "*But*," he went on, "in future, Mr Pyecroft, I should take it kindly of you if you'd confine your remarks to the drinks set before you. Otherwise," he says, "with the best will in the world towards you, I may find myself guilty of murder! Do you understand?" he says. "Perfectly," I says, "but would it at all soothe you to know that in such a case the chances o' your being killed are precisely equivalent to the chances o' me being outed." "Why, no," he says, "I'm almost afraid that 'ud be a temptation." Then I said—we was right under the lamp by that arch at the end o' the Gardens where the trams come round—"Assumin' murder was done—or attempted murder—I put it to you that you would still be left so badly crippled, as one might say, that your subsequent capture by the police—to 'oom you would 'ave to explain—would be largely inevitable." "That's better," 'e says, passin' 'is hands over his forehead. "That's much better, because," he says, "do you know, as I am now, Pye, I'm not so sure if I could explain anything much." Those were the only particular words I had with 'im in our walks as I remember.'

'What walks!' said Hooper. 'Oh my soul, what walks!'

'They were chronic,' said Pyecroft gravely, 'but I didn't anticipate any danger till the Circus left. Then I anticipated that, bein' deprived of 'is stimulant, he might react on me, so to say, with a hatchet. Consequently, after the final performance an' the ensuin' wet walk, I kep' myself aloof from my superior officer on board in the execution of 'is duty, as you might put it. Consequently, I was interested when the sentry informs me while I was passin' on my lawful occasions that Click had asked to see the captain. As a general rule warrant officers don't dissipate much of the owner's time, but Click put in an hour and more be'ind that door. My duties kep' me within eyeshot of it. Vickery came out first, an' 'e actually nodded at me an' smiled. This knocked me out o' the boat, because, havin' seen 'is face for five consecutive nights, I didn't anticipate any change there more than a condenser in hell, so to speak. The owner emerged later. His face didn't read off at all, so I fell back on his cox, 'oo'd been eight years with him and knew him better than boat signals. Lamson—that was the cox's name—crossed 'is bows once or twice at low speeds an' dropped down to me visibly concerned. "He's shipped 'is court-martial face," says Lamson. "Some one's goin' to be 'ung. I've never seen that look but once before when they chucked the gun-sights overboard in the *Fantastic*." Throwin' gun-sights overboard, Mr Hooper, is the equivalent for mutiny in these degenerate days. It's done to attract the notice of the authorities an' the *Western Mornin' News*—generally by a stoker. Naturally, word went round the lower deck an' we had a private over'aul of our little consciences. But, barrin' a shirt which a second-class stoker said 'ad walked into 'is bag from the marines' flat by itself, nothin' vital transpired. The owner went about flyin' the signal for "attend public execution," so to say, but there was no corpse at the yard-arm. 'E lunched on the beach an' 'e returned with 'is regulation harbour-routine face about 3 p.m. Thus Lamson lost prestige for raising false alarms. The only person 'oo might 'ave connected the epicycloidal* gears correctly was one Pyecroft, when he was told that Mr Vickery would go up-country that same evening to take over certain naval ammunition left after the war* in Bloemfontein Fort. No details was ordered to accompany Master Vickery. He was told off first person singular—as a unit—by himself.'

The marine whistled penetratingly.

'That's what I thought,' said Pyecroft. 'I went ashore with him in the cutter an' 'e asked me to walk through the station. He was clickin' audibly, but otherwise seemed happy-ish.

' "You might like to know," he says, stoppin' just opposite the Admiral's front gate, "that Phyllis's Circus will be performin' at Worcester to-morrow night. So I shall see 'er yet once again. You've been very patient with me," he says.

' "Look here, Vickery," I said, "this thing's come to be just as much as I can stand. Consume your own smoke. I don't want to know any more."

' "You!" he said. "What have you got to complain of?—you've only 'ad to watch. I'm *it*," he says, "but that's neither

here nor there," he says. "I've one thing to say before shakin'
'ands. Remember," 'e says—we were just by the Admiral's
garden-gate then—"remember, that I am *not* a murderer,
because my lawful wife died in childbed six weeks after I came
out. That much at least I am clear of," 'e says.

' "Then what have you done that signifies?" I said. "What's
the rest of it?"

' "The rest," 'e says, "is silence,"* an' he shook 'ands and
went clickin' into Simonstown station.'

'Did he stop to see Mrs Bathurst at Worcester?' I asked.

'It's not known. He reported at Bloemfontein, saw the
ammunition into the trucks, and then 'e disappeared. Went
out—deserted, if you care to put it so—within eighteen months
of his pension, an' if what 'e said about 'is wife was true he was
a free man as 'e then stood. How do you read it off?'

'Poor devil!' said Hooper. 'To see her that way every night!
I wonder what it was.'

'I've made my 'ead ache in that direction many a long night.'

'But I'll swear Mrs B. 'ad no 'and in it,' said the Sergeant,
unshaken.

'No. Whatever the wrong or deceit was, he did it, I'm sure
o' that. I 'ad to look at 'is face for five consecutive nights. I'm
not so fond o' navigatin' about Cape Town with a South-Easter
blowin' these days. I can hear those teeth click, so to say.'

'Ah, those teeth,' said Hooper, and his hand went to his
waistcoat-pocket once more. 'Permanent things false teeth are.
You read about 'em in all the murder trials.'

'What d'you suppose the captain knew—or did?' I asked.

'I've never turned my searchlight that way,' Pyecroft
answered unblushingly.

We all reflected together, and drummed on empty beer
bottles as the picnic-party, sunburned, wet, and sandy, passed
our door singing 'The Honeysuckle and the Bee'.*

'Pretty girl under that kapje,'* said Pyecroft.

'They never circulated his description?' said Pritchard.

'I was askin' you before these gentlemen came,' said Hooper
to me, 'whether you knew Wankies—on the way to the Zam-
besi—beyond Bulawayo?'

'Would he pass there—tryin' to get to that Lake what's 'is
name?' said Pritchard.

Hooper shook his head and went on: 'There's a curious bit o' line there, you see. It runs through solid teak forest—a sort o' mahogany really—seventy-two miles without a curve.* I've had a train derailed there twenty-three times in forty miles. I was up there a month ago relievin' a sick inspector, you see. He told me to look out for a couple of tramps in the teak.'

'Two?' Pyecroft said. 'I don't envy that other man if——'

'We get heaps of tramps up there since the war. The inspector told me I'd find 'em at M'Bindwe siding waiting to go North. He'd given 'em some grub and quinine, you see. I went up on a construction train. I looked out for 'em. I saw them miles ahead along the straight, waiting in the teak. One of 'em was standin' up by the dead-end of the siding an' the other was squattin' down lookin' up at 'im, you see.'

'What did you do for 'em?' said Pritchard.

'There wasn't much I could do, except bury 'em. There'd been a bit of a thunderstorm in the teak, you see, and they were both stone dead and as black as charcoal.* That's what they really were, you see—charcoal. They fell to bits when we tried to shift 'em. The man who was standin' up had the false teeth. I saw 'em shinin' against the black. Fell to bits he did too, like his mate* squatting down an' watchin' him, both of 'em all wet in the rain. Both burned to charcoal, you see. And—that's what made me ask about marks just now—the false-toother was tattooed on the arms and chest—a crown and foul anchor with M. V. above.'

'I've seen that,' said Pyecroft quickly. 'It was so.'

'But if he was all charcoal-like?' said Pritchard, shuddering.

'You know how writing shows up white on a burned letter? Well, it was like that, you see. We buried 'em in the teak and I kept . . . But he was a friend of you two gentlemen, you see.'

Mr Hooper brought his hand away from his waistcoat-pocket—empty.

Pritchard covered his face with his hands for a moment, like a child shutting out an ugliness.

'And to think of her at Hauraki!' he murmured—'with 'er 'air-ribbon on my beer. "Ada," she said to her niece . . . Oh, my Gawd!' . . .

'On a summer afternoon, when the honeysuckle blooms,
    And all Nature seems at rest,
Underneath the bower, 'mid the perfume of the flower,
    Sat a maiden with the one she loves the best——'

sang the picnic-party waiting for their train at Glengariff.

'Well, I don't know how you feel about it,' said Pyecroft, 'but
'avin' seen 'is face for five consecutive nights on end, I'm
inclined to finish what's left of the beer an' thank Gawd he's
dead!'

'WIRELESS'*

KASPAR'S SONG IN 'VARDA'

(From the Swedish of Stagnelius.) *

Eyes aloft, over dangerous places,
   The children follow where Psyche* flies,
And, in the sweat of their upturned faces,
   Slash with a net at the empty skies.

So it goes they fall amid brambles,
   And sting their toes on the nettle-tops,
Till after a thousand scratches and scrambles
   They wipe their brows, and the hunting stops.

Then to quiet them comes their father
   And stills the riot of pain and grief,
Saying, 'Little ones, go and gather
   Out of my garden a cabbage leaf.

'You will find on it whorls and clots of
   Dull grey eggs that, properly fed,
Turn, by way of the worm, to lots of
   Radiant Psyches raised from the dead.'

         *   *   *

'Heaven is beautiful, Earth is ugly,'
   The three-dimensioned preacher saith,
So we must not look where the snail and the slug lie
   For Psyche's birth. . . . And that is our death!

'Wireless'

'IT's a funny thing, this Marconi business, isn't it?' said Mr Shaynor, coughing heavily. 'Nothing seems to make any difference, by what they tell me—storms, hills, or anything; but if that's true we shall know before morning.'

'Of course it's true,' I answered, stepping behind the counter. 'Where's old Mr Cashell?'

'He's had to go to bed on account of his influenza. He said you'd very likely drop in.'

'Where's his nephew?'

'Inside, getting the things ready. He told me that the last time they experimented they put the pole * on the roof of one of the big hotels here, and the batteries electrified all the water-supply, and'—he giggled—'the ladies got shocks when they took their baths.'

'I never heard of that.'

'The hotel wouldn't exactly advertise it, would it? Just now, by what Mr Cashell tells me, they're trying to signal from here to Poole, * and they're using stronger batteries than ever. But, you see, he being the guvnor's nephew and all that (and it will be in the papers too), it doesn't matter how they electrify things in this house. Are you going to watch?'

'Very much. I've never seen this game. Aren't you going to bed?'

'We don't close till ten on Saturdays. There's a good deal of influenza in town, too, and there'll be a dozen prescriptions coming in before morning. I generally sleep in the chair here. It's warmer than jumping out of bed every time. Bitter cold, isn't it?'

'Freezing hard. I'm sorry your cough's worse.'

'Thank you. I don't mind cold so much. It's this wind that fair cuts me to pieces.' He coughed again hard and hackingly, as an old lady came in for ammoniated quinine. 'We've just run out of it in bottles, madam,' said Mr Shaynor, returning to the professional tone, 'but if you will wait two minutes, I'll make it up for you, madam.'

I had used the shop for some time, and my acquaintance with the proprietor had ripened into friendship. It was Mr Cashell who revealed to me the purpose and power of Apothecaries' Hall* what time a fellow-chemist had made an error in a prescription of mine, had lied to cover his sloth, and when error and lie were brought home to him had written vain letters.

'A disgrace to our profession,' said the thin, mild-eyed man, hotly, after studying the evidence. 'You couldn't do a better service to the profession than report him to Apothecaries' Hall.'

I did so, not knowing what djinns I should evoke; and the result was such an apology as one might make who had spent a night on the rack. I conceived great respect for Apothecaries' Hall, and esteem for Mr Cashell, a zealous craftsman who magnified his calling. Until Mr Shaynor came down from the North his assistants had by no means agreed with Mr Cashell. 'They forget,' said he, 'that, first and foremost, the compounder is a medicine-man. On him depends the physician's reputation. He holds it literally in the hollow of his hand, Sir.'

Mr Shaynor's manners had not, perhaps, the polish of the grocery and Italian warehouse next door, but he knew and loved his dispensary work in every detail. For relaxation he seemed to go no farther afield than the romance of drugs—their discovery, preparation, packing, and export—but it led him to the ends of the earth, and on this subject, and the Pharmaceutical Formulary,* and Nicholas Culpepper,* most confident of physicians, we met.

Little by little I grew to know something of his beginnings and his hopes—of his mother, who had been a school-teacher in one of the northern counties, and of his red-headed father, a small job-master* at Kirby Moors, who died when he was a child; of the examinations he had passed and of their exceeding and increasing difficulty; of his dreams of a shop in London; of his hate for the price-cutting Co-operative stores; and, most interesting, of his mental attitude towards customers.

'There's a way you get into,' he told me, 'of serving them carefully, and I hope, politely, without stopping your own thinking. I've been reading Christy's *New Commercial Plants**
all this autumn, and that needs keeping your mind on it, I can

tell you. So long as it isn't a prescription, of course, I can carry as much as half a page of Christy in my head, and at the same time I could sell out all that window twice over, and not a penny wrong at the end. As to prescriptions, I think I could make up the general run of 'em in my sleep, almost.'

For reasons of my own, I was deeply interested in Marconi experiments at their outset in England; and it was of a piece with Mr Cashell's unvarying thoughtfulness that, when his nephew the electrician appropriated the house for a long-range installation, he should, as I have said, invite me to see the result.

The old lady went away with her medicine, and Mr Shaynor and I stamped on the tiled floor behind the counter to keep ourselves warm. The shop, by the light of the many electrics, looked like a Paris-diamond * mine, for Mr Cashell believed in all the ritual of his craft. Three superb glass jars *—red, green, and blue—of the sort that led Rosamond * to parting with her shoes—blazed in the broad plate-glass windows, and there was a confused smell of orris, Kodak Wlms, vulcanite, tooth-powder, sachets, and almond-cream in the air. Mr Shaynor fed the dispensary stove, and we sucked cayenne-pepper jujubes and menthol lozenges. The brutal east wind had cleared the streets, and the few passers-by were muffled to their puckered eyes. In the Italian warehouse next door some gay feathered birds and game, hung upon hooks, sagged to the wind across the left edge of our window-frame.

'They ought to take these poultry in—all knocked about like that,' said Mr Shaynor. 'Doesn't it make you feel fair perishing? See that old hare! The wind's nearly blowing the fur off him.'

I saw the belly-fur of the dead beast blown apart in ridges and streaks as the wind caught it, showing bluish skin underneath. 'Bitter cold,' said Mr Shaynor, shuddering. 'Fancy going out on a night like this! Oh, here's young Mr Cashell.'

The door of the inner office behind the dispensary opened, and an energetic, spade-bearded man stepped forth, rubbing his hands.

'I want a bit of tin-foil, Shaynor,' he said. 'Good-evening. My uncle told me you might be coming.' This to me, as I began the first of a hundred questions.

'I've everything in order,' he replied. 'We're only waiting until Poole calls us up. Excuse me a minute. You can come in whenever you like—but I'd better be with the instruments. Give me that tin-foil. Thanks.'

While we were talking, a girl—evidently no customer—had come into the shop, and the face and bearing of Mr Shaynor changed. She leaned confidently across the counter.

'But I can't,' I heard him whisper uneasily—the flush on his cheek was dull red, and his eyes shone like a drugged moth's. 'I can't. I tell you I'm alone in the place.'

'No, you aren't. Who's *that*? Let him look after it for half an hour. A brisk walk will do you good. Ah, come now, John.'

'But he isn't——'

'I don't care. I want you to; we'll only go round by St Agnes. If you don't——'

He crossed to where I stood in the shadow of the dispensary counter, and began some sort of broken apology about a lady-friend.

'Yes,' she interrupted. 'You take the shop for half an hour—to oblige *me*, won't you?'

She had a singularly rich and promising voice that well matched her outline.

'All right,' I said. 'I'll do it—but you'd better wrap yourself up, Mr Shaynor.'

'Oh, a brisk walk ought to help me. We're only going round by the church.' I heard him cough grievously as they went out together.

I refilled the stove, and, after reckless expenditure of Mr Cashell's coal, drove some warmth into the shop. I explored many of the glass-knobbed drawers that lined the walls, tasted some disconcerting drugs, and, by the aid of a few cardamoms, ground ginger, chloric-ether, and dilute alcohol, manufactured a new and wildish drink, of which I bore a glassful to young Mr Cashell, busy in the back office. He laughed shortly when I told him that Mr Shaynor had stepped out—but a frail coil of wire held all his attention, and he had no word for me bewildered among the batteries and rods. The noise of the sea on the beach began to make itself heard as the traffic in the street ceased. Then briefly, but very lucidly, he gave me the names and uses of the mechanism that crowded the tables and the floor.

'When do you expect to get the message from Poole?' I demanded, sipping my liquor out of a graduated glass.

'About midnight, if everything is in order. We've got our installation-pole fixed to the roof of the house. I shouldn't advise you to turn on a tap or anything tonight. We've connected up with the plumbing, and all the water will be electrified.' He repeated to me the history of the agitated ladies at the hotel at the time of the first installation.

'But what *is* it?' I asked. 'Electricity is out of my beat altogether.'

'Ah, if you knew *that* you'd know something nobody knows. It's just—It—what we call Electricity, but the magic—the manifestations—the Hertzian waves—are all revealed by *this*. The coherer, we call it.'

He picked up a glass tube not much thicker than a thermometer, in which, almost touching, were two tiny silver plugs, and between them an infinitesimal pinch of metallic dust. 'That's all,' he said, proudly, as though himself responsible for the wonder. 'That is the thing that will reveal to us the Powers—whatever the Powers may be—at work—through space—a long distance away.'

Just then Mr Shaynor returned alone and stood coughing his heart out on the mat.

'Serves you right for being such a fool,' said young Mr Cashell, as annoyed as myself at the interruption. 'Never mind—we've all the night before us to see wonders.'

Shaynor clutched the counter, his handkerchief to his lips. When he brought it away I saw two bright red stains.

'I—I've got a bit of a rasped throat from smoking cigarettes,' he panted. 'I think I'll try a cubeb.'*

'Better take some of this. I've been compounding while you've been away.' I handed him the brew.

''Twon't make me drunk, will it? I'm almost a teetotaller. My word! That's grateful and comforting.'

He set down the empty glass to cough afresh.

'Brr! But it was cold out there! I shouldn't care to be lying in my grave a night like this. Don't *you* ever have a sore throat from smoking?' He pocketed the handkerchief after a furtive peep.

'Oh, yes, sometimes,' I replied, wondering, while I spoke, into what agonies of terror I should fall if ever I saw those bright-red danger-signals* under my nose. Young Mr Cashell among the batteries coughed slightly to show that he was quite ready to continue his scientific explanations, but I was thinking still of the girl with the rich voice and the significantly cut mouth, at whose command I had taken charge of the shop. It flashed across me that she distantly resembled the seductive shape on a gold-framed toilet-water advertisement whose charms were unholily heightened by the glare from the red bottle in the window. Turning to make sure, I saw Mr Shaynor's eyes bent in the same direction, and by instinct recognized that the flamboyant thing was to him a shrine. 'What do you take for your—cough?' I asked.

'Well, I'm the wrong side of the counter to believe much in patent medicines. But there are asthma cigarettes and there are pastilles. To tell you the truth, if you don't object to the smell, which is very like incense, I believe, though I'm not a Roman Catholic, Blaudett's Cathedral Pastilles relieve me as much as anything.'

'Let's try.' I had never raided a chemist's shop before, so I was thorough. We unearthed the pastilles—brown, gummy cones of benzoin—and set them alight under the toilet-water advertisement, where they fumed in thin blue spirals.

'Of course,' said Mr Shaynor, to my question, 'what one uses in the shop for one's self comes out of one's pocket. Why, stock-taking in our business is nearly the same as with jewellers—and I can't say more than that. But one gets them'—he pointed to the pastille-box—'at trade prices.' Evidently the censing of the gay, seven-tinted wench with the teeth was an established ritual which cost something.

'And when do we shut up shop?'

'We stay like this all night. The guv—old Mr Cashell—doesn't believe in locks and shutters as compared with electric light. Besides, it brings trade. I'll just sit here in the chair by the stove and write a letter, if you don't mind. Electricity isn't my prescription.'

The energetic young Mr Cashell snorted within, and Shaynor settled himself up in his chair over which he had thrown a staring red, black, and yellow Austrian jute blanket, rather like a table-cover. I cast about, amid patent-medicine pamphlets, for something to read, but finding little, returned to the manufacture of the new drink. The Italian warehouse took down its

game and went to bed. Across the street blank shutters flung
back the gaslight in cold smears; the dried pavement seemed
to rough up in goose-flesh under the scouring of the savage
wind, and we could hear, long ere he passed, the policeman
flapping his arms to keep himself warm. Within, the flavours
of cardamoms and chloric-ether disputed those of the pastilles
and a score of drugs and perfume and soap scents. Our electric
lights, set low down in the windows before the tun-bellied
Rosamond jars, flung inward three monstrous daubs of red,
blue, and green, that broke into kaleidoscopic lights on the
facetted knobs of the drug-drawers, the cut-glass scent flagons,
and the bulbs of the sparklet bottles. They flushed the white-
tiled floor in gorgeous patches; splashed along the nickel-silver
counter-rails, and turned the polished mahogany counter-
panels to the likeness of intricate grained marbles—slabs of
porphyry and malachite. Mr Shaynor unlocked a drawer, and
ere he began to write, took out a meagre bundle of letters. From
my place by the stove, I could see the scalloped edges of the
paper with a flaring monogram in the corner and could even
smell the reek of chypre. At each page he turned toward the
toilet-water lady of the advertisement and devoured her with
over-luminous eyes. He had drawn the Austrian blanket over
his shoulders, and among those warring lights he looked more
than ever the incarnation of a drugged moth—a tiger-moth as
I thought.

He put his letter into an envelope, stamped it with stiff
mechanical movements, and dropped it in the drawer. Then I
became aware of the silence of a great city asleep—the silence
that underlaid the even voice of the breakers along the sea-
front—a thick, tingling quiet of warm life stilled down for its
appointed time, and unconsciously I moved about the glittering
shop as one moves in a sick-room. Young Mr Cashell was
adjusting some wire that crackled from time to time with the
tense, knuckle-stretching sound of the electric spark. Upstairs,
where a door shut and opened swiftly, I could hear his uncle
coughing abed.

'Here,' I said, when the drink was properly warmed, 'take
some of this, Mr Shaynor.'

He jerked in his chair with a start and a wrench, and held out his hand for the glass. The mixture, of a rich port-wine colour, frothed at the top.

'It looks,' he said, suddenly, 'it looks—those bubbles—like a string of pearls winking at you—rather like the pearls round that young lady's neck.' He turned again to the advertisement where the female in the dove-coloured corset had seen fit to put on all her pearls before she cleaned her teeth.

'Not bad, is it?' I said.

'Eh?'

He rolled his eyes heavily full on me, and, as I stared, I beheld all meaning and consciousness die out of the swiftly dilating pupils. His figure lost its stark rigidity, softened into the chair, and, chin on chest, hands dropped before him, he rested open-eyed, absolutely still.

'I'm afraid I've rather cooked Shaynor's goose,' I said, bearing the fresh drink to young Mr Cashell. 'Perhaps it was the chloric-ether.'

'Oh, he's all right.' The spade-bearded man glanced at him pityingly. 'Consumptives go off in those sort of doses very often. It's exhaustion . . . I don't wonder. I daresay the liquor will do him good. It's grand stuff,' he finished his share appreciatively. 'Well, as I was saying—before he interrupted—about this little coherer. The pinch of dust, you see, is nickel-filings. The Hertzian waves, you see, come out of space from the station that despatches 'em, and all these little particles are attracted together—cohere, we call it—for just so long as the current passes through them. Now, it's important to remember that the current is an induced current. There are a good many kinds of induction——'

'Yes, but what *is* induction?'

'That's rather hard to explain untechnically. But the long and the short of it is that when a current of electricity passes through a wire there's a lot of magnetism present round that wire; and if you put another wire parallel to, and within what we call its magnetic field—why then, the second wire will also become charged with electricity.'

'On its own account?'

'On its own account.'

'Then let's see if I've got it correctly. Miles off, at Poole, or wherever it is——'

'It will be anywhere in ten years.'

'You've got a charged wire——'

'Charged with Hertzian waves which vibrate, say, two hundred and thirty million times a second.' Mr Cashell snaked his forefinger rapidly through the air.

'All right—a charged wire at Poole, giving out these waves into space. Then this wire of yours sticking out into space—on the roof of the house—in some mysterious way gets charged with those waves from Poole——'

'Or anywhere—it only happens to be Poole tonight.'

'And those waves set the coherer at work, just like an ordinary telegraph-office ticker?'

'No! That's where so many people make the mistake. The Hertzian waves wouldn't be strong enough to work a great heavy Morse instrument like ours. They can only just make that dust cohere, and while it coheres (a little while for a dot and a longer while for a dash) the current from this battery—the home battery'—he laid his hand on the thing—'can get through to the Morse printing-machine to record the dot or dash. Let me make it clearer. Do you know anything about steam?'

'Very little. But go on.'

'Well, the coherer is like a steam-valve. Any child can open a valve and start a steamer's engines, because a turn of the hand lets in the main steam, doesn't it? Now, this home battery here ready to print is the main steam. The coherer is the valve, always ready to be turned on. The Hertzian wave is the child's hand that turns it.'

'I see. That's marvellous.'

'Marvellous, isn't it? And, remember, we're only at the beginning. There's nothing we shan't be able to do in ten years. I want to live—my God, how I want to live, and see it develop?' He looked through the door at Shaynor breathing lightly in his chair. 'Poor beast! And he wants to keep company with Fanny Brand.'

'Fanny *who*?' I said, for the name struck an obscurely familiar chord in my brain—something connected with a stained handkerchief, and the word 'arterial'.

'Fanny Brand—the girl you kept shop for.' He laughed. 'That's all I know about her, and for the life of me I can't see what Shaynor sees in her, or she in him.'

'*Can't* you see what he sees in her?' I insisted.

'Oh, yes, if *that's* what you mean. She's a great, big, fat lump of a girl, and so on. I suppose that's why he's so crazy after her. She isn't his sort. Well, it doesn't matter. My uncle says he's bound to die before the year's out. Your drink's given him a good sleep, at any rate.' Young Mr Cashell could not catch Mr Shaynor's face, which was half turned to the advertisement.

I stoked the stove anew, for the room was growing cold, and lighted another pastille. Mr Shaynor in his chair, never moving, looked through and over me with eyes as wide and lustreless as those of a dead hare.

'Poole's late,' said young Mr Cashell, when I stepped back. 'I'll just send them a call.'

He pressed a key in the semi-darkness, and with a rending crackle there leaped between two brass knobs a spark, streams of sparks, and sparks again.

'Grand, isn't it? *That's* the Power—our unknown Power—kicking and fighting to be let loose,' said young Mr Cashell. 'There she goes—kick—kick—kick into space. I never get over the strangeness of it when I work a sending-machine—waves going into space, you know. T. R. is our call. Poole ought to answer with L. L. L.'

We waited two, three, five minutes. In that silence, of which the boom of the tide was an orderly part, I caught the clear '*kiss—kiss—kiss*' of the halliards on the roof, as they were blown against the installation-pole.

'Poole is not ready. I'll stay here and call you when he is.'

I returned to the shop, and set down my glass on a marble slab with a careless clink. As I did so, Shaynor rose to his feet, his eyes fixed once more on the advertisement, where the young woman bathed in the light from the red jar simpered pinkly over her pearls. His lips moved without cessation. I stepped nearer to listen. 'And threw—and threw—and threw,' he repeated, his face all sharp with some inexplicable agony.

I moved forward astonished. But it was then he found words—delivered roundly and clearly. These:—

And threw warm gules on Madeleine's young breast.*

The trouble passed off his countenance, and he returned lightly to his place, rubbing his hands.

It had never occurred to me, though we had many times discussed reading and prize-competitions as a diversion, that Mr Shaynor ever read Keats, or could quote him at all appositely. There was, after all, a certain stained-glass effect of light on the high bosom of the highly-polished picture which might, by stretch of fancy, suggest, as a vile chromo* recalls some incomparable canvas, the line he had spoken. Night, my drink, and solitude were evidently turning Mr Shaynor into a poet. He sat down again and wrote swiftly on his villainous note-paper, his lips quivering.

I shut the door into the inner office and moved up behind him. He made no sign that he saw or heard. I looked over his shoulder, and read, amid half-formed words, sentences, and wild scratches:—

> ——Very cold it was. Very cold
> The hare—the hare—the hare—
> The birds——*

He raised his head sharply, and frowned toward the blank shutters of the poulterer's shop where they jutted out against our window. Then one clear line came:—

> The hare, in spite of fur, was very cold.

The head, moving machine-like, turned right to the advertisement where the Blaudett's Cathedral pastille reeked abominably. He grunted, and went on:—

> Incense in a censer—
> Before her darling picture framed in gold—
> Maiden's picture—angel's portrait—*

'Hsh!' said Mr Cashell guardedly from the inner office, as though in the presence of spirits. 'There's something coming through from somewhere; but it isn't Poole.' I heard the crackle of sparks as he depressed the keys of the transmitter. In my own brain, too, something crackled, or it might have been the hair on my head. Then I heard my own voice, in a harsh whisper:

'Mr Cashell, there is something coming through here, too. Leave me alone till I tell you.'

'But I thought you'd come to see this wonderful thing—Sir,' indignantly at the end.

'Leave me alone till I tell you. Be quiet.'

I watched—I waited. Under the blue-veined hand—the dry hand of the consumptive—came away clear, without erasure:—

> And my weak spirit fails
> To think how the dead must freeze—

he shivered as he wrote—

> Beneath the churchyard mould.*

Then he stopped, laid the pen down, and leaned back.

For an instant, that was half an eternity, the shop spun before me in a rainbow-tinted whirl, in and through which my own soul most dispassionately considered my own soul as that fought with an over-mastering fear. Then I smelt the strong smell of cigarettes from Mr Shaynor's clothing, and heard, as though it had been the rending of trumpets, the rattle of his breathing. I was still in my place of observation, much as one would watch a rifle-shot at the butts, half-bent, hands on my knees, and head within a few inches of the black, red, and yellow blanket of his shoulder. I was whispering encouragement, evidently to my other self, sounding sentences, such as men pronounce in dreams.

'If he has read Keats, it proves nothing. If he hasn't—like causes *must* beget like effects. There is no escape from this law. *You* ought to be grateful that you know "St Agnes' Eve" without the book; because, given the circumstances, such as Fanny Brand, who is the key of the enigma, and approximately represents the latitude and longitude of Fanny Brawne; allowing also for the bright red colour of the arterial blood upon the handkerchief, which was just what you were puzzling over in the shop just now; and counting the effect of the professional environment,* here almost perfectly duplicated—the result is logical and inevitable. As inevitable as induction.'

Still, the other half of my soul refused to be comforted. It was cowering in some minute and inadequate corner—at an immense distance.

Hereafter, I found myself one person again, my hands still gripping my knees, and my eyes glued on the page before Mr Shaynor. As dreamers accept and explain the upheaval of landscapes and the resurrection of the dead, with excerpts from the evening hymn or the multiplication-table, so I had accepted the facts, whatever they might be, that I should witness, and had devised a theory, sane and plausible to my mind, that explained them all. Nay, I was even in advance of my facts, walking hurriedly before them, assured that they would fit my theory. And all that I now recall of that epoch-making theory are the lofty words: 'If he has read Keats it's the chloric-ether. If he hasn't, it's the identical bacillus, or Hertzian wave of tuberculosis, *plus* Fanny Brand and the professional status which, in conjunction with the main-stream of subconscious thought common to all mankind, has thrown up temporarily an induced Keats.'

Mr Shaynor returned to his work, erasing and rewriting as before with swiftness. Two or three blank pages he tossed aside. Then he wrote, muttering:—

The little smoke of a candle that goes out.

'No,' he muttered. 'Little smoke—little smoke—little smoke. What else?' He thrust his chin forward toward the advertisement, whereunder the last of the Blaudett's Cathedral pastilles fumed in its holder. 'Ah!' Then with relief:—

The little smoke that dies in moonlight cold.

Evidently he was snared by the rhymes of his first verse, for he wrote and rewrote 'gold—cold—mould' many times. Again he sought inspiration from the advertisement, and set down, without erasure, the line I had overheard:—

And threw warm gules on Madeleine's young breast.

As I remembered the original it is 'fair'—a trite word—instead of 'young', and I found myself nodding approval, though I admitted that the attempt to reproduce 'its little smoke in pallid moonlight died' was a failure.

Followed without a break ten or fifteen lines of bald prose— the naked soul's confession of its physical yearning for its beloved—unclean as we count uncleanliness; unwholesome, but human exceedingly; the raw material, so it seemed to me in that hour and in that place, whence Keats wove the twenty-sixth, seventh, and eighth stanzas of his poem. Shame I had none in overseeing this revelation; and my fear had gone with the smoke of the pastille.

'That's it,' I murmured. 'That's how it's blocked out. Go on! Ink it in, man. Ink it in!'

Mr Shaynor returned to broken verse wherein 'loveliness' was made to rhyme with a desire to look upon 'her empty dress'. He picked up a fold of the gay, soft blanket, spread it over one hand, caressed it with infinite tenderness, thought, muttered, traced some snatches which I could not decipher, shut his eyes drowsily, shook his head, and dropped the stuff. Here I found myself at fault, for I could not then see (as I do now) in what manner a red, black, and yellow Austrian blanket coloured his dreams.*

In a few minutes he laid aside his pen, and, chin on hand, considered the shop with thoughtful and intelligent eyes. He threw down the blanket, rose, passed along a line of drug-drawers, and read the names on the labels aloud. Returning, he took from his desk Christy's *New Commercial Plants* and the old Culpepper that I had given him, opened and laid them side by side with a clerky air, all trace of passion gone from his face, read first in one and then in the other, and paused with pen behind his ear.

'What wonder of Heaven's coming now?' I thought.

'Manna—manna—manna,' he said at last, under wrinkled brows. 'That's what I wanted. Good! Now then! Now then! Good! Good! Oh, by God, that's good!' His voice rose and he spoke rightly and fully without a falter:—

> Candied apple, quince and plum and gourd,
> And jellies smoother than the creamy curd,
> And lucent syrups tinct with cinnamon,
> Manna and dates in Argosy transferred
> From Fez; and spiced dainties, every one
> From silken Samarcand to cedared Lebanon.*

He repeated it once more, using 'blander' for 'smoother' in the second line; then wrote it down without erasure, but this time (my set eyes missed no stroke of any word) he substituted

...other' for his atrocious second thought, so that it came away under his hand as it is written in the book—as it is written in the book.

A wind went shouting down the street, and on the heels of the wind followed a spurt and rattle of rain.

After a smiling pause—and good right had he to smile—he began anew, always tossing the last sheet over his shoulder:—

> The sharp rain falling on the window-pane,
> Rattling sleet—the wind-blown sleet. *

Then prose: 'It is very cold of mornings when the wind brings rain and sleet with it. I heard the sleet on the window-pane outside, and thought of you, my darling. I am always thinking of you. I wish we could both run away like two lovers into the storm and get that little cottage by the sea which we are always thinking about, my own dear darling. We could sit and watch the sea beneath our windows. It would be a fairyland all of our own—a fairy sea—a fairy sea. . . .'

He stopped, raised his head, and listened. The steady drone of the Channel along the sea-front that had borne us company so long leaped up a note to the sudden fuller surge that signals the change from ebb to flood. It beat in like the change of step throughout an army—this renewed pulse of the sea—and filled our ears till they, accepting it, marked it no longer.

> A fairyland for you and me
> Across the foam—beyond . . .
> A magic foam, a perilous sea. *

He grunted again with effort and bit his underlip. My throat dried, but I dared not gulp to moisten it lest I should break the spell that was drawing him nearer and nearer to the high-water mark but two of the sons of Adam have reached. Remember that in all the millions permitted there are no more than five—five little lines—of which one can say: 'These are the pure Magic. These are the clear Vision. The rest is only poetry.' And Mr Shaynor was playing hot and cold with two of them!

I vowed no unconscious thought of mine should influence the blindfold soul, and pinned myself desperately to the other three, repeating and re-repeating:—

> A savage spot as holy and enchanted
> As e'er beneath a waning moon was haunted
> By woman wailing for her demon lover.*

But though I believed my brain thus occupied, my every sense hung upon the writing under the dry, bony hand, all brown-fingered with chemicals and cigarette-smoke.

> Our windows fronting on the dangerous foam,

(he wrote, after long, irresolute snatches), and then—

> Our open casements facing desolate seas
> Forlorn—forlorn—

Here again his face grew peaked and anxious with that sense of loss I had first seen when the Power snatched him. But this time the agony was tenfold keener. As I watched it mounted like mercury in the tube. It lighted his face from within till I thought the visibly scourged soul must leap forth naked between his jaws, unable to endure. A drop of sweat trickled from my forehead down my nose and splashed on the back of my hand.

> Our windows facing on the desolate seas
> And pearly foam of magic fairyland—

'Not yet—not yet,' he muttered, 'wait a minute. *Please* wait a minute. I shall get it then—

> Our magic windows fronting on the sea,
> The dangerous foam of desolate seas . . .
>   For aye.

Ouh, my God!'
From head to heel he shook—shook from the marrow of his bones outwards—then leaped to his feet with raised arms, and slid the chair screeching across the tiled floor where it struck the drawers behind and fell with a jar. Mechanically, I stooped to recover it.

As I rose, Mr Shaynor was stretching and yawning at leisure.

'I've had a bit of a doze,' he said. 'How did I come to knock the chair over? You look rather——'

'The chair startled me,' I answered. 'It was so sudden in this quiet.'

Young Mr Cashell behind his shut door was offendedly silent.

'I suppose I must have been dreaming,' said Mr Shaynor.

'I suppose you must,' I said. 'Talking of dreams—I—I noticed you writing—before——'

He flushed consciously.

'I meant to ask you if you've ever read anything written by a man called Keats.'

'Oh! I haven't much time to read poetry, and I can't say that I remember the name exactly. Is he a popular writer?'

'Middling. I thought you might know him because he's the only poet who was ever a druggist. And he's rather what's called the lover's poet.'

'Indeed. I must dip into him. What did he write about?'

'A lot of things. Here's a sample that may interest you.'

Then and there, carefully, I repeated the verse he had twice spoken and once written not ten minutes ago.

'Ah! Anybody could see he was a druggist from that line about the tinctures and syrups. It's a fine tribute to our profession.'

'I don't know,' said young Mr Cashell, with icy politeness, opening the door one half-inch, 'if you still happen to be interested in our trifling experiments. But, should such be the case——'

I drew him aside, whispering, 'Shaynor seemed going off into some sort of fit when I spoke to you just now. I thought, even at the risk of being rude, it wouldn't do to take you off your instruments just as the call was coming through. Don't you see?'

'Granted—granted as soon as asked,' he said, unbending. 'I *did* think it a shade odd at the time. So that was why he knocked the chair down?'

'I hope I haven't missed anything,' I said.

'I'm afraid I can't say that, but you're just in time for the end of a rather curious performance. You can come in too, Mr Shaynor. Listen, while I read it off.'

The Morse instrument was ticking furiously. Mr Cashell interpreted: ' "*K.K.V. Can make nothing of your signals.*" ' A pause. ' "*M.M.V. M.M.V. Signals unintelligible. Purpose anchor Sandown Bay. Examine instruments tomorrow.*" Do you know what that means? It's a couple of men-o'-war working Marconi signals off the Isle of Wight. They are trying to talk to each other. Neither can read the other's messages, but all their messages are being taken in by our receiver here. They've been going on for ever so long. I wish you could have heard it.'

'How wonderful!' I said. 'Do you mean we're overhearing Portsmouth ships trying to talk to each other—that we're eavesdropping across half South England?'

'Just that. Their transmitters are all right, but their receivers are out of order, so they only get a dot here and a dash there. Nothing clear.'

'Why is that?'

'God knows—and Science will know tomorrow. Perhaps the induction is faulty; perhaps the receivers aren't tuned to receive just the number of vibrations per second that the transmitter sends. Only a word here and there. Just enough to tantalize.'

Again the Morse sprang to life.

'That's one of 'em complaining now. Listen: "*Disheartening—most disheartening.*" It's quite pathetic. Have you ever seen a spiritualistic seance? It reminds me of that sometimes—odds and ends of messages coming out of nowhere—a word here and there—no good at all.'

'But mediums are all impostors,' said Mr Shaynor, in the doorway, lighting an asthma-cigarette. 'They only do it for the money they can make. I've seen 'em.'

'Here's Poole, at last—clear as a bell. L. L. L. *Now* we shan't be long.' Mr Cashell rattled the keys merrily. 'Anything you'd like to tell 'em?'

'No, I don't think so,' I said. 'I'll go home and get to bed. I'm feeling a little tired.'

'THEY'*

THE RETURN OF THE CHILDREN

Neither the harps nor the crowns amused, nor the cherubs'
dove-winged races—
Holding hands forlornly the Children wandered beneath the
Dome;
Plucking the radiant robes of the passers-by, and with pitiful
faces
Begging what Princes and Powers refused:—'Ah, please will
you let us go home?'

Over the jewelled floor, nigh weeping, ran to them Mary the
Mother,
Kneeled and caressed and made promise with kisses, and drew
them along to the gateway—
Yea, the all-iron unbribeable Door which Peter must guard and
none other.
Straightway She took the Keys from his keeping, and opened
and freed them straightway.

Then to Her Son, Who had seen and smiled, She said: 'On the
night that I bore Thee
What didst Thou care for a love beyond mine or a heaven that
was not my arm?
Didst Thou push from the nipple, O Child, to hear the angels
adore Thee?
When we two lay in the breath of the kine?' And He said:—
'Thou hast done no harm.'

So through the Void the Children ran homeward merrily hand
in hand,
Looking neither to left nor right where the breathless Heavens
stood still;
And the Guards of the Void resheathed their swords, for they
heard the Command
'Shall I that have suffered the children to come to me hold them
against their will?'

'They'

ONE view called me to another; one hill top to its fellow, half
across the county, and since I could answer at no more trouble
than the snapping forward of a lever, I let the county flow under
my wheels.* The orchid-studded flats of the East gave way to
the thyme, ilex, and grey grass of the Downs; these again to the
rich cornland and fig-trees of the lower coast, where you carry
the beat of the tide on your left hand for fifteen level miles; and
when at last I turned inland through a huddle of rounded hills
and woods I had run myself clean out of my known marks.
Beyond that precise hamlet which stands godmother to the
capital of the United States, I found hidden villages where bees,
the only things awake, boomed in eighty-foot lindens that
overhung grey Norman churches; miraculous brooks diving
under stone bridges built for heavier traffic* than would ever
vex them again; tithe-barns larger than their churches, and an
old smithy that cried out aloud how it had once been a hall of
the Knights of the Temple.* Gipsies I found on a common
where the gorse, bracken, and heath fought it out together up
a mile of Roman road; and a little farther on I disturbed a red
fox rolling dog-fashion in the naked sunlight.

As the wooded hills closed about me I stood up in the car to
take the bearings of that great Down* whose ringed head is a
landmark for fifty miles across the low countries. I judged that
the lie of the country would bring me across some westward-
running road that went to his feet, but I did not allow for the
confusing veils of the woods. A quick turn plunged me first into
a green cutting brim-full of liquid sunshine, next into a gloomy
tunnel where last year's dead leaves whispered and scuffled
about my tyres. The strong hazel stuff meeting overhead had
not been cut for a couple of generations at least, nor had any
axe helped the moss-cankered oak and beech to spring above
them. Here the road changed frankly into a carpeted ride on
whose brown velvet spent primrose-clumps showed like jade,
and a few sickly, white-stalked blue-bells nodded together. As

the slope favoured I shut off the power and slid over the whirled leaves, expecting every moment to meet a keeper; but I only heard a jay, far off, arguing against the silence under the twilight of the trees.

Still the track descended. I was on the point of reversing and working my way back on the second speed ere I ended in some swamp, when I saw sunshine through the tangle ahead and lifted the brake.

It was down again at once. As the light beat across my face my fore-wheels took the turf of a great still lawn from which sprang horsemen ten feet high with levelled lances, monstrous peacocks, and sleek round-headed maids of honour—blue, black, and glistening—all of clipped yew. Across the lawn—the marshalled woods besieged it on three sides—stood an ancient house of lichened and weather-worn stone, with mullioned windows and roofs of rose-red tile. It was Xanked by semi-circular walls, also rose-red, that closed the lawn on the fourth side, and at their feet a box hedge grew man-high. There were doves on the roof about the slim brick chimneys, and I caught a glimpse of an octagonal dove-house behind the screening wall.

Here, then, I stayed; a horseman's green spear laid at my breast; held by the exceeding beauty of that jewel in that setting.

'If I am not packed off for a trespasser, or if this knight does not ride a wallop at me,' thought I, 'Shakespeare and Queen Elizabeth at least must come out of that half-open garden door and ask me to tea.'

A child appeared at an upper window, and I thought the little thing waved a friendly hand. But it was to call a companion, for presently another bright head showed. Then I heard a laugh among the yew-peacocks, and turning to make sure (till then I had been watching the house only) I saw the silver of a fountain behind a hedge thrown up against the sun. The doves on the roof cooed to the cooing water; but between the two notes I caught the utterly happy chuckle of a child absorbed in some light mischief.

The garden door—heavy oak sunk deep in the thickness of the wall—opened further: a woman in a big garden hat set her foot slowly on the time-hollowed stone step and as slowly walked across the turf. I was forming some apology when she lifted up her head and I saw that she was blind.

'I heard you,' she said. 'Isn't that a motor car?'

'I'm afraid I've made a mistake in my road. I should have turned off up above—I never dreamed——' I began.

'But I'm very glad. Fancy a motor car coming into the garden! It will be such a treat——' She turned and made as though looking about her. 'You—you haven't seen any one, have you—perhaps?'

'No one to speak to, but the children seemed interested at a distance.'

'Which?'

'I saw a couple up at the window just now, and I think I heard a little chap in the grounds.'

'Oh, lucky you!' she cried, and her face brightened. 'I hear them, of course, but that's all. You've seen them and heard them?'

'Yes,' I answered. 'And if I know anything of children, one of them's having a beautiful time by the fountain yonder. Escaped, I should imagine.'

'You're fond of children?'

I gave her one or two reasons why I did not altogether hate them.

'Of course, of course,' she said. 'Then you understand. Then you won't think it foolish if I ask you to take your car through the gardens, once or twice—quite slowly. I'm sure they'd like to see it. They see so little, poor things. One tries to make their life pleasant, but——' she threw out her hands towards the woods. 'We're so out of the world here.'

'That will be splendid,' I said. 'But I can't cut up your grass.'

She faced to the right. 'Wait a minute,' she said. 'We're at the South gate, aren't we? Behind those peacocks there's a flagged path. We call it the Peacocks' Walk. You can't see it from here, they tell me, but if you squeeze along by the edge of the wood you can turn at the first peacock and get on to the flags.'

It was sacrilege to wake that dreaming house-front with the clatter of machinery, but I swung the car to clear the turf, brushed along the edge of the wood and turned in on the broad stone path where the fountain-basin lay like one star-sapphire.

'May I come too?' she cried. 'No, please don't help me. They'll like it better if they see me.'

She felt her way lightly to the front of the car, and with one foot on the step she called: 'Children, oh, children! Look and see what's going to happen!'

The voice would have drawn lost souls from the Pit, for the yearning that underlay its sweetness, and I was not surprised to hear an answering shout behind the yews. It must have been the child by the fountain, but he fled at our approach, leaving a little toy boat in the water. I saw the glint of his blue blouse among the still horsemen.

Very disposedly we paraded the length of the walk and at her request backed again. This time the child had got the better of his panic, but stood far off and doubting.

'The little fellow's watching us,' I said. 'I wonder if he'd like a ride.'

'They're very shy still. Very shy. But, oh, lucky you to be able to see them! Let's listen.'

I stopped the machine at once, and the humid stillness, heavy with the scent of box, cloaked us deep. Shears I could hear where some gardener was clipping; a mumble of bees and broken voices that might have been the doves.

'Oh, unkind!' she said weariedly.

'Perhaps they're only shy of the motor. The little maid at the window looks tremendously interested.'

'Yes?' She raised her head. 'It was wrong of me to say that. They are really fond of me. It's the only thing that makes life worth living—when they're fond of you, isn't it? I daren't think what the place would be without them. By the way, is it beautiful?'

'I think it is the most beautiful place I have ever seen.'

'So they all tell me. I can feel it, of course, but that isn't quite the same thing.'

'Then have you never——?' I began, but stopped abashed.

'Not since I can remember. It happened when I was only a few months old, they tell me. And yet I must remember something, else how could I dream about colours. I see light in my dreams, and colours, but I never see *them*. I only hear them just as I do when I'm awake.'

'It's difficult to see faces in dreams. Some people can, but most of us haven't the gift,' I went on, looking up at the window where the child stood all but hidden.

'I've heard that too,' she said. 'And they tell me that one never sees a dead person's face in a dream. Is that true?'

'I believe it is—now I come to think of it.'

'But how is it with yourself—yourself?' The blind eyes turned towards me.

'I have never seen the faces of my dead in any dream,' I answered.

'Then it must be as bad as being blind.'

The sun had dipped behind the woods and the long shades were possessing the insolent horsemen one by one. I saw the light die from off the top of a glossy-leaved lance and all the brave hard green turn to soft black. The house, accepting another day at end, as it had accepted an hundred thousand gone, seemed to settle deeper into its rest among the shadows.

'Have you ever wanted to?' she said after the silence.

'Very much sometimes,' I replied. The child had left the window as the shadows closed upon it.

'Ah! So've I, but I don't suppose it's allowed. . . . Where d'you live?'

'Quite the other side of the county—sixty miles and more, and I must be going back. I've come without my big lamp.'

'But it's not dark yet. I can feel it.'

'I'm afraid it will be by the time I get home. Could you lend me someone to set me on my road at first? I've utterly lost myself.'

'I'll send Madden with you to the cross-roads. We are so out of the world, I don't wonder you were lost! I'll guide you round to the front of the house; but you will go slowly, won't you, till you're out of the grounds? It isn't foolish, do you think?'

'I promise you I'll go like this,' I said, and let the car start herself down the flagged path.

We skirted the left wing of the house, whose elaborately cast lead guttering alone was worth a day's journey; passed under a great rose-grown gate in the red wall, and so round to the high front of the house which in beauty and stateliness as much excelled the back as that all others I had seen.

'Is it so very beautiful?' she said wistfully when she heard my raptures. 'And you like the lead-figures too? There's the old azalea garden behind. They say that this place must have been made for children. Will you help me out, please? I should like to come with you as far as the cross-roads, but I mustn't leave them. Is that you, Madden? I want you to show this gentleman the way to the cross-roads. He has lost his way but—he has seen them.'

A butler appeared noiselessly at the miracle of old oak that must be called the front door, and slipped aside to put on his hat. She stood looking at me with open blue eyes in which no sight lay, and I saw for the first time that she was beautiful.

'Remember,' she said quietly, 'if you are fond of them you will come again,' and disappeared within the house.

The butler in the car said nothing till we were nearly at the lodge gates, where catching a glimpse of a blue blouse in a shrubbery I swerved amply lest the devil that leads little boys to play should drag me into child-murder.

'Excuse me,' he asked of a sudden, 'but why did you do that, Sir?'

'The child yonder.'

'Our young gentleman in blue?'

'Of course.'

'He runs about a good deal. Did you see him by the fountain, Sir?'

'Oh, yes, several times. Do we turn here?'

'Yes, Sir. And did you 'appen to see them upstairs too?'

'At the upper window? Yes.'

'Was that before the mistress come out to speak to you, Sir?'

'A little before that. Why d'you want to know?'

He paused a little. 'Only to make sure that—that they had seen the car, Sir, because with children running about, though I'm sure you're driving particularly careful, there might be an accident. That was all, Sir. Here are the cross-roads. You can't miss your way from now on. Thank you, Sir, but that isn't *our* custom, not with——'

'I beg your pardon,' I said, and thrust away the British silver.

'Oh, it's quite right with the rest of 'em as a rule. Good-bye, Sir.'

He retired into the armour-plated conning tower of his caste and walked away. Evidently a butler solicitous for the honour of his house, and interested, probably through a maid, in the nursery.

Once beyond the signposts at the cross-roads I looked back, but the crumpled hills interlaced so jealously that I could not see where the house had lain. When I asked its name at a cottage along the road, the fat woman who sold sweetmeats there gave me to understand that people with motor cars had small right to live—much less to 'go about talking like carriage folk.' They were not a pleasant-mannered community.

When I retraced my route on the map that evening I was little wiser. Hawkin's Old Farm appeared to be the Survey title of the place, and the old County Gazetteer, generally so ample, did not allude to it. The big house of those parts was Hodnington Hall, Georgian with early Victorian embellishments, as an atrocious steel engraving attested. I carried my difficulty to a neighbour—a deep-rooted tree of that soil—and he gave me a name of a family which conveyed no meaning.

A month or so later—I went again, or it may have been that my car took the road of her own volition. She over-ran the fruitless Downs, threaded every turn of the maze of lanes below the hills, drew through the high-walled woods, impenetrable in their full leaf, came out at the cross-roads where the butler had left me, and a little farther on developed an internal trouble which forced me to turn her in on a grass way-waste that cut into a summer-silent hazel wood. So far as I could make sure by the sun and a six-inch Ordnance map, this should be the road flank of that wood which I had first explored from the heights above. I made a mighty serious business of my repairs and a glittering shop of my repair kit, spanners, pump, and the like, which I spread out orderly upon a rug. It was a trap to catch all childhood, for on such a day, I argued, the children would not be far off. When I paused in my work I listened, but the wood was so full of the noises of summer (though the birds had mated) that I could not at first distinguish these from the tread of small cautious feet stealing across the dead leaves. I rang my bell in an alluring manner, but the feet fled, and I repented, for to a child a sudden noise is very real terror. I must have been at work half an hour when I heard in the wood the voice of the blind woman crying: 'Children, oh, children! Where are you?' and the stillness made slow to close on the perfection of that cry. She came towards me, half feeling her way between the tree boles, and though a child it seemed clung to her skirt, it swerved into the leafage like a rabbit as she drew nearer.

'Is that you?' she said, 'from the other side of the county?'

'Yes, it's me from the other side of the county.'

'Then why didn't you come through the upper woods? They were there just now.'

'They were here a few minutes ago. I expect they knew my car had broken down, and came to see the fun.'

'Nothing serious, I hope? How do cars break down?'

'In fifty different ways. Only mine has chosen the fifty first.'

She laughed merrily at the tiny joke, cooed with delicious laughter, and pushed her hat back.

'Let me hear,' she said.

'Wait a moment,' I cried, 'and I'll get you a cushion.'

She set her foot on the rug all covered with spare parts, and stooped above it eagerly. 'What delightful things!' The hands through which she saw glanced in the chequered sunlight. 'A box here—another box! Why you've arranged them like playing shop!'

'I confess now that I put it out to attract them. I don't need half those things really.'

'How nice of you! I heard your bell in the upper wood. You say they were here before that?'

'I'm sure of it. Why are they so shy? That little fellow in blue who was with you just now ought to have got over his fright. He's been watching me like a Red Indian.'

'It must have been your bell,' she said. 'I heard one of them go past me in trouble when I was coming down. They're shy—so shy even with me.' She turned her face over her shoulder and cried again: 'Children, oh, children! Look and see!'

'They must have gone off together on their own affairs,' I suggested, for there was a murmur behind us of lowered voices broken by the sudden squeaking giggles of childhood. I returned to my tinkerings and she leaned forward, her chin on her hand, listening interestedly.

'How many are they?' I said at last. The work was finished, but I saw no reason to go.

Her forehead puckered a little in thought. 'I don't quite know,' she said simply. 'Sometimes more—sometimes less. They come and stay with me because I love them, you see.'

'That must be very jolly,' I said, replacing a drawer, and as I spoke I heard the inanity of my answer.

'You—you aren't laughing at me,' she cried. 'I—I haven't any of my own. I never married. People laugh at me sometimes about them because—because—'

'Because they're savages,' I returned. 'It's nothing to fret for. That sort laugh at everything that isn't in their own fat lives.'

'I don't know. How should I? I only don't like being laughed at about *them*. It hurts; and when one can't see. . . . I don't want to seem silly,' her chin quivered like a child's as she spoke, 'but we blindies have only one skin, I think. Everything outside hits straight at our souls. It's different with you. You've such good defences in your eyes—looking out—before anyone can really pain you in your soul. People forget that with us.'

I was silent reviewing that inexhaustible matter—the more than inherited (since it is also carefully taught) brutality of the Christian peoples, beside which the mere heathendom of the West Coast nigger is clean and restrained. It led me a long distance into myself.

'Don't do that!' she said of a sudden, putting her hands before her eyes.

'What?'

She made a gesture with her hand.

'That! It's—it's all purple and black. Don't! That colour hurts.'

'But, how in the world do you know about colours?' I exclaimed, for here was a revelation indeed.

'Colours as colours?' she asked.

'No. *Those* Colours* which you saw just now.'

'You know as well as I do,' she laughed, 'else you wouldn't have asked that question. They aren't in the world at all. They're in *you*—when you went so angry.'

'D'you mean a dull purplish patch, like port wine mixed with ink?' I said.

'I've never seen ink or port wine, but the colours aren't mixed. They are separate—all separate.'

'Do you mean black streaks and jags across the purple?'

She nodded. 'Yes—if they are like this,' and zig-zagged her finger again, 'but it's more red than purple—that bad colour.'

'And what are the colours at the top of the—whatever you see?'

Slowly she leaned forward and traced on the rug the figure of the Egg * itself.

'I see them so,' she said, pointing with a grass stem, 'white, green, yellow, red, purple, and when people are angry or bad, black across the red—as you were just now.'

'Who told you anything about it—in the beginning?' I demanded.

'About the colours? No one. I used to ask what colours were when I was little—in table-covers and curtains and carpets, you see—because some colours hurt me and some made me happy. People told me; and when I got older that was how I saw people.' Again she traced the outline of the Egg which it is given to very few of us to see.

'All by yourself?' I repeated.

'All by myself. There wasn't anyone else. I only found out afterwards that other people did not see the Colours.'

She leaned against the tree-bole plaiting and unplaiting chance-plucked grass stems. The children in the wood had drawn nearer. I could see them with the tail of my eye frolicking like squirrels.

'Now I am sure you will never laugh at me,' she went on after a long silence. 'Nor at *them*.'

'Goodness! No!' I cried, jolted out of my train of thought. 'A man who laughs at a child—unless the child is laughing too—is a heathen!'

'I didn't mean that, of course. You'd never laugh *at* children, but I thought—I used to think—that perhaps you might laugh about *them*. So now I beg your pardon. . . . What are you going to laugh at?'

I had made no sound, but she knew.

'At the notion of your begging my pardon. If you had done your duty as a pillar of the State and a landed proprietress you ought to have summoned me for trespass when I barged

through your woods the other day. It was disgraceful of me—
inexcusable.'

She looked at me, her head against the tree trunk—long and
steadfastly—this woman who could see the naked soul.

'How curious,' she half whispered. 'How very curious.'

'Why, what have I done?'

'You don't understand . . . and yet you understood about
the Colours. Don't you understand?'

She spoke with a passion that nothing had justified, and I
faced her bewilderedly as she rose. The children had gathered
themselves in a roundel behind a bramble bush. One sleek head
bent over something smaller, and the set of the little shoulders
told me that fingers were on lips. They, too, had some child's
tremendous secret. I alone was hopelessly astray there in the
broad sunlight.

'No,' I said, and shook my head as though the dead eyes
could note. 'Whatever it is, I don't understand yet. Perhaps I
shall later—if you'll let me come again.'

'You will come again,' she answered. 'You will surely come
again and walk in the wood.'

'Perhaps the children will know me well enough by that time
to let me play with them—as a favour. You know what children
are like.'

'It isn't a matter of favour but of right,' she replied, and while
I wondered what she meant, a dishevelled woman plunged
round the bend of the road, loose-haired, purple, almost lowing
with agony as she ran. It was my rude, fat friend of the
sweetmeat shop. The blind woman heard and stepped forward.
'What is it, Mrs Madehurst?' she asked.

The woman flung her apron over her head and literally
grovelled in the dust, crying that her grandchild was sick to
death, that the local doctor was away fishing, that Jenny the
mother was at her wits' end, and so forth, with repetitions and
bellowings.

'Where's the next nearest doctor?' I asked between paroxysms.

'Madden will tell you. Go round to the house and take him
with you. I'll attend to this. Be quick!' She half supported the
fat woman into the shade. In two minutes I was blowing all the

horns of Jericho* under the front of the House Beautiful, and Madden, in the pantry, rose to the crisis like a butler and a man.

A quarter of an hour at illegal speeds caught us a doctor five miles away. Within the half-hour we had decanted him, much interested in motors, at the door of the sweetmeat shop, and drew up the road to await the verdict.

'Useful things cars,' said Madden, all man and no butler. 'If I'd had one when mine took sick she wouldn't have died.'

'How was it?' I asked.

'Croup. Mrs Madden was away. No one knew what to do. I drove eight miles in a tax cart for the doctor. She was choked when we came back. This car 'd ha' saved her. She'd have been close on ten now.'

'I'm sorry,' I said. 'I thought you were rather fond of children from what you told me going to the cross-roads the other day.'

'Have you seen 'em again, Sir—this mornin'?'

'Yes, but they're well broke to cars. I couldn't get any of them within twenty yards of it.'

He looked at me carefully as a scout considers a stranger—not as a menial should lift his eyes to his divinely appointed* superior.

'I wonder why,' he said just above the breath that he drew.

We waited on. A light wind from the sea wandered up and down the long lines of the woods, and the wayside grasses, whitened already with summer dust, rose and bowed in sallow waves.

A woman, wiping the suds off her arms, came out of the cottage next the sweetmeat shop.

'I've be'n listenin' in de back-yard,' she said cheerily. 'He says Arthur's unaccountable bad. Did ye hear him shruck just now? Unaccountable bad. I reckon t'will come Jenny's turn to walk in de wood nex' week along, Mr Madden.'

'Excuse me, Sir, but your lap-robe is slipping,' said Madden deferentially. The woman started, dropped a curtsey, and hurried away.

'What does she mean by "walking in the wood"?' I asked.

'It must be some saying they use hereabouts. I'm from Norfolk myself,' said Madden. 'They're an independent lot in this county. She took you for a chauffeur, Sir.'

I saw the Doctor come out of the cottage followed by a draggle-tailed wench who clung to his arm as though he could make treaty for her with Death. 'Dat sort,' she wailed—'dey're just as much to us dat has 'em as if dey was lawful born. Just as much—just as much! An' God he'd be just as pleased if you saved 'un, Doctor. Don't take it from me. Miss Florence will tell ye de very same. Don't leave 'im, Doctor!'

'I know, I know,' said the man; 'but he'll be quiet for a while now. We'll get the nurse and the medicine as fast as we can.' He signalled me to come forward with the car, and I strove not to be privy to what followed; but I saw the girl's face, blotched and frozen with grief, and I felt the hand without a ring clutching at my knees when we moved away.

The Doctor was a man of some humour, for I remember he claimed my car under the Oath of Æsculapius,* and used it and me without mercy. First we convoyed Mrs Madehurst and the blind woman to wait by the sick bed till the nurse should come. Next we invaded a neat county town for prescriptions (the Doctor said the trouble was cerebro-spinal meningitis), and when the County Institute, banked and flanked with scared market cattle, reported itself out of nurses for the moment we literally flung ourselves loose upon the county. We conferred with the owners of great houses—magnates at the ends of overarching avenues whose big-boned womenfolk strode away from their tea-tables to listen to the imperious Doctor. At last a white-haired lady sitting under a cedar of Lebanon and surrounded by a court of magnificent Borzois*—all hostile to motors—gave the Doctor, who received them as from a princess, written orders which we bore many miles at top speed, through a park, to a French nunnery, where we took over in exchange a pallid-faced and trembling Sister. She knelt at the bottom of the tonneau* telling her beads without pause till, by short cuts of the Doctor's invention, we had her to the sweet-meat shop once more. It was a long afternoon crowded with mad episodes that rose and dissolved like the dust of our wheels; cross-sections of remote and incomprehensible lives through which we raced at right angles; and I went home in the dusk, wearied out, to dream of the clashing horns of cattle; round-eyed nuns walking in a garden of graves; pleasant tea-parties beneath shaded trees; the carbolic-scented, grey-painted corridors of the County Institute; the steps of shy children in the wood, and the hands that clung to my knees as the motor began to move.

* * *

I had intended to return in a day or two, but it pleased Fate to hold me from that side of the county, on many pretexts, till the elder and the wild rose had fruited. There came at last a brilliant day, swept clear from the south-west, that brought the hills within hand's reach—a day of unstable airs and high filmy clouds. Through no merit of my own I was free, and set the car for the third time on that known road. As I reached the crest of the Downs I felt the soft air change, saw it glaze under the sun; and, looking down at the sea, in that instant beheld the blue of the Channel turn through polished silver and dulled steel to dingy pewter. A laden collier hugging the coast steered outward for deeper water, and, across copper-coloured haze, I saw sails rise one by one on the anchored fishing-fleet. In a deep dene behind me an eddy of sudden wind drummed through sheltered oaks, and spun aloft the first dry sample of autumn leaves. When I reached the beach road the sea-fog fumed over the brickfields, and the tide was telling all the groins of the gale beyond Ushant. In less than an hour summer England vanished in chill grey. We were again the shut island of the North, all the ships of the world bellowing at our perilous gates; and between their outcries ran the piping of bewildered gulls. My cap dripped moisture, the folds of the rug held it in pools or sluiced it away in runnels, and the salt-rime stuck to my lips.

Inland the smell of autumn loaded the thickened fog among the trees, and the drip became a continuous shower. Yet the late flowers—mallow of the wayside, scabious of the field, and dahlia of the garden—showed gay in the mist, and beyond the sea's breath there was little sign of decay in the leaf. Yet in the villages the house doors were all open, and bare-legged, bare-headed children sat at ease on the damp doorsteps to shout 'pip-pip' at the stranger.

I made bold to call at the sweetmeat shop, where Mrs Madehurst met me with a fat woman's hospitable tears. Jenny's child, she said, had died two days after the nun had come. It was, she felt, best out of the way, even though insurance offices, for reasons which she did not pretend to follow, would not willingly insure* such stray lives. 'Not but what Jenny didn't tend to Arthur as though he'd come all proper at de end of de first year—like Jenny herself.' Thanks to Miss Florence, the child had been buried with a pomp which, in Mrs Madehurst's opinion, more than covered the small irregularity of its birth. She described the coffin, within and without, the glass hearse, and the evergreen* lining of the grave.

'But how's the mother?' I asked.

'Jenny? Oh, she'll get over it. I've felt dat way with one or two o' my own. She'll get over. She's walkin' in de wood now.'

'In this weather?'

Mrs Madehurst looked at me with narrowed eyes across the counter.

'I dunno but it opens de 'eart like. Yes, it opens de 'eart. Dat's where losin' and bearin' comes so alike in de long run, we do say.'

Now the wisdom of the old wives is greater than that of all the Fathers, and this last oracle sent me thinking so extendedly as I went up the road, that I nearly ran over a woman and a child at the wooded corner by the lodge gates of the House Beautiful.

'Awful weather!' I cried, as I slowed dead for the turn.

'Not so bad,' she answered placidly out of the fog. 'Mine's used to 'un. You'll find yours indoors, I reckon.'

Indoors, Madden received me with professional courtesy, and kind inquiries for the health of the motor, which he would put under cover.

I waited in a still, nut-brown hall, pleasant with late flowers and warmed with a delicious wood fire—a place of good influence and great peace. (Men and women may sometimes, after great effort, achieve a creditable lie; but the house, which is their temple, cannot say anything save the truth of those who have lived in it.)*A child's cart and a doll lay on the black-and-white floor, where a rug had been kicked back. I felt that the children had only just hurried away—to hide themselves, most like—in the many turns of the great adzed staircase that climbed statelily out of the hall, or to crouch at gaze behind the lions and roses of the carven gallery above. Then I heard her voice above me, singing as the blind sing—from the soul:—

> In the pleasant orchard-closes.

And all my early summer came back at the call. *

> In the pleasant orchard-closes,
> God bless all our gains say we—
> But may God bless all our losses,
> Better suits with our degree.

She dropped the marring fifth line, * and repeated—

> Better suits with our degree!

I saw her lean over the gallery, her linked hands white as pearl against the oak.

'Is that you—from the other side of the county?' she called.

'Yes, me—from the other side of the county,' I answered, laughing.

'What a long time before you had to come here again.' She ran down the stairs, one hand lightly touching the broad rail. 'It's two months and four days. Summer's gone!'

'I meant to come before, but Fate prevented.'

'I knew it. Please do something to that fire. They won't let me play with it, but I can feel it's behaving badly. Hit it!'

I looked on either side of the deep fireplace, and found but a half-charred hedge-stake with which I punched a black log into flame.

'It never goes out, day or night,' she said, as though explaining. 'In case any one comes in with cold toes, you see.'

'It's even lovelier inside than it was out,' I murmured. The red light poured itself along the age-polished dusky panels till the Tudor roses and lions of the gallery took colour and motion. An old eagle-topped convex mirror gathered the picture into its mysterious heart, distorting afresh the distorted shadows, and curving the gallery lines into the curves of a ship. The day was shutting down in half a gale as the fog turned to stringy scud. Through the uncurtained mullions of the broad window I could see valiant horsemen of the lawn rear and recover against the wind that taunted them with legions of dead leaves.

'Yes, it must be beautiful,' she said. 'Would you like to go over it? There's still light enough upstairs.'

I followed her up the unflinching, wagon-wide staircase to the gallery whence opened the thin fluted Elizabethan doors.

'Feel how they put the latch low down for the sake of the children.' She swung a light door inward.

'By the way, where are they?' I asked. 'I haven't even heard them today.'

She did not answer at once. Then, 'I can only hear them,' she replied softly. 'This is one of their rooms—everything ready, you see.'

She pointed into a heavily-timbered room. There were little low gate tables and children's chairs. A doll's house, its hooked front half open, faced a great dappled rocking-horse, from whose padded saddle it was but a child's scramble to the broad window-seat overlooking the lawn. A toy gun lay in a corner beside a gilt wooden cannon.

'Surely they've only just gone,' I whispered. In the failing light a door creaked cautiously. I heard the rustle of a frock and the patter of feet—quick feet through a room beyond.

'I heard that,' she cried triumphantly. 'Did you? Children, oh, children! Where are you?'

The voice filled the walls that held it lovingly to the last perfect note, but there came no answering shout such as I had heard in the garden. We hurried on from room to oak-floored room; up a step here, down three steps there; among a maze of passages; always mocked by our quarry. One might as well have tried to work an unstopped warren with a single ferret. There were bolt-holes innumerable—recesses in walls, embrasures of deep slitten windows now darkened, whence they could start up behind us; and abandoned fireplaces, six feet deep in the masonry, as well as the tangle of communicating doors. Above all, they had the twilight for their helper in our game. I had caught one or two joyous chuckles of evasion, and once or twice had seen the silhouette of a child's frock against some darkening window at the end of a passage; but we returned empty-handed to the gallery, just as a middle-aged woman was setting a lamp in its niche.

'No, I haven't seen her* either this evening, Miss Florence,' I heard her say, 'but that Turpin he says he wants to see you about his shed.'

'Oh, Mr Turpin must want to see me very badly. Tell him to come to the hall, Mrs Madden.'

I looked down into the hall whose only light was the dulled fire, and deep in the shadow I saw them at last. They must have slipped down while we were in the passages, and now thought themselves perfectly hidden behind an old gilt leather screen. By child's law, my fruitless chase was as good as an introduction, but since I had taken so much trouble I resolved to force them to come forward later by the simple trick, which children detest, of pretending not to notice them. They lay close, in a little huddle, no more than shadows except when a quick flame betrayed an outline.

'And now we'll have some tea,' she said. 'I believe I ought to have offered it you at first, but one doesn't arrive at manners somehow when one lives alone and is considered—h'm—peculiar.' Then with very pretty scorn, 'Would you like a lamp to see to eat by?'

'The firelight's much pleasanter, I think.' We descended into that delicious gloom and Madden brought tea.

I took my chair in the direction of the screen ready to surprise or be surprised as the game should go, and at her permission, since a hearth is always sacred, bent forward to play with the fire.

'Where do you get these beautiful short faggots from?' I asked idly. 'Why, they are tallies!'

'Of course,' she said. 'As I can't read or write I'm driven back on the early English tally for my accounts. Give me one and I'll tell you what it meant.'

I passed her an unburned hazel-tally, about a foot long, and she ran her thumb down the nicks.

'This is the milk-record for the home farm for the month of April last year, in gallons,' said she. 'I don't know what I should have done without tallies. An old forester of mine taught me the system. It's out of date now for every one else; but my tenants respect it. One of them's coming now to see me. Oh, it doesn't matter. He has no business here out of office hours. He's a greedy, ignorant man—very greedy or—he wouldn't come here after dark.'

'Have you much land then?'

'Only a couple of hundred acres in hand, thank goodness. The other six hundred are nearly all let to folk who knew my folk before me, but this Turpin is quite a new man—and a highway robber.'

'But are you sure I shan't be——?'

'Certainly not. You have the right. He hasn't any children.'

'Ah, the children!' I said, and slid my low chair back till it nearly touched the screen that hid them. 'I wonder whether they'll come out for me.'

There was a murmur of voices—Madden's and a deeper note—at the low, dark side door, and a ginger-headed, canvas-gaitered giant of the unmistakable tenant-farmer type stumbled or was pushed in.

'Come to the fire, Mr Turpin,' she said.

'If—if you please, Miss, I'll—I'll be quite as well by the door.' He clung to the latch as he spoke like a frightened child. Of a sudden I realised that he was in the grip of some almost overpowering fear.

'Well?'

'About that new shed for the young stock—that was all. These first autumn storms settin' in . . . but I'll come again, Miss.' His teeth did not chatter much more than the door latch.

'I think not,' she answered levelly. 'The new shed—m'm. What did my agent write you on the 15th?'

'I—fancied p'raps that if I came to see you—ma—man to man like, Miss. But——'

His eyes rolled into every corner of the room wide with horror. He half opened the door through which he had entered, but I noticed it shut again—from without and firmly.

'He wrote what I told him,' she went on. 'You are over-stocked already. Dunnett's Farm never carried more than fifty bullocks—even in Mr Wright's time. And *he* used cake.* You've sixty-seven and you don't cake. You've broken the lease in that respect. You're dragging the heart out of the farm.'

'I'm—I'm getting some minerals—superphosphates—next week. I've as good as ordered a truck-load already. I'll go down to the station tomorrow about 'em. Then I can come and see you man to man like, Miss, in the daylight. . . . That gentle-man's not going away, is he?' He almost shrieked.

I had only slid the chair a little farther back, reaching behind me to tap on the leather of the screen, but he jumped like a rat.

'No. Please attend to me, Mr Turpin.' She turned in her chair and faced him with his back to the door. It was an old and sordid little piece of scheming that she forced from him— his plea for the new cow-shed at his landlady's expense, that he might with the covered manure pay his next year's rent out of the valuation after, as she made clear, he had bled the enriched pastures to the bone. I could not but admire the intensity of his greed, when I saw him out-facing for its sake whatever terror it was that ran wet on his forehead.

I ceased to tap the leather—was, indeed, calculating the cost of the shed—when I felt my relaxed hand taken and turned softly between the soft hands of a child. So at last I had triumphed. In a moment I would turn and acquaint myself with those quick-footed wanderers. . . .

The little brushing kiss fell in the centre of my palm—as a gift on which the fingers were, once, expected to close: as the all-faithful half-reproachful signal of a waiting child not used to neglect even when grown-ups were busiest—a fragment of the mute code devised very long ago.

Then I knew. And it was as though I had known from the first day when I looked across the lawn at the high window.

I heard the door shut. The woman turned to me in silence, and I felt that she knew.

What time passed after this I cannot say. I was roused by the fall of a log, and mechanically rose to put it back. Then I returned to my place in the chair very close to the screen.*

'Now you understand,' she whispered, across the packed shadows.

'Yes, I understand—now.* Thank you.'

'I—I only hear them.' She bowed her head in her hands. 'I have no right, you know—no other right. I have neither borne nor lost—neither borne nor lost!'

'Be very glad then,' said I, for my soul was torn open within me.

'Forgive me!'

She was still, and I went back to my sorrow and my joy.

'It was because I loved them so,' she said at last, brokenly. '*That* was why it was, even from the first—even before I knew that they—they were all I should ever have. And I love them so!'

She stretched out her arms to the shadows and the shadows within the shadow.

'They came because I loved them—because I needed them. I—I must have made them come. Was that wrong, think you?'

'No—no.'

'I—I grant you that the toys and—and all that sort of thing were nonsense, but—but I used to so hate empty rooms myself when I was little.' She pointed to the gallery. 'And the passages all empty. . . . And how could I ever bear the garden door shut? Suppose——'

'Don't! For pity's sake, don't!' I cried. The twilight had brought a cold rain with gusty squalls that plucked at the leaded windows.

'And the same thing with keeping the fire in all night. *I* don't think it so foolish—do you?'

I looked at the broad brick hearth, saw, through tears I believe, that there was no unpassable iron* on or near it, and bowed my head.

'I did all that and lots of other things—just to make believe. Then they came. I heard them, but I didn't know that they were not mine by right till Mrs Madden told me——'

'The butler's wife? What?'

'One of them—I heard—she saw. And knew. Hers! *Not* for me. I didn't know at first. Perhaps I was jealous.*Afterwards, I began to understand that it was only because I loved them, not because—— . . . Oh, you *must* bear or lose,' she said piteously. 'There is no other way—and yet they love me. They must! Don't they?'

There was no sound in the room except the lapping voices of the fire, but we two listened intently, and she at least took comfort from what she heard. She recovered herself and half rose. I sat still in my chair by the screen.

'Don't think me a wretch to whine about myself like this, but—but I'm all in the dark, you know, and *you* can see.'

In truth I could see, and my vision confirmed me in my resolve, though that was like the very parting of spirit and flesh. Yet a little longer I would stay since it was the last time.

'You think it is wrong, then?' she cried sharply, though I had said nothing.

'Not for you. A thousand times no. For you it is right. . . . I am grateful to you beyond words. For me it would be wrong. For me only. . . .'

'Why?' she said, but passed her hand before her face as she had done at our second meeting in the wood. 'Oh, I see,' she went on simply as a child. 'For you it would be wrong.' Then with a little indrawn laugh, 'and, d'you remember, I called you lucky—once—at first. You who must never come here again!'

She left me to sit a little longer by the screen, and I heard the sound of her feet die out along the gallery above.

THE EDGE OF THE EVENING*

Ah! What avails the classic bent,
    And what the chosen word,
Against the undoctored incident
    That actually occurred?

And what is Art whereto we press
    Through paint and prose and rhyme—
When Nature in her nakedness
    Defeats us every time?*

'Hı! Hı! Hold your horses! Stop! . . . Well! Well!' A lean man
in a sable-lined overcoat leaped from a private car and barred
my way up Pall Mall. 'You don't know me? You're excusable.
I wasn't wearing much of anything last time we met—in South
Africa.'

The scales fell from my eyes, and I saw him once more in
a sky-blue army shirt, behind barbed wire, among Dutch
prisoners bathing at Simonstown, more than a dozen years
ago.* 'Why, it's Zigler—Laughton O. Zigler!' I cried. 'Well, I
am glad to see you.'

'Oh no! You don't work any of your English on me. "So glad
to see you, doncher know—an' ta-ta!" Do you reside in this
village?'

'No. I'm up here buying stores.'

'Then you take my automobile. Where to? . . . Oh, I know
them! My Lord Marshalton is one of the Directors. Pigott, drive
to the Army and Navy Co-operative Supply Association
Limited, Victoria Street, Westminster.'

He settled himself on the deep dove-colour pneumatic
cushions, and his smile was like the turning on of all the
electrics. His teeth were whiter than the ivory fittings. He smelt
of rare soap and cigarettes—such cigarettes as he handed me
from a golden box with an automatic lighter. On my side of the
car was a gold-mounted mirror, card and toilette case. I looked
at him inquiringly.

'Yes,' he nodded, 'two years after I quit the Cape. She's not an Ohio girl, though. She's in the country now. Is that right? She's at our little place in the country. We'll go there as soon as you're through with your grocery-list. Engagements? The only engagement you've got is to grab your grip—get your bag from your hotel, I mean—and come right along and meet her. You are the captive of *my* bow and spear now.'

'I surrender,' I said meekly. 'Did the Zigler automatic gun do all this?' I pointed to the car fittings.

'Psha! Think of your rememberin' that! Well, no. The Zigler is a great gun—the greatest ever—but life's too short, an' too interestin', to squander on pushing her in military society. I've leased my rights in her to a Pennsylvanian-Transylvanian citizen full of mentality and moral uplift. If those things weigh with the Chancelleries of Europe, he will make good and—I shall be surprised. Excuse me!'

He bared his head as we passed the statue of the Great Queen outside Buckingham Palace.

'A very great lady!' said he. 'I have enjoyed her hospitality. She represents one of the most wonderful institutions in the world. The next is the one we are going to. Mrs Zigler uses 'em, and they break her up every week on returned empties.'

'Oh, you mean the Stores?' I said.

'Mrs Zigler means it more. They are quite ambassadorial in their outlook. I guess I'll wait outside and pray while you wrestle with 'em.'

My business at the Stores finished, and my bag retrieved from the hotel, his moving palace slid us into the country.

'I owe it to you,' Zigler began as smoothly as the car, 'to tell you what I am now. I represent the business end of the American Invasion. Not the blame cars themselves—I wouldn't be found dead in one—but the tools that make 'em. I am the Zigler Higher-Speed Tool and Lathe Trust. The Trust, sir, is entirely my own—in my own inventions. I am the Renzalaer ten-cylinder aerial—the lightest aeroplane-engine on the market—one price, one power, one guarantee. I am the Orlebar Paper-welt, Pulp-panel Company for aeroplane bodies; and I am the Rush Silencer* for military aeroplanes— absolutely silent—which the Continent leases under royalty. With three exceptions, the British aren't wise to it yet. That's all I represent at present. You saw me take off my hat to your late Queen? I owe every cent I have to that great an' good Lady. Yes, sir, I came out of Africa, after my eighteen months' rest-cure and open-air treatment and sea-bathing, as her prisoner of war, like a giant refreshed. There wasn't anything could hold me, when I'd got my hooks into it, after that experience. And to you as a representative British citizen, I say here and now that I regard you as the founder of the family fortune—Tommy's and mine.'

'But I only gave you some papers and tobacco.'

'What more does any citizen need? The Cullinan diamond wouldn't have helped me as much then; an'—talking about South Africa, tell me——'

We talked about South Africa till the car stopped at the Georgian lodge of a great park.

'We'll get out here. I want to show you a rather sightly view,' said Zigler.

We walked, perhaps, half a mile, across timber-dotted turf, past a lake, entered a dark rhododendron-planted wood, ticking with the noise of pheasants' feet, and came out suddenly, where five rides met, at a small classic temple between lichened stucco statues which faced a circle of turf, several acres in extent. Irish yews, of a size that I had never seen before, walled the sunless circle like cliffs of riven obsidian, except at the lower end, where it gave on to a stretch of undulating bare ground ending in a timbered slope half-a-mile away.

'That's where the old Marshalton race-course used to be,' said Zigler. 'That ice-house is called Flora's Temple. Nell Gwynne and Mrs Siddons an' Taglioni an' all that crowd used to act plays here for King George the Third. Wasn't it? Well, George is the only king I play. Let it go at that. This circle was the stage, I guess. The kings an' the nobility sat in Flora's Temple. I forget who sculped these statues at the door. They're the Comic and Tragic Muse. But it's a sightly view, ain't it?'

The sunlight was leaving the park. I caught a glint of silver to the southward beyond the wooded ridge.

'That's the ocean—the Channel, I mean,' said Zigler. 'It's twenty-three miles as a man flies. A sightly view, ain't it?'

I looked at the severe yews, the dumb yelling mouths of the two statues, at the blue-green shadows on the unsunned grass, and at the still bright plain in front where some deer were feeding.

'It's a most dramatic contrast, but I think it would be better on a summer's day,' I said, and we went on, up one of the noiseless rides, a quarter of a mile at least, till we came to the porticoed front of an enormous Georgian pile. Four footmen revealed themselves in a hall hung with pictures.

'I hired this off of my Lord Marshalton,' Zigler explained, while they helped us out of our coats under the severe eyes of ruffed and periwigged ancestors. 'Ya-as. They always look at *me* too, as if I'd blown in from the gutter. Which, of course, I have. That's Mary, Lady Marshalton. Old man Joshua* painted her. Do you see any likeness to my Lord Marshalton? Why, haven't you ever met up with him? He was Captain Mankeltow—my Royal British Artillery captain that blew up my gun in the war, an' then tried to bury me against my religious principles.* Ya-as. His father died and he got the lordship. That was about all he got by the time that your British death-duties were through with him. So he said I'd oblige him by hiring his ranch. It's a hell an' a half of a proposition to handle, but Tommy—Mrs Laughton—understands it. Come right in to the parlour and be very welcome.'

He guided me, hand on shoulder, into a babble of high-pitched talk and laughter that filled a vast drawing-room. He introduced me as the founder of the family fortunes to a little, lithe, dark-eyed woman whose speech and greeting were of the soft-lipped South. She in turn presented me to her mother, a black-browed, snowy-haired old lady with a cap of priceless Venetian point,* hands that must have held many hearts in their time, and a dignity as unquestioned and unquestioning as an empress. She was, indeed, a Burton of Savannah, who, on their own ground, out-rank the Lees of Virginia. The rest of the company came from Buffalo, Cincinnati, Cleveland, and Chicago, with here and there a softening southern strain. A party of young folk popped corn beneath a mantelpiece surmounted by a Gainsborough. Two portly men, half hidden by a cased harp, discussed, over sheaves of typewritten documents, the terms of some contract. A knot of matrons talked servants—Irish *versus* German—across the grand piano. A youth ravaged an old bookcase, while beside him a tall girl stared at the portrait of a woman of many loves, dead three hundred years, but now leaping to life and warning under the shaded frame-light. In a corner half-a-dozen girls examined the glazed tables that held the decorations—English and foreign—of the late Lord Marshalton.

'See heah! Would this be the Ordeh of the Gyartah?' one said, pointing.

'I presoom likely. No! The Garter has "*Honey swore*" *—I know that much. This is "*Tria juncta*" * something.'

'Oh, what's that cunning little copper cross with "For Valurr"?' * a third cried.

'Say! Look at here!' said the young man at the bookcase. 'Here's a first edition of *Handley Cross* * and a Beewick's *Birds* right next to it—just like so many best sellers. Look, Maidie!'

The girl beneath the picture half turned her body but not her eyes.

'You don't tell *me*!' she said slowly. 'Their women amounted to something after all.'

'But Woman's scope and outlook was vurry limmutted in those days,' one of the matrons put in, from the piano.

'Limutted? For *her*? If they whurr, I guess she was the limmut. Who was she? Peters, whurr's the cat'log?'

A thin butler, in charge of two footmen removing the tea-batteries, slid to a table and handed her a blue-and-gilt book. He was buttonholed by one of the men behind the harp, who wished to get a telephone call through to Edinburgh.

'The local office shuts at six,' said Peters. 'But I can get through to'—he named some town—'in ten minutes, sir.'

'That suits me. You'll find me here when you've hitched up. Oh, say, Peters! We—Mister Olpherts an' me—ain't goin' by that early morning train tomorrow—but the other one—on the other line—whatever they call it.'

'The nine twenty-seven, sir. Yes, sir. Early breakfast will be at half-past eight and the car will be at the door at nine.'

'Peters!' an imperious young voice called. 'What's the matteh with Lord Marshalton's Ordeh of the Gyartah? We cyan't find it anywheah.'

'Well, miss, I *have* heard that that Order is usually returned to His Majesty on the death of the holder. Yes, miss.' Then in a whisper to a footman, 'More butter for the pop-corn in King

Charles's Corner.' He stopped behind my chair. 'Your room is Number Eleven, sir. May I trouble you for your keys?'

He left the room with a six-year-old maiden called Alice who had announced she would not go to bed "less Peter, Peter, Punkin-eater* takes me—so there!'

He very kindly looked in on me for a moment as I was dressing for dinner. 'Not at all, sir,' he replied to some compliment I paid him. 'I valeted the late Lord Marshalton for fifteen years. He was very abrupt in his movements, sir. As a rule I never received more than an hour's notice of a journey. We used to go to Syria frequently. I have been twice to Babylon. Mr and Mrs Zigler's requirements are, comparatively speaking, few.'

'But the guests?'

'Very little out of the ordinary as soon as one knows their ordinaries. Extremely simple, if I may say so, sir.'

I had the privilege of taking Mrs Burton in to dinner, and was rewarded with an entirely new, and to me rather shocking, view of Abraham Lincoln, who, she said, had wasted the heritage of his land by blood and fire, and had surrendered the remnant to aliens. 'My brother, suh,' she said, 'fell at Gettysburg in order that Armenians should colonize New England today. If I took any interest in any dam-Yankee outside of my son-in-law Laughton yondah, I should say that my brother's death had been amply avenged.'

The man at her right took up the challenge, and the war spread. Her eyes twinkled over the flames she had lit.

'Don't these folk,' she said a little later, 'remind you of Arabs picnicking under the Pyramids?'

'I've never seen the Pyramids,' I replied.

'Hm! I didn't know you were as English as all that.' And when I laughed, 'Are you?'

'Always. It saves trouble.'

'Now that's just what I find so significant among the English'—this was Alice's mother, I think, with one elbow well forward among the salted almonds. 'Oh, I know how *you* feel, Madam Burton, but a Northerner like myself—I'm Buffalo— even though we come over every year— notices the desire for comfort in England. There's so little conflict or uplift in British society.'

'But we like being comfortable,' I said.

'I know it. It's very characteristic. But ain't it a little, just a little, lacking in adaptability an' imagination?'

'They haven't any need for adaptability,' Madam Burton struck in. 'They haven't any Ellis Island* standards to live up to.'

'But we can assimilate,' the Buffalo woman charged on.

'Now you *have* done it!' I whispered to the old lady as the blessed word 'assimilation' woke up all the old arguments for and against.

There was not a dull moment in that dinner for me—nor afterwards when the boys and girls at the piano played the rag-time tunes of their own land, while their elders, inexhaustibly interested, replunged into the discussion of that land's future, till there was talk of coon-can.* When all the company had been set to tables Zigler led me into his book-lined study, where I noticed he kept his golf-clubs, and spoke simply as a child, gravely as a bishop, of the years that were past since our last meeting. . . .

'That's about all, I guess—up to date,' he said when he had unrolled the bright map of his fortunes across three continents. 'Bein' rich suits me. So does your country, sir. My own country? You heard what that Detroit man said at dinner. "A Government of the alien, by the alien, for the alien." Mother's right, too. Lincoln killed us. From the highest motives—but he killed us. Oh, say, that reminds me. 'J'ever kill a man from the highest motives?'

'Not from any motive—as far as I remember.'

'Well, I have. It don't weigh on my mind any, but it was interesting. Life *is* interesting for a rich—for any—man in England. Ya-as! Life in England is like settin' in the front row at the theatre and never knowin' when the whole blame drama won't spill itself into your lap. I didn't always know that. I lie abed now, and I blush to think of some of the breaks I made in South Africa. About the British. Not your official method of doin' business. But the Spirit. I was 'way, 'way off on the Spirit. Are you acquainted with any other country where you'd have to kill a man or two to get at the National Spirit?'

'Well,' I answered, 'next to marrying one of its women, killing one of its men makes for pretty close intimacy with any country. I take it you killed a British citizen.'

'Why, no. Our syndicate confined its operations to aliens—dam-fool aliens. . . . 'J'ever know an English lord called Lundie?* Looks like a frame-food and soap advertisement. I imagine he was in your Supreme Court before he came into his lordship.'

'He is a lawyer—what we call a Law Lord—a Judge of Appeal—not a real hereditary lord.'

'That's as much beyond me as *this*!' Zigler slapped a fat Debrett* on the table. 'But I presoom this unreal Law Lord Lundie is kind o' real in his decisions? I judged so. And—one more question. 'Ever meet a man called Walen?'

'D'you mean Burton-Walen, the editor of——,' I mentioned the journal.

'That's him. 'Looks like a tough, talks like a Maxim, and trains with kings.'

'He does,' I said. 'Burton-Walen knows all the crowned heads of Europe intimately. It's his hobby.'

'Well, there's the whole outfit for you—exceptin' my Lord Marshalton, *née* Mankeltow, an' me. All active murderers—specially the Law Lord—or accessories after the fact. And what do they hand you out for *that*, in this country?'

'Twenty years, I believe,' was my reply.

He reflected a moment.

'No-o-o,' he said, and followed it with a smoke-ring. 'Twenty months at the Cape is my limit. Say, murder ain't the soul-shatterin' event those nature-fakers in the magazines make out. It develops naturally like any other proposition. . . . Say, 'j'ever play this golf game? It's come up in the States from Maine to California, an' we're prodoocin' all the champions in sight. Not a business man's play, but interestin'. I've got a golf-links in the park here that they tell me is the finest inland course ever. I had to pay extra for that when I hired the ranch—last year. It was just before I signed the papers that our murder eventuated. My Lord Marshalton he asked me down for the week-end to fix up something or other—about Peters and the linen, I think 'twas. Mrs Zigler took a holt of the proposition. She understood Peters from the word "go." There wasn't any house-party; only fifteen or twenty folk. A full house is thirty-two, Tommy tells me. 'Guess we must be near on that tonight. In the smoking-room here, my Lord Marshalton— Mankeltow that was—introduces me to this Walen man with the nose. He'd been in the War too, from start to finish. He knew all the columns and generals that I'd battled with in the days of my Zigler gun. We kinder fell into each other's arms an' let the harsh world go by for a while.

'Walen he introduces me to your Lord Lundie. *He* was a new proposition to me. If he hadn't been a lawyer he'd have made a lovely cattle-king. I thought I had played poker some. Another of my breaks. Ya-as! It cost me eleven hundred dollars besides what Tommy said when I retired. I have no fault to find with your hereditary aristocracy, or your judiciary, or your press.

'Sunday we all went to Church across the Park here. . . . Psha! Think o' your rememberin' my religion! I've become an Episcopalian since I married. Ya-as. . . . After lunch Walen did his crowned-heads-of-Europe stunt in the smokin'-room here. He was long on Kings. And Continental crises. I do not pretend to follow British domestic politics, but in the aeroplane business a man has to know something of international possibilities. At present, you British are settin' in kimonoes on dynamite kegs. Walen's talk put me wise on the location and size of some of the kegs. Ya-as!

'After that, we four went out to look at those golf-links I was hirin'. We each took a club. Mine'—he glanced at a great tan bag by the fireplace—'was the beginner's friend—the cleek. Well, sir, this golf proposition took a holt of me as quick as—quick as death. They had to prise me off the greens when it got too dark to see, and then we went back to the house. I was walkin' ahead with my Lord Marshalton talkin' beginners' golf. (*I* was the man who ought to have been killed by rights.) We cut 'cross lots through the woods to Flora's Temple—that place I showed you this afternoon. Lundie and Walen were, maybe, twenty or thirty rod * behind us in the dark. Marshalton and I stopped at the theatre to admire at the ancestral yew-trees. He took me right under the biggest—King Somebody's Yew— and while I was spannin' it with my handkerchief, he says, "Look heah!" just as if it was a rabbit—and down comes a bi-plane into the theatre with no more noise than the dead. My

Rush Silencer is the only one on the market that allows that sort of gumshoe work. . . . What? A bi-plane—with two men in it. Both men jump out and start fussin' with the engines. I was starting to tell Mankeltow—I can't remember to call him Marshalton any more—that it looked as if the Royal British Flying Corps had got on to my Rush Silencer at last; but he steps out from under the yew to these two Stealthy Steves and says, "What's the trouble? Can I be of any service?" He thought—so did I—'twas some of the boys from Aldershot or Salisbury.* Well, sir, from there on, the situation developed like a motion-picture in Hell. The man on the nigh side of the machine whirls round, pulls his gun and fires into Mankeltow's face. I laid him out with my cleek automatically. Any one who shoots a friend of mine gets what's comin' to him if I'm within reach. He drops. Mankeltow rubs his neck with his handkerchief. The man the far side of the machine starts to run. Lundie down the ride, or it might have been Walen, shouts, "What's happened?" Mankeltow says, "Collar that chap."

'The second man runs ring-a-ring-o'-roses round the machine, one hand reachin' behind him. Mankeltow heads him off to me. He breaks blind for Walen and Lundie, who are runnin' up the ride. There's some sort of mix-up among 'em, which it's too dark to see, and a thud. Walen says, "Oh, well collared!" Lundie says, "That's the only thing I never learned at Harrow!" . . . Mankeltow runs up to 'em, still rubbin' his neck, and says, "*He* didn't fire at me. It was the other chap. Where is he?"

'"I've stretched him alongside his machine," I says.

'"Are they poachers?" says Lundie.

'"No. Airmen. I can't make it out," says Mankeltow.

'"Look at here," says Walen, kind of brusque. "This man ain't breathin' at all. Didn't you hear somethin' crack when he lit, Lundie?"

'"My God!" says Lundie. "Did I? I thought it was my suspenders"—no, he said "braces."

'Right there I left them and sort o' tip-toed back to my man, hopin' he'd revived and quit. But he hadn't. That darned cleek had hit him on the back of the neck just where his helmet stopped. He'd got *his*. I knew it by the way the head rolled in my hands. Then the others came up the ride totin' *their* load.

No mistakin' that shuffle on grass. D'you remember it—in South Africa? Ya-as.

' "Hsh!" says Lundie. "Do you know I've broken this man's neck?"

' "Same here," I says.

' "What? Both?" says Mankeltow.

' "Nonsense!" says Lord Lundie. "Who'd have thought he was that out of training? A man oughtn't to fly if he ain't fit."

' "What did they want here, anyway?" said Walen; and Mankeltow says, "We can't leave them in the open. Some one'll come. Carry 'em to Flora's Temple."

'We toted 'em again and laid 'em out on a stone bench. They was still dead in spite of our best attentions. We knew it, but we went through the motions till it was quite dark. 'Wonder if all murderers do that? "We want a light on this," says Walen after a spell. "There ought to be one in the machine. Why didn't they light it?"

'We came out of Flora's Temple, and shut the doors behind us. Some stars were showing then—same as when Cain * did his little act, I guess. I climbed up and searched the machine. She was very well equipped. I found two electric torches in clips alongside her barometers by the rear seat.

' "What make is she?" says Mankeltow.

' "Continental Renzalaer," I says. "My engines and my Rush Silencer."

'Walen whistles. "Here—let me look," he says, and grabs the other torch. She was sure well equipped. We gathered up an armful of cameras an' maps an' note-books an' an album of mounted photographs which we took to Flora's Temple and spread on a marble-topped table (I'll show you tomorrow) which the King of Naples had presented to grandfather Marshalton. Walen starts to go through 'em. We wanted to know why our friends had been so prejudiced against our society.

' "Wait a minute," says Lord Lundie. "Lend me a handkerchief."

'He pulls out his own, and Walen contributes his green-and-red bandanna, and Lundie covers their faces. "Now," he says, "we'll go into the evidence."

'There wasn't any flaw in that evidence. Walen read out their last observations, and Mankeltow asked questions, and Lord

Lundie sort o' summarized, and I looked at the photos in the album. 'J'ever see a bird's-eye telephoto-survey of England for military purposes? It's interestin' but indecent—like turnin' a man upside down. None of those close-range panoramas of forts could have been taken without my Rush Silencer.

' "I wish *we* was as thorough as they are," says Mankeltow, when Walen stopped translatin'.

' "We've been thorough enough," says Lord Lundie. "The evidence against both accused is conclusive. Any other country would give 'em seven years in a fortress. We should probably give 'em eighteen months as first-class misdemeanants. But their case," he says, "is out of our hands. We must review our own. Mr Zigler," he said, "will you tell us what steps you took to bring about the death of the first accused?" I told him. He wanted to know specially whether I'd stretched first accused before or after he had fired at Mankeltow. Mankeltow testified he'd been shot at, and exhibited his neck as evidence. It was scorched.

' "Now, Mr Walen," says Lord Lundie. "Will you kindly tell us what steps you took with regard to the second accused?"

' "The man ran directly at me, me lord," says Walen. "I said, 'Oh no, you don't,' and hit him in the face."

'Lord Lundie lifts one hand and uncovers second accused's face. There was a bruise on one cheek and the chin was all greened with grass. He was a heavy-built man.

' "What happened after that?" says Lord Lundie.

' "To the best of my remembrance he turned from me towards your lordship."

'Then Lundie goes ahead. "I stooped, and caught the man round the ankles," he says. "The sudden check threw him partially over my left shoulder. I jerked him off that shoulder, still holding his ankles, and he fell heavily on, it would appear, the point of his chin, death being instantaneous."

' "Death being instantaneous," says Walen.

'Lord Lundie takes off his gown and wig—you could see him do it—and becomes our fellow-murderer. "That's our case," he says. "I know how *I* should direct the jury, but it's an undignified business for a Lord of Appeal to lift his hand to, and some of my learned brothers," he says, "might be disposed to be facetious."

'I guess I can't be properly sensitized. Any one who steered me out of that trouble might have had the laugh on me for generations. But I'm only a millionaire. I said we'd better search second accused in case he'd been carryin' concealed weapons.

' "That certainly is a point," says Lord Lundie. "But the question for the jury would be whether I exercised more force than was necessary to prevent him from usin' them." *I* didn't say anything. He wasn't talkin' my language. Second accused had his gun on him sure enough, but it had jammed in his hip-pocket. He was too fleshy to reach behind for business purposes, and he didn't look a gun-man anyway. Both of 'em carried wads of private letters. By the time Walen had translated, we knew how many children the fat one had at home and when the thin one reckoned to be married. Too bad! Ya-as.

'Says Walen to me while we was rebuttonin' their jackets (they was not in uniform): "Ever read a book called *The Wrecker,** Mr Zigler?"

' "Not that I recall at the present moment," I says.

' "Well, do," he says. "You'd appreciate it. You'd appreciate it now, I assure you."

' "I'll remember," I says. "But I don't see how this song and dance helps us any. Here's our corpses, here's their machine, and daylight's bound to come."

' "Heavens! That reminds me," says Lundie. "What time's dinner?"

' "Half-past eight," says Mankeltow. "It's half-past five now. We knocked off golf at twenty to, and if they hadn't been such silly asses, firin' pistols like civilians, we'd have had them to dinner. Why, they might be sitting with us in the smoking-room this very minute," he says. Then he said that no man had a right to take his profession so seriously as these two mountebanks.

' "How interestin'!" says Lundie. "I've noticed this impatient attitude toward their victim in a good many murderers. I never understood it before. Of course, it's the disposal of the body that annoys 'em. Now, I wonder," he says, "who our case will come up before? Let's run through it again."

M.B.-6

'Then Walen whirls in. He'd been bitin' his nails in a corner. We was all nerved up by now. . . . Me? The worst of the bunch. I had to think for Tommy as well.

' "We *can't* be tried," says Walen. "We *mustn't* be tried! It'll make an infernal international stink. What did I tell you in the smoking-room after lunch? The tension's at breaking-point already. This 'ud snap it. Can't you see that?"

' "I was thinking of the legal aspect of the case," says Lundie. "With a good jury we'd likely be acquitted."

' "Acquitted!" says Walen. "Who'd dare acquit us in the face of what 'ud be demanded by—the other party? Did you ever hear of the War of Jenkins' ear?* 'Ever hear of Mason and Slidell?* 'Ever hear of an ultimatum? You know who *these* two idiots are; you know who *we* are—a Lord of Appeal, a Viscount of the English peerage, and me—*me* knowing all I know, which the men who know dam' well know that I *do* know! It's our necks or Armageddon. Which do you think this Government would choose? We *can't* be tried!" he says.

' "Then I expect I'll have to resign me club," Lundie goes on. "I don't think that's ever been done before by an *ex-officio** member. I must ask the secretary." I guess he was kinder bunkered for the minute, or maybe 'twas the lordship comin' out on him.

' "Rot!" says Mankeltow. "Walen's right. We can't afford to be tried. We'll have to bury them; but my head-gardener locks up all the tools at five o'clock."

' "Not on your life!" says Lundie. He was on deck again—as the high-class lawyer. "Right or wrong, if we attempt conceal-ment of the bodies we're done for."

' "I'm glad of that," says Mankeltow, "because, after all, it ain't cricket to bury 'em."

'Somehow—but I know I ain't English—that consideration didn't worry me as it ought. An' besides, I was thinkin'—I had to—an' I'd begun to see a light 'way off—a little glimmerin' light o' salvation.

' "Then what *are* we to do?" says Walen. "Zigler, what do you advise? Your neck's in it too."

' "Gentlemen," I says, "something Lord Lundie let fall a while back gives me an idea. I move that this committee empowers Big Claus and Little Claus,* who have elected to

commit suicide in our midst, to leave the premises *as* they came.
I'm asking you to take big chances," I says, "but they're all
we've got," and then I broke for the bi-plane.

'Don't tell me the English can't think as quick as the next
man when it's up to them! They lifted 'em out o' Flora's
Temple—reverent, but not wastin' time—whilst I found out
what had brought her down. One cylinder was misfirin'. I
didn't stop to fix it. My Renzalaer will hold up on six. We've
proved that. If her crew had relied on my guarantees, they'd
have been half-way home by then, instead of takin' their seats
with hangin' heads like they was ashamed. They ought to have
been ashamed too, playin' gun-men in a British peer's park! I
took big chances startin' her without controls, but 'twas a dead
still night an' a clear run—you saw it—across the Theatre into
the park, and I prayed she'd rise before she hit high timber. I
set her all I dared for a quick lift. I told Mankeltow that if I gave
her too much nose she'd be liable to up-end and flop. He didn't
want another inquest on his estate. No, sir! So I had to fix her
up in the dark. Ya-as!

'I took big chances, too, while those other three held on to
her and I worked her up to full power. My Renzalaer's no
ventilation-fan to pull against. But I climbed out just in time.
I'd hitched the signallin' lamp to her tail so's we could track
her. Otherwise, with my Rush Silencer, we might's well have
shooed an owl out of a barn. She left just that way when we let
her go. No sound except the propellers—*Whoo-oo-oo! Whoo-
oo-oo!* There was a dip in the ground ahead. It hid her lamp for
a second—but there's no such thing as time in real life. Then
that lamp travelled up the far slope slow—too slow. Then it
kinder lifted, we judged. Then it sure was liftin'. Then it lifted
good. D'you know why? Our four naked perspirin' souls was
out there underneath her, hikin' her heavens high. Yes, sir. *We*
did it! . . . And that lamp kept liftin' and liftin'. Then she
side-slipped! My God, she side-slipped twice, which was what
I'd been afraid of all along! Then she straightened up, and went
away climbin' to glory, for that blessed star of our hope got
smaller and smaller till we couldn't track it any more. Then we
breathed. We hadn't breathed any since their arrival, but we
didn't know it till we breathed that time—all together. Then

we dug our finger-nails out of our palms an' came alive again—in instalments.

'Lundie spoke first. "We therefore commit their bodies to the air,"* he says, an' puts his cap on.

' "The deep—the deep," says Walen. "It's just twenty-three miles to the Channel."

' "Poor chaps! Poor chaps!" says Mankeltow. "We'd have had 'em to dinner if they hadn't lost their heads. I can't tell you how this distresses me, Laughton."

' "Well, look at here, Arthur," I says, "It's only God's Own Mercy you an' me ain't lyin' in Flora's Temple now, and if that fat man had known enough to fetch his gun around while he was runnin', Lord Lundie and Walen would have been alongside us."

' "I see that," he says. "But we're alive and they're dead, don't ye know."

' "I know it," I says. "That's where the dead are always so damned unfair on the survivors."

' "I see that too," he says. "But I'd have given a good deal if it hadn't happened, poor chaps!"

' "Amen!" says Lundie. Then? Oh, then we sorter walked back two an' two to Flora's Temple an' lit matches to see we hadn't left anything behind. Walen, he had confiscated the note-books before they left. There was the first man's pistol, which we'd forgot to return him, lyin' on the stone bench. Mankeltow puts his hand on it—he never touched the trigger—an', bein' an automatic, of course the blame thing jarred off—spiteful as a rattler!

' "Look out! They'll have one of us yet," says Walen in the dark. But they didn't—the Lord hadn't quit being our shepherd—and we heard the bullet zip across the veldt—quite like old times. Ya-as!

' "Swine!" says Mankeltow.

'After that I didn't hear any more "Poor chap" talk. . . . Me? I never worried about killing *my* man. I was too busy figurin' how a British jury might regard the proposition. I guess Lundie felt that way too.

'Oh, but say! We had an interestin' time at dinner. Folks was expected whose auto had hung up on the road. They hadn't wired, and Peters had laid two extra places. We noticed 'em as soon as we sat down. I'd hate to say how noticeable they were. Mankeltow with his neck bandaged (he'd caught a relaxed throat golfin') sent for Peters and told him to take those empty places away—*if you please*. It takes something to rattle Peters. He was rattled that time. Nobody else noticed anything. And now . . .'

'Where did they come down?' I asked, as he rose.

'In the Channel, I guess. There was nothing in the papers about 'em. Shall we go into the drawin'-room, and see what these boys and girls are doin'? But say, ain't life in England interestin'?'

REBIRTH

If any God should say
        'I will restore
The world her yesterday
        Whole as before
My Judgment blasted it'—who would not lift
Heart, eye, and hand in passion o'er the gift?

If any God should will
        To wipe from mind
The memory of this ill
        Which is mankind
In soul and substance now—who would not bless
Even to tears His loving-tenderness

If any God should give
        Us leave to fly
These present deaths we live,
        And safely die
In those lost lives we lived ere we were born—
What man but would not laugh the excuse to scorn?

For we are what we are—
        So broke to blood
And the strict works of war—
        So long subdued
To sacrifice, that threadbare Death commands
Hardly observance at our busier hands.

Yet we were what we were,
        And, fashioned so,
It pleases us to stare
        At the far show
Of unbelievable years and shapes that flit,
In our own likeness, on the edge of it.

THE DOG HERVEY*

My friend Attley, who would give away his own head if you told him you had lost yours, was giving away a six-months-old litter of Bettina's pups, and half-a-dozen women were in raptures at the show on Mittleham lawn.

We picked by lot. Mrs Godfrey drew first choice; her married daughter, second. I was third, but waived my right because I was already owned by Malachi, Bettina's full brother, whom I had brought over in the car to visit his nephews and nieces, and he would have slain them all if I had taken home one. Milly, Mrs Godfrey's younger daughter, pounced on my rejection with squeals of delight, and Attley turned to a dark, sallow-skinned, slack-mouthed girl, who had come over for tennis, and invited her to pick. She put on a pair of pince-nez that made her look like a camel, knelt clumsily, for she was long from the hip to the knee, breathed hard, and considered the last couple.

'I think I'd like that sandy-pied one,' she said.

'Oh, not him, Miss Sichliffe!' Attley cried. 'He was overlaid or had sunstroke or something. They call him The Looney in the kennels. Besides, he squints.'*

'I think that's rather fetching,' she answered. Neither Malachi nor I had ever seen a squinting dog before.

'That's chorea—St Vitus's dance,' Mrs Godfrey put in. 'He ought to have been drowned.'

'But I like his cast of countenance,'* the girl persisted.

'He doesn't look a good life,' I said, 'but perhaps he can be patched up.' Miss Sichliffe turned crimson; I saw Mrs Godfrey exchange a glance with her married daughter, and knew I had said something which would have to be lived down.

'Yes,' Miss Sichliffe went on, her voice shaking, 'he isn't a good life, but perhaps I can—patch him up. Come here, sir.' The misshapen beast lurched toward her, squinting down his own nose till he fell over his own toes. Then, luckily, Bettina ran across the lawn and reminded Malachi of their puppyhood. All that family are as queer as Dick's hatband,* and fight like

man and wife. I had to separate them, and Mrs Godfrey helped
me till they retired under the rhododendrons and had it out in
silence.

'D'you know what that girl's father was?' Mrs Godfrey asked.

'No,' I replied. 'I loathe her for her own sake. She breathes
through her mouth.'

'He was a retired doctor,' she explained. 'He used to pick up
stormy young men in the repentant stage, take them home, and
patch them up till they were sound enough to be insured. Then
he insured them heavily,* and let them out into the world
again—with an appetite. Of course, no one knew him while he
was alive, but he left pots of money to his daughter.'

'Strictly legitimate—highly respectable,' I said. 'But what a
life for the daughter!'

'Mustn't it have been! *Now* d'you realize what you said just
now?'

'Perfectly; and now you've made me quite happy, shall we
go back to the house?'

When we reached it they were all inside, sitting on committee
of names.

'What shall you call yours?' I heard Milly ask Miss Sichliffe.

'Harvey,' she replied—'Harvey's Sauce, you know. He's
going to be quite saucy when I've'—she saw Mrs Godfrey and
me coming through the French window—'when he's stronger.'

Attley, the well-meaning man, to make me feel at ease, asked
what I thought of the name.

'Oh, splendid,' I said at random. 'H with an A, A with an R,
R with a——'

'But that's Little Bingo,'* some one said, and they all
laughed.

Miss Sichliffe, her hands joined across her long knees,
drawled, 'You ought always to verify your quotations.'

It was not a kindly thrust, but something in the word
'quotation' set the automatic side of my brain at work on some
shadow of a word or phrase that kept itself out of memory's
reach as a cat sits just beyond a dog's jump. When I was going
home, Miss Sichliffe came up to me in the twilight, the pup on
a leash, swinging her big shoes at the end of her tennis-racket.

''Sorry,' she said in her thick schoolboy-like voice. 'I'm sorry for what I said to you about verifying quotations. I didn't know you well enough and—anyhow, I oughtn't to have.'

'But you were quite right about Little Bingo,' I answered. 'The spelling ought to have reminded me.'

'Yes, of course. It's the spelling,' she said, and slouched off with the pup sliding after her. Once again my brain began to worry after something that would have meant something if it had been properly spelled. I confided my trouble to Malachi on the way home, but Bettina had bitten him in four places, and he was busy.

Weeks later, Attley came over to see me, and before his car stopped Malachi let me know that Bettina was sitting beside the chauffeur. He greeted her by the scruff of the neck as she hopped down; and I greeted Mrs Godfrey, Attley, and a big basket.

'You've got to help me,' said Attley tiredly. We took the basket into the garden, and there staggered out the angular shadow of a sandy-pied, broken-haired terrier, with one imbecile and one delirious ear, and two most hideous squints. Bettina and Malachi, already at grips on the lawn, saw him, let go, and fled in opposite directions.

'Why have you brought that fetid hound here?' I demanded.

'Harvey? For you to take care of,' said Attley. 'He's had distemper, but *I'm* going abroad.'

'Take him with you. I won't have him. He's mentally afflicted.'

'Look here,' Attley almost shouted, 'do I strike you as a fool?'

'Always,' said I.

'Well, then, if you say so, and Ella says so, that proves I ought to go abroad.'

'Will's wrong, quite wrong,' Mrs Godfrey interrupted; 'but you must take the pup.'

'My dear boy, my dear boy, don't you ever give anything to a woman,' Attley snorted.

Bit by bit I got the story out of them in the quiet garden (never a sign from Bettina and Malachi), while Harvey stared me out of countenance, first with one cuttlefish eye and then with the other.

It appeared that, a month after Miss Sichliffe took him, the dog Harvey developed distemper. Miss Sichliffe had nursed him herself for some time; then she carried him in her arms the two miles to Mittleham, and wept—actually wept—at Attley's feet, saying that Harvey was all she had or expected to have in this world, and Attley must cure him. Attley, being by wealth, position, and temperament guardian to all lame dogs, had put everything aside for this unsavoury job, and, he asserted, Miss Sichliffe had virtually lived with him ever since.

'She went home at night, of course,' he exploded, 'but the rest of the time she simply infested the premises. Goodness knows, I'm not particular, but it was a scandal. Even the servants! . . . Three and four times a day, and notes in between, to know how the beast was. Hang it all, don't laugh! And wanting to send me flowers and goldfish. Do I look as if I wanted goldfish? Can't you two stop for a minute?' (Mrs Godfrey and I were clinging to each other for support.) 'And it isn't as if I was—was so alluring a personality, is it?'

Attley commands more trust, goodwill, and affection than most men, for he is that rare angel, an absolutely unselfish bachelor, content to be run by contending syndicates of zealous friends. His situation seemed desperate, and I told him so.

'Instant flight is your only remedy,' was my verdict. 'I'll take care of both your cars while you're away, and you can send me over all the greenhouse fruit.'

'But why should I be chased out of my house by a she-dromedary?' he wailed.

'Oh, stop! Stop!' Mrs Godfrey sobbed. 'You're both wrong. I admit you're right, but I *know* you're wrong.'

'Three *and* four times a day,' said Attley, with an awful countenance. 'I'm not a vain man, but—look here, Ella, I'm not sensitive, I hope, but if you persist in making a joke of it——'

'Oh, be quiet!' she almost shrieked. 'D'you imagine for one instant that your friends would ever let Mittleham pass out of their hands? I quite agree it is unseemly for a grown girl to come to Mittleham at all hours of the day and night——'

'I told you she went home o' nights,' Attley growled.

'Specially if she goes home o' nights. Oh, but think of the life she must have led, Will!'

'I'm not interfering with it; only she must leave me alone.'

'She may want to patch you up and insure you,' I suggested.

'D'you know what *you* are?' Mrs Godfrey turned on me with the smile I have feared for the last quarter of a century. 'You're the nice, kind, wise, doggy friend. You don't know how wise and nice you are supposed to be. Will has sent Harvey to you to complete the poor angel's convalescence. You know all about dogs, or Will wouldn't have done it. He's written her that. You're too far off for her to make daily calls on you. P'r'aps she'll drop in two or three times a week, and write on other days. But it doesn't matter what she does, because you don't own Mittleham, don't you see?'

I told her I saw most clearly.

'Oh, you'll get over that in a few days,' Mrs Godfrey countered. 'You're the sporting, responsible, doggy friend who——'

'He used to look at me like that at first,' said Attley, with a visible shudder, 'but he gave it up after a bit. It's only because you're new to him.'

'But, confound you! he's a ghoul——' I began.

'And when he gets quite well, you'll send him back to her direct with your love, and she'll give you some pretty four-tailed goldfish,' said Mrs Godfrey, rising. 'That's all settled. Car, please. We're going to Brighton to lunch together.

They ran before I could get into my stride, so I told the dog Harvey what I thought of them and his mistress. He never shifted his position, but stared at me, an intense, lopsided stare, eye after eye. Malachi came along when he had seen his sister off, and from a distance counselled me to drown the brute and consort with gentlemen again. But the dog Harvey never even cocked his cockable ear.

And so it continued as long as he was with me. Where I sat, he sat and stared; where I walked, he walked beside, head stiffly slewed over one shoulder in single-barrelled contemplation of me. He never gave tongue, never closed in for a caress, seldom let me stir a step alone. And, to my amazement, Malachi, who suffered no stranger to live within our gates, saw this gaunt, growing, green-eyed devil wipe him out of my service and company without a whimper. Indeed, one would have said the situation interested him, for he would meet us returning from grim walks together, and look alternately at Harvey and at me with the same quivering interest that he showed at the mouth of a rat-hole. Outside these inspections, Malachi withdrew himself as only a dog or a woman can.

Miss Sichliffe came over after a few days (luckily I was out) with some elaborate story of paying calls in the neighbourhood. She sent me a note of thanks next day. I was reading it when Harvey and Malachi entered and disposed themselves as usual, Harvey close up to stare at me, Malachi half under the sofa, watching us both. Out of curiosity I returned Harvey's stare, then pulled his lopsided head on to my knee, and took his eye for several minutes. Now, in Malachi's eye I can see at any hour all that there is of the normal decent dog, flecked here and there with that strained half-soul which man's love and association have added to his nature. But with Harvey the eye was perplexed, as a tortured man's. * Only by looking far into its deeps could one make out the spirit of the proper animal, beclouded and cowering beneath some unfair burden.

Leggatt, my chauffeur, came in for orders.

'How d'you think Harvey's coming on?' I said, as I rubbed the brute's gulping neck. The vet had warned me of the possibilities of spinal trouble following distemper.

'He ain't *my* fancy,' was the reply. 'But *I* don't question his comings and goings so long as I 'aven't to sit alone in a room with him.'

'Why? He's as meek as Moses,' * I said.

'He fair gives me the creeps. P'r'aps he'll go out in fits.'

But Harvey, as I wrote his mistress from time to time, throve, and when he grew better, would play by himself grisly games of spying, walking up, hailing, and chasing another dog. From these he would break off of a sudden and return to his normal stiff gait, with the air of one who had forgotten some matter of life and death, which could be reached only by staring at me. I left him one evening posturing with the unseen on the lawn, and went inside to finish some letters for the post. I must have been at work nearly an hour, for I was going to turn on the lights, when I felt there was somebody in the room whom, the short hairs at the back of my neck warned me, I was not in the least anxious to face. There was a mirror on the wall. As I lifted my eyes to it I saw the dog Harvey reflected near the shadow by the closed door. He had reared himself full-length on his hind legs, his head a little one side to clear a sofa between us, and he was looking at me. The face, with its knitted brows and drawn lips, was the face of a dog, but the look, for the fraction of time that I caught it, was human—wholly and horribly human. When the blood in my body went forward again he had dropped to the floor, and was merely studying me in his usual one-eyed fashion. Next day I returned him to Miss Sichliffe. I would not have kept him another day for the wealth of Asia, or even Ella Godfrey's approval.

Miss Sichliffe's house I discovered to be a mid-Victorian mansion of peculiar villainy even for its period, surrounded by gardens of conflicting colours, all dazzling with glass and fresh paint on ironwork. Striped blinds, for it was a blazing autumn morning, covered most of the windows, and a voice sang to the piano an almost forgotten song of Jean Ingelow's *—

> Methought that the stars were blinking bright,
> And the old brig's sails unfurled—

Down came the loud pedal, and the unrestrained cry swelled out across a bed of tritomas * consuming in their own fires—

> When I said I will sail to my love this night
> On the other side of the world.

I have no music, but the voice drew. I waited till the end: *

> Oh, maid most dear, I am not here
> I have no place apart—
> No dwelling more on sea or shore,
> But only in thy heart.

It seemed to me a poor life that had no more than that to do at eleven o'clock of a Tuesday forenoon. Then Miss Sichliffe suddenly lumbered through a French window in clumsy haste, her brows contracted against the light.

'Well?' she said, delivering the word like a spear-thrust, with the full weight of a body behind it.

'I've brought Harvey back at last,' I replied. 'Here he is.'

But it was at me she looked, not at the dog who had cast himself at her feet—looked as though she would have fished my soul out of my breast on the instant.

'Wha—what did you think of him? What did *you* make of him?' she panted. I was too taken aback for the moment to reply. Her voice broke as she stooped to the dog at her knees. 'O Harvey, Harvey! You utterly worthless old devil!' she cried, and the dog cringed and abased himself in servility that one could scarcely bear to look upon. I made to go.

'Oh, but please, you mustn't!' She tugged at the car's side. 'Wouldn't you like some flowers or some orchids? We've really splendid orchids, and'—she clasped her hands—'there are Japanese goldfish—real Japanese goldfish, with four tails. If you don't care for 'em, perhaps your friends or somebody—oh, please!'

Harvey had recovered himself, and I realized that this woman beyond the decencies was fawning on me as the dog had fawned on her.

'Certainly,' I said, ashamed to meet her eye. 'I'm lunching at Mittleham, but——'

'There's plenty of time,' she entreated. 'What do *you* think of Harvey?'

'He's a queer beast,' I said, getting out. 'He does nothing but stare at me.'

'Does he stare at you all the time he's with you?'

'Always. He's doing it now. Look!'

We had halted. Harvey had sat down, and was staring from one to the other with a weaving motion of the head.

'He'll do that all day,' I said. 'What is it, Harvey?'' Yes, what *is* it, Harvey?' she echoed. The dog's throat twitched, his body stiffened and shook as though he were going to have a fit. Then he came back with a visible wrench to his unwinking watch.

''Always so?' she whispered.

'Always,' I replied, and told her something of his life with me. She nodded once or twice, and in the end led me into the house.

There were unaging pitch-pine doors of Gothic design in it; there were inlaid marble mantel-pieces and cut-steel fenders; there were stupendous wall-papers, and octagonal, medal-lioned Wedgewood what-nots, and black-and-gilt Austrian images holding candelabra, with every other refinement that Art had achieved or wealth had bought between 1851 and 1878. And everything reeked of varnish.

'Now!' she opened a baize door, and pointed down a long corridor flanked with more Gothic doors. 'This was where we used to—to patch 'em up. You've heard of us. Mrs Godfrey told you in the garden the day I got Harvey given me. I'—she drew in her breath—'I live here by myself, and I have a very large income. * Come back, Harvey.'

He had tiptoed down the corridor, as rigid as ever, and was sitting outside one of the shut doors. 'Look here!' she said, and planted herself squarely in front of me. 'I tell you this because you—you've patched up Harvey, too. Now, I want you to remember that my name is Moira. Mother calls me Marjorie because it's more refined; but my real name is Moira, and I am in my thirty-fourth year.'

'Very good,' I said. 'I'll remember all that.'

'Thank you.' Then with a sudden swoop into the humility of an abashed boy—''Sorry if I haven't said the proper things. You see—there's Harvey looking at us again. Oh, I want to say—if ever you want anything in the way of orchids or goldfish or—or anything else that would be useful to you, you've only to come to me for it. Under the will I'm perfectly independent, and we're a long-lived family, worse luck!' She looked at me, and her face worked like glass behind driven flame. 'I may reasonably expect to live another fifty years,' she said.

'Thank you, Miss Sichliffe,' I replied. 'If I want anything, you may be sure I'll come to you for it.' She nodded. 'Now I must get over to Mittleham,' I said.

'Mr Attley will ask you all about this.' For the first time she laughed aloud. 'I'm afraid I frightened him nearly out of the county. I didn't think, of course. But I dare say he knows by this time he was wrong. Say good-bye to Harvey.'

'Good-bye, old man,' I said. 'Give me a farewell stare, so we shall know each other when we meet again.'

The dog looked up, then moved slowly toward me, and stood, head bowed to the floor, shaking in every muscle as I patted him; and when I turned, I saw him crawl back to her feet.

That was not a good preparation for the rampant boy-and-girl-dominated lunch at Mittleham, which, as usual, I found in possession of everybody except the owner.

'But what did the dromedary say when you brought her beast back?' Attley demanded.

'The usual polite things,' I replied. 'I'm posing as the nice doggy friend nowadays.'

'I don't envy you. She's never darkened my doors, thank goodness, since I left Harvey at your place. I suppose she'll run about the county now swearing you cured him. That's a woman's idea of gratitude.' Attley seemed rather hurt, and Mrs Godfrey laughed.

'That proves you were right about Miss Sichliffe, Ella,' I said. 'She had no designs on anybody.'

'I'm always right in these matters. But didn't she even offer you a goldfish?'

'Not a thing,' said I. 'You know what an old maid's like where her precious dog's concerned.' And though I have tried vainly to lie to Ella Godfrey for many years, I believe that in this case I succeeded.

When I turned into our drive that evening, Leggatt observed half aloud:

'I'm glad Svengali's* back where he belongs. It's time our Mike had a look in.'

Sure enough, there was Malachi back again in spirit as well as flesh, but still with that odd air of expectation he had picked up from Harvey.

* * *

It was in January that Attley wrote me that Mrs Godfrey, wintering in Madeira with Milly, her unmarried daughter, had been attacked with something like enteric; that the hotel, anxious for its good name, had thrust them both out into a cottage annexe; that he was off with a nurse, and that I was not to leave England till I heard from him again. In a week he wired that Milly was down as well, and that I must bring out two more nurses, with suitable delicacies.

Within seventeen hours I had got them all aboard the Cape boat, and had seen the women safely collapsed into sea-sickness. The next few weeks were for me, as for the invalids, a low delirium, clouded with fantastic memories of Portuguese officials trying to tax calves'-foot jelly; voluble doctors insisting that true typhoid was unknown in the island; nurses who had

to be exercised, taken out of themselves, and return
tick of change of guard; night slides down glassy, co
streets, smelling of sewage and flowers, between walls whose
every stone and patch Attley and I knew; vigils in stucco
verandahs, watching the curve and descent of great stars or
drawing auguries from the break of dawn; insane interludes of
gambling at the local Casino, where we won heaps of uncon-
soling silver; blasts of steamers arriving and departing in the
roads; help offered by total strangers, grabbed at or thrust aside;
the long nightmare crumbling back into sanity one forenoon
under a vine-covered trellis, where Attley sat hugging a nurse,
while the others danced a noiseless, neat-footed break-down*
never learned at the Middlesex Hospital. At last, as the tension
came out all over us in aches and tingles that we put down to
the country wine, a vision of Mrs Godfrey, her grey hair turned
to spun-glass, but her eyes triumphant over the shadow of
retreating death beneath them, with Milly, enormously grown,
and clutching life back to her young breast, both stretched out
on cane chairs, clamouring for food.

In this ungirt hour there imported himself into our life a
youngish-looking middle-aged man of the name of Shend, with
a blurred face and deprecating eyes. He said he had gambled
with me at the Casino, which was no recommendation, and I
remember that he twice gave me a basket of champagne and
liqueur brandy for the invalids, which a sailor in a red-tasselled
cap carried up to the cottage for me at 3 a.m. He turned out to
be the son of some merchant prince in the oil and colour line,
and the owner of a four-hundred-ton steam yacht, into which,
at his gentle insistence, we later shifted our camp, staff, and
equipage, Milly weeping with delight to escape from the horrible cottage. There we lay off Funchal for weeks, while Shend
did miracles of luxury and attendance through deputies, and
never once asked how his guests were enjoying themselves.
Indeed, for several days at a time we would see nothing of him.
He was, he said, subject to malaria. Giving as they do with both
hands, I knew that Attley and Mrs Godfrey could take nobly;
but I never met a man who so nobly gave and so nobly received
thanks as Shend did.

'Tell us why you have been so unbelievably kind to us
gipsies,' Mrs Godfrey said to him one day on deck.

He looked up from a diagram of some Thames-mouth shoals
which he was explaining to me, and answered with his gentle
smile:

'I will. It's because it makes me happy—it makes me more
than happy—to be with you. It makes me comfortable. You
know how selfish men are? If a man feels comfortable all over
with certain people, he'll bore them to death, just like a dog.
You always make me feel as if pleasant things were going to
happen to me.'

'Haven't any ever happened before?' Milly asked.

'This is the most pleasant thing that has happened to me in
ever so many years,' he replied. 'I feel like the man in the Bible,
"It's good for me to be here." * Generally, I don't feel that it's
good for me to be anywhere in particular.' Then, as one begging
a favour. 'You'll let me come home with you—in the same boat,
I mean? I'd take you back in this thing of mine, and that would
save you packing your trunks, but she's too lively for spring
work across the Bay.'

We booked our berths, and when the time came, he wafted
us and ours aboard the Southampton mail-boat with the pomp
of plenipotentiaries and the precision of the Navy. Then he
dismissed his yacht, and became an inconspicuous passenger
in a cabin opposite to mine, on the port side.

We ran at once into early British spring weather, followed by
sou'west gales. Mrs Godfrey, Milly, and the nurses disappeared. Attley stood it out, visibly yellowing, till the next
meal, and followed suit, and Shend and I had the little table all
to ourselves. I found him even more attractive when the women
were away. The natural sweetness of the man, his voice, and
bearing all fascinated me, and his knowledge of practical
seamanship (he held an extra master's certificate) was a real
joy. We sat long in the empty saloon and longer in the
smoking-room, making dashes downstairs over slippery decks
at the eleventh hour.

It was on Friday night, just as I was going to bed, that he
came into my cabin, after cleaning his teeth, which he did half
a dozen times a day.

'I say,' he began hurriedly, 'do you mind if I come in here
for a little? I'm a bit edgy.' I must have shown surprise. 'I'm
ever so much better about liquor than I used to be, but—it's

the whisky in the suitcase that throws me. For God's sake, old man, don't go back on me tonight! Look at my hands!'

They were fairly jumping at the wrists. He sat down on a trunk that had slid out with the roll. We had reduced speed, and were surging in confused seas that pounded on the black port-glasses. The night promised to be a pleasant one!

'You understand, of course, don't you?' he chattered.

'Oh yes,' I said cheerily; 'but how about——'

'No, no; on no account the doctor. 'Tell a doctor, tell the whole ship. Besides, I've only got a touch of 'em. You'd never have guessed it, would you? The tooth-wash does the trick. I'll give you the prescription.'

'I'll send a note to the doctor for a prescription, shall I?' I suggested.

'Right! I put myself unreservedly in your hands. 'Fact is, I always did. I said to myself—'sure I don't bore you?—the minute I saw you, I said, "Thou art the man." '* He repeated the phrase as he picked at his knees. 'All the same, you can take it from me that the ewe-lamb* business is a rotten bad one. I don't care how unfaithful the shepherd may be. Drunk or sober, 'tisn't cricket.'

A surge of the trunk threw him across the cabin as the steward answered my bell. I wrote my requisition to the doctor while Shend was struggling to his feet.

'What's wrong?' he began. 'Oh, I know. We're slowing for soundings off Ushant. It's about time, too. You'd better ship the dead-lights* when you come back, Matchem. It'll save you waking us later. This sea's going to get up when the tide turns. That'll show you,' he said as the man left, 'that I am to be trusted. You—you'll stop me if I say anything I shouldn't, won't you?'

'Talk away,' I replied, 'if it makes you feel better.'

'That's it; you've hit it exactly. You always make me feel better. I can rely on you. It's awkward soundings but you'll see me through it. We'll defeat him yet. . . . I may be an utterly worthless devil, but I'm not a brawler. . . . I told him so at breakfast. I said, "Doctor, I detest brawling, but if ever you allow that girl to be insulted again as Clements insulted her, I will break your neck with my own hands." You think I was right?'

'Absolutely,' I agreed.

'Then we needn't discuss the matter any further. That man was a murderer in intention—outside the law, you understand, as it was then. They've changed it since *—but he never deceived *me*. I told him so. I said to him at the time, "I don't know what price you're going to put on my head, but if ever you allow Clements to insult her again, you'll never live to claim it." '

'And what did he do?' I asked, to carry on the conversation, for Matchem entered with the bromide.

'Oh, crumpled up at once. 'Lead still going, Matchem?'

'I 'aven't 'eard,' said that faithful servant of the Union-Castle Company.

'Quite right. Never alarm the passengers. Ship the deadlight, will you?' Matchem shipped it, for we were rolling very heavily. There were tramplings and gull-like cries from on deck. Shend looked at me with a mariner's eye.

'That's nothing,' he said protectingly.

'Oh, it's all right for you,' I said, jumping at the idea. '*I* haven't an extra master's certificate. I'm only a passenger. I confess it funks me.'

Instantly his whole bearing changed to answer the appeal.

'My dear fellow, it's as simple as houses. We're hunting for sixty-five fathom water. Anything short of sixty, with a sou'west wind means—but I'll get my Channel Pilot out of my cabin and give you the general idea. I'm only too grateful to do anything to put your mind at ease.'

And so, perhaps, for another hour—he declined the drink—Channel Pilot in hand, he navigated us round Ushant, and at my request up-channel to Southampton, light by light, with explanations and reminiscences. I professed myself soothed at last, and suggested bed.

'In a second,' said he. 'Now, you wouldn't think, would you'—he glanced off the book toward my wildly swaying dressing-gown on the door—'that I've been seeing things for the last half-hour? 'Fact is, I'm just on the edge of 'em, skating on thin ice round the corner—nor'east as near as nothing—where that dog's looking at me.'

'What's the dog like?' I asked.

'Ah, that *is* comforting of you! Most men walk through 'em to show me they aren't real. As if I didn't know! But *you*'re

different. Anybody could see that with half an eye.' He stiffened
and pointed. 'Damn it all! The dog sees it too with half an——
Why, he knows you! Knows you perfectly. D'you know *him*?'

'How can I tell if he isn't real?' I insisted.

'But you can! *You*'re all right. I saw that from the first. Don't
go back on me now or I shall go to pieces like the *Drummond
Castle*.* I beg your pardon, old man; but, you see, you *do* know
the dog. I'll prove it. What's that dog doing? Come on! *You*
know.' A tremor shook him, and he put his hand on my knee,
and whispered with great meaning: 'I'll letter or halve it* with
you. There! You begin.'

'S,' said I to humour him, for a dog would most likely be
standing or sitting, or may be scratching or sniffing or staring.

'Q,' he went on, and I could feel the heat of his shaking hand.

'U,' said I. There was no other letter possible; but I was
shaking too.

'I.'

'N.'

'T-i-n-g,' he ran out. 'There! That proves it. I knew you knew
him. You don't know what a relief that is. Between ourselves,
old man, he—he's been turning up lately a—a damn sight more
often than I cared for. And a squinting dog—a dog that squints!
I mean that's a bit *too* much. Eh? What?' He gulped and half
rose, and I thought that the full tide of delirium would be on
him in another sentence.

'Not a bit of it,' I said as a last chance, with my hand over
the bellpush. 'Why, you've just proved that I know him; so there
are two of us in the game, anyhow.'

'By Jove! that *is* an idea! Of course there are. I knew you'd
see me through. We'll defeat them yet. Hi, pup! . . . He's gone.
Absolutely disappeared!' He sighed with relief, and I caught
the lucky moment.

'Good business! I expect he only came to have a look at me,'
I said. 'Now, get this drink down and turn in to the lower bunk.'

He obeyed, protesting that he could not inconvenience me,
and in the midst of apologies sank into a dead sleep. I expected
a wakeful night, having a certain amount to think over; but no
sooner had I scrambled into the top-bunk than sleep came on
me like a wave from the other side of the world.

In the morning there were apologies, which we got over at breakfast before our party were about.

'I suppose—after this—well, I don't blame you. I'm rather a lonely chap, though.' His eyes lifted dog-like across the table.

'Shend,' I replied, 'I'm not running a Sunday school. You're coming home with me in my car as soon as we land.'

'That is kind of you—kinder than you think.'

'That's because you're a little jumpy still. Now, I don't want to mix up in your private affairs——'

'But I'd like you to,' he interrupted.

'Then, would you mind telling me the Christian name of a girl who was insulted by a man called Clements?'

'Moira,' he whispered; and just then Mrs Godfrey and Milly came to table with their shore-going hats on.

We did not tie up till noon, but the faithful Leggatt had intrigued his way down to the dock-edge, and beside him sat Malachi, wearing his collar of gold, * or Leggatt makes it look so, as eloquent as Demosthenes. * Shend flinched a little when he saw him. We packed Mrs Godfrey and Milly into Attley's car—they were going with him to Mittleham, of course—and drew clear across the railway lines to find England all lit and perfumed for spring. Shend sighed with happiness.

'D'you know,' he said, 'if—if you'd chucked me—I should have gone down to my cabin after breakfast and cut my throat. And now—it's like a dream—a good dream, you know.'

We lunched with the other three at Romsey. Then I sat in front for a little while to talk to my Malachi. When I looked back, Shend was solidly asleep, and stayed so for the next two hours, while Leggatt chased Attley's fat Daimler along the green-speckled hedges. He woke up when we said good-bye at Mittleham, with promises to meet again very soon.

'And I hope,' said Mrs Godfrey, 'that everything pleasant will happen to you.'

'Heaps and heaps—all at once,' cried long, weak Milly, waving her wet handkerchief.

'I've just got to look in at a house near here for a minute to inquire about a dog,' I said, 'and then we will go home.'

'I used to know this part of the world,' he replied, and said no more till Leggatt shot past the lodge at the Sichliffes's gate. Then I heard him gasp.

Miss Sichliffe, in a green waterproof, an orange jersey, and a pinkish leather hat, was working on a bulb-border. She straightened herself as the car stopped, and breathed hard. Shend got out and walked towards her. They shook hands, turned round together, and went into the house. Then the dog Harvey pranced out corkily from under the lee of a bench. Malachi, with one joyous swoop, fell on him as an enemy and an equal. Harvey, for his part, freed from all burden whatsoever except the obvious duty of a man-dog on his own ground, met Malachi without reserve or remorse, and with six months' additional growth to come and go on.

'Don't check 'em!' cried Leggatt, dancing round the flurry. 'They've both been saving up for each other all this time. It'll do 'em worlds of good.'

'Leggatt,' I said, 'will you take Mr Shend's bag and suitcase up to the house and put them down just inside the door? Then we will go on.'

So I enjoyed the finish alone. It was a dead heat, and they licked each other's jaws in amity till Harvey, one imploring eye on me, leaped into the front seat and Malachi backed his appeal. It was theft, but I took him, and we talked all the way home of r-rats and r-rabbits and bones and baths and the other basic facts of life. That evening after dinner they slept before the fire, with their warm chins across the hollows of my ankles—to each chin an ankle—till I kicked them upstairs to bed.

I was not at Mittleham when she came over to announce her engagement, but I heard of it when Mrs Godfrey and Attley came, forty miles an hour, over to me, and Mrs Godfrey called me names of the worst for suppression of information.

'As long as it wasn't me, I don't care,' said Attley.

'I believe you knew it all along,' Mrs Godfrey repeated. 'Else what made you drive that man literally into her arms?'

'To ask after the dog Harvey,' I replied.

'Then, what's the beast doing here?' Attley demanded, for Malachi and the dog Harvey were deep in a council of the family with Bettina, who was being out-argued.

'Oh, Harvey seemed to think himself *de trop* where he was,' I said. 'And she hasn't sent after him. You'd better save Bettina before they kill her.'

'There's been enough lying about that dog,' said Mrs Godfrey to me. 'If he wasn't born in lies, he was baptized in 'em. D'you know why she called him Harvey? It only occurred to me in those dreadful days when I was ill, and one can't keep from thinking, and thinks everything. D'you know your Boswell? What did Johnson say about Hervey—with an e?'

'Oh, *that's* it, is it?' I cried incautiously. 'That was why I ought to have verified my quotations. The spelling defeated me. Wait a moment, and it will come back. Johnson said: "He was a vicious man," ' I began.

' "But very kind to me," ' Mrs Godfrey prompted. Then, both together, ' "If you call a dog Hervey, I shall love him." '*

'So you *were* mixed up in it. At any rate, you had your suspicions from the first? Tell me,' she said.

'Ella,' I said, 'I don't know anything rational or reasonable about any of it. It was all—all woman-work, and it scared me horribly.'

'Why?' she asked.

That was six years ago. I have written this tale to let her know—wherever she may be.

THE COMFORTERS

Until thy feet have trod the Road
   Advise not wayside folk,
Nor till thy back has borne the Load
   Break in upon the Broke.

Chase not with undesired largesse
   Of sympathy the heart
Which, knowing her own bitterness,
   Presumes to dwell apart.

Employ not that glad hand to raise
   The God-forgotten head
To Heaven, and all the neighbours' gaze—
   Cover thy mouth instead.

The quivering chin, the bitten lip,
   The cold and sweating brow,
Later may yearn for fellowship—
   Not now, you ass, not now!

Time, not thy ne'er so timely speech,
   Life, not thy views thereon,
Shall furnish or deny to each
   His consolation.

Or, if impelled to interfere,
   Exhort, uplift, advise,
Lend not a base, betraying ear
   To all the victim's cries.

Only the Lord can understand
   When those first pangs begin,
How much is reflex action and
   How much is really sin.

E'en from good words thyself refrain,
   And tremblingly admit
There is no anodyne for pain
   Except the shock of it.

So, when thine own dark hour shall fall,
  Unchallenged canst thou say:
'I never worried *you* at all,
  For God's sake go away!'

MARY POSTGATE *

OF Miss Mary Postgate, Lady McCausland wrote that she was 'thoroughly conscientious, tidy, companionable, and ladylike. I am very sorry to part with her, and shall always be interested in her welfare.'

Miss Fowler engaged her on this recommendation, and to her surprise, for she had had experience of companions, found that it was true. Miss Fowler was nearer sixty than fifty at the time, but though she needed care she did not exhaust her attendant's vitality. On the contrary, she gave out, stimulatingly and with reminiscences. Her father had been a minor Court official in the days when the Great Exhibition of 1851 had just set its seal on Civilization made perfect. Some of Miss Fowler's tales, none the less, were not always for the young. Mary was not young, and though her speech was as colourless as her eyes or her hair, she was never shocked. She listened unflinchingly to every one; said at the end, 'How interesting!' or 'How shocking!' as the case might be, and never again referred to it, for she prided herself on a trained mind, which 'did not dwell on these things'. She was, too, a treasure at domestic accounts, for which the village tradesmen, with their weekly books, loved her not. Otherwise she had no enemies; provoked no jealousy even among the plainest; neither gossip nor slander had ever been traced to her; she supplied the odd place at the Rector's or the Doctor's table at half an hour's notice; she was a sort of public aunt to very many small children of the village street, whose parents, while accepting everything, would have been swift to resent what they called 'patronage'; she served on the Village Nursing Committee as Miss Fowler's nominee when Miss Fowler was crippled by rheumatoid arthritis, and came out of six months' fortnightly meetings equally respected by all the cliques.

And when Fate threw Miss Fowler's nephew, an unlovely orphan of eleven, on Miss Fowler's hands, Mary Postgate stood to her share of the business of education as practised in private and public schools. She checked printed clothes-lists, and unitemized bills of extras; wrote to Head and House masters, matrons, nurses, and doctors, and grieved or rejoiced over half-term reports. Young Wyndham Fowler repaid her in his holidays by calling her 'Gatepost,' 'Postey', or 'Packthread', by thumping her between her narrow shoulders, or by chasing her bleating, round the garden, her large mouth open, her large nose high in air, at a stiff-necked shamble very like a camel's. Later on he filled the house with clamour, argument, and harangues as to his personal needs, likes and dislikes, and the limitations of 'you women', reducing Mary to tears of physical fatigue, or, when he chose to be humorous, of helpless laughter. At crises, which multiplied as he grew older, she was his ambassadress and his interpretress to Miss Fowler, who had no large sympathy with the young; a vote in his interest at the councils on his future; his sewing-woman, strictly accountable for mislaid boots and garments; always his butt and his slave.

And when he decided to become a solicitor, and had entered an office in London; when his greeting had changed from 'Hullo, Postey, you old beast', to 'Mornin', Packthread', there came a war which, unlike all wars that Mary could remember, did not stay decently outside England and in the newspapers, but intruded on the lives of people whom she knew. As she said to Miss Fowler, it was 'most vexatious'. It took the Rector's son who was going into business with his elder brother; it took the Colonel's nephew on the eve of fruit-farming in Canada; it took Mrs Grant's son who, his mother said, was devoted to the ministry; and, very early indeed, it took Wynn Fowler, who announced on a postcard that he had joined the Flying Corps *, and wanted a cardigan waistcoat.

'He must go, and he must have the waistcoat,' said Miss Fowler. So Mary got the proper-sized needles and wool, while Miss Fowler told the men of her establishment—two gardeners and an odd man, aged sixty—that those who could join the Army had better do so. The gardeners left. Cheape, the odd man, stayed on, and was promoted to the gardener's cottage. The cook, scorning to be limited in luxuries, also left, after a spirited scene with Miss Fowler, and took the housemaid with her. Miss Fowler gazetted Nellie, Cheape's seventeen-year-old daughter, to the vacant post; Mrs Cheape to the rank of cook, with occasional cleaning bouts; and the reduced establishment moved forward smoothly.

Wynn demanded an increase in his allowance. Miss Fowler, who always looked facts in the face, said, 'He must have it. The chances are he won't live long to draw it, and if three hundred makes him happy——'

Wynn was grateful, and came over, in his tight-buttoned uniform, to say so. His training centre was not thirty miles away, and his talk was so technical that it had to be explained by charts of the various types of machines. He gave Mary such a chart.

'And you'd better study it, Postey,' he said. 'You'll be seeing a lot of 'em soon.' So Mary studied the chart, but when Wynn next arrived to swell and exalt himself before his womenfolk, she failed badly in cross-examination, and he rated her as in the old days.

'You *look* more or less like a human being,' he said in his new Service voice. 'You *must* have had a brain at some time in your past. What have you done with it? Where d'you keep it? A sheep would know more than you do, Postey. You're lamentable. You are less use than an empty tin can, you dowey* old cassowary.'

'I suppose that's how your superior officer talks to *you*?' said Miss Fowler from her chair.

'But Postey doesn't mind,' Wynn replied. 'Do you, Pack-thread?'

'Why? Was Wynn saying anything? I shall get this right next time you come,' she muttered, and knitted her pale brows again over the diagrams of Taubes, Farmans, and Zeppelins. *

In a few weeks the mere land and sea battles which she read to Miss Fowler after breakfast passed her like idle breath. Her heart and her interest were high in the air with Wynn, who had finished 'rolling' (whatever that might be) and had gone on from a 'taxi' to a machine more or less his own. * One morning it circled over their very chimneys, alighted on Vegg's Heath, almost outside the garden gate, and Wynn came in, blue with cold, shouting for food. He and she drew Miss Fowler's bath-chair, as they had often done, along the Heath foot-path to look at the biplane. Mary observed that 'it smelt very badly.'

'Postey, I believe you think with your nose,' said Wynn. 'I know you don't with your mind. Now, what type's that?'

'I'll go and get the chart,' said Mary.

'You're hopeless! You haven't the mental capacity of a white mouse,' he cried, and explained the dials and the sockets for bomb-dropping till it was time to mount and ride the wet clouds once more.

'Ah!' said Mary, as the stinking thing flared upward. 'Wait till our Flying Corps gets to work! Wynn says it's much safer than in the trenches.'

'I wonder,' said Miss Fowler. 'Tell Cheape to come and tow me home again.'

'It's all downhill. I can do it,' said Mary, 'if you put the brake on.' She laid her lean self against the pushing-bar and home they trundled.

'Now, be careful you aren't heated and catch a chill,' said overdressed Miss Fowler.

'Nothing makes me perspire,' said Mary. As she bumped the chair under the porch she straightened her long back. The exertion had given her a colour, and the wind had loosened a wisp of hair across her forehead. Miss Fowler glanced at her. *

'What do you ever think of, Mary?' she demanded suddenly.

'Oh, Wynn says he wants another three pairs of stockings—as thick as we can make them.'

'Yes. But I mean the things that women think about. Here you are, more than forty——'

'Forty-four,' said truthful Mary.

'Well?'

'Well?' Mary offered Miss Fowler her shoulder as usual.

'And you've been with me ten years now.'

'Let's see,' said Mary. 'Wynn was eleven when he came. He's twenty now, and I came two years before that. It must be eleven.'

'Eleven! And you've never told me anything that matters in all that while. Looking back, it seems to me that I've done all the talking.'

'I'm afraid I'm not much of a conversationalist. As Wynn says, I haven't the mind. Let me take your hat.'

Miss Fowler, moving stiZy from the hip, stamped her rubber-tipped stick on the tiled hall floor. 'Mary, aren't you *anything* except a companion? Would you *ever* have been anything except a companion?'

Mary hung up the garden hat on its proper peg. 'No,' she said after consideration. 'I don't imagine I ever should. But I've no imagination, I'm afraid.'

She fetched Miss Fowler her eleven-o'clock glass of Contrexeville.*

That was the wet December when it rained six inches to the month, and the women went abroad as little as might be. Wynn's flying chariot visited them several times, and for two mornings (he had warned her by postcard) Mary heard the thresh of his propellers at dawn. The second time she ran to the window, and stared at the whitening sky. A little blur passed overhead. She lifted her lean arms towards it.

That evening at six o'clock there came an announcement in an official envelope that Second Lieutenant W. Fowler had been killed during a trial flight. Death was instantaneous. She read it and carried it to Miss Fowler.

'I never expected anything else,' said Miss Fowler; 'but I'm sorry it happened before he had done anything.'

The room was whirling round Mary Postgate, but she found herself quite steady in the midst of it.

'Yes,' she said. 'It's a great pity he didn't die in action after he had killed somebody.'

'He was killed instantly. That's one comfort,' Miss Fowler went on.

'But Wynn says the shock of a fall kills a man at once—whatever happens to the tanks,' quoted Mary.

The room was coming to rest now. She heard Miss Fowler say impatiently, 'But why can't we cry, Mary?' and herself replying, 'There's nothing to cry for. He has done his duty as much as Mrs Grant's son did.'

'And when he died, *she* came and cried all the morning,' said Miss Fowler. 'This only makes me feel tired—terribly tired. Will you help me to bed, please, Mary?—And I think I'd like the hot-water bottle.'

So Mary helped her and sat beside, talking of Wynn in his riotous youth.

'I believe,' said Miss Fowler suddenly, 'that old people and young people slip from under a stroke like this. The middle-aged feel it most.'

'I expect that's true,' said Mary, rising. 'I'm going to put away the things in his room now. Shall we wear mourning?'

'Certainly not,' said Miss Fowler. 'Except, of course, at the funeral. I can't go. You will. I want you to arrange about his being buried here. What a blessing it didn't happen at Salisbury!'*

Every one, from the Authorities of the Flying Corps to the Rector, was most kind and sympathetic. Mary found herself for the moment in a world where bodies were in the habit of being despatched by all sorts of conveyances to all sorts of places. And at the funeral two young men in buttoned-up uniforms stood beside the grave and spoke to her afterwards.

'You're Miss Postgate, aren't you?' said one. 'Fowler told me about you. He was a good chap—a first-class fellow—a great loss.'

'Great loss!' growled his companion. 'We're all awfully sorry.'

'How high did he fall from?' Mary whispered.

'Pretty nearly four thousand feet, I should think, didn't he? You were up that day, Monkey?'

'All of that,' the other child replied. 'My bar made three thousand, and I wasn't as high as him by a lot.'

'Then *that's* all right,' said Mary. 'Thank you very much.'

They moved away as Mrs Grant flung herself weeping on Mary's flat chest, under the lych-gate, and cried, '*I* know how it feels! *I* know how it feels!'

'But both his parents are dead,' Mary returned, as she fended her off. 'Perhaps they've all met by now,' she added vaguely as she escaped towards the coach.

'I've thought of that too,' wailed Mrs Grant; 'but then he'll be practically a stranger to them. Quite embarrassing!'

Mary faithfully reported every detail of the ceremony to Miss Fowler, who, when she described Mrs Grant's outburst, laughed aloud.

'Oh, how Wynn would have enjoyed it! He was always utterly unreliable at funerals. D'you remember——' And they talked of him again, each piecing out the other's gaps. 'And now,' said Miss Fowler, 'we'll pull up the blinds and we'll have a general tidy. That always does us good. Have you seen to Wynn's things?'

'Everything—since he first came,' said Mary. 'He was never destructive—even with his toys.'

They faced that neat room.

'It can't be natural not to cry,' Mary said at last. 'I'm *so* afraid you'll have a reaction.'

'As I told you, we old people slip from under the stroke. It's you I'm afraid for. Have you cried yet?'

'I can't. It only makes me angry with the Germans.'

'That's sheer waste of vitality,' said Miss Fowler. 'We must live till the war's finished.' She opened a full wardrobe. 'Now, I've been thinking things over. This is my plan. All his civilian clothes can be given away—Belgian refugees, and so on.'

Mary nodded. 'Boots, collars, and gloves?'

'Yes. We don't need to keep anything except his cap and belt.'

'They came back yesterday with his Flying Corps clothes'—Mary pointed to a roll on the little iron bed.

'Ah, but keep his Service things. Some one may be glad of them later. Do you remember his sizes?'

'Five feet eight and a half; thirty-six inches round the chest. But he told me he's just put on an inch and a half. I'll mark it on a label and tie it on his sleeping-bag.'

'So that disposes of *that*,' said Miss Fowler, tapping the palm of one hand with the ringed third finger of the other. 'What waste it all is! We'll get his old school trunk tomorrow and pack his civilian clothes.'

'And the rest?' said Mary. 'His books and pictures and the games and the toys—and—and the rest?'

'My plan is to burn every single thing,' said Miss Fowler. 'Then we shall know where they are and no one can handle them afterwards. What do you think?'

'I think that would be much the best,' said Mary. 'But there's such a lot of them.'

'We'll burn them in the destructor,' said Miss Fowler.

This was an open-air furnace for the consumption of refuse; a little circular four-foot tower of pierced brick over an iron grating. Miss Fowler had noticed the design in a gardening journal years ago, and had had it built at the bottom of the garden. It suited her tidy soul, for it saved unsightly rubbish-heaps, and the ashes lightened the stiff clay soil.

Mary considered for a moment, saw her way clear, and nodded again. They spent the evening putting away well-remembered civilian suits, underclothes that Mary had marked, and the regiments of very gaudy socks and ties. A second trunk was needed, and, after that, a little packing-case, and it was late next day when Cheape and the local carrier lifted them to the cart. The Rector luckily knew of a friend's son, about Wve feet eight and a half inches high, to whom a complete Flying Corps outWt would be most acceptable, and sent his gardener's son down with a barrow to take delivery of it. The cap was hung up in Miss Fowler's bedroom, the belt in Miss Postgate's; for, as Miss Fowler said, they had no desire to make tea-party talk of them.

'That disposes of *that*,' said Miss Fowler. 'I'll leave the rest to you, Mary. I can't run up and down the garden. You'd better take the big clothes-basket and get Nellie to help you.'

'I shall take the wheel-barrow and do it myself,' said Mary, and for once in her life closed her mouth.

Miss Fowler, in moments of irritation, had called Mary deadly methodical. She put on her oldest waterproof and gardening-hat and her ever-slipping galoshes, for the weather was on the edge of more rain. She gathered fire-lighters from the kitchen, a half-scuttle of coals, and a faggot of brushwood. These she wheeled in the barrow down the mossed paths to the dank little laurel shrubbery where the destructor stood under the drip of three oaks. She climbed the wire fence into the Rector's glebe just behind, and from his tenant's rick pulled two large armfuls of good hay, which she spread neatly on the fire-bars. Next, journey by journey, passing Miss Fowler's white face at the morning-room window each time, she brought down in the towel-covered clothes-basket, on the wheelbarrow, thumbed and used Hentys, Marryats, Levers, Stevensons, Baroness Orczys, Garvices,* schoolbooks, and atlases, unrelated piles of the *Motor Cyclist*, the *Light Car*, and catalogues of Olympia Exhibitions; the remnants of a fleet of sailing-ships from nine-penny cutters to a three-guinea yacht; a prep.-school dressing-gown; bats from three-and-sixpence to twenty-four shillings; cricket and tennis balls; disintegrated steam and clockwork locomotives with their twisted rails; a grey and red tin model of a submarine; a dumb gramophone and cracked records; golf-clubs that had to be broken across the knee, like his walking-sticks, and an assegai; photographs of private and public school cricket and football elevens, and his OTC* on the line of march; kodaks, and film-rolls; some pewters, and one real silver cup, for boxing competitions and Junior Hurdles; sheaves of school photographs; Miss Fowler's photograph; her own which he had borne off in fun and (good care she took not to ask!) had never returned; a playbox with a secret drawer; a load of flannels, belts, and jerseys, and a pair of spiked shoes unearthed in the attic; a packet of all the letters that Miss Fowler and she had ever written to him, kept for some absurd reason through all these years; a five-day attempt at a diary; framed pictures of racing motors in full Brooklands* career, and load upon load of undistinguishable wreckage of tool-boxes, rabbit-hutches, electric batteries, tin soldiers, fret-saw outfits, and jig-saw puzzles.

Miss Fowler at the window watched her come and go, and said to herself, 'Mary's an old woman. I never realized it before.'

After lunch she recommended her to rest.

'I'm not in the least tired,' said Mary. 'I've got it all arranged. I'm going to the village at two o'clock for some paraffin. Nellie hasn't enough, and the walk will do me good.'

She made one last quest round the house before she started, and found that she had overlooked nothing. It began to mist as soon as she had skirted Vegg's Heath, where Wynn used to descend—it seemed to her that she could almost hear the beat of his propellers overhead, but there was nothing to see. She hoisted her umbrella and lunged into the blind wet till she had reached the shelter of the empty village. As she came out of Mr Kidd's shop with a bottle full of paraffin in her string shopping-bag, she met Nurse Eden, the village nurse, and fell into talk with her, as usual, about the village children. They were just parting opposite the 'Royal Oak', when a gun, they fancied, was fired immediately behind the house. It was followed by a child's shriek dying into a wail.

'Accident!' said Nurse Eden promptly, and dashed through the empty bar, followed by Mary. They found Mrs Gerritt, the publican's wife, who could only gasp and point to the yard, where a little cart-lodge was sliding sideways amid a clatter of tiles. Nurse Eden snatched up a sheet drying before the fire, ran out, lifted something from the ground, and flung the sheet round it. The sheet turned scarlet and half her uniform too, as she bore the load into the kitchen. It was little Edna Gerritt, aged nine, whom Mary had known since her perambulator days.

'Am I hurted bad?' Edna asked, and died between Nurse Eden's dripping hands. The sheet fell aside and for an instant, before she could shut her eyes, Mary saw the ripped and shredded body.

'It's a wonder she spoke at all,' said Nurse Eden. 'What in God's name was it?'

'A bomb,'* said Mary.

'One o' the Zeppelins?'

'No. An aeroplane. I thought I heard it on the Heath, but I fancied it was one of ours. It must have shut off its engines* as it came down. That's why we didn't notice it.'

'The filthy pigs!' said Nurse Eden, all white and shaken. 'See the pickle I'm in! Go and tell Dr Hennis, Miss Postgate.' Nurse looked at the mother, who had dropped face down on the floor. 'She's only in a fit. Turn her over.'

Mary heaved Mrs Gerritt right side up, and hurried off for the doctor. When she told her tale, he asked her to sit down in the surgery till he got her something.

'But I don't need it, I assure you," said she. 'I don't think it would be wise to tell Miss Fowler about it, do you? Her heart is so irritable in this weather.'

Dr Hennis looked at her admiringly as he packed up his bag.

'No. Don't tell anybody till we're sure,' he said, and hastened to the 'Royal Oak', while Mary went on with the paraffin. The village behind her was as quiet as usual, for the news had not yet spread. She frowned a little to herself, her large nostrils expanded uglily, and from time to time she muttered a phrase which Wynn, who never restrained himself before his women-folk, had applied to the enemy. 'Bloody pagans! They *are* bloody pagans. But,' she continued, falling back on the teaching that had made her what she was, 'one mustn't let one's mind dwell on these things.'

Before she reached the house Dr Hennis, who was also a special constable, overtook her in his car.

'Oh, Miss Postgate,' he said, 'I wanted to tell you that that accident at the "Royal Oak" was due to Gerritt's stable tumbling down. It's been dangerous for a long time. It ought to have been condemned.'

'I thought I heard an explosion too,' said Mary.

'You might have been misled by the beams snapping. I've been looking at 'em. They were dry-rotted through and through. Of course, as they broke, they would make a noise just like a gun.'

'Yes?' said Mary politely.

'Poor little Edna was playing underneath it,' he went on, still holding her with his eyes, 'and that and the tiles cut her to pieces, you see?'

'I saw it,' said Mary, shaking her head. 'I heard it too.'

'Well, we cannot be sure.' Dr Hennis changed his tone completely. 'I know both you and Nurse Eden (I've been speaking to her) are perfectly trustworthy, and I can rely on you not to say anything—yet at least. It is no good to stir up people unless——'

'Oh, I never do—anyhow,' said Mary, and Dr Hennis went on to the county town.

After all, she told herself, it might, just possibly, have been the collapse of the old stable that had done all those things to poor little Edna. She was sorry she had even hinted at other things, but Nurse Eden was discretion itself. By the time she reached home the affair seemed increasingly remote by its very monstrosity. As she came in, Miss Fowler told her that a couple of aeroplanes had passed half an hour ago.

'I thought I heard them,' she replied, 'I'm going down to the garden now. I've got the paraffin.'

'Yes, but—what *have* you got on your boots? They're soaking wet. Change them at once.'

Not only did Mary obey but she wrapped the boots in a newspaper, and put them into the string bag with the bottle. So, armed with the longest kitchen poker, she left.

'It's raining again,' was Miss Fowler's last word, 'but—I know you won't be happy till that's disposed of.'

'It won't take long. I've got everything down there, and I've put the lid on the destructor to keep the wet out.'

The shrubbery was filling with twilight by the time she had completed her arrangements and sprinkled the sacrificial oil. As she lit the match that would burn her heart to ashes, she heard * a groan or a grunt behind the dense Portugal laurels.

'Cheape?' she called impatiently, but Cheape, with his ancient lumbago, in his comfortable cottage would be the last man to profane the sanctuary. 'Sheep,' she concluded, and threw in the match. The pyre went up in a roar, and the immediate flame hastened night around her.

'How Wynn would have loved this!' she thought, stepping back from the blaze.

By its light she saw, half hidden behind a laurel not five paces away, a bareheaded man sitting very stiffly at the foot of one of the oaks. A broken branch lay across his lap—one booted leg protruding from beneath it. His head moved ceaselessly from side to side, but his body was as still as the tree's trunk. He was dressed—she moved sideways to look more closely—in a uniform something like Wynn's, with a flap buttoned across the chest. For an instant, she had some idea that it might be one of the young flying men she had met at the funeral. But their heads were dark and glossy. This man's was as pale as a baby's, and so closely cropped that she could see the disgusting pinky skin beneath. His lips moved.

'What do you say?' Mary moved towards him and stooped.

'Laty! Laty! Laty!' he muttered, while his hands picked at the dead wet leaves. There was no doubt as to his nationality. It made her so angry that she strode back to the destructor, though it was still too hot to use the poker there. Wynn's books seemed to be catching well. She looked up at the oak behind the man; several of the light upper and two or three rotten lower branches had broken and scattered their rubbish on the shrubbery path. On the lowest fork a helmet with dependent strings, showed like a bird's-nest in the light of a long-tongued flame. Evidently this person had fallen through the tree. Wynn had told her that it was quite possible for people to fall out of aeroplanes. Wynn told her too, that trees were useful things to break an aviator's fall, but in this case the aviator must have been broken or he would have moved from his queer position. He seemed helpless except for his horrible rolling head. On the other hand, she could see a pistol case at his belt—and Mary

loathed pistols. Months ago, after reading certain Belgian
reports together, she and Miss Fowler had had dealings with
one—a huge revolver with flat-nosed bullets, which latter,
Wynn said, were forbidden by the rules of war to be used
against civilized enemies. 'They're good enough for us,' Miss
Fowler had replied. 'Show Mary how it works.' And Wynn,
laughing at the mere possibility of any such need, had led the
craven winking Mary into the Rector's disused quarry, and had
shown her how to fire the terrible machine. It lay now in the
top-left-hand drawer of her toilet-table—a memento not included in the burning. Wynn would be pleased to scc how she
was not afraid.

She slipped up to the house to get it. When she came through
the rain, the eyes in the head were alive with expectation. The
mouth even tried to smile. But at sight of the revolver its corners
went down just like Edna Gerritt's. A tear trickled from one
eye, and the head rolled from shoulder to shoulder as though
trying to point out something.

'Cassée. Tout cassée,' it whimpered.

'What do you say?' said Mary disgustedly, keeping well to
one side, though only the head moved.

'Cassée,' it repeated. 'Che me rends. Le médicin!* Toctor!'

'Nein!' said she, bringing all her small German to bear with
the big pistol. 'Ich haben der todt Kinder gesehn.'*

The head was still. Mary's hand dropped. She had been
careful to keep her finger off the trigger for fear of accidents.
After a few moments' waiting, she returned to the destructor,
where the flames were falling, and churned up Wynn's charring
books with the poker. Again the head groaned for the doctor.

'Stop that!' said Mary, and stamped her foot. 'Stop that, you
bloody pagan!'

The words came quite smoothly and naturally. They were
Wynn's own words, and Wynn was a gentleman who for no
consideration on earth would have torn little Edna into those
vividly coloured strips and strings. But this thing hunched
under the oak-tree had done that thing. It was no question of
reading horrors out of newspapers to Miss Fowler. Mary had
seen it with her own eyes on the 'Royal Oak' kitchen table. She
must not allow her mind to dwell upon it. Now Wynn was dead,
and everything connected with him was lumping and rustling

and tinkling under her busy poker into red black dust and grey leaves of ash. The thing beneath the oak would die too. Mary had seen death more than once. She came of a family that had a knack of dying under, as she told Miss Fowler, 'most distressing circumstances'. She would stay where she was till she was entirely satisfied that It was dead—dead as dear papa in the late 'eighties; aunt Mary in 'eighty-nine; mamma in 'ninety-one; cousin Dick in 'ninety-five; Lady McCausland's housemaid in 'ninety-nine; Lady McCausland's sister in nineteen hundred and one; Wynn buried five days ago; and Edna Gerritt still waiting for decent earth to hide her. As she thought—her underlip caught up by one faded canine, brows knit and nostrils wide—she wielded the poker with lunges that jarred the grating at the bottom, and careful scrapes round the brickwork above. She looked at her wrist-watch. It was getting on to half-past four, and the rain was coming down in earnest. Tea would be at five. If It did not die before that time, she would be soaked and would have to change. Meantime, and this occupied her, Wynn's things were burning well in spite of the hissing wet, though now and again a book-back with a quite distinguishable title would be heaved up out of the mass. The exercise of stoking had given her a glow which seemed to reach to the marrow of her bones. She hummed—Mary never had a voice— to herself. She had never believed in all those advanced views— though Miss Fowler herself leaned a little that way—of woman's work in the world; but now she saw there was much to be said for them. This, for instance, was *her* work—work which no man, least of all Dr Hennis, would ever have done. A man, at such a crisis, would be what Wynn called a 'sportsman'; would leave everything to fetch help,* and would certainly bring It into the house. Now a woman's business was to make a happy home for—for a husband and children. Failing these—it was not a thing one should allow one's mind to dwell upon—but——

'Stop it!' Mary cried once more across the shadows. 'Nein, I tell you! Ich haben der todt Kinder gesehn.'

But it was a fact. A woman who had missed these things could still be useful—more useful than a man in certain respects. She thumped like a pavior through the settling ashes at the secret thrill of it. The rain was damping the fire, but she could feel—it was too dark to see—that her work was done. There was a dull red glow at the bottom of the destructor, not enough to char the wooden lid if she slipped it half over against the driving wet. This arranged, she leaned on the poker and waited, while an increasing rapture laid hold on her. She ceased to think. She gave herself up to feel. Her long pleasure was broken by a sound that she had waited for in agony several times in her life. She leaned forward and listened, smiling. There could be no mistake. She closed her eyes and drank it in. Once it ceased abruptly.

'Go on,' she murmured, half aloud. 'That isn't the end.'

Then the end came very distinctly in a lull between two rain-gusts. Mary Postgate drew her breath short between her teeth and shivered from head to foot. '*That's* all right,' said she contentedly, and went up to the house, where she scandalized the whole routine by taking a luxurious hot bath before tea, and came down looking, as Miss Fowler said when she saw her lying all relaxed on the other sofa, 'quite handsome!'

THE BEGINNINGS

It was not part of their blood,
    It came to them very late
With long arrears to make good,
    When the English began to hate.

They were not easily moved,
    They were icy willing to wait
Till every count should be proved,
    Ere the English began to hate.

Their voices were even and low,
    Their eyes were level and straight.
There was neither sign nor show,
    When the English began to hate.

It was not preached to the crowd,
    It was not taught by the State.
No man spoke it aloud,
    When the English began to hate.

It was not suddenly bred,
    It will not swiftly abate,
Through the chill years ahead,
    When Time shall count from the date
    That the English began to hate.

REGULUS *

Regulus, a Roman general, defeated the Carthaginians 256 BC, but was next year defeated and taken prisoner by the Carthaginians, who sent him to Rome with an embassy to ask for peace or an exchange of prisoners. Regulus strongly advised the Roman Senate to make no terms with the enemy. He then returned to Carthage and was put to death.

THE Fifth Form had been dragged several times in its collective life, from one end of the school Horace * to the other. Those were the years when Army examiners gave thousands of marks for Latin, and it was Mr King's hated business to defeat them.

Hear him, then, on a raw November morning at second lesson.

'Aha!' he began, rubbing his hands. '*Cras ingens iterabimus aequor.* * Our portion today is the Fifth Ode of the Third Book, I believe—concerning one Regulus, a gentleman. And how often have we been through it?'

'Twice, sir,' said Malpass, head of the Form.

Mr King shuddered. 'Yes, twice, quite literally,' he said. 'Today, with an eye to your Army *viva-voce* * examinations— ugh!—I shall exact somewhat freer and more florid renditions. With feeling and comprehension if that be possible. I except'— here his eye swept the back benches—'our friend and companion Beetle, from whom, now as always, I demand an absolutely literal translation.' The form laughed subserviently.

'Spare his blushes! Beetle charms us first.'

Beetle stood up, confident in the possession of a guaranteed construe, left behind by M'Turk, who had that day gone into the sick-house with a cold. Yet he was too wary a hand to show confidence.

'*Credidimus*, we—believe—we have believed,' he opened in hesitating slow time, '*tonantem Jovem*, thundering Jove—*regnare*, to reign—*caelo*, in heaven. *Augustus*, Augustus—*habebitur*, will be held or considered—*praesens divus*, a present God—*adjectis Britannis*, the Britons being added—*imperio*, to the Empire—*gravibusque Persis*, with the heavy—er, stern Persians.'

'What?'

'The grave or stern Persians.' Beetle pulled up with the 'Thank-God-I-have-done-my-duty' air of Nelson in the cockpit.

'I am quite aware,' said King, 'that the first stanza is about the extent of your knowledge, but continue, sweet one, continue. *Gravibus*, by the way, is usually translated as "troublesome".'

Beetle drew a long and tortured breath. The second stanza (which carries over to the third) of that Ode is what is technically called a 'stinker'. But M'Turk had done him handsomely.

'*Milesne Crassi*,* had—has the soldier of Crassus—*vixit*, lived—*turpis maritus*, a disgraceful husband——'

'You slurred the quantity* of the word after *turpis*,' said King. 'Let's hear it.'

Beetle guessed again, and for a wonder hit the correct quantity. 'Er—a disgraceful husband—*conjuge barbara*, with a barbarous spouse.'

'Why do you select *that* disgustful equivalent out of all the dictionary?' King snapped. 'Isn't "wife" good enough for you?'

'Yes, sir. But what do I do about this bracket, sir? Shall I take it now?'

'Confine yourself at present to the soldier of Crassus.'

'Yes, sir. *Et*, and—*consenuit*, has he grown old—*in armis*, in the—er—arms—*hostium socerorum*, of his father-in-law's enemies.'

'Who? How? Which?'

'Arms of his enemies' fathers-in-law, sir.'

'Tha-anks. By the way, what meaning might you attach to *in armis*?'

'Oh, weapons—weapons of war, sir.' There was a virginal note in Beetle's voice as though he had been falsely accused of uttering indecencies. 'Shall I take the bracket now, sir?'

'Since it seems to be troubling you.'

'*Pro Curia*, O for the Senate House—*inversique mores*, and manners upset—upside down.'

'Ve-ry like your translation. Meantime, the soldier of Crassus?'

'*Sub rege Medo*, under a Median King—*Marsus et Apulus*, he being a Marsian and an Apulian.'

'Who? The Median King?'

'No, sir. The soldier of Crassus. *Oblittus* agrees with *milesne Crassi*, sir,' volunteered too hasty Beetle.

'Does it? It doesn't with *me*.'

'*Oh-blight-us*,' Beetle corrected hastily, 'forgetful—*anciliorum*, of the shields, or trophies—*et nominis*, and the—his name—*et togae*, and the toga—*eternaeque Vestae*, and eternal Vesta—*incolumi Jove*, Jove being safe—*et urbe Roma*, and the Roman city.' With an air of hardly restrained zeal—'Shall I go on, sir?'

Mr King winced. 'No, thank you. You have indeed given us a translation! May I ask if it conveys any meaning whatever to your so-called mind?'

'Oh, I think so, sir.' This with gentle toleration for Horace and all his works.

'We envy you. Sit down.'

Beetle sat down relieved, well knowing that a reef of uncharted genitives stretched ahead of him, on which in spite of M'Turk's sailing-directions he would infallibly have been wrecked.

Rattray, who took up the task, steered neatly through them and came unscathed to port.

'Here we require drama,' said King. 'Regulus himself is speaking now. Who shall represent the provident-minded Regulus? Winton, will you kindly oblige?'

Winton of King's House, a long, heavy, tow-headed Second Fifteen forward, overdue for his First Fifteen colours, and in aspect like an earnest, elderly horse, rose up, and announced, among other things, that he had seen 'signs affixed to Punic deluges'. Half the Form shouted for joy, and the other half for joy that there was something to shout about.

Mr King opened and shut his eyes with great swiftness. '*Signa adfixa delubris*,'* he gasped. 'So *delubris* is "deluges" is it? Winton, in all our dealings, have I ever suspected you of a jest?'

'No, sir,' said the rigid and angular Winton, while the Form rocked about him.

'And yet you assert *delubris* means "deluges". Whether I am a fit subject for such a jape is, of course, a matter of opinion, but. . . . Winton, you are normally conscientious. May we assume you looked out *delubris*?'

'No, sir.' Winton was privileged to speak that truth dangerous to all who stand before Kings.

''Made a shot at it then?'

Every line of Winton's body showed he had done nothing of the sort. Indeed, the very idea that 'Pater' Winton (and a boy is not called 'Pater' by companions for his frivolity) would make a shot at anything was beyond belief. But he replied, 'Yes', and all the while worked with his right heel as though he were heeling a ball at punt-about.

Though none dared to boast of being a favourite with King, the taciturn, three-cornered Winton stood high in his House-Master's opinion. It seemed to save him neither rebuke nor punishment, but the two were in some fashion sympathetic.

'Hm!' said King drily. 'I was going to say—*Flagitio additis damnum*,* but I think—I think I see the process. Beetle, the translation of *delubris*, please.'

Beetle raised his head from his shaking arm long enough to answer: 'Ruins, sir.'

There was an impressive pause while King checked off crimes on his fingers. Then to Beetle the much-enduring man * addressed winged words:

'Guessing,' said he. 'Guessing, Beetle, as usual, from the look of *delubris* that it bore some relation to *diluvium* or deluge, you imparted the result of your half-baked lucubrations to Winton who seems to have been lost enough to have accepted it. Observing next, your companion's fall, from the presumed security of your undistinguished position in the rear-guard, you took another pot-shot. The turbid chaos of your mind threw up some memory of the word "dilapidations" which you have pitifully attempted to disguise under the synonym of "ruins".'

As this was precisely what Beetle had done he looked hurt but forgiving. 'We will attend to this later,' said King. 'Go on, Winton, and retrieve yourself.'

Delubris happened to be the one word which Winton had not looked out and had asked Beetle for, when they were settling into their places. He forged ahead with no further trouble. Only when he rendered *scilicet* as 'forsooth', King erupted.

'Regulus', he said, 'was not a leader-writer for the penny press, nor, for that matter, was Horace. Regulus says: "The soldier ransomed by gold will come keener for the fight—will he by—by gum!" *That's* the meaning of *scilicet*. It indicates contempt—bitter contempt. "Forsooth", forsooth! You'll be talking about "speckled beauties" and "eventually transpire" next. Howell, what do you make of that doubled "Vidi ego—ego vidi"? It wasn't put in to fill up the metre, you know.'

'Isn't it intensive, sir?' said Howell, afflicted by a genuine interest in what he read. 'Regulus was a bit in earnest about Rome making no terms with Carthage—and he wanted to let the Romans understand it, didn't he, sir?'

'Less than your usual grace, but the fact. Regulus *was* in earnest. He was also engaged at the same time in cutting his own throat with every word he uttered. He knew Carthage which (your examiners won't ask you this so you needn't take notes) was a sort of God-forsaken nigger Manchester. Regulus was not thinking about his own life. He was telling Rome the truth. He was playing for his side. Those lines from the eighteenth to the fortieth ought to be written in blood. Yet there are things in human garments which will tell you that Horace was a flaneur—a man about town. Avoid such beings. Horace knew a very great deal. *He* knew! *Erit ille fortis*—"will he be brave who once to faithless foes has knelt?" And again (stop pawing with your hooves, Thornton!) *hic unde vitam sumeret inscius.* * That means roughly—but I perceive I am ahead of my translators. Begin at *hic unde*, Vernon, and let us see if you have the spirit of Regulus.'

Now no one expected fireworks from gentle Paddy Vernon, sub-prefect of Hartopp's House, but, as must often be the case with growing boys, his mind was in abeyance for the time being, and he said, all in a rush, on behalf of Regulus: '*O magna Carthago probrosis altior Italiae ruinis,* * O Carthage, thou wilt stand forth higher than the ruins of Italy.'

Even Beetle, most lenient of critics, was interested at this point, though he did not join the half-groan of reprobation from the wiser heads of the Form.

'*Please* don't mind me,' said King, and Vernon very kindly did not. He ploughed on thus: 'He (Regulus) is related to have removed from himself the kiss of the shameful wife and of his small children as less by the head, and, being stern, to have placed his virile visage on the ground.'*

Since King loved 'virile' about as much as he did 'spouse' or 'forsooth' the Form looked up hopefully. But Jove thundered not.

'Until,' Vernon continued, 'he should have confirmed the sliding fathers as being the author of counsel never given under an alias.'*

He stopped, conscious of stillness round him like the dread calm of the typhoon's centre. King's opening voice was sweeter than honey.

'I am painfully aware by bitter experience that I cannot give you any idea of the passion, the power, the—the essential guts of the lines which you have so foully outraged in our presence. But——' the note changed, 'so far as in me lies, I will strive to bring home to you, Vernon, the fact that there exist in Latin a few pitiful rules of grammar, of syntax, nay, even of declension, which were not created for your incult sport—your Bœotian diversion. You will, therefore, Vernon, write out and bring to me tomorrow a word-for-word English–Latin translation of the Ode, together with a full list of all adjectives—an adjective is not a verb, Vernon, as the Lower Third will tell you—all adjectives, their number, case, and gender. Even now I haven't begun to deal with you faithfully.'

'I—I'm very sorry, sir,' Vernon stammered.

'You mistake the symptoms, Vernon. You are possibly discomfited by the imposition, but sorrow postulates some sort of mind, intellect, *nous*. Your rendering of *probrosis* alone stamps you as lower than the beasts of the field. Will some one take the taste out of our mouths? And—talking of tastes——' He coughed. There was a distinct flavour of chlorine gas in the air. Up went an eyebrow, though King knew perfectly well what it meant.

'Mr Hartopp's st—science class next door,' said Malpass.

'Oh yes. I had forgotten. Our newly established Modern Side, of course. Perowne, open the windows; and Winton, go on once more from *interque maerentes*.'

'And hastened away,' said Winton, 'surrounded by his mourning friends, into—into illustrious banishment. But I got that out of Conington,* sir,' he added in one conscientious breath.

'I am aware. The master generally knows his ass's crib,* though I acquit *you* of any intention that way. Can you suggest anything for *egregius exul?* Only "egregious exile"? I fear "egregious" is a good word ruined. No! You can't in this case improve on Conington. Now then for *atqui sciebat quae sibi barbarus tortor pararet.* The whole force of it lies in the *atqui.*'

'Although he knew,' Winton suggested.

'Stronger than that, I think.'

'He who knew well,' Malpass interpolated.

'Ye-es. "Well though he knew." I don't like Conington's "well-witting". It's Wardour Street.'

'Well though he knew what the savage torturer was—was getting ready for him,' said Winton.

'Ye-es. Had in store for him.'

'Yet he brushed aside his kinsmen and the people delaying his return.'

'Ye-es; but then how do you render *obstantes*?'

'If it's a free translation mightn't *obstantes* and *morantem* come to about the same thing, sir?'

'Nothing comes to "about the same thing" with Horace, Winton. As I have said, Horace was not a journalist. No, I take it that his kinsmen bodily withstood his departure, whereas the crowd—*populumque*—the democracy stood about futilely pitying him and getting in the way. Now for that noblest of endings—*quam si clientum,*' and King ran off into the quotation:

'As though some tedious business o'er
Of clients' court, his journey lay
Towards Venafrum's grassy floor
Or Sparta-built Tarentum's bay.*

All right, Winton. Beetle, when you've quite finished dodging the fresh air yonder, give me the meaning of *tendens*—and turn down your collar.'

'Me, sir? *Tendens*, sir? Oh! Stretching away in the direction of, sir.'

'Idiot! Regulus was not a feature of the landscape. He was a man, self-doomed to death by torture. *Atqui sciebat*—knowing it—having achieved it for his country's sake—can't you hear that *atqui* cut like a knife?—he moved off with some dignity. That is why Horace out of the whole golden Latin tongue chose the one word "tendens"—which is utterly untranslatable.'

The gross injustice of being asked to translate it, converted Beetle into a young Christian martyr, till King buried his nose in his handkerchief again.

'I think they've broken another gas-bottle next door, sir,' said Howell. 'They're always doing it.' The Form coughed as more chlorine came in.

'Well, I suppose we must be patient with the Modern Side,' said King. 'But it is almost insupportable for this Side. Vernon, what are you grinning at?'

Vernon's mind had returned to him glowing and inspired. He chuckled as he underlined his Horace.

'It appears to amuse you,' said King. 'Let us participate. What is it?'

'The last two lines of the Tenth Ode, in this book, sir,' was Vernon's amazing reply.

'What? Oh, I see. *Non hoc semper erit liminis aut aquae caelestis patiens latus*.' * King's mouth twitched to hide a grin. 'Was that done with intention?'

'I—I thought it fitted, sir.'

'It does. It's distinctly happy. What put it into your thick head, Paddy?'

'I don't know, sir, except we did the Ode last term.'

'And you remembered? The same head that minted *probrosis* as a verb! Vernon, you are an enigma. No! This Side will *not* always be patient of unheavenly gases and waters. I will make representations to our so-called Moderns. Meantime (who shall say I am not just?) I remit you your accrued pains and penalties in regard to *probrosim, probrosis, probrosit*, and other enormities. I oughtn't to do it, but this Side is occasionally human. By no means bad, Paddy.'

'Thank you, sir,' said Vernon, wondering how inspiration had visited him.

Then King, with a few brisk remarks about Science, headed them back to Regulus, of whom and of Horace and Rome and

evil-minded commercial Carthage and of the democracy eternally futile, he explained, in all ages and climes, he spoke for ten
minutes; passing thence to the next Ode—*Delicta majorum*—
where he fetched up, full-voiced, upon—'*Dis te minorem quod
geris imperas*' (Thou rulest because thou bearest thyself as lower
than the Gods)—making it a text for a discourse on manners,
morals, and respect for authority as distinct from bottled gases,
which lasted till the bell rang. Then Beetle, concertinaing his
books, observed to Winton, 'When King's really on tap he's an
interestin' dog. Hartopp's chlorine uncorked him.'

'Yes; but why did you tell me *delubris* was "deluges", you silly
ass?' said Winton.

'Well, that uncorked him too. Look out, you hoof-handed
old owl!' Winton had cleared for action as the Form poured
out like puppies at play and was scragging Beetle. Stalky from
behind collared Winton low. The three fell in confusion.

'*Dis te minorem quod geris imperas*,' quoth Stalky, ruffling
Winton's lint-white locks. ''Mustn't jape with Number Five
study. Don't be too virtuous. Don't brood over it. 'Twon't
count against you in your future caree-ah. Cheer up, Pater.'

'Pull him off my—er—essential guts, will you?' said Beetle
from beneath. 'He's squashin' 'em.'

They dispersed to their studies.

* * *

No one, the owner least of all, can explain what is in a growing
boy's mind. It might have been the blind ferment of adolescence; Stalky's random remarks about virtue might have stirred
him; like his betters he might have sought popularity by way of
clowning; or, as the Head asserted years later, the only known
jest of his serious life might have worked on him, as a sober-
sided man's one love colours and dislocates all his after days.
But, at the next lesson, mechanical drawing with Mr Lidgett
who as drawing-master had very limited powers of punishment,
Winton fell suddenly from grace and let loose a live mouse in
the form-room. The whole form, shrieking and leaping high,
threw at it all the plaster cones, pyramids, and fruit in high
relief—not to mention ink-pots—that they could lay hands on.
Mr Lidgett reported at once to the Head; Winton owned up to
his crime, which, venial in the Upper Third, pardonable at a

price in the Lower Fourth, was, of course, rank ruffianism on the part of a Fifth Form boy; and so, by graduated stages, he arrived at the Head's study just before lunch, penitent, perturbed, annoyed with himself and—as the Head said to King in the corridor after the meal—more human than he had known him in seven years.

'You see,' the Head drawled on, 'Winton's only fault is a certain costive and unaccommodating virtue. So this comes very happily.'

'I've never noticed any sign of it,' said King. Winton was in King's House, and though King as pro-consul might, and did, infernally oppress his own Province, once a black and yellow cap was in trouble at the hands of the Imperial authority King fought for him to the very last steps of Caesar's throne.

'Well, you yourself admitted just now that a mouse was beneath the occasion,' the Head answered.

'It was.' Mr King did not love Mr Lidgett. 'It should have been a rat. But—but—I hate to plead it—it's the lad's first offence.'

'Could you have damned him more completely, King?'

'Hm. What is the penalty?' said King, in retreat, but keeping up a rear-guard action.

'Only my usual few lines of Virgil to be shown up by tea-time.'

The Head's eyes turned slightly to that end of the corridor where Mullins, Captain of the Games ('Pot', 'old Pot', or 'Potiphar' Mullins), was pinning up the usual Wednesday notice—'Big, Middle, and Little Side Football—A to K, L to Z, 3 to 4.45 p.m.'

You cannot write out the Head's usual few (which means five hundred) Latin lines and play football for one hour and three-quarters between the hours of 1.30 and 5 p.m. Winton had evidently no intention of trying to do so, for he hung about the corridor with a set face and an uneasy foot. Yet it was law in the school, compared with which that of the Medes and Persians* was no more than a non-committal resolution, that any boy, outside the First Fifteen, who missed his football for any reason whatever, and had not a written excuse, duly signed by competent authority to explain his absence, would receive not less than three strokes with a ground-ash from the Captain of the Games, generally a youth between seventeen and eighteen years, rarely under eleven stone ('Pot' was nearer thirteen), and always in hard condition.

King knew without inquiry that the Head had given Winton no such excuse.

'But he is practically a member of the First Fifteen. He has played for it all this term,' said King. 'I believe his Cap should have arrived last week.'

'His Cap has not been given him. Officially, therefore, he is naught. I rely on old Pot.'

'But Mullins is Winton's study-mate,' King persisted.

Pot Mullins and Pater Winton were cousins and rather close friends.

'That will make no difference to Mullins—or Winton, if I know 'em,' said the Head.

'But—but,' King played his last card desperately, 'I was going to recommend Winton for extra sub-prefect in my House, now Carton has gone.'

'Certainly,' said the Head. 'Why not? He will be excellent by tea-time, I hope.'

At that moment they saw Mr Lidgett, tripping down the corridor, waylaid by Winton.

'It's about that mouse-business at mechanical drawing,' Winton opened, swinging across his path.

'Yes, yes, highly disgraceful,' Mr Lidgett panted.

'I know it was,' said Winton. 'It—it was a cad's trick because——'

'Because you knew I couldn't give you more than fifty lines,' said Mr Lidgett.

'Well, anyhow I've come to apologize for it.'

'Certainly,' said Mr Lidgett, and added, for he was a kindly man, 'I think that shows quite right feeling. I'll tell the Head at once I'm satisfied.'

'No—no!' The boy's still unmended voice jumped from the growl to the squeak. 'I didn't mean *that*! I—I did it on principle. Please don't—er—do anything of that kind.'

Mr Lidgett looked him up and down and, being an artist, understood.

'Thank you, Winton,' he said. 'This shall be between ourselves.'

'You heard?' said King, indecent pride in his voice.

'Of course. You thought he was going to get Lidgett to beg him off the impot.'

King denied this with so much warmth that the Head laughed and King went away in a huff.

'By the way,' said the Head, 'I've told Winton to do his lines in your form-room—not in his study.'

'Thanks,' said King over his shoulder, for the Head's orders had saved Winton and Mullins, who was doing extra Army work in the study, from an embarrassing afternoon together.

An hour later, King wandered into his still form-room as though by accident. Winton was hard at work.

'Aha!' said King, rubbing his hands. 'This does not look like games, Winton. Don't let me arrest your facile pen. Whence this sudden love for Virgil?'

'Impot from the Head, sir, for that mouse-business this morning.'

'Rumours thereof have reached us. That was a lapse on your part into Lower Thirdery which I don't quite understand.'

The 'tump-tump' of the puntabouts before the sides settled to games came through the open window. Winton, like his House-master, loved fresh air. Then they heard Paddy Vernon, sub-prefect on duty, calling the roll in the field and marking defaulters. Winton wrote steadily. King curled himself up on a desk, hands round knees. One would have said that the man was gloating over the boy's misfortune, but the boy understood.

'*Dis te minorem quod geris imperas,*' King quoted presently. 'It is necessary to bear oneself as lower than the local gods—even than drawing-masters who are precluded from effective retaliation. I *do* wish you'd tried that mouse-game with me, Pater.'

Winton grinned; then sobered. 'It was a cad's trick, sir, to play on Mr Lidgett.' He peered forward at the page he was copying.

'Well, "the sin *I* impute to each frustrate ghost"*——' King stopped himself. 'Why do you goggle like an owl? Hand me the Mantuan* and I'll dictate. No matter. Any rich Virgilian measures will serve. I may peradventure recall a few.' He began:

'Tu regere imperio populos Romane memento
Hae tibi erunt artes pacisque imponere morem,
Parcere subjectis et debellare superbos.*

There you have it all, Winton. Write that out twice and yet once
again.'

For the next forty minutes, with never a glance at the book,
King paid out the glorious hexameters (and King could read
Latin as though it were alive), Winton hauling them in and
coiling them away behind him as trimmers in a telegraph-ship's
hold coil away deep-sea cable. King broke from the Aeneid to
the Georgics and back again, pausing now and then to translate
some specially loved line or to dwell on the treble-shot texture
of the ancient fabric. He did not allude to the coming interview
with Mullins except at the last, when he said, 'I think at this
juncture, Pater, I need not ask you for the precise significance
of *atqui sciebat quae sibi barbarus tortor.*'

The ungrateful Winton flushed angrily, and King loafed out
to take five o'clock call-over, after which he invited little
Hartopp to tea and a talk on chlorine-gas. Hartopp accepted
the challenge like a bantam, and the two went up to King's
study about the same time as Winton returned to the form-
room beneath it to finish his lines.

Then half a dozen of the Second Fifteen who should have
been washing strolled in to condole with 'Pater' Winton, whose
misfortune and its consequences were common talk. No one
was more sincere than the long, red-headed, knotty-knuckled
'Paddy' Vernon, but, being a careless animal, he joggled Winton's desk.

'Curse you for a silly ass!' said Winton. 'Don't do that.'

No one is expected to be polite while under punishment, so
Vernon, sinking his sub-prefectship, replied peacefully enough:

'Well, don't be wrathy, Pater.'

'I'm not,' said Winton. 'Get out! This ain't your House
form-room.'

''Form-room don't belong to you. Why don't you go to your
own study?' Vernon replied.

'Because Mullins is there waitin' for the victim,' said Stalky
delicately, and they all laughed. 'You ought to have shaken that
mouse out of your trouser-leg, Pater. That's the way *I* did in

my youth. Pater's revertin' to his second childhood. Never mind, Pater, we all respect you and your future caree-ah.'

Winton, still writhing, growled. Vernon leaning on the desk somehow shook it again. Then he laughed.

'What are you grinning at?' Winton asked.

'I was only thinkin' of *you* being sent up to take a lickin' from Pot. I swear I don't think it's fair. You've never shirked a game in your life, and you're as good as in the First Fifteen already. Your Cap ought to have been delivered last week, oughtn't it?'

It was law in the school that no man could by any means enjoy the privileges and immunities of the First Fifteen till the black velvet cap with the gold tassel, made by dilatory Exeter outfitters, had been actually set on his head. Ages ago, a large-built and unruly Second Fifteen had attempted to change this law, but the prefects of that age were still larger, and the lively experiment had never been repeated.

'Will you,' said Winton very slowly, 'kindly mind your own damned business, you cursed, clumsy, fat-headed fool?'

The form-room was as silent as the empty field in the darkness outside. Vernon shifted his feet uneasily.

'Well, *I* shouldn't like to take a lickin' from Pot,' he said.

'Wouldn't you?' Winton asked, as he paged the sheets of lines with hands that shook.

'No, I shouldn't,' said Vernon, his freckles growing more distinct on the bridge of his white nose.

'Well, I'm going to take it'—Winton moved clear of the desk as he spoke. 'But *you*'re going to take a lickin' from me first.' Before any one realized it, he had flung himself neighing against Vernon. No decencies were observed on either side, and the rest looked on amazed. The two met confusedly, Vernon trying to do what he could with his longer reach; Winton, insensible to blows, only concerned to drive his enemy into a corner and batter him to pulp. This he managed over against the fireplace, where Vernon dropped half-stunned. 'Now I'm going to give you your lickin',' said Winton. 'Lie there till I get a ground-ash and I'll cut you to pieces. If you move, I'll chuck you out of the window.' He wound his hands into the boy's collar and waist-band, and had actually heaved him half off the ground before the others with one accord dropped on his head, shoulders, and legs. He fought them crazily in an awful hissing silence. Stalky's sensitive nose was rubbed along the floor; Beetle received a jolt in the wind that sent him whistling and crowing against the wall; Perowne's forehead was cut, and Malpass came out with an eye that explained itself like a dying rainbow through a whole week.

'Mad! Quite mad!' said Stalky, and for the third time wriggled back to Winton's throat. The door opened and King came in, Hartopp's little figure just behind him. The mound on the floor panted and heaved but did not rise, for Winton still squirmed vengefully. 'Only a little play, sir,' said Perowne. ''Only hit my head against a form.' This was quite true.

'Oh,' said King. '*Dimovit obstantes propinquos.* You, I presume, are the *populus* delaying Winton's return to—Mullins, eh?'

'No, sir,' said Stalky beind his claret-coloured handkerchief. 'We're the *maerentes amicos*.'

'Not bad! You see, some of it sticks after all,' King chuckled to Hartopp, and the two masters left without further inquiries.

The boys sat still on the now passive Winton.

'Well,' said Stalky at last, 'of all the putrid he-asses, Pater, you are the——'

'I'm sorry. I'm awfully sorry,' Winton began, and they let him rise. He held out his hand to the bruised and bewildered Vernon. 'Sorry, Paddy. I—I must have lost my temper. I—I don't know what's the matter with me.'

''Fat lot of good that'll do my face at tea,' Vernon grunted. 'Why couldn't you say there was something wrong with you instead of lamming out like a lunatic? Is my lip puffy?'

'Just a trifle. Look at my beak! Well, we got all these pretty marks at footer—owin' to the zeal with which we played the game,' said Stalky, dusting himself. 'But d'you think you're fit to be let loose again, Pater? 'Sure you don't want to kill another sub-prefect? I wish *I* was Pot. I'd cut your sprightly young soul out.'

'I s'pose I ought to go to Pot now,' said Winton.

'And let all the other asses see you lookin' like this! Not much. We'll all come up to Number Five Study and wash off in hot water. Beetle, you aren't damaged. Go along and light the gas-stove.'

'There's a tin of cocoa in my study somewhere,' Perowne shouted after him. 'Rootle round till you find it, and take it up.'

Separately, by different roads, Vernon's jersey pulled half over his head, the boys repaired to Number Five Study. Little Hartopp and King, I am sorry to say, leaned over the banisters of King's landing and watched.

'Ve-ry human,' said little Hartopp. 'Your virtuous Winton, having got himself into trouble, takes it out of my poor old Paddy. I wonder what precise lie Paddy will tell about his face.'

'But surely you aren't going to embarrass him by asking?' said King.

'*Your* boy won,' said Hartopp.

'To go back to what we were discussing,' said King quickly, 'do you pretend that your modern system of inculcating un-related facts about chlorine, for instance, all of which may be proved fallacies by the time the boys grow up, can have any real bearing on education—even the low type of it that examiners expect?'

'I maintain nothing. But is it any worse than your Chinese reiteration of uncomprehended syllables in a dead tongue?'

'Dead, forsooth!' King fairly danced. 'The only living tongue on earth! Chinese! On my word, Hartopp!'

'And at the end of seven years—how often have I said it?' Hartopp went on,—'seven years of two hundred and twenty days of six hours each, your victims go away with nothing, absolutely nothing, except, perhaps, if they've been very attent-ive, a dozen—no, I'll grant you twenty—one score of totally unrelated Latin tags which any child of twelve could have absorbed in two terms.'

'But—but can't you realize that if our system brings later—at any rate—at a pinch—a simple understanding—grammar and Latinity apart—a mere glimpse of the significance (foul word!) of, we'll say, one Ode of Horace, one twenty lines of Virgil, we've got what we poor devils of ushers are striving after?'

'And what might that be?' said Hartopp.

'Balance, proportion, perspective—life. Your scientific man is the unrelated animal—the beast without background. Haven't you ever realized *that* in your atmosphere of stinks?'

'Meantime you make them lose life for the sake of living, eh?'

'Blind again, Hartopp! I told you about Paddy's quotation this morning. (But he made *probrosis* a verb, he did!) You yourself heard young Corkran's reference to *maerentes amicos*. It sticks—a little of it sticks among the barbarians.'

'Absolutely and essentially Chinese,' said little Hartopp, who, alone of the common-room, refused to be outfaced by King. 'But I don't yet understand how Paddy came to be licked by Winton. Paddy's supposed to be something of a boxer.'

'Beware of vinegar made from honey,' King replied. 'Pater, like some other people, is patient and long-suffering, but he has his limits. The Head is oppressing him damnably, too. As I pointed out, the boy has practically been in the First Fifteen since term began.'

'But, my dear fellow, I've known you give a boy an impot and refuse him leave off games, again and again.'

'Ah, but that was when there was real need to get at some oaf who couldn't be sensitized in any other way. Now, in our esteemed Head's action I see nothing but——'

The conversation from this point does not concern us.

Meantime Winton, very penitent and especially polite towards Vernon, was being cheered with cocoa in Number Five Study. They had some difficulty in stemming the flood of his apologies. He himself pointed out to Vernon that he had attacked a sub-prefect for no reason whatever, and, therefore, deserved official punishment.

'I can't think what was the matter with me today,' he mourned. 'Ever since that blasted mouse-business——'

'Well, then, don't think,' said Stalky. 'Or do you want Paddy to make a row about it before all the school?'

Here Vernon was understood to say that he would see Winton and all the school somewhere else.

'And if you imagine Perowne and Malpass and me are goin' to give evidence at a prefects' meeting just to soothe your beastly conscience, you jolly well err,' said Beetle. 'I know what you did.'

'What?' croaked Pater, out of the valley of his humiliation.

'You went Berserk. I've read all about it in *Hypatia*.'*

'What's "going Berserk"?' Winton asked.

'Never you mind,' was the reply. 'Now, don't you feel awfully weak and seedy?'

'I *am* rather tired,' said Winton, sighing.

'That's what you ought to be. You've gone Berserk and pretty soon you'll go to sleep. But you'll probably be liable to fits of it all your life,' Beetle concluded. ''Shouldn't wonder if you murdered some one some day.'

'Shut up—you and your Berserks!' said Stalky. 'Go to Mullins now and get it over, Pater.'

'I call it filthy unjust of the Head,' said Vernon. 'Anyhow, you've given me my lickin', old man. I hope Pot'll give you yours.'

'I'm awfully sorry—awfully sorry,' was Winton's last word.

It was the custom in that consulship to deal with games' defaulters between five o'clock call-over and tea. Mullins, who was old enough to pity, did not believe in letting boys wait through the night till the chill of the next morning for their punishments. He was finishing off the last of the small fry and their excuses when Winton arrived.

'But, please, Mullins'—this was Babcock tertius, a dear little twelve-year-old mother's darling—'I had an awful hack on the knee. I've been to the Matron about it and she gave me some iodine. I've been rubbing it in all day. I thought that would be an excuse off.'

'Let's have a look at it,' said the impassive Mullins. 'That's a shin-bruise—about a week old. Touch your toes. I'll give you the iodine.'

Babcock yelled loudly as he had many times before. The face of Jevons, aged eleven, a new boy that dark wet term, low in the House, low in the Lower School, and lowest of all in his homesick little mind, turned white at the horror of the sight. They could hear his working lips part stickily as Babcock wailed his way out of hearing.

'Hullo, Jevons! What brings you here?' said Mullins.

'Pl-ease, sir, I went for a walk with Babcock tertius.'

'Did you? Then I bet you went to the tuck-shop—and you paid, didn't you?'

A nod. Jevons was too terrified to speak.

'Of course, and I bet Babcock told you that old Pot 'ud let you off because it was the first time.'

Another nod with a ghost of a smile in it.

'All right.' Mullins picked Jevons up before he could guess what was coming, laid him on the table with one hand, with the other gave him three emphatic spanks, then held him high in air.

'Now you tell Babcock tertius that he's got you a licking from me, and see you jolly well pay it back to him. And when you're prefect of games don't you let any one shirk his footer without a written excuse. Where d'you play in your game?'

'Forward, sir.'

'You can do better than that. I've seen you run like a young buck-rabbit. Ask Dickson from me to try you as three-quarter next game, will you? Cut along.'

Jevons left, warm for the first time that day, enormously set up in his own esteem, and very hot against the deceitful Babcock.

Mullins turned to Winton. 'Your name's on the list, Pater.' Winton nodded.

'I know it. The Head landed me with an impot for that mouse-business at mechanical drawing. No excuse.'

'He meant it then?' Mullins jerked his head delicately towards the ground-ash on the table. 'I heard something about it.'

Winton nodded. 'A rotten thing to do,' he said. 'Can't think what I was doing ever to do it. It counts against a fellow so; and there's some more too——'

'All right, Pater. Just stand clear of our photo-bracket, will you?'

The little formality over, there was a pause. Winton swung round, yawned in Pot's astonished face and staggered towards the window-seat.

'What's the matter with you, Dick? Ill?'

'No. Perfectly all right, thanks. Only—only a little sleepy.' Winton stretched himself out, and then and there fell deeply and placidly asleep.

'It isn't a faint,' said the experienced Mullins, 'or his pulse wouldn't act. 'Tisn't a fit or he'd snort and twitch. It can't be sunstroke, this term, and he hasn't been over-training for anything.' He opened Winton's collar, packed a cushion under his head, threw a rug over him and sat down to listen to the regular breathing. Before long Stalky arrived, on pretence of borrowing a book. He looked at the window-seat.

''Noticed anything wrong with Winton lately?' said Mullins.

''Notice anything wrong with my beak?' Stalky replied. 'Pater went Berserk after call-over, and fell on a lot of us for jesting with him about his impot. You ought to see Malpass's eye.'

'You mean that Pater fought?' said Mullins.

'Like a devil. Then he nearly went to sleep in our study just now. I expect he'll be all right when he wakes up. Rummy business! Conscientious old bargee. You ought to have heard his apologies.'

'But Pater can't fight one little bit,' Mullins repeated.

''Twasn't fighting. He just tried to murder every one.' Stalky described the affair, and when he left Mullins went off to take counsel with the Head, who, out of a cloud of blue smoke, told him that all would yet be well.

'Winton,' said he, 'is a little stiff in his moral joints. He'll get over that. If he asks you whether today's doings will count against him in his——'

'But you know it's important to him, sir. His people aren't—very well off,' said Mullins.

'That's why I'm taking all this trouble. You must reassure him, Pot. I have overcrowded him with new experiences. Oh, by the way, has his Cap come?'

'It came at dinner, sir.' Mullins laughed.

Sure enough, when he waked at tea-time, Winton proposed to take Mullins all through every one of his day's lapses from grace, and 'Do you think it will count against me?' said he.

'Don't you fuss so much about yourself and your silly career,' said Mullins. 'You're all right. And oh—here's your First Cap at last. Shove it up on the bracket and come on to tea.'

They met King on their way, stepping statelily and rubbing his hands. 'I have applied,' said he, 'for the services of an additional sub-prefect in Carton's unlamented absence. Your name, Winton, seems to have found favour with the powers that be, and—and all things considered—I am disposed to give my support to the nomination. You are therefore a quasi-lictor.'

'Then it didn't count against me,' Winton gasped as soon as they were out of hearing.

A Captain of Games can jest with a sub-prefect publicly.

'You utter ass!' said Mullins, and caught him by the back of his stiff neck and ran him down to the hall where the sub-prefects, who sit below the salt, made him welcome with the economical bloater-paste of mid-term.

* * *

King and little Hartopp were sparring in the Reverend John Gillett's study at 10 p.m.—classical *versus* modern as usual.

'Character—proportion—background,' snarled King. 'That is the essence of the Humanities.'

'Analects of Confucius,' little Hartopp answered.

'Time,' said the Reverend John behind the soda-water. 'You men oppress me. Hartopp, what did you say to Paddy in your dormitories tonight? Even *you* couldn't have overlooked his face.'

'But I did,' said Hartopp calmly. 'I wasn't even humorous about it, as some clerics might have been. I went straight through and said naught.'

'Poor Paddy! Now, for my part,' said King, 'and you know I am not lavish in my praises, I consider Winton a first-class type; absolutely first-class.'

'Ha-ardly,' said the Reverend John. 'First-class of the second class, I admit. The very best type of second class but'—he shook his head—'it should have been a rat. Pater'll never be anything more than a Colonel of Engineers.'

'What do you base that verdict on?' said King stiffly.

'He came to me after prayers—with all his conscience.'

'Poor old Pater. Was it the mouse?' said little Hartopp.

'That, and what he called his uncontrollable temper, and his responsibilities as sub-prefect.'

'And you?'

'If we had had what is vulgarly called a pi-jaw he'd have had hysterics. So I recommended a dose of Epsom salts. * He'll take it, too—conscientiously. Don't eat me, King. Perhaps he'll be a KCB'*

Ten o'clock struck and the Army class boys in the further studies coming to their houses after an hour's extra work passed along the gravel path below. Some one was chanting, to the tune of 'White sand and grey sand,' *Dis te minorem quod geris imperas.* He stopped outside Mullins' study. They heard Mullins' window slide up and then Stalky's voice:

'Ah! Good-evening, Mullins, my *barbarus tortor.* We're the waits. We have come to inquire after the local Berserk. Is he doin' as well as can be expected in his new caree-ah?'

'Better than you will, in a sec, Stalky,' Mullins grunted.

''Glad of that. We thought he'd like to know that Paddy has been carried to the sick-house in ravin' delirium. They think it's concussion of the brain.'

'Why, he was all right at prayers,' Winton began earnestly, and they heard a laugh in the background as Mullins slammed down the window.

''Night, Regulus,' Stalky sang out, and the light footsteps went on.

'You see. It sticks. A little of it sticks among the barbarians,' said King.

'Amen,' said the Reverend John. 'Go to bed.'

A TRANSLATION

HORACE, Bk. V. Ode 3*

There are whose study is of smells,
    And to attentive schools rehearse
How something mixed with something else
    Makes something worse.

Some cultivate in broths impure
    The clients of our body—these,
Increasing without Venus, cure,
    Or cause, disease.

Others the heated wheel extol,
    And all its offspring, whose concern
Is how to make it farthest roll
    And fastest turn.

Me, much incurious if the hour
    Present, or to be paid for, brings
Me to Brundusium by the power
    Of wheels or wings;

Me, in whose breast no flame hath burned
    Life-long, save that by Pindar* lit,
Such lore leaves cold: I am not turned
    Aside to it

More than when, sunk in thought profound
    Of what the unaltering Gods require,
My steward (friend but slave) brings round
    Logs for my fire.

THE WISH HOUSE *

'LATE CAME THE GOD'

Late came the God, having sent his forerunners who were not
    regarded—
  Late, but in wrath;
Saying: 'The wrong shall be paid, the contempt be rewarded
  On all that she hath.'
He poisoned the blade and struck home, the full bosom
    receiving
The wound and the venom in one, past cure or relieving.

He made treaty with Time to stand still that the grief might be
    fresh—
Daily renewed and nightly pursued through her soul to her
    flesh—
Mornings of memory, noontides of agony, midnights unslaked
    for her,
Till the stones of the streets of her Hells and her Paradise
    ached for her.

So she lived while her body corrupted upon her.
  And she called on the Night for a sign, and a Sign was
    allowed,
And she built an Altar and served by the light of her Vision—
  Alone, without hope of regard or reward, but uncowed,
Resolute, selfless, divine.
  These things she did in Love's honour . . .
What is a God beside Woman? Dust and derision!

The Wish House

THE new Church Visitor had just left after a twenty minutes'
call. During that time, Mrs Ashcroft had used such English as
an elderly, experienced, and pensioned cook should, who had
seen life in London. She was the readier, therefore, to slip back
into easy, ancient Sussex ('t's softening to 'd's as one warmed)
when the 'bus brought Mrs Fettley from thirty miles away for
a visit, that pleasant March Saturday. The two had been friends
since childhood; but, of late, destiny had separated their meetings by long intervals.

Much was to be said, and many ends, loose since last time,
to be ravelled up on both sides, before Mrs Fettley, with her
bag of quilt-patches, took the couch beneath the window
commanding the garden, and the football-ground in the valley
below.

'Most folk got out at Bush Tye for the match there,' she
explained, 'so there weren't no one for me to cushion agin, the
last five mile. An' she *do* just-about bounce ye.'

'You've took no hurt,' said her hostess. 'You don't brittle by
agein', Liz.'

Mrs Fettley chuckled and made to match a couple of patches
to her liking. 'No, or I'd ha' broke twenty year back. You can't
ever mind when I was so's to be called round, can ye?'

Mrs Ashcroft shook her head slowly—she never hurried—
and went on stitching a sack-cloth lining into a list-bound rush
tool-basket. Mrs Fettley laid out more patches in the Spring
light through the geraniums on the window-sill, and they were
silent awhile.

'What like's this new Visitor o' yourn?' Mrs Fettley inquired,
with a nod towards the door. Being very short-sighted, she had,
on her entrance, almost bumped into the lady.

Mrs Ashcroft suspended the big packing-needle judicially on
high, ere she stabbed home. 'Settin' aside she don't bring much
news with her yet, I dunno as I've anythin' special agin her.'

'Ourn, at Keyneslade,' said Mrs Fettley, 'she's full o' words an' pity, but she don't stay for answers. Ye can get on with your thoughts while she clacks.'

'This 'un don't clack. She's aimin' to be one o' those High Church nuns, like.'

'Ourn's married, but, by what they say, she've made no great gains of it . . .' Mrs Fettley threw up her sharp chin. 'Lord! How they dam' cherubim do shake the very bones o' the place!'

The tile-sided cottage trembled at the passage of two specially chartered forty-seat charabancs on their way to the Bush Tye match; a regular Saturday 'shopping' 'bus, for the county's capital, fumed behind them; while, from one of the crowded inns, a fourth car backed out to join the procession, and held up the stream of through pleasure-traffic.

'You're as free-tongued as ever, Liz,' Mrs Ashcroft observed.

'Only when I'm with you. Otherwhiles, I'm Granny—three times over. I lay that basket's for one o' your gran'chiller—ain't it?'

''Tis for Arthur—my Jane's eldest.'

'But he ain't workin' nowheres, is he?'

'No. 'Tis a picnic-basket.'

'You're let off light. My Willie, he's allus at me for money for them aireated wash-poles * folk puts up in their gardens to draw the music from Lunnon, like. An' I give it 'im—pore fool me!'

'An' he forgets to give you the promise-kiss after, don't he?' Mrs Ashcroft's heavy smile seemed to strike inwards.

'He do. 'No odds 'twixt boys now an' forty year back. 'Take all an' give naught—an' we to put up with it! Pore fool we! Three shillin' at a time Willie'll ask me for!'

'They don't make nothin' o' money these days,' Mrs Ashcroft said.

'An' on'y last week,' the other went on, 'me daughter, she ordered a quarter pound suet at the butchers's; an' she sent it back to 'im to be chopped. She said she couldn't bother with choppin' it.'

'I lay he charged her, then.'

'I lay he did. She told me there was a whisk-drive that afternoon at the Institute, an' she couldn't bother to do the choppin'.'

'Tck!'

Mrs Ashcroft put the last firm touches to the basket-lining. She had scarcely finished when her sixteen-year-old grandson, a maiden of the moment in attendance, hurried up the garden-path shouting to know if the thing were ready, snatched it, and made off without acknowledgement. Mrs Fettley peered at him closely.

'They're goin' picnickin' somewheres,' Mrs Ashcroft explained.

'Ah,' said the other, with narrowed eyes. 'I lay *he* won't show much mercy to any he comes across, either. Now 'oo the dooce do he remind me of, all of a sudden?'

'They must look arter theirselves—'same as we did.' Mrs Ashcroft began to set out the tea.

'No denyin' *you* could, Gracie,' said Mrs Fettley. 'What's in your head now?'

'Dunno . . . But it come over me, sudden-like—about dat woman from Rye—I've slipped the name—Barnsley, wadn't it?'

'Batten—Polly Batten, you're thinkin' of.'

'That's it—Polly Batten. That day she had it in for you with a hay-fork—'time we was all hayin' at Smalldene—for stealin' her man.'

'But you heered me tell her she had my leave to keep him?' Mrs Ashcroft's voice and smile were smoother than ever.

'I did—an' we was all looking that she'd prod the fork spang through your breastes when you said it.'

'No-oo. She'd never go beyond bounds—Polly. She shruck too much for reel doin's.'

'Allus seems to *me*,' Mrs Fettley said after a pause, 'that a man 'twixt two fightin' women is the foolishest thing on earth. 'Like a dog bein' called two ways.'

'Mebbe. But what set ye off on those times, Liz?'

'That boy's fashion o' carryin' his head an' arms. I haven't rightly looked at him since he's growed. Your Jane never showed it, but—*him*! Why, 'tis Jim Batten and his tricks come to life again! . . . Eh?'

'Mebbe. There's some that would ha' made it out so—bein' barren-like, themselves.'

'Oho! Ah well! Dearie, dearie me, now! . . . An' Jim Batten's been dead this———'

'Seven and twenty year,' Mrs Ashcroft answered briefly. 'Won't ye draw up, Liz?'

Mrs Fettley drew up to buttered toast, currant bread, stewed tea, bitter as leather, some home-preserved pears, and a cold boiled pig's tail to help down the muffins. She paid all the proper compliments.

'Yes. I dunno as I've ever owed me belly much,' said Mrs Ashcroft thoughtfully. 'We only go through this world once.'

'But don't it lay heavy on ye, sometimes?' her guest suggested.

'Nurse says I'm a sight liker to die o' me indigestion than me leg.' For Mrs Ashcroft had a long-standing ulcer on her shin, which needed regular care from the Village Nurse, who boasted (or others did, for her) that she had dressed it one hundred and three times already during her term of office.

'An' you that *was* so able, too! It's all come on ye before your full time, like. *I*'ve watched ye goin'.' Mrs Fettley spoke with real affection.

'Somethin's bound to find ye sometime. I've me 'eart left me still,' Mrs Ashcroft returned.

'You was always big-hearted enough for three. That's somethin' to look back on at the day's eend.'

'I reckon you've *your* back-lookin's, too,' was Mrs Ashcroft's answer.

'You know it. But I don't think much regardin' such matters excep' when I'm along with you, Gra'. 'Takes two sticks to make a fire.'*

Mrs Fettley stared, with jaw half-dropped, at the grocer's bright calendar on the wall. The cottage shook again to the roar of the motor-traffic, and the crowded football-ground below the garden roared almost as loudly; for the village was well set to its Saturday leisure.

*   *   *

Mrs Fettley had spoken very precisely for some time without interruption, before she wiped her eyes. 'And,' she concluded, 'they read 'is death-notice to me, out o' the paper last month. O' course it wadn't any o' *my* becomin' concerns—let be I 'adn't set eyes on him for so long. O' course *I* couldn't say nor show nothin'. Nor I've no rightful call to go to Eastbourne to see 'is grave, either. I've been schemin' to slip over there by the 'bus some day; but they'd ask questions at 'ome past endurance. So I 'aven't even *that* to stay me.'

'But you've 'ad your satisfactions?'

'Godd! Yess! Those four years 'e was workin' on the rail near us. An' the other drivers they gave him a brave funeral, too.'

'Then you've naught to cast-up about. 'Nother cup o' tea?'

* * *

The light and air had changed a little with the sun's descent, and the two elderly ladies closed the kitchen-door against chill. A couple of jays squealed and skirmished through the undraped apple-trees in the garden. This time, the word was with Mrs Ashcroft, her elbows on the tea-table, and her sick leg propped on a stool. . . .

'Well I never! But what did your 'usband say to that?' Mrs Fettley asked, when the deep-toned recital halted.

''E said I might go where I pleased for all of 'im. But seein' 'e was bedrid, I said I'd 'tend 'im out. 'E knowed I wouldn't take no advantage of 'im in that state. 'E lasted eight or nine week. Then he was took with a seizure-like; an' laid stone-still for days. Then 'e propped 'imself up abed an' says: "You pray no man'll ever deal with you like you've dealed with some." "An' you?" I says, for *you* know, Liz, what a rover 'e was. "It cuts both ways," says 'e, "but *I*'m death-wise, an' I can see what's comin' to you." He died a-Sunday an' was buried a-Thursday . . . An' yet I'd set a heap by him—one time or—did I ever?'

'You never told me that before,' Mrs Fettley ventured.

'I'm payin' ye for what ye told me just now. Him bein' dead, I wrote up, sayin' I was free for good, to that Mrs Marshall in Lunnon—which gave me my first place as kitchen-maid— Lord, how long ago! She was well pleased, for they two was both gettin' on, an' I knowed their ways. You remember, Liz, I used to go to 'em in service between whiles, for years—when we wanted money, or—or my 'usband was away—on occasion.'

''E *did* get that six months at Chichester, didn't 'e?' Mrs Fettley whispered. 'We never rightly won to the bottom of it.'

''E'd ha' got more, but the man didn't die.'

''None o' your doin's, was it, Gra'?'

'No! 'Twas the woman's husband this time. An' so, my man bein' dead, I went back to them Marshall's, as cook, to get me legs under a gentleman's table again, and be called with a handle to me name. That was the year you shifted to Portsmouth.'

'Cosham,' Mrs Fettley corrected. 'There was a middlin' lot o' new buildin' bein' done there. My man went first, an' got the room, an' I follered.'

'Well, then, I was a year-abouts in Lunnon, all at a breath, like, four meals a day an' livin' easy. Then, 'long towards autumn, they two went travellin', like, to France; keepin' me on, for they couldn't do without me. I put the house to rights for the caretaker, an' then I slipped down 'ere to me sister Bessie—me wages in me pockets, an' all 'ands glad to be'old of me.'

'That would be when I was at Cosham,' said Mrs Fettley.

'*You* know, Liz, there wasn't no cheap-dog pride to folk, those days, no more than there was cinemas nor whisk-drives. Man or woman 'ud lay hold o' any job that promised a shillin' to the backside of it, didn't they? I was all peaked up after Lunnon, an' I thought the fresh airs 'ud serve me. So I took on at Smalldene, obligin' with a hand at the early potato-liftin', stubbin' hens,* an' such-like. They'd ha' mocked me sore in my kitchen in Lunnon, to see me in men's boots, an' me petticoats all shorted.'

'Did it bring ye any good?' Mrs Fettley asked.

''Twadn't for that I went. You know, 's'well's me, that na'un happens to ye till it '*as* 'appened. Your mind don't warn ye before'and of the road ye've took, till you're at the far eend of it. We've only a backwent view of our proceedin's.'

''Oo was it?'

''Arry Mockler.' Mrs Ashcroft's face puckered to the pain of her sick leg.

Mrs Fettley gasped. ''Arry? Bert Mockler's son!* An' *I* never guessed!'

Mrs Ashcroft nodded. 'An' I told myself—*an*' I beleft it—that I wanted field-work.'

'What did ye get out of it?'

'The usuals. Everythin' at first—worse than naught after. I had signs an' warnings a-plenty, but I took no heed of 'em. For we was burnin' rubbish one day, just when we'd come to know how 'twas with—with both of us. 'Twas early in the year for burnin', an' I said so. "No!" says he. "The sooner dat old stuff's off an' done with," 'e says, "the better." 'Is face was harder'n rocks when he spoke. Then it come over me that I'd found me master, which I 'adn't ever before. I'd allus owned 'em, like.'

'Yes! Yes! They're yourn or you're theirn,' the other sighed. 'I like the right way best.'

'I didn't. But 'Arry did . . . 'Long then, it come time for me to go back to Lunnon. I couldn't. I clean couldn't! So, I took an' tipped a dollop o' scaldin' water out o' the copper one Monday mornin' over me left 'and and arm. Dat stayed me where I was for another fortnight.'

'Was it worth it?' said Mrs Fettley, looking at the silvery scar on the wrinkled fore-arm.

Mrs Ashcroft nodded. 'An' after that, we two made it up 'twixt us so's 'e could come to Lunnon for a job in a liv'ry-stable not far from me. 'E got it. *I* 'tended to that. There wadn't no talk nowhere. His own mother never suspicioned how 'twas. He just slipped up to Lunnon, an' there we abode that winter, not 'alf a mile 'tother from each.'

'Ye paid 'is fare an' all, though'; Mrs Fettley spoke convincedly.

Again Mrs Ashcroft nodded. 'Dere wadn't much I didn't do for him. 'E was me master, an'—O God, help us!—we'd laugh over it walkin' together after dark in them paved streets, an' me corns fair wrenchin' in me boots! I'd never been like that before. Ner he! Ner he!'

Mrs Fettley clucked sympathetically.

'An' when did ye come to the eend?' she asked.

'When 'e paid it all back again, every penny. Then I knowed, but I wouldn't *suffer* meself to know. "You've been mortal kind to me," he says. "Kind!" I said. " 'Twixt *us*?" But 'e kep' all on tellin' me 'ow kind I'd been an' 'e'd never forget it all his days. I held it from off o' me for three evenin's, because I would *not* believe. Then 'e talked about not bein' satisfied with 'is job in the stables, an' the men there puttin' tricks on 'im, an' all they lies which a man tells when 'e's leavin' ye. I heard 'im out, neither 'elpin' nor 'inderin'. At the last, I took off a liddle brooch which he'd give me an' I says: "Dat'll do. *I* ain't askin' na'un'." An' I turned me round an' walked off to me own sufferin's. 'E didn't make 'em worse. 'E didn't come nor write after that. 'E slipped off 'ere back 'ome to 'is mother again.'

'An' 'ow often did ye look for 'en to come back?' Mrs Fettley demanded mercilessly.

'More'n once—more'n once! Goin' over the streets we'd used, I thought de very pave-stones 'ud shruck out under me feet.'

'Yes,' said Mrs Fettley. 'I dunno but dat don't 'urt as much as aught else. An' dat was all ye got?'

'No. 'Twadn't. That's the curious part, if you'll believe it, Liz.'

'I do. I lay you're further off lyin' now than in all your life, Gra'.'

'I am . . . An' I suffered, like I'd not wish my most arrantest enemies to. God's Own Name! I went through the hoop that spring! One part of it was headaches which I'd never known all me days before. Think o' *me* with an 'eddick! But I come to be grateful for 'em. They kep' me from thinkin' . . .'

''Tis like a tooth,' Mrs Fettley commented. 'It must rage an' rugg* till it tortures itself quiet on ye; an' then—then there's na'un left.'

'*I* got enough lef' to last me all *my* days on earth. It come about through our charwoman's liddle girl—Sophy Ellis was 'er name—all eyes an' elbers an' hunger. I used to give 'er vittles.* Otherwhiles, I took no special notice of 'er, an' a sight less, o' course, when me trouble about 'Arry was on me. But—you know how liddle maids first feel it sometimes—she come to be crazy-fond o' me, pawin' an' cuddlin' all whiles; an' I 'adn't the 'eart to beat 'er off . . . One afternoon, early in spring 'twas, 'er mother 'ad sent 'er round to scutchel up what vittles she could off of us. I was settin' by the fire, me apern over me head, half-mad with the 'eddick, when she slips in. I reckon I was middlin' short with 'er. "Lor'!" she says. "Is that all? I'll take it off you in two-twos!" I told her not to lay a finger

on me, for I thought she'd want to stroke my forehead; an'—I
ain't that make. "*I* won't tech ye," she says, an' slips out again.
She 'adn't been gone ten minutes 'fore me old 'eddick took off
quick as bein' kicked. So I went about my work. Prasin'ly,
Sophy comes back, an' creeps into my chair quiet as a mouse.
'Er eyes was deep in 'er 'ead an' 'er face all drawed. I asked 'er
what 'ad 'appened. "Nothin'," she says. "On'y *I*'ve got it now."
"Got what?" I says. "Your 'eddick," she says, all hoarse an'
sticky-lipped. "I've took it on me." "Nonsense," I says, "it went
of itself when you was out. Lay still an' I'll make ye a cup o'
tea." " ' 'Twon't do no good," she says, "till your time's up. 'Ow
long do *your* 'eddicks last?" "Don't talk silly," I says, "or I'll
send for the Doctor." It looked to me like she might be hatchin'
de measles. "Oh, Mrs Ashcroft," she says, stretchin' out 'er
liddle thin arms. "I *do* love ye." There wasn't any holdin' agin
that. I took 'er into me lap an' made much of 'er. "Is it truly
gone?" she says. "Yes," I says, "an' if 'twas you took it away,
I'm truly grateful." "'*Twas* me," she says, layin' 'er cheek to
mine. "No one but me knows how." An' then she said she'd
changed me 'eddick for me at a Wish 'Ouse.'

'Whatt?' Mrs Fettley spoke sharply.

'A Wish House. No! *I* 'adn't 'eard o' such things, either. I
couldn't get it straight at first, but, puttin' all together, I made
out that a Wish 'Ouse 'ad to be a house which 'ad stood unlet
an' empty long enough for Some One, like, to come an in'abit
there. She said, a liddle girl that she'd played with in the
livery-stables where 'Arry worked 'ad told 'er so. She said the
girl 'ad belonged in a caravan that laid up, o' winters, in
Lunnon. Gipsy, I judge.'

'Ooh! There's no sayin' what Gippos know, but *I*'ve never
'eard of a Wish 'Ouse, an' I know—some things,' said Mrs
Fettley.

'Sophy said there was a Wish 'Ouse in Wadloes Road—just
a few streets off, on the way to our green-grocer's. All you 'ad
to do, she said, was to ring the bell an' wish your wish through
the slit o' the letter-box. I asked 'er if the fairies give it 'er?
"Don't ye know," she says, "there's no fairies in a Wish 'Ouse?
There's on'y a Token." '*

'Goo' Lord A'mighty! Where did she come by *that* word?' cried Mrs Fettley; for a Token is a wraith of the dead or, worse still, of the living.

'The caravan-girl 'ad told 'er, she said. Well, Liz, it troubled me to 'ear 'er, an' lyin' in me arms she must ha' felt it. "That's very kind o' you," I says, holdin' 'er tight, "to wish me 'eddick away. But why didn't ye ask somethin' nice for yourself?" "You can't do that," she says. "All you'll get at a Wish 'Ouse is leave to take some one else's trouble. I've took Ma's 'eadaches, when she's been kind to me; but this is the first time I've been able to do aught for you. Oh, Mrs Ashcroft, I *do* just-about love you." An' she goes on all like that. Liz, I tell you my 'air e'en a'most stood on end to 'ear 'er. I asked 'er what like a Token was. "I dunno," she says, "but after you've ringed the bell, you'll 'ear it run up from the basement, to the front door. Then say your wish," she says, "an' go away." "The Token don't open de door to ye, then?" I says. "Oh no," she says. "You on'y 'ear gigglin', like, be'ind the front door. Then you say you'll take the trouble off of 'oo ever 'tis you've chose for your love; an' ye'll get it," she says. I didn't ask no more—she was too 'ot an' fevered. I made much of 'er till it come time to light de gas, an' a liddle after that, 'er 'eddick—mine, I suppose—took off, an' she got down an' played with the cat.'

'Well, I never!' said Mrs Fettley. 'Did—did ye foller it up, anyways?'

'She askt me to, but I wouldn't 'ave no such dealin's with a child.'

'What *did* ye do, then?'

''Sat in me own room 'stid o' the kitchen when me 'eddicks come on. But it lay at de back o' me mind.'

'Twould. Did she tell ye more, ever?'

'No. Besides what the Gippo girl 'ad told 'er, she knew naught, 'cept that the charm worked. An', next after that—in May 'twas—I suffered the summer out in Lunnon. 'Twas hot an' windy for weeks, an' the streets stinkin' o' dried 'orse-dung blowin' from side to side an' lyin' level with the kerb. We don't get that nowadays. I 'ad my 'ol'day just before hoppin',* an' come down 'ere to stay with Bessie again. She noticed I'd lost flesh, an' was all poochy under the eyes.'

'Did ye see 'Arry?'

Mrs Ashcroft nodded. 'The fourth—no, the fifth day. Wednesday 'twas. I knowed 'e was workin' at Smalldene again. I asked 'is mother in the street, bold as brass. She 'adn't room to say much, for Bessie—you know 'er tongue—was talkin' full-clack. But that Wednesday, I was walkin' with one o' Bessie's chillern hangin' on me skirts, at de back o' Chanter's Tot. Prasin'ly, I felt 'e was be'ind me on the footpath, an' I knowed by 'is tread 'e'd changed 'is nature. I slowed, an' I heard 'im slow. Then I fussed a piece with the child, to force him past me, like. So 'e *ad* to come past. 'E just says "Good-evenin'," and goes on, tryin' to pull 'isself together.'

'Drunk, was he?' Mrs Fettley asked.

'Never! S'runk an' wizen; 'is clothes 'angin' on 'im like bags, an' the back of 'is neck whiter'n chalk. 'Twas all I could do not to oppen my arms an' cry after him. But I swallered me spittle till I was back 'ome again an' the chillern abed. Then I says to Bessie, after supper, "What in de world's come to 'Arry Mock-ler?" Bessie told me 'e'd been a-Hospital for two months, 'long o' cuttin' 'is foot wid a spade, muckin' out the old pond at Smalldene. There was poison in de dirt, an' it rooshed up 'is leg, like an' come out all over him.* 'E 'adn't been back to 'is job—carterin' at Smalldene—more'n a fortnight. She told me the Doctor said he'd go off, likely, with the November frostes; an' 'is mother 'ad told 'er that 'e didn't rightly eat nor sleep, an' sweated 'imself into pools, no odds 'ow chill 'e lay. An' spit terrible o' mornin's. "Dearie me," I says. "But, mebbe, hoppin' 'll set 'im right again," an' I licked me thread-point an' I fetched me needle's eye up to it an' I threads me needle under de lamp, steady as rocks. An' dat night (me bed was in de wash-house) I cried an' I cried. An' *you* know, Liz—for you've been with me in my throes—it takes summat to make me cry.'

'Yes; but chile-bearin' is on'y just pain,' said Mrs Fettley.

'I come round by cock-crow, an' dabbed cold tea on me eyes to take away the signs. Long towards nex' evenin'—I was settin' out to lay some flowers on me 'usband's grave, for the look o' the thing—I met 'Arry over against where the War Memorial is now. 'E was comin' back from 'is 'orses, so 'e couldn't *not* see me. I looked 'im all over, an' " 'Arry," I says twix' me teeth, "come back an' rest-up in Lunnon." "I won't take it," he says, "for I can give ye naught." "I don't ask it," I says. "By God's

Own Name, I don't ask na'un! On'y come up an' see a Lunnon
doctor." 'E lifts 'is two 'eavy eyes at me: "'Tis past that, Gra',"
'e says. "I've but a few months left." "'Arry!" I says. "*My* man!"
I says. I couldn't say no more. 'Twas all up in me throat.
"Thank ye kindly, Gra'," 'e says (but 'e never says "my
woman"), an' 'e went on up-street an' 'is mother—Oh, damn
'er!—she was watchin' for 'im, an' she shut de door be'ind 'im.'

Mrs Fettley stretched an arm across the table, and made to
finger Mrs Ashcroft's sleeve at the wrist, but the other moved
it out of reach.

'So I went on to the churchyard with my flowers, an' I
remembered my 'usband's warnin' that night he spoke. 'E *was*
death-wise, an' it '*ad* 'appened as 'e said. But as I was settin'
down de jam-pot on the grave-mound, it come over me there
was one thing I *could* do for 'Arry. Doctor or no Doctor, I
thought I'd make a trial of it. So I did. Nex' mornin', a bill
came down from our Lunnon green-grocer. Mrs Marshall,
she'd lef' me petty cash for suchlike—o'course—but I tole Bess
'twas me to come an' open the 'ouse. So I went up, afternoon
train.'

'An'—but I know you 'adn't—'adn't you no fear?'

'What for? There was nothin' front o' me but my own shame
an' God's croolty. I couldn't ever get 'Arry—'ow *could* I? I
knowed it must go on burnin' till it burned me out.'

'Aie!' said Mrs Fettley, reaching for the wrist again, and this
time Mrs Ashcroft permitted it.

'Yit 'twas a comfort to know I could try *this* for 'im. So I went
an' I paid the green-grocer's bill, an' put 'is receipt in me
hand-bag, an' then I stepped round to Mrs Ellis—our char—
an' got the 'ouse-keys an' opened the 'ouse. First, I made me
bed to come back to (God's Own Name! Me bed to lie upon!).
Nex' I made me a cup o' tea an' sat down in the kitchen
thinkin', till 'long towards dusk. Terrible close, 'twas. Then I
dressed me an' went out with the receipt in me 'and-bag,
feignin' to study it for an address, like. Fourteen, Wadloes
Road, was the place—a liddle basement-kitchen 'ouse, in a row
of twenty-thirty such, an' tiddy strips o' walled garden in
front—the paint off the front doors, an' na'un done to na'un
since ever so long. There wasn't 'ardly no one in the streets
'cept the cats. '*Twas* 'ot, too! I turned into the gate bold as

brass; up de steps I went an' I ringed the front-door bell. She pealed loud, like it do in an empty house. When she'd all ceased, I 'eard a cheer, like, pushed back on de floor o' the kitchen. Then I 'eard feet on de kitchen-stairs, like it might ha' been a heavy woman in slippers. They come up to de stair-head, acrost the hall—I 'eard the bare boards creak under 'em—an' at de front door dey stopped. I stooped me to the letter-box slit, an' I says: "Let me take everythin' bad that's in store for my man, 'Arry Mockler, for love's sake." Then, whatever it was 'tother side de door let its breath out, like, as if it 'ad been holdin' it for to 'ear better.'

'Nothin' was *said* to ye?' Mrs Fettley demanded.

'Na'un. She just breathed out—a sort of *A-ah*, like. Then the steps went back an' downstairs to the kitchen—all draggy—an' I heard the cheer drawed up again.'

'An' you abode on de doorstep, throughout all, Gra'?'

Mrs Ashcroft nodded.

'Then I went away, an' a man passin' says to me: "Didn't you know that house was empty?" "No," I says. "I must ha' been give the wrong number." An' I went back to our 'ouse, an' I went to bed; for I was fair flogged out. 'Twas too 'ot to sleep more'n snatches, so I walked me about, lyin' down betweens, till crack o' dawn. Then I went to the kitchen to make me a cup o' tea, an' I hitted meself just above the ankle on an old roastin'-jack o' mine that Mrs Ellis had moved out from the corner, her last cleanin'. An' so—nex' after that—I waited till the Marshalls come back o' their holiday.'

'Alone there? I'd ha' thought you'd 'ad enough of empty houses,' said Mrs Fettley, horrified.

'Oh, Mrs Ellis an' Sophy was runnin' in an' out soon's I was back, an' 'twixt us we cleaned de house again top-to-bottom. There's allus a hand's turn more to do in every house. An' that's 'ow 'twas with me that autumn an' winter, in Lunnon.'

'Then na'un hap—overtook ye for your doin's?'

Mrs Ashcroft smiled. 'No. Not then. 'Long in November I sent Bessie ten shillin's.'

'You was allus free-'anded,' Mrs Fettley interrupted.

'An' I got what I paid for, with the rest o' the news. She said the hoppin' 'ad set 'im up wonderful. 'E'd 'ad six weeks of it, and now 'e was back again carterin' at Smalldene. No odds to

me 'ow it 'ad 'appened—'slong's it 'ad. But I dunno as my ten
shillin's eased me much. 'Arry bein' *dead*, like, 'e'd ha' been
mine, till Judgement. 'Arry bein' alive, 'e'd like as not pick up
with some woman middlin' quick. I raged over that. Come
spring, I 'ad somethin' else to rage for. I'd growed a nasty little
weepin' boil, * like, on me shin, just above the boot-top, that
wouldn't heal no shape. It made me sick to look at it, for I'm
clean-fleshed by nature. Chop me all over with a spade, an' I'd
heal like turf. Then Mrs Marshall she set 'er own doctor at me.
'E said I ought to ha' come to him at first go-off, 'stead o'
drawin' all manner o' dyed stockin's over it for months. 'E said
I'd stood up too much to me work, for it was settin' very close
atop of a big swelled vein, like, behither the small o' me ankle.
"Slow come, slow go,' 'e says. "Lay your leg up on high an'
rest it," he says, "an' 'twill ease off. Don't let it close up too
soon. You've got a very fine leg, Mrs Ashcroft," 'e says. An' he
put wet dressin's on it.'

"E done right.' Mrs Fettley spoke firmly. 'Wet dressin's to
wet wounds. They draw de humours, same's a lamp-wick
draws de oil.'

'That's true. An' Mrs Marshall was allus at me to make me
set down more, an' dat nigh healed it up. An' then after a while
they packed me off down to Bessie's to finish the cure; for I
ain't the the sort to sit down when I ought to stand up. You
was back in the village then, Liz.'

'I was. I was, but—never did I guess!'

'I didn't desire ye to.' Mrs Ashcroft smiled. 'I saw 'Arry once
or twice in de street, wonnerful fleshed up an' restored back.
Then, one day I didn't see 'im, an' 'is mother told me one of
'is 'orses 'ad lashed out an' caught 'im on the 'ip. So 'e was
abed an' middlin' painful. An' Bessie, she says to his mother,
'twas a pity 'Arry 'adn't a woman of 'is own to take the nursin'
off 'er. And the old lady *was* mad! She told us that 'Arry 'ad
never looked after any woman in 'is born days, an' as long as
she was atop the mowlds, she'd contrive for 'im till 'er two 'ands
dropped off. So I knowed she'd do watch-dog for me, 'thout
askin' for bones.'

Mrs Fettley rocked with small laughter.

'That day,' Mrs Ashcroft went on, 'I'd stood on me feet nigh all the time, watchin' the doctor go in an' out; for they thought it might be 'is ribs, too. That made my boil break again, issuin' an' weepin'. But it turned out 'twadn't ribs at all, an' 'Arry 'ad a good night. When I heard that, nex' mornin', I says to meself, "I won't lay two an' two together *yit*. I'll keep me leg down a week, an' see what comes of it." It didn't hurt me that day, to speak of—'seemed more to draw the strength out o' me like—an' 'Arry 'ad another good night. That made me persevere; but I didn't dare lay two an' two together till the week-end, an' then, 'Arry come forth e'en a'most 'imself again—na'un hurt outside ner in of him. I nigh fell on me knees in de wash-house when Bessie was up-street. "I've got ye now, my man," I says. "You'll take your good from me 'thout knowin' it till my life's end. O God send me long to live for 'Arry's sake!" I says. An' I dunno that didn't still me ragin's.'

'For good?' Mrs Fettley asked.

'They come back, plenty times, but, let be how 'twould, I knowed I was doin' for 'im. I *knowed* it. I took an' worked me pains on an' off, like regulatin' my own range, till I learned to 'ave 'em at my commandments. An' that was funny, too. There was times, Liz, when my trouble 'ud all s'rink an' dry up, like. First, I used to try an' fetch it on again; bein' fearful to leave 'Arry alone too long for anythin' to lay 'old of. Prasin'ly I come to see that was a sign he'd do all right awhile, an' so I saved myself.'

''Ow long for?' Mrs Fettley asked, with deepest interest.

I've gone de better part of a year onct or twice with na'un more to show than the liddle weepin' core of it, like. *All* s'rinked up an' dried off. Then he'd inflame up—for a warnin'—an' I'd suffer it. When I couldn't no more—an' I '*ad* to keep on goin' with my Lunnon work—I'd lay me leg high on a cheer till it eased. Not too quick. I knowed by the feel of it, those times, dat 'Arry was in need. Then I'd send another five shillin's to Bess, or somethin' for the chillern, to find out if, mebbe, 'e'd took any hurt through my neglects. 'Twas *so*! Year in, year out, I worked it dat way, Liz, an' 'e got 'is good from me 'thout knowin'—for years and years.'

'But what did *you* get out of it, Gra'?' Mrs Fettley almost wailed. 'Did ye see 'im reg'lar?'

'Times—when I was 'ere on me 'ol'days. An' more, now that I'm 'ere for good. But 'e's never looked at me, ner any other woman 'cept 'is mother. 'Ow I used to watch an' listen! So did she.'

'Years an' years!' Mrs Fettley repeated. 'An' where's 'e workin' at now?'

'Oh, 'e's give up carterin' quite a while. He's workin' for one o' them big tractorizin' firms—plowin' sometimes, an' sometimes off with lorries—fur as Wales, I've 'eard. He comes 'ome to 'is mother 'tween whiles; but I don't set eyes on him now, fer weeks on end. No odds! 'Is job keeps 'im from continuin' in one stay anywheres.'

'But—just for de sake o' sayin' somethin'—s'pose 'Arry *did* get married?' said Mrs Fettley.

Mrs Ashcroft drew her breath sharply between her still even and natural teeth. '*Dat* ain't been required of me,' she answered. 'I reckon my pains 'ull be counted agin that. Don't *you*, Liz?'

'It ought to be, dearie. It ought to be.'

'It *do* 'urt sometimes. You shall see it when Nurse comes. She thinks I don't know it's turned.'*

Mrs Fettley understood. Human nature seldom walks up to the word 'cancer'.

'Be ye certain sure, Gra'?' she asked.

'I was sure of it when old Mr Marshall 'ad me up to 'is study an' spoke a long piece about my faithful service. I've obliged 'em on an' off for a goodish time, but not enough for a pension. But they give me a weekly 'lowance for life. I knew what *that* sinnified—as long as three years ago.'

'Dat don't *prove* it, Gra'.'

'To give fifteen bob a week to a woman 'oo'd live twenty year in the course o' nature? It *do*!'

'You're mistook! You're mistook!' Mrs Fettley insisted.

'Liz, there's *no* mistakin' when the edges are all heaped up, like—same as a collar. You'll see it. An' I laid out Dora Wickwood, too. *She* 'ad it under the arm-pit, like.'

Mrs Fettley considered awhile, and bowed her head in finality.

''Ow long d'you reckon 'twill allow ye, countin' from now, dearie?'

'Slow come, slow go. But if I don't set eyes on ye 'fore next hoppin', this'll be good-bye, Liz.'

'Dunno as I'll be able to manage by then—not 'thout I have a liddle dog to lead me. For de chillern, dey won't be troubled, an'—O Gra'!—I'm blindin' up—I'm blindin' up!'

'Oh, *dat* was why you didn't more'n finger with your quilt-patches all this while! I was wonderin' . . . But the pain *do* count, don't ye think, Liz? The pain *do* count to keep 'Arry—where I want 'im. Say it can't be wasted, like.'

'I'm sure of it—sure of it, dearie. You'll 'ave your reward.'

'I don't want no more'n this—*if* de pain is taken into de reckonin'.'

''Twill be—'twill be, Gra'.'

There was a knock on the door.

'That's Nurse. She's before 'er time,' said Mrs Ashcroft. 'Open to 'er.'

The young lady entered briskly, all the bottles in her bag clicking. 'Evenin', Mrs Ashcroft,' she began. 'I've come raound a little earlier than usual because of the Institute dance to-na-ite. You won't ma-ind, will you?'

'Oh, no. Me dancin' days are over.' Mrs Ashcroft was the self-contained domestic at once. 'My old friend, Mrs Fettley 'ere, has been settin' talkin' with me a while.'

'I hope she 'asn't been fatiguing you?' said the Nurse a little frostily.

'Quite the contrary. It 'as been a pleasure. Only—only—just at the end I felt a bit—a bit flogged out like.'

'Yes, yes.' The Nurse was on her knees already, with the washes to hand. 'When old ladies get together they talk a deal too much, I've noticed.'

'Mebbe we do,' said Mrs Fettley, rising. 'So, now, I'll make myself scarce.'

'Look at it first, though,' said Mrs Ashcroft feebly. 'I'd like ye to look at it.'

Mrs Fettley looked, and shivered. Then she leaned over, and kissed Mrs Ashcroft once on the waxy yellow forehead, and again on the faded grey eyes.

'It *do* count, don't it—de pain?' The lips that still kept trace of their original moulding hardly more than breathed the words.

Mrs Fettley kissed them and moved towards the door.

RAHERE*

RAHERE, King Henry's Jester, feared by all the Norman Lords
For his eye that pierced their bosoms, for his tongue that
  shamed their swords;
Feed and flattered by the Churchmen—well they knew how
  deep he stood
In dark Henry's crooked counsels—fell upon an evil mood.

Suddenly, his days before him and behind him seemed to stand
Stripped and barren, fixed and fruitless, as those leagues of
  naked sand
When St Michael's ebb slinks outward to the bleak horizon-
  bound,
And the trampling wide-mouthed waters are withdrawn from
  sight and sound.

Then a Horror of Great Darkness sunk his spirit and, anon,
(Who had seen him wince and whiten as he turned to walk
  alone)
Followed Gilbert* the Physician, and muttered in his ear,
'Thou hast it, O my brother?' 'Yea, I have it,' said Rahere.

'So it comes,' said Gilbert smoothly, 'man's most immanent
  distress.
'Tis a humour of the Spirit which abhorreth all excess;
And, whatever breed the surfeit—Wealth, or Wit, or Power, or
  Fame
(And thou hast each) the Spirit laboureth to expel the same.

'Hence the dulled eye's deep self-loathing—hence the loaded
  leaden brow;
Hence the burden of Wanhope* that aches thy soul and body
  now.
Ay, the merriest fool must face it, and the wisest Doctor learn;
For it comes—it comes,' said Gilbert, 'as it passes—to
  return.'

But Rahere was in his torment, and he wandered, dumb and
    far,
Till he came to reeking Smithfield where the crowded gallows
    are.
(Followed Gilbert the Physician) and beneath the wry-necked
    dead,
Sat a leper and his woman, very merry, breaking bread.

He was cloaked from chin to ankle—faceless, fingerless,
    obscene—
Mere corruption swaddled man-wise, but the woman whole
    and clean;
And she waited on him crooning, and Rahere beheld the twain,
Each delighting in the other, and he checked and groaned
    again.

'So it comes,—it comes,' said Gilbert, 'as it came when Life
    began.
'Tis a motion of the Spirit that revealeth God to man
In the shape of Love exceeding, which regards not taint or fall,
Since in perfect Love, saith Scripture, can be no excess at all.

'Hence the eye that sees no blemish—hence the hour that holds
    no shame.
Hence the Soul assured the Essence and the Substance are the
    same.
Nay, the meanest need not miss it, though the mightier pass it
    by;
For it comes—it comes,' said Gilbert, 'and, thou seest, it does
    not die!'

THE BULL THAT THOUGHT *

WESTWARD from a town by the Mouths of the Rhône, runs a road* so mathematically straight, so barometrically level, that it ranks among the world's measured miles and motorists use it for records.

I had attacked the distance several times, but always with a Mistral blowing, or the unchancy cattle of those parts on the move. But once, running from the East, into a high-piled, almost Egyptian, sunset, there came a night which it would have been sin to have wasted. It was warm with the breath of summer in advance; moonlit till the shadow of every rounded pebble and pointed cypress wind-break lay solid on that vast flat-floored waste; and my Mr Leggatt, who had slipped out to make sure, reported that the road-surface was unblemished.

'*Now*,' he suggested, 'we might see what she'll do under strict road-conditions. She's been pullin' like the Blue de Luxe* all day. Unless I'm all off, it's her night out.'

We arranged the trial for after dinner—thirty kilometres as near as might be; and twenty-two of them without even a level crossing.*

There sat beside me at table d'hôte an elderly, bearded Frenchman wearing the rosette of by no means the lowest grade of the Legion of Honour,* who had arrived in a talkative Citroën. I gathered that he had spent much of his life in the French Colonial Service in Annam and Tonquin.* When the war came, his years barring him from the front line, he had supervised Chinese woodcutters* who, with axe and dynamite, deforested the centre of France for trench-props. He said my chauffeur had told him that I contemplated an experiment. He was interested in cars—had admired mine—would, in short, be greatly indebted to me if I permitted him to assist as an observer. One could not well refuse; and, knowing my Mr Leggatt, it occurred to me there might also be a bet in the background.

While he went to get his coat, I asked the proprietor his name. 'Voiron—Monsieur André Voiron,' was the reply. 'And his business?' 'Mon Dieu! He is Voiron! He is all those things, there!' The proprietor waved his hands at brilliant advertisements on the dining-room walls, which declared that Voiron Frères dealt in wines, agricultural implements, chemical manures, provisions, and produce throughout that part of the globe.

He said little for the first five minutes of our trip, and nothing at all for the next ten—it being, as Leggatt had guessed, Esmeralda's night out. But, when her indicator climbed to a certain figure and held there for three blinding kilometres, he expressed himself satisfied, and proposed to me that we should celebrate the event at the hotel. 'I keep yonder,' said he, 'a wine on which I should value your opinion.'

On our return, he disappeared for a few minutes, and I heard him rumbling in a cellar. The proprietor presently invited me to the dining-room, where, beneath one frugal light, a table had been set with local dishes of renown. There was, too, a bottle beyond most known sizes, marked black on red, with a date. Monsieur Voiron opened it, and we drank to the health of my car. The velvety, perfumed liquor, between fawn and topaz, neither too sweet nor too dry, creamed in its generous glass. but I knew no wine composed of the whispers of angels' wings, the breath of Eden and the foam and pulse of Youth renewed. So I asked what it might be.

'It is champagne,' he said gravely.

'Then what have I been drinking all my life?'

'If you were lucky, before the War, and paid thirty shillings a bottle, it is possible you may have drunk one of our better-class *tisanes*.'*

'And where does one get this?'

'Here, I am happy to say. Elsewhere, perhaps, it is not so easy. We growers exchange these real wines among ourselves.'

I bowed my head in admiration, surrender, and joy. There stood the most ample bottle, and it was not yet eleven o'clock. Doors locked and shutters banged throughout the establishment. Some last servant yawned on his way to bed. Monsieur Voiron opened a window and the moonlight flooded in from a small pebbled court outside. One could almost hear the town of Chambres breathing in its first sleep. Presently, there was a thick noise in the air, the passing of feet and hooves, lowings, and a stifled bark or two. Dust rose over the courtyard wall, followed by the strong smell of cattle.

'They are moving some beasts,' said Monsieur Voiron, cocking an ear. 'Mine, I think. Yes, I hear Christophe. Our beasts do not like automobiles—so we move at night. You do not know our country—the Crau, here, or the Camargue? I was—I am now, again—of it. All France is good; but this is the best.' He spoke, as only a Frenchman can, of his own loved part of his own lovely land.

'For myself, if I were not so involved in all these affairs'—he pointed to the advertisements—'I would live on our farm with my cattle, and worship them like a Hindu. You know our cattle of the Camargue, Monsieur? No? It is not an acquaintance to rush upon lightly. There are no beasts like them. They have a mentality superior to that of others. They graze and they ruminate, by choice, facing our Mistral, which is more than some automobiles will do. Also they have in them the potentiality of thought—and when cattle think—I have seen what arrives.'

'Are they so clever as all that?' I asked idly.

'Monsieur, when your sportif chauffeur camouflaged your limousine so that she resembled one of your Army lorries, I would not believe her capacities. I bet him—ah—two to one—she would not touch ninety kilometres. It was proved that she could. I can give you no proof, but will you believe me if I tell you what a beast who thinks can achieve?'

'After the War,' said I spaciously, 'everything is credible.'

'That is true! Everything inconceivable has happened; but still we learn nothing and we believe nothing. When I was a child in my father's house—before I became a Colonial Administrator—my interest and my affection were among our cattle. We of the old rock live here—have you seen?—in big farms like castles. Indeed, some of them may have been Saracenic. The barns group round them—great white-walled barns, and yards solid as our houses. One gate shuts all. It is a world apart; an administration of all that concerns beasts. It was there I learned something about cattle. You see, they are our playthings in the Camargue and the Crau. The boy measures his strength against the calf that butts him in play among the manure-heaps. He moves in and out among the cows, who are—not so amiable. He rides with the herdsmen in the open to shift the herds. Sooner or later, he meets as bulls the little calves that knocked him over. So it was with me—till it became necessary that I should go to our Colonies.' He laughed. 'Very necessary. That is a good time in youth, Monsieur, when one does these things which shock our parents. Why is it always Papa who is so shocked and has never heard of such things—and Mamma who supplies the excuses? . . . And when my brother—my elder who stayed and created the business—begged me to return and help him, I resigned my Colonial career gladly enough. I returned to our own lands and my well-loved, wicked white and yellow cattle of the Camargue and the Crau. My Faith, I could talk of them all night, for this stuff unlocks the heart, without making repentance in the morning. . . . Yes! It was after the War that this happened. There was a calf, among Heaven knows how many of ours—a bull-calf—an infant indistinguishable from his companions. He was sick, and he had been taken up with his mother into the big farmyard at home with us. Naturally the children of our herdsmen practised on him from the first. It is in their blood. The Spaniards make a cult of bull-fighting. Our little devils down here bait bulls as automatically as the English child kicks or throws balls. This calf would chase them with his eyes open, like a cow when she hunts a man. They would take refuge behind our tractors and wine-carts in the centre of the yard: he would chase them in and out as a dog hunts rats. More than that, he would study their psychology, his eyes in their eyes. Yes, he watched their faces to divine which way they would run. He himself, also, would pretend sometimes to charge directly at a boy. Then he would wheel right or left—one could never tell—and knock over some child pressed against a wall who thought himself safe. After this, he would stand over him, knowing that his companions must come to his aid; and when they were all together, waving their jackets across his eyes and pulling his tail, he would scatter them—how he would scatter them! He could kick, too, sideways like a cow. He knew his ranges as well as our gunners, and he was as quick on his feet as our Carpentier.* I observed him often. Christophe—the man who passed just now—our chief herdsman, who had taught me to ride with our beasts when I was ten—Christophe told me that he was descended from a yellow cow of those days that had chased us once into the marshes. "He kicks just like her," said Christophe. "He can side-kick as he jumps. Have you seen, too, that he is not deceived by the jacket when a boy waves it? He uses it to find the boy. They think they are feeling him. He is feeling them always. He thinks, that one." I had come to the same conclusion. Yes—the creature was a thinker along the lines necessary to his sport; and he was a humorist also, like so many natural murderers. One knows the type among beasts as well as among men. It possesses a curious truculent mirth—almost indecent but infallibly significant——'

Monsieur Voiron replenished our glasses with the great wine that went better at each descent.

'They kept him for some time in the yards to practise upon. Naturally he became a little brutal; so Christophe turned him out to learn manners among his equals in the grazing lands, where the Camargue joins the Crau. How old was he then? About eight or nine months, I think. We met again a few months later—he and I. I was riding one of our little half-wild horses, along a road of the Crau, when I found myself almost unseated. It was he! He had hidden himself behind a wind-break till we passed, and had then charged my horse from behind. Yes, he had deceived even my little horse! But I recognized him. I gave him the whip across the nose, and I said: "Apis,* for this thou goest to Arles! It was unworthy of thee, between us two." But that creature had no shame. He went away laughing, like an Apache. If he had dismounted me, I do not think it is I who would have laughed—yearling as he was.'

'Why did you want to send him to Arles?' I asked.

'For the bull-ring. When your charming tourists leave us, we institute our little amusements there. Not a real bull-fight, you understand, but young bulls with padded horns, and our boys from hereabouts and in the city go to play with them. Naturally, before we send them we try them in our yards at home. So we brought up Apis from his pastures. He knew at once that he was among the friends of his youth—he almost shook hands with them—and he submitted like an angel to padding his horns. He investigated the carts and tractors in the yards, to choose his lines of defence and attack. And then—he attacked with an *élan*, and he defended with a tenacity and forethought that delighted us. In truth, we were so pleased that I fear we trespassed upon his patience. We desired him to repeat himself, which no true artist will tolerate. But he gave us fair warning. He went out to the centre of the yard, where there was some dry earth; he kneeled down and—you have seen a calf whose horns fret him thrusting and rooting into a bank? He did just that, very deliberately, till he had rubbed the pads off his horns. Then he rose, dancing on those wonderful feet that twinkled, and he said: "Now, my friends, the buttons are off the foils. Who begins?" We understood. We finished at once. He was turned out again on the pastures till it should be time to amuse them at our little metropolis. But, some time before he went to Arles—yes, I think I have it correctly—Christophe, who had been out on the Crau, informed me that Apis had assassinated a young bull who had given signs of developing into a rival. That happens, of course, and our herdsmen should prevent it. But Apis had killed in his own style—at dusk, from the ambush of a wind-break—by an oblique charge from behind which knocked the other over. He had then disembowelled him. All very possible, *but*—the murder accomplished—Apis went to the bank of a wind-break, knelt, and carefully, as he had in our yard, cleaned his horns in the earth. Christophe, who had never seen such a thing, at once borrowed (do you know, it is most efficacious when taken that way?) some Holy Water from our little chapel in those pastures, sprinkled Apis (whom it did not affect), and rode in to tell me. It was obvious that a thinker of that bull's type would also be meticulous in his toilette; so, when he was sent to Arles, I warned our consignees to exercise caution with him. Happily, the change of scene, the music, the general attention, and the meeting again with old friends—all our bad boys attended—agreeably distracted him. He became for the time a pure *farceur** again; but his wheelings, his rushes, his rat-huntings were more superb than ever. There was in them now, you understand, a breadth of technique that comes of reasoned art, and, above all, the passion that arrives after experience. Oh, he had learned, out there on the Crau! At the end of his little turn, he was, according to local rules, to be handled in all respects except for the sword, which was a stick, as a professional bull who must die. He was manœuvred into, or he posed himself in, the proper attitude; made his rush; received the point on his shoulder and then—turned about and cantered toward the door by which he had entered the arena. He said to the world: "My friends, the representation is ended. I thank you for your applause. I go to repose myself." But our Arlesians, who are—not so clever as some, demanded an encore, and Apis was headed back again. We others from his country, we knew what would happen. He went to the centre of the ring, kneeled, and, slowly, with full parade, plunged his horns alternately in the dirt till the pads came off. Christophe shouts: "Leave him alone, you straight-nosed imbeciles! Leave him before you must." But they required emotion; for Rome has always debauched her loved Provincia with bread and circuses.* It was given. Have you, Monsieur, ever seen a servant, with pan and broom, sweeping round the base-board of a room? In a half-minute Apis has them all swept out and over the barrier. Then he demands once more that the door shall be opened to him. It is opened and he retires as though— which, truly, is the case—loaded with laurels.'

Monsieur Voiron refilled the glasses, and allowed himself a cigarette, which he puffed for some time.

'And afterwards?' I said.

'I am arranging it in my mind. It is difficult to do it justice. Afterwards—yes, afterwards—Apis returned to his pastures and his mistresses and I to my business. I am no longer a scandalous old "sportif" in shirt-sleeves howling encouragement to the yellow son of a cow. I revert to Voiron Frères— wines, chemical manures, *et cetera*. And next year, through some chicane which I have not the leisure to unravel, and also, thanks to our patriarchal system of paying our older men out of the increase of the herds, old Christophe possesses himself of Apis. Oh, yes, he proves it through descent from a certain cow that my father had given his father before the Republic.* Beware, Monsieur, of the memory of the illiterate man! An ancestor of Christophe had been a soldier under our Soult against your Beresford,* near Bayonne. He fell into the hands of Spanish guerrillas. Christophe and his wife used to tell me the details on certain Saints' Days when I was a child. Now, as compared with our recent war, Soult's campaign and retreat across the Bidassoa——'

'But did you allow Christophe just to annex the bull?' I demanded.

'You do not know Christophe. He had sold him to the Spaniards before he informed me. The Spaniards pay in coin— douros* of very pure silver. Our peasants mistrust our paper. You know the saying: "A thousand francs paper; eight hundred metal, and the cow is yours." Yes, Christophe sold Apis, who was then two and a half years old, and to Christophe's knowledge thrice at least an assassin.'

'How was that?' I said.

'Oh, his own kind only; and always, Christophe told me, by the same oblique rush from behind, the same sideways over-throw, and the same swift disembowelment, followed by this levitical cleaning of the horns. In human life he would have kept a manicurist—this Minotaur. And so, Apis disappears from our country. That does not trouble me. I know in due time I shall be advised. Why? Because, in this land, Monsieur, not a hoof moves between Berre and the Saintes Maries* without the knowledge of specialists such as Christophe. The beasts are the substance and the drama of their lives to them. So when Christophe tells me, a little before Easter Sunday, that Apis makes his début in the bull-ring of a small Catalan town on the road to Barcelona, it is only to pack my car and trundle there across the frontier with him. The place lacked importance and manufactures, but it had produced a matador of some reputation, who was condescending to show his art in his native town. They were even running one special train to the place. Now our French railway system is only execrable, but the Spanish——'

'You went down by road, didn't you?' said I.

'Naturally. It was not too good. Villamarti was the matador's name. He proposed to kill two bulls for the honour of his birthplace. Apis, Christophe told me, would be his second. It was an interesting trip, and that little city by the sea was ravishing. Their bull-ring dates from the middle of the seven-teenth century. It is full of feeling. The ceremonial too—when the horsemen enter and ask the Mayor in his box to throw down the keys of the bull-ring—that was exquisitely conceived. You know, if the keys are caught in the horseman's hat, it is considered a good omen. They were perfectly caught. Our seats were in the front row beside the gates where the bulls enter, so we saw everything.

'Villamarti's first bull was not too badly killed. The second matador, whose name escapes me, killed his without distinction—a foil to Villamarti. And the third, Chisto, a laborious, middle-aged professional who had never risen beyond a certain dull competence, was equally of the background. Oh, they are as jealous as the girls of the Comédie Française, * these matadors! Villamarti's troupe stood ready for his second bull. The gates opened, and we saw Apis, beautifully balanced on his feet, peer coquettishly round the corner, as though he were at home. A picador—a mounted man with the long lance-goad—stood near the barrier on his right. He had not even troubled to turn his horse, for the capeadors—the men with the cloaks—were advancing to play Apis—to feel his psychology and intentions, according to the rules that are made for bulls who do not think. . . . I did not realize the murder before it was accomplished! The wheel, the rush, the oblique charge from behind, the fall of horse and man were simultaneous. Apis leaped the horse, with whom he had no quarrel, and alighted, all four feet together (it was enough), between the man's shoulders, changed his beautiful feet on the carcass, and was away, pretending to fall nearly on his nose. Do you follow me? In that instant, by that stumble, he produced the impression that his adorable assassination was a mere bestial blunder. Then, Monsieur, I began to comprehend that it was an artist we had to deal with. He did not stand over the body to draw the rest of the troupe. He chose to reserve that trick. He let the attendants bear out the dead, and went on to amuse himself among the capeadors. Now to Apis, trained among our children in the yards, the cloak was simply a guide to the boy behind it. He pursued, you understand, the person, not the propaganda—the proprietor, not the journal. If a third of our electors of France were as wise, my friend! . . . But it was done leisurely, with humour and a touch of truculence. He romped after one man's cloak as a clumsy dog might do, but I observed that he kept the man on his terrible left side. Christophe whispered to me:

"Wait for his mother's kick. When he has made the fellow confident it will arrive." It arrived in the middle of a gambol. My God! He lashed out in the air as he frisked. The man dropped like a sack, lifted one hand a little towards his head, and—that was all. So you see, a body was again at his disposition; a second time the cloaks ran up to draw him off, but, a second time, Apis refused his grand scene. A second time he acted that his murder was accident and—he convinced his audience! It was as though he had knocked over a bridge-gate in the marshes by mistake. Unbelievable? I saw it.'

The memory sent Monsieur Voiron again to the champagne, and I accompanied him.

'But Apis was not the sole artist present. They say Villamarti comes of a family of actors. I saw him regard Apis with a new eye. He, too, began to understand. He took his cloak and moved out to play him before they should bring on another picador. He had his reputation. Perhaps Apis knew it. Perhaps Villamarti reminded him of some boy with whom he has practised at home. At any rate Apis permitted it—up to a certain point; but he did not allow Villamarti the stage. He cramped him throughout. He dived and plunged clumsily and slowly, but always with menace and always closing in. We could see that the man was conforming to the bull—not the bull to the man; for Apis was playing him towards the centre of the ring, and, in a little while—I watched his face—Villamarti knew it. But I could not fathom the creature's motive. "Wait," said old Christophe. "He wants that picador on the white horse yonder. When he reaches his proper distance he will get him. Villamarti is his cover. He used me once that way." And so it was, my friend! With the clang of one of our own Seventy-fives,* Apis dismissed Villamarti with his chest—breasted him over—and had arrived at his objective near the barrier. The same oblique charge; the head carried low for the sweep of the horns; the immense sideways fall of the horse, broken-legged and half-paralysed; the senseless man on the ground, and—behold Apis between them, backed against the barrier—his right covered by the horse; his left by the body of the man at his feet. The simplicity of it! Lacking the carts and tractors of his early parade-grounds he, being a genius, had extemporized with the materials at hand, and dug himself in. The troupe closed up again, their left wing broken by the kicking horse, their right immobilized by the man's body which Apis bestrode with significance. Villamarti almost threw himself between the horns, but—it was more an appeal than an attack. Apis refused him. He held his base. A picador was sent at him—necessarily from the front, which alone was open. Apis charged—he who, till then, you realize, had not used the horn! The horse went over backwards, the man half beneath him. Apis halted, hooked him under the heart, and threw him to the barrier. We heard his head crack, but he was dead before he hit the wood. There was no demonstration from the audience. They, also, had begun to realize this Foch* among bulls! The arena occupied itself again with the dead. Two of the troupe irresolutely tried to play him—God knows in what hope!—but he moved out to the centre of the ring. "Look!" said Christophe. "Now he goes to clean himself. That always frightened me." He knelt down; he began to clean his horns. The earth was hard. He worried at it in an ecstasy of absorption. As he laid his head along and rattled his ears, it was as though he were interrogating the Devils themselves upon their secrets, and always saying impatiently: "Yes, I know that—and *that*—and *that*! Tell me more—*more*!' In the silence that covered us, a woman cried: "He digs a grave! Oh, Saints, he digs a grave!" Some others echoed this—not loudly—as a wave echoes in a grotto of the sea.

'And when his horns were cleaned, he rose up and studied poor Villamarti's troupe, eyes in eyes, one by one, with the gravity of an equal in intellect and the remote and merciless resolution of a master in his art. This was more terrifying than his toilette.'

'And they—Villamarti's men?' I asked.

'Like the audience, were dominated. They had ceased to posture, or stamp, or address insults to him. They conformed to him. The two other matadors stared. Only Chisto, the oldest, broke silence with some call or other, and Apis turned his head towards him. Otherwise he was isolated, immobile—sombre—meditating on those at his mercy. Ah!

'For some reason the trumpet sounded for the *banderillas*— those gay hooked darts that are planted in the shoulders of bulls who do not think, after their neck-muscles are tired by lifting horses. When such bulls feel the pain, they check for an instant, and, in that instant, the men step gracefully aside. Villamarti's banderillero answered the trumpet mechanically—like one condemned. He stood out, poised the darts and stammered the usual patter of invitation. . . . And after? I do not assert that Apis shrugged his shoulders, but he reduced the episode to its lowest elements, as could only a bull of Gaul. With his truculence was mingled always—owing to the shortness of his tail—a certain Rabelaisian abandon, especially when viewed from the rear. Christophe had often commented upon it. Now, Apis brought that quality into play. He circulated round that boy, forcing him to break up his beautiful poses. He studied him from various angles, like an incompetent photographer. He presented to him every portion of his anatomy except his shoulders. At intervals he feigned to run in upon him. My God, he was cruel! But his motive was obvious. He was playing for a laugh from the spectators which should synchronize with the fracture of the human morale. It was achieved. The boy turned and ran towards the barrier. Apis was on him before the laugh ceased; passed him; headed him—what do I say?—herded him off to the left, his horns beside and a little in front of his chest: he did not intend him to escape into a refuge. Some of the troupe would have closed in, but Villamarti cried: "If he wants him he will take him. Stand!" They stood. Whether the boy slipped or Apis nosed him over I could not see. But he dropped, sobbing. Apis halted like a car with four brakes, struck a pose, smelt him very completely and turned away. It was dismissal more ignominious than degradation at the head of one's battalion. The representation was finished. Remained only for Apis to clear his stage of the subordinate characters.

'Ah! His gesture then! He gave a dramatic start—this Cyrano* of the Camargue—as though he was aware of them for the first time. He moved. All their beautiful breeches twinkled for an instant along the top of the barrier. He held the stage alone! But Christophe and I, we trembled! For, observe, he had now involved himself in a stupendous drama of which he only could supply the third act. And, except for an audience on the razor-edge of emotion, he had exhausted his material. Molière* himself—we have forgotten, my friend, to drink to the health of that great soul—might have been at a loss. And Tragedy is but a step behind Failure. We could see the four or five Civil Guards, who are sent always to keep order, fingering the breeches of their rifles. They were but waiting a word from the Mayor to fire on him, as they do sometimes at a bull who leaps the barrier among the spectators. They would, of course, have killed or wounded several people—but that would not have saved Apis.'

Monsieur Voiron drowned the thought at once, and wiped his beard.

'At that moment Fate—the Genius of France, if you will—sent to assist in the incomparable finale, none other than Chisto, the eldest, and I should have said (but never again will I judge!) the least inspired of all; mediocrity itself but, at heart—and it is the heart that conquers always, my friend—at heart an artist. He descended stiffly into the arena, alone and assured. Apis regarded him, his eyes in his eyes. The man took stance, with his cloak, and called to the bull as to an equal: "Now, Señor, we will show these honourable caballeros something together." He advanced thus against this thinker who at a plunge—a kick—a thrust—could, we all knew, have extinguished him. My dear friend, I wish I could convey to you something of the unaffected bonhomie, the humour, the delicacy, the consideration bordering on respect even, with which Apis, the supreme artist, responded to this invitation. It was the Master, wearied after a strenuous hour in the atelier, unbuttoned and at ease with some not inexpert but limited disciple. The telepathy was instantaneous between them. And for good reason! Christophe said to me: "All's well. That Chisto began among the bulls. I was sure of it when I heard him call just now. He has been a herdsman. He'll pull it off." There was a little feeling and adjustment, at first, for mutual distances and allowances.

'Oh, yes! And here occurred a gross impertinence of Villamarti. He had, after an interval, followed Chisto—to retrieve his reputation. My Faith! I can conceive the elder Dumas* slamming his door on an intruder precisely as Apis did. He raced Villamarti into the nearest refuge at once. He stamped his feet outside it, and he snorted: "Go! I am engaged with an artist." Villamarti went—his reputation left behind for ever.

'Apis returned to Chisto saying: "Forgive the interruption. I am not always master of my time, but you were about to observe, my dear confrère . . .?" Then the play began. Out of compliment to Chisto, Apis chose as his objective (every bull varies in this respect) the inner edge of the cloak—that nearest to the man's body. This allows but a few millimetres clearance in charging. But Apis trusted himself as Chisto trusted him, and, this time, he conformed to the man, with inimitable judgement and temper. He allowed himself to be played into the shadow or the sun, as the delighted audience demanded. He raged enormously; he feigned defeat; he despaired in statuesque abandon, and thence flashed into fresh paroxysms of wrath—but always with the detachment of the true artist who knows he is but the vessel of an emotion whence others, not he, must drink. And never once did he forget that honest Chisto's cloak was to him the gauge by which to spare even a hair on the skin. He inspired Chisto too. My God! His youth returned to that meritorious beef-sticker—the desire, the grace, and the beauty of his early dreams. One could almost see that girl of the past for whom he was rising, rising to these present heights of skill and daring. It was his hour too—a miraculous hour of dawn returned to gild the sunset. All he knew was at Apis' disposition. Apis acknowledged it with all that he had learned at home, at Arles and in his lonely murders on our grazing-grounds. He flowed round Chisto like a river of death—round his knees, leaping at his shoulders, kicking just clear of one side or the other of his head; behind his back hissing as he shaved by; and once or twice—inimitable!—he reared wholly up before him while Chisto slipped back from beneath the avalanche of that instructed body. Those two, my dear friend, held five thousand people dumb with no sound but of their breathings—regular as pumps. It was unbearable. Beast and man realized together that we needed a change of note—a détente. They relaxed to pure buffoonery. Chisto fell back and talked to him outrageously. Apis pretended he had never heard such language. The audience howled with delight. Chisto slapped him; he took liberties with his short tail, to the end of which he clung while Apis pirouetted; he played about him in all postures; he had become the herdsman again—gross, care-less, brutal, but comprehending. Yet Apis was always the more

consummate clown. All that time (Christophe and I saw it)
Apis drew off towards the gates of the *toril** where so many
bulls enter but—have you ever heard of one that returned? *We*
knew that Apis knew that as he had saved Chisto, so Chisto
would save him. Life is sweet to us all; to the artist who lives
many lives in one, sweetest. Chisto did not fail him. At the last,
when none could laugh any longer, the man threw his cape
across the bull's back, his arm round his neck. He flung up a
hand at the gate, as Villamarti, young and commanding but *not*
a herdsman, might have raised it, and he cried: "Gentlemen,
open to me and my honourable little donkey." They opened—I
have misjudged Spaniards in my time!—those gates opened to
the man and the bull together, and closed behind them. And
then? From the Mayor to the Guardia Civil they went mad for
five minutes, till the trumpets blew and the fifth bull rushed
out—an unthinking black Andalusian. I suppose some one
killed him. My friend, my very dear friend, to whom I have
opened my heart, I confess that I did not watch. Christophe
and I, we were weeping together like children of the same
Mother.* Shall we drink to Her?'

ALNASCHAR* AND THE OXEN

There's a pasture in a valley where the hanging woods divide,
  And a Herd lies down and ruminates in peace;
Where the pheasant rules the nooning, and the owl the twilight
    tide,
  And the war-cries of our world die out and cease.
Here I cast aside the burden that each weary week-day brings
  And, delivered from the shadows I pursue,
On peaceful, postless Sabbaths I consider Weighty Things—
  Such as Sussex Cattle feeding in the dew!

At the gate beside the river where the trouty shallows brawl,
  I know the pride that Lobengula* felt,
When he bade the bars be lowered of the Royal Cattle Kraal,
  And fifteen mile of oxen took the veldt.
From the walls of Bulawayo in unbroken file they came
  To where the Mount of Council cuts the blue . . .
I have only six and twenty, but the principle's the same
  With my Sussex Cattle feeding in the dew!

To a luscious sound of tearing, where the clovered herbage rips,
  Level-backed and level-bellied watch 'em move—
See those shoulders, guess that heart-girth, praise those loins,
    admire those hips,
  And the tail set low for flesh to make above!
Count the broad unblemished muzzles, test the kindly mellow
    skin
  And, where yon heifer lifts her head at call,
Mark the bosom's just abundance 'neath the gay and clean-cut
    chin,
  And those eyes of Juno, overlooking all!

Here is colour, form and substance! I will put it to the proof
  And, next season, in my lodges shall be born
Some very Bull of Mithras,* flawless from his agate hoof
  To his even-branching, ivory, dusk-tipped horn.

He shall mate with block-square virgins—kings shall seek his
    like in vain,
  While I multiply his stock a thousandfold,
Till an hungry world extol me, builder of a lofty strain
  That turns one standard ton at two years old!

There's a valley, under oakwood, where a man may dream his
    dream,
  In the milky breath of cattle laid at ease,
Till the moon o'ertops the alders, and her image chills the stream,
  And the river-mist runs silver round their knees!
Now the footpaths fade and vanish; now the ferny clumps deceive;
  Now the hedgerow-folk possess their fields anew;
Now the Herd is lost in darkness, and I bless them as I leave,
  My Sussex Cattle feeding in the dew!

THE GARDENER *

One grave to me was given,
  One watch till Judgment Day;
And God looked down from Heaven
  And rolled the stone away. *

One day in all the years,
  One hour in that one day,
His Angel saw my tears,
  And rolled the stone away!

EVERY one in the village knew that Helen Turrell did her duty
by all her world, and by none more honourably than by her
only brother's unfortunate child. The village knew, too, that
George Turrell had tried his family severely since early youth,
and were not surprised to be told that, after many fresh starts
given and thrown away, he, an Inspector of Indian Police,
had entangled himself with the daughter of a retired non-
commissioned officer, and had died of a fall from a horse a few
weeks before his child was born. Mercifully, George's father
and mother were both dead, and though Helen, thirty-five and
independent, might well have washed her hands of the whole
disgraceful affair, she most nobly took charge, though she was,
at the time, under threat of lung trouble which had driven her
to the South of France. She arranged for the passage of the
child and a nurse from Bombay, met them at Marseilles, nursed
the baby through an attack of infantile dysentery due to the
carelessness of the nurse, whom she had had to dismiss, and at
last, thin and worn but triumphant, brought the boy late in the
autumn, wholly restored, to her Hampshire home.

All these details were public property, for Helen was as open
as the day, and held that scandals are only increased by hushing
them up. She admitted that George had always been rather a
black sheep, but things might have been much worse if the
mother had insisted on her right to keep the boy. Luckily, it
seemed that people of that class would do almost anything for

money, and, as George had always turned to her in his scrapes,
she felt herself justified—her friends agreed with her—in cutting the whole non-commissioned officer connection, and giving the child every advantage. A christening, by the Rector,
under the name of Michael, was the first step. So far as she
knew herself, she was not, she said, a child-lover, but, for all
his faults, she had been very fond of George, and she pointed
out that little Michael had his father's mouth to a line; which
made something to build upon.

As a matter of fact, it was the Turrell forehead, broad, low,
and well-shaped, with the widely spaced eyes beneath it, that
Michael had most faithfully reproduced. His mouth was somewhat better cut than the family type. But Helen, who would
concede nothing good to his mother's side, vowed he was a
Turrell all over, and, there being no one to contradict, the
likeness was established.

In a few years Michael took his place, as accepted as Helen
had always been—fearless, philosophical, and fairly good-
looking. At six, he wished to know why he could not call her
'Mummy', as other boys called their mothers. She explained
that she was only his auntie, and that aunties were not quite
the same as mummies, but that, if it gave him pleasure, he might
call her 'Mummy' at bedtime, for a pet-name between themselves.

Michael kept his secret most loyally, but Helen, as usual,
explained* the fact to her friends; which when Michael heard,
he raged.

'Why did you tell? *Why* did you tell?' came at the end of the
storm.

'Because it's always best to tell the truth,' Helen answered,
her arm round him as he shook in his cot.

'All right, but when the troof's ugly I don't think it's nice.'

'Don't you, dear?'

'No, I don't, and'—she felt the small body stiffen—'now
you've told, I won't call you "Mummy" any more—not even
at bedtimes.'

'But isn't that rather unkind?' said Helen softly.

'I don't care! I don't care! You've hurted me in my insides
and I'll hurt you back. I'll hurt you as long as I live!'

'Don't, oh, don't talk like that, dear! You don't know what——'

'I will! And when I'm dead I'll hurt you worse!'

'Thank goodness, I shall be dead long before you, darling.'

'Huh! Emma says, " 'Never know your luck." ' (Michael had been talking to Helen's elderly, flat-faced maid.) 'Lots of little boys die quite soon. So'll I. *Then* you'll see!'

Helen caught her breath and moved towards the door, but the wail of 'Mummy! Mummy!' drew her back again, and the two wept together.

At ten years old, after two terms at a prep. school, something or somebody gave him the idea that his civil status was not quite regular. He attacked Helen on the subject, breaking down her stammered defences with the family directness.

''Don't believe a word of it,' he said, cheerily, at the end. 'People wouldn't have talked like they did if my people had been married. But don't you bother, Auntie. I've found out all about my sort in English Hist'ry and the Shakespeare bits. There was William the Conqueror to begin with, and—oh, heaps more, and they all got on first-rate. 'Twon't make any difference to you, my being *that*—will it?'

'As if anything could——' she began.

'All right. We won't talk about it any more if it makes you cry.' He never mentioned the thing again of his own will, but when, two years later, he skilfully managed to have measles in the holidays, as his temperature went up to the appointed one hundred and four he muttered of nothing else, till Helen's voice, piercing at last his delirium, reached him with assurance that nothing on earth or beyond could make any difference between them.

The terms at his public school and the wonderful Christmas, Easter, and Summer holidays followed each other, variegated and glorious as jewels on a string; and as jewels Helen treasured them. In due time Michael developed his own interests, which ran their courses and gave way to others; but his interest in Helen was constant and increasing throughout. She repaid it with all that she had of affection or could command of counsel and money; and since Michael was no fool, the War took him just before what was like to have been a most promising career.

He was to have gone up to Oxford, with a scholarship, in October. At the end of August he was on the edge of joining the first holocaust of public-school boys who threw themselves into the Line; but the captain of his OTC,* where he had been sergeant for nearly a year, headed him off and steered him directly to a commission in a battalion so new that half of it still wore the old Army red,* and the other half was breeding meningitis through living overcrowdedly in damp tents. Helen had been shocked at the idea of direct enlistment.

'But it's in the family,' Michael laughed.

'You don't mean to tell me that you believed that old story all this time?' said Helen. (Emma, her maid, had been dead now several years.) 'I gave you my word of honour—and I give it again—that—that it's all right. It is indeed.'

'Oh, *that* doesn't worry me. It never did,' he replied valiantly. 'What I meant was, I should have got into the show earlier if I'd enlisted—like my grandfather.'

'Don't talk like that! Are you afraid of its ending so soon, then?'

'No such luck. You know what K.* says.'

'Yes. But my banker told me last Monday it couldn't *possibly* last beyond Christmas—for financial reasons.'

''Hope he's right, but our Colonel—and he's a Regular—says it's going to be a long job.'

Michael's battalion was fortunate in that, by some chance which meant several 'leaves', it was used for coast-defence among shallow trenches on the Norfolk coast; thence sent north to watch the mouth of a Scotch estuary, and, lastly, held for weeks on a baseless rumour of distant service.* But, the very day that Michael was to have met Helen for four whole hours at a railway-junction up the line, it was hurled out, to help make good the wastage of Loos, and he had only just time to send her a wire of farewell.

In France luck again helped the battalion. It was put down near the Salient, where it led a meritorious and unexacting life, while the Somme was being manufactured; and enjoyed the peace of the Armentières and Laventie sectors when that battle began. Finding that it had sound views on protecting its own flanks and could dig, a prudent Commander stole it out of its own Division, under pretence of helping to lay telegraphs, and used it round Ypres at large.

A month later, and just after Michael had written Helen that there was nothing special doing and therefore no need to worry, a shell-splinter dropping out of a wet dawn killed him at once. The next shell uprooted and laid down over the body what had been the foundation of a barn wall, so neatly that none but an expert would have guessed that anything unpleasant had happened.

By this time the village was old in experience of war, and, English fashion, had evolved a ritual to meet it. When the postmistress handed her seven-year-old daughter the official telegram to take to Miss Turrell, she observed to the Rector's gardener: 'It's Miss Helen's turn now.' He replied, thinking of his own son: 'Well, he's lasted longer than some.' The child herself came to the front-door weeping aloud, because Master Michael had often given her sweets. Helen, presently, found herself pulling down the house-blinds one after one with great care, and saying earnestly to each: 'Missing *always* means dead.' Then she took her place in the dreary procession that was impelled to go through an inevitable series of unprofitable emotions. The Rector, of course, preached hope and prophesied word, very soon, from a prison camp. Several friends, too, told her perfectly truthful tales, but always about other women, to whom, after months and months of silence, their missing had been miraculously restored. Other people urged her to communicate with infallible Secretaries of organizations* who could communicate with benevolent neutrals, who could extract accurate information from the most secretive of Hun prison commandants. Helen did and wrote and signed everything that was suggested or put before her.

Once, on one of Michael's leaves, he had taken her over a munition factory, where she saw the progress of a shell from blank-iron to the all but finished article. It struck her at the time that the wretched thing was never left alone for a single second; and 'I'm being manufactured into a bereaved next of kin,' she told herself, as she prepared her documents.

In due course, when all the organizations had deeply or sincerely regretted their inability to trace, etc., something gave way within her and all sensation—save of thankfulness for the release—came to an end in blessed passivity. Michael had died and her world had stood still and she had been one with the full shock of that arrest. Now she was standing still and the world was going forward, but it did not concern her—in no way or relation did it touch her. She knew this by the ease with which she could slip Michael's name into talk and incline her head to the proper angle, at the proper murmur of sympathy.

In the blessed realization of that relief, the Armistice with all its bells broke over her and passed unheeded. At the end of another year she had overcome her physical loathing of the living and returned young, so that she could take them by the hand and almost sincerely wish them well. She had no interest in any aftermath, national or personal, of the war, but, moving at an immense distance, she sat on various relief committees and held strong views—she heard herself delivering them— about the site of the proposed village War Memorial.

Then there came to her, as next of kin, an official intimation, backed by a page of a letter to her in indelible pencil, a silver identity-disc, and a watch, to the effect that the body of Lieutenant Michael Turrell had been found, identified, and re-interred in Hagenzeele* Third Military Cemetery—the letter of the row and the grave's number in that row duly given.

So Helen found herself moved on to another process of the manufacture—to a world full of exultant or broken relatives, now strong in the certainty that there was an altar upon earth where they might lay their love. These soon told her, and by means of time-tables made clear, how easy it was and how little it interfered with life's affairs to go and see one's grave.

'*So* different,' as the Rector's wife said, 'if he'd been killed in Mesopotamia, or even Gallipoli.'

The agony of being waked up to some sort of second life drove Helen across the Channel, where, in a new world of abbreviated titles, she learnt that Hagenzeele Third could be comfortably reached by an afternoon train which fitted in with the morning boat, and that there was a comfortable little hotel not three kilometres from Hagenzeele itself, where one could spend quite a comfortable night and see one's grave next morning. All this she had from a Central Authority who lived in a board and tar-paper shed on the skirts of a razed city full of whirling lime-dust and blown papers.

'By the way,' said he, 'you know your grave, of course?'

'Yes, thank you,' said Helen, and showed its row and number typed on Michael's own little typewriter. The officer would have checked it, out of one of his many books; but a large Lancashire woman thrust between them and bade him tell her where she might find her son, who had been corporal in the ASC.* His proper name, she sobbed, was Anderson, but, coming of respectable folk, he had of course enlisted under the name of Smith; and had been killed at Dickiebush, in early 'Fifteen. She had not his number nor did she know which of his two Christian names he might have used with his alias; but her Cook's tourist ticket expired at the end of Easter week, and if by then she could not find her child she should go mad. Whereupon she fell forward on Helen's breast; but the officer's wife came out quickly from a little bedroom behind the office, and the three of them lifted the woman on to the cot.

'They are often like this,' said the officer's wife, loosening the tight bonnet-strings. 'Yesterday she said he'd been killed at Hooge. Are you sure you know your grave? It makes such a difference.'

'Yes, thank you,' said Helen, and hurried out before the woman on the bed should begin to lament again.

Tea in a crowded mauve and blue striped wooden structure, with a false front, carried her still further into the nightmare. She paid her bill beside a stolid, plain-featured Englishwoman, who, hearing her inquire about the train to Hagenzeele, volunteered to come with her.

'I'm going to Hagenzeele myself,' she explained. 'Not to Hagenzeele Third; mine is Sugar Factory, but they call it La Rosière now. It's just south of Hagenzeele Three. Have you got your room at the hotel there?'

'Oh yes, thank you. I've wired.'

'That's better. Sometimes the place is quite full, and at others there's hardly a soul. But they've put bathrooms into the old Lion d'Or—that's the hotel on the west side of Sugar Factory—and it draws off a lot of people, luckily.'

'It's all new to me. This is the first time I've been over.'

'Indeed! This is my ninth time since the Armistice. Not on my own account. *I* haven't lost any one, thank God—but, like every one else, I've a lot of friends at home who have. Coming over as often as I do, I find it helps them to have some one just look at the—the place and tell them about it afterwards. And one can take photos for them, too. I get quite a list of commissions to execute.' She laughed nervously and tapped her slung Kodak. 'There are two or three to see at Sugar Factory this time, and plenty of others in the cemeteries all about. My system is to save them up, and arrange them, you know. And when I've got enough commissions for one area to make it worth while, I pop over and execute them. It *does* comfort people.'

'I suppose so,' Helen answered, shivering as they entered the little train.

'Of course it does. (Isn't it lucky we've got window-seats?) It must do or they wouldn't ask one to do it, would they? I've a list of quite twelve or fifteen commissions here'—she tapped the Kodak again—'I must sort them out tonight. Oh, I forgot to ask you. What's yours?'

'My nephew,' said Helen. 'But I was very fond of him.'

'Ah, yes! I sometimes wonder whether *they* know after death? What do you think?'

'Oh, I don't—I haven't dared to think much about that sort of thing,' said Helen, almost lifting her hands to keep her off.

'Perhaps that's better,' the woman answered. 'The sense of loss must be enough, I expect. Well, I won't worry you any more.'

Helen was grateful, but when they reached the hotel Mrs Scarsworth (they had exchanged names) insisted on dining at the same table with her, and after the meal, in the little, hideous salon full of low-voiced relatives, took Helen through her 'commissions' with biographies of the dead, where she happened to know them, and sketches of their next of kin. Helen endured till nearly half-past nine, ere she fled to her room.

Almost at once there was a knock at her door and Mrs Scarsworth entered; her hands, holding the dreadful list, clasped before her.

'Yes—yes—*I* know,' she began. 'You're sick of me, but I want to tell you something. You—you aren't married, are you? Then perhaps you won't . . . But it doesn't matter. I've *got* to tell some one. I can't go on any longer like this.'

'But please——' Mrs Scarsworth had backed against the shut door, and her mouth worked dryly.

'In a minute,' she said. 'You—you know about these graves of mine I was telling you about downstairs, just now? They really *are* commissions. At least several of them are.' Her eye wandered round the room. 'What extraordinary wall-papers they have in Belgium, don't you think? . . . Yes. I swear they are commissions. But there's *one*, d'you see, and—and he was more to me than anything else in the world. Do you understand?'

Helen nodded.

'More than any one else. And, of course, he oughtn't to have been. He ought to have been nothing to me. But he *was*. He *is*. That's why I do the commissions, you see. That's all.'

'But why do you tell me?' Helen asked desperately.

'Because I'm *so* tired of lying. Tired of lying—always lying—year in and year out. When I don't tell lies I've got to act 'em and I've got to think 'em, always. *You* don't know what that means. He was everything to me that he oughtn't to have been—the one real thing—the only thing that ever happened to me in all my life; and I've had to pretend he wasn't. I've had to watch every word I said, and think out what lie I'd tell next, for years and years!'

'How many years?' Helen asked.

'Six years and four months before, and two and three-quarters after. I've gone to him eight times, since. Tomorrow'll make the ninth, and—and I can't—I *can't* go to him again with nobody in the world knowing. I want to be honest with some one before I go. Do you understand? It doesn't matter about *me*. I was never truthful, even as a girl. But it isn't worthy of *him*. So—so I—I had to tell you. I can't keep it up any longer. Oh, I can't!'

She lifted her joined hands almost to the level of her mouth, and brought them down sharply, still joined, to full arms' length below her waist. Helen reached forward, caught them, bowed her head over them, and murmured: 'Oh, my dear! My dear!' Mrs Scarsworth stepped back, her face all mottled.

'My God!' said she. 'Is *that* how you take it?'

Helen could not speak, and the woman went out; but it was a long while before Helen was able to sleep.

Next morning Mrs Scarsworth left early on her round of commissions, and Helen walked alone to Hagenzeele Third. The place was still in the making, and stood some five or six feet above the metalled road, which it flanked for hundreds of yards. Culverts across a deep ditch served for entrances through the unfinished boundary wall. She climbed a few wooden-faced earthen steps and then met the entire crowded level of the thing in one held breath. She did not know that Hagenzeele Third counted twenty-one thousand dead already. All she saw was a merciless sea of black crosses, bearing little strips of stamped tin at all angles across their faces. She could distinguish no order or arrangement in their mass; nothing but a waist-high wilderness as of weeds stricken dead, rushing at her. She went forward, moved to the left and the right hopelessly, wondering by what guidance she should ever come to her own. A great distance away there was a line of whiteness. It proved to be a block of some two or three hundred graves whose headstones had already been set, whose flowers were planted out, and whose new-sown grass showed green. Here she could see clear-cut letters at the ends of the rows, and, referring to her slip, realized that it was not here she must look.

A man knelt behind a line of headstones—evidently a gardener, for he was firming a young plant in the soft earth. She went towards him, her paper in her hand. He rose at her approach and without prelude or salutation asked: 'Who are you looking for?'

'Lieutenant Michael Turrell—my nephew,' said Helen slowly and word for word, as she had many thousands of times in her life.

The man lifted his eyes and looked at her with infinite compassion before he turned from the fresh-sown grass toward the naked black crosses.

'Come with me,' he said, 'and I will show you where your son lies.'

When Helen left the Cemetery she turned for a last look. In the distance she saw the man bending over his young plants; and she went away, supposing him to be the gardener.*

THE BURDEN

One grief on me is laid
    Each day of every year,
Wherein no soul can aid,
    Whereof no soul can hear:
Whereto no end is seen
    Except to grieve again—
Ah, Mary Magdalene, *
    Where is there greater pain?

To dream on dear disgrace
    Each hour of every day—
To bring no honest face
    To aught I do or say:
To lie from morn till e'en—
    To know my lies are vain—
Ah, Mary Magdalene,
    Where can be greater pain?

To watch my steadfast fear
    Attend my every way
Each day of every year—
    Each hour of every day:
To burn, and chill between—
    To quake and rage again—
Ah, Mary Magdalene,
    Where shall be greater pain?

One grave to me was given—
To guard till Judgment Day—
But God looked down from Heaven
    And rolled the Stone away!
One day of all my years—
    One hour of that one day—
His Angel saw my tears
    And rolled the Stone away!

THE EYE OF ALLAH *

UNTIMELY

Nothing in life has been made by man for man's using
But it was shown long since to man in ages
Lost as the name of the maker of it,

Who received oppression and scorn for his wages—
Hate, avoidance, and scorn in his daily dealings—
Until he perished, wholly confounded.

More to be pitied than he are the wise
Souls which foresaw the evil of loosing
Knowledge or Art before time, and aborted
Noble devices and deep-wrought healings,
Lest offence should arise.

Heaven delivers on earth the Hour that cannot be thwarted,
Neither advanced, at the price of a world or a soul, and
    its Prophet
Comes through the blood of the vanguards who
    dreamed—too soon—it had sounded.

The Eye of Allah

THE Cantor* of St Illod's being far too enthusiastic a musician to concern himself with its Library, the Sub-Cantor, who idolized every detail of the work, was tidying up, after two hours' writing and dictation in the Scriptorium. The copying-monks handed him in their sheets—it was a plain Four Gospels ordered by an Abbot at Evesham—and filed out to vespers. John Otho, better known as John of Burgos, took no heed. He was burnishing a tiny boss of gold in his miniature of the Annunciation for his Gospel of St Luke, which it was hoped that Cardinal Falcodi, the Papal Legate, might later be pleased to accept.

'Break off, John,' said the Sub-Cantor in an undertone.

'Eh? Gone, have they? I never heard. Hold a minute, Clement.'

The Sub-Cantor waited patiently. He had known John more than a dozen years, coming and going at St Illod's, to which monastery John, when abroad, always said he belonged. The claim was gladly allowed for, more even than other Fitz Otho's, he seemed to carry all the Arts under his hand, and most of their practical receipts under his hood.

The Sub-Cantor looked over his shoulder at the pinned-down sheet where the first words of the Magnificat* were built up in gold washed with red-lac for a background to the Virgin's hardly yet fired halo. She was shown, hands joined in wonder, at a lattice of infinitely intricate arabesque, round the edges of which sprays of orange-bloom seemed to load the blue hot air that carried back over the minute parched landscape in the middle distance.

'You've made her all Jewess,' said the Sub-Cantor, studying the olive-flushed cheek and the eyes charged with fore-knowledge.

'What else was Our Lady?' John slipped out the pins. 'Listen, Clement. If I do not come back, this goes into my Great Luke, whoever finishes it.' He slid the drawing between its guard-papers.

'Then you're for Burgos again—as I heard?'

'In two days. The new Cathedral* yonder—but they're slower than the Wrath of God, those masons—is good for the soul.'

'*Thy* soul?' The Sub-Cantor seemed doubtful.

'Even mine, by your permission. And down south—on the edge of the Conquered Countries—Granada* way—there's some Moorish diaper-work that's wholesome. It allays vain thought and draws it toward the picture—as you felt, just now, in my Annunciation.'

'She—it was very beautiful. No wonder you go. But you'll not forget your absolution, John?'

'Surely.' This was a precaution John no more omitted on the eve of his travels than he did the recutting of the tonsure which he had provided himself with in his youth, somewhere near Ghent. The mark gave him privilege of clergy* at a pinch, and a certain consideration on the road always.

'You'll not forget, either, what we need in the Scriptorium. There's no more true ultramarine in this world now. They mix it with that German blue. And as for vermilion——'

'I'll do my best always.'

'And Brother Thomas' (this was the Infirmarian in charge of the monastery hospital) 'he needs——'

'He'll do his own asking. I'll go over his side now, and get me re-tonsured.'

John went down the stairs to the lane that divides the hospital and cook-house from the back-cloisters. While he was being barbered, Brother Thomas (St Illod's meek but deadly persistent Infirmarian)* gave him a list of drugs that he was to bring back from Spain by hook, crook, or lawful purchase. Here they were surprised by the lame, dark Abbot Stephen, in his fur-lined night-boots.* Not that Stephen de Sautré was any spy; but as a young man he had shared an unlucky Crusade, which had ended, after a battle at Mansura,* in two years' captivity among the Saracens at Cairo where men learn to walk softly. A fair huntsman and hawker, a reasonable disciplinarian, but a man of science above all, and a Doctor of Medicine under one Ranulphus, Canon of St Paul's, his heart was more in the monastery's hospital work than its religious. He checked their list interestedly, adding items of his own. After the Infirmarian had withdrawn, he gave John generous absolution, to cover lapses by the way; for he did not hold with chance-bought Indulgences.

'And what seek you *this* journey?' he demanded, sitting on the bench beside the mortar and scales in the little warm cell for stored drugs.

'Devils, mostly,' said John, grinning.

'In Spain? Are not Abana and Pharpar——?' *

John, to whom men were but matter for drawings, and well-born to boot (since he was a de Sanford * on his mother's side), looked the Abbot full in the face and—'Did *you* find it so?' said he.

'No. They were in Cairo too. But what's your special need of 'em?'

'For my Great Luke. He's the masterhand of all Four when it comes to devils.'

'No wonder. He was a physician. You're not.'

'Heaven forbid! But I'm weary of our Church-pattern devils. They're only apes and goats and poultry conjoined. 'Good enough for plain red-and-black Hells and Judgement Days— but not for me.'

'What makes you so choice in them?'

'Because it stands to reason and Art that there are all musters of devils in Hell's dealings. Those Seven, for example, that were haled out of the Magdalene. * They'd be she-devils—no kin at all to the beaked and horned and bearded devils-general.'

The Abbot laughed.

'And see again! The devil that came out of the dumb man. What use is snout or bill to *him*? He'd be faceless as a leper. Above all—God send I live to do it!—the devils that entered the Gadarene swine. They'd be—they'd be—I know not yet what they'd be, but they'd be surpassing devils. I'd have 'em diverse as the Saints themselves. But now, they're all one pattern for wall, window, or picture-work.'

'Go on, John. You're deeper in this mystery than I.'

'Heaven forbid! But I say there's respect due to devils, damned tho' they be.'

'Dangerous doctrine.'

'My meaning is that if the shape of anything be worth man's thought to picture to man, it's worth his best thought.'

'That's safer. But I'm glad I've given you Absolution.'

'There's less risk for a craftsman who deals with the outside shapes of things—for Mother Church's glory.'

'Maybe so, but John'—the Abbot's hand almost touched John's sleeve—'tell me, now, is—is she Moorish or—or Hebrew?'

'She's mine,' John returned.

'Is that enough?'

'I have found it so.'

'Well—ah well! It's out of my jurisdiction, but—how do they look at it down yonder?'

'Oh, they drive nothing to a head in Spain—neither Church nor King, bless them! There's too many Moors and Jews to kill them all, and if they chased 'em away there'd be no trade nor farming. Trust me, in the Conquered Countries, from Seville to Granada, we live lovingly enough together—Spaniard, Moor, and Jew. Ye see, *we* ask no questions.'

'Yes—yes,' Stephen sighed. 'And always there's the hope, she may be converted.'

'Oh yes, there's always hope.'

The Abbot went on into the hospital. It was an easy age before Rome tightened the screw as to clerical connections. If the lady were not too forward, or the son too much his father's beneficiary in ecclesiastical preferments and levies, a good deal was overlooked. But, as the Abbot had reason to recall, unions between Christian and Infidel led to sorrow. None the less, when John with mule, mails, and man, clattered off down the lane for Southampton and the sea, Stephen envied him.

*　　*　　*

He was back, twenty months later, in good hard case, and loaded down with fairings. A lump of richest lazuli, a bar of orange-hearted vermilion, and a small packet of dried beetles which make most glorious scarlet, for the Sub-Cantor. Besides that, a few cubes of milky marble, with yet a pink flush in them, which could be slaked and ground down to incomparable background-stuff. There were quite half the drugs that the Abbot and Thomas had demanded, and there was a long deep-red cornelian* necklace for the Abbot's Lady—Anne of Norton. She received it graciously, and asked where John had come by it.

'Near Granada,' he said.

'You left all well there?' Anne asked. (Maybe the Abbot had told her something of John's confession.)

'I left all in the hands of God.'

'Ah me! How long since?'

'Four months less eleven days.'

'Were you—with her?'

'In my arms. Childbed.'

'And?'

'The boy too. There is nothing now.'

Anne of Norton caught her breath.

'I think you'll be glad of that,' she said after a while.

'Give me time, and maybe I'll compass it. But not now.'

'You have your handwork and your art and—John—remember there's no jealousy in the grave.'

'Ye-es! I have my Art, and Heaven knows I'm jealous of none.'

'Thank God for that at least,' said Anne of Norton, the always ailing woman who followed the Abbot with her sunk eyes. 'And be sure I shall treasure this'—she touched the beads—'as long as I shall live.'

'I brought—trusted—it to you for that,' he replied, and took leave. When she told the Abbot how she had come by it, he said nothing, but as he and Thomas were storing the drugs that John handed over in the cell which backs on to the hospital kitchen-chimney, he observed, of a cake of dried poppy-juice: 'This has power to cut off all pain from a man's body.'

'I have seen it,' said John.

'But for pain of the soul there is, outside God's Grace, but one drug; and that is a man's craft, learning, or other helpful motion of his own mind.'

'That is coming to me, too,' was the answer.

John spent the next fair May day out in the woods with the monastery swineherd and all the porkers; and returned loaded with flowers and sprays of spring, to his own carefully kept place in the north bay of the Scriptorium. There, with his travelling sketch-books under his left elbow, he sunk himself past all recollections in his Great Luke.

Brother Martin, Senior Copyist (who spoke about once a fortnight), ventured to ask, later, how the work was going.

'All here!' John tapped his forehead with his pencil. 'It has been only waiting these months to—ah God!—be born. Are ye free of your plain-copying, Martin?'

Brother Martin nodded. It was his pride that John of Burgos turned to him, in spite of his seventy years, for really good page-work.

'Then see!' John laid out a new vellum—thin but flawless. 'There's no better than this sheet from here to Paris. Yes! Smell it if you choose. Wherefore—give me the compasses and I'll set it out for you—if ye make one letter lighter or darker than its next, I'll stick ye like a pig.'

'Never, John!' the old man beamed happily.

'But I will! Now, follow! Here and here, as I prick, and in script of just this height to the hair's-breadth, ye'll scribe the thirty-first and thirty-second verses of Eighth Luke.'

'Yes, the Gadarene Swine! "*And they besought him that he would not command them to go out into the deep. And there was an herd of many swine*" '—— Brother Martin naturally knew all the Gospels by heart.

'Just so! Down to "*And he suffered them.*" Take your time to it. My Magdalene has to come off my heart first.'

Brother Martin achieved the work so perfectly that John stole some soft sweetmeats from the Abbot's kitchen for his reward. The old man ate them; then repented; then confessed and insisted on penance. At which, the Abbot, knowing there was but one way to reach the real sinner, set him a book called *De Virtutibus Herbarum** to fair-copy. St Illod's had borrowed it from the gloomy Cistercians,* who do not hold with pretty things, and the crabbed text kept Martin busy just when John wanted him for some rather specially spaced letterings.

'See now,' said the Sub-Cantor improvingly. 'You should not do such things, John. Here's Brother Martin on penance for your sake——'

'No—for my Great Luke. But I've paid the Abbot's cook. I've drawn him till his own scullions cannot keep straight-faced. *He*'ll not tell again.'

'Unkindly done! And you're out of favour with the Abbot too. He's made no sign to you since you came back—never asked you to high table.'

'I've been busy. Having eyes in his head, Stephen knew it. Clement, there's no Librarian from Durham to Torre* fit to clean up after you.'

The Sub-Cantor stood on guard; he knew where John's compliments generally ended.

'But outside the Scriptorium——'

'Where I never go.' The Sub-Cantor had been excused even digging in the garden, lest it should mar his wonderful book-binding hands.

'In all things outside the Scriptorium you are the master-fool of Christendie. Take it from me, Clement. I've met many.'

'I take everything from you,' Clement smiled benignly. 'You use me worse than a singing-boy.'

They could hear one of that suffering breed in the cloister below, squalling as the Cantor pulled his hair. *

'God love you! So I do! But have you ever thought how I lie and steal daily on my travels—yes, and for aught you know, murder—to fetch you colours and earths?'

'True,' said just and conscience-stricken Clement. 'I have often thought that were I in the world—which God forbid!—I might be a strong thief in some matters.'

Even Brother Martin, bent above his loathed De Virtutibus, laughed.

* * *

But about mid-summer, Thomas the Infirmarian conveyed to John the Abbot's invitation to supper in his house that night, with the request that he would bring with him anything that he had done for his Great Luke.

'What's toward?' said John, who had been wholly shut up in his work.

'Only one of his "wisdom" dinners. You've sat at a few since you were a man.'

'True: and mostly good. How would Stephen have us——?'

'Gown and hood over all. There will be a doctor from Salerno—one Roger,* an Italian. Wise and famous with the knife on the body. He's been in the Infirmary some ten days, helping me—even me!'

''Never heard the name. But our Stephen's *physicus* before *sacerdos*,* always.'

'And his Lady has a sickness of some time. Roger came hither in chief because of her.'

'Did he? Now I think of it, I have not seen the Lady Anne for a while.'

'Ye've seen nothing for a long while. She has been housed near a month—they have to carry her abroad now.'

'So bad as that, then?'

'Roger of Salerno will not yet say what he thinks. But——'

'God pity Stephen! . . . Who else at table, beside thee?'

'An Oxford friar.* Roger is his name also. A learned and famous philosopher. And he holds his liquor too, valiantly.'

'Three doctors—counting Stephen. I've always found that means two atheists.'

Thomas looked uneasily down his nose. 'That's a wicked proverb,' he stammered. 'You should not use it.'

'Hoh! Never come you the monk over me, Thomas! You've been Infirmarian at St Illod's eleven years—and a lay-brother still. Why have you never taken orders, all this while?'

'I—I am not worthy.'

'Ten times worthier than that new fat swine—Henry Who's-his-name—that takes the Infirmary Masses. He bullocks in with the Viaticum, under your nose, when a sick man's only faint from being bled. So the man dies—of pure fear. Ye know it! I've watched your face at such times. Take Orders, Didymus.* You'll have a little more medicine and a little less Mass with your sick then; and they'll live longer.'

'I am unworthy—unworthy,' Thomas repeated pitifully.

'Not you—but—to your own master you stand or fall. And now that my work releases me for awhile, I'll drink with any philosopher out of any school. And Thomas,' he coaxed, 'a hot bath for me in the Infirmary before vespers.'

*   *   *

When The Abbot's perfectly cooked and served meal had
ended, and the deep-fringed naperies were removed, and the
Prior had sent in the keys with word that all was fast in the
Monastery, and the keys had been duly returned with the
word, 'Make it so till Prime,' the Abbot and his guests went
out to cool themselves in an upper cloister that took them,
by way of the leads, to the South Choir side of the Triforium.
The summer sun was still strong, for it was barely six o'clock,
but the Abbey Church, of course, lay in her wonted darkness. Lights were being lit for choir-practice thirty feet
below.

'Our Cantor gives them no rest,' the Abbot whispered.
'Stand by this pillar and we'll hear what he's driving them at
now.'

'Remember all!' the Cantor's hard voice came up. 'This is
the soul of Bernard * himself, attacking our evil world. Take it
quicker than yesterday, and throw all your words clean-bitten
from you. In the loft there! Begin!'

The organ broke out for an instant, alone and raging. Then
the voices crashed together into that first fierce line of the '*De
Contemptu Mundi.*' *

'*Hora novissima—tempora pessima*'—a dead pause till the
assenting *sunt* broke, like a sob, out of the darkness, and one
boy's voice, clearer than silver trumpets, returned the long-
drawn *vigilemus*.

'*Ecce minaciter, imminet Arbiter*' (organ and voices were
leashed together in terror and warning, breaking away liquidly
to the '*ille supremus*'). Then the tone-colours shifted for the
prelude to—'*Imminet, imminet, ut mala terminet*——'

'Stop! Again!' cried the Cantor; and gave his reasons a little
more roundly than was natural at choir-practice.

'Ah! Pity o' man's vanity! He's guessed we are here. Come
away!' said the Abbot. Anne of Norton, in her carried chair,
had been listening too, further along the dark Triforium, with
Roger of Salerno. John heard her sob. On the way back, he
asked Thomas how her health stood. Before Thomas could
reply the sharp-featured Italian doctor pushed between them.
'Following on our talk together, I judged it best to tell her,' said
he to Thomas.

'What?' John asked simply enough.

'What she knew already.' Roger of Salerno launched into a Greek quotation to the effect that every woman knows all about everything.

'I have no Greek,' said John stiffly. Roger of Salerno had been giving them a good deal of it, at dinner.

'Then I'll come to you in Latin. Ovid hath it neatly. *"Utque malum late solet immedicabile cancer——"* * but doubtless you know the rest, worthy Sir.'

'Alas! My school-Latin's but what I've gathered by the way from fools professing to heal sick women. *"Hocus-pocus——"* but doubtless you know the rest, worthy Sir.'

Roger of Salerno was quite quiet till they regained the dining-room, where the fire had been comforted and the dates, raisins, ginger, figs, and cinnamon-scented sweetmeats set out, with the choicer wines, on the after-table. The Abbot seated himself, drew off his ring, dropped it, that all might hear the tinkle, into an empty silver cup, stretched his feet towards the hearth, and looked at the great gilt and carved rose in the barrel-roof. The silence that keeps from Compline to Matins had closed on their world. The bull-necked Friar watched a ray of sunlight split itself into colours on the rim of a crystal salt-cellar; Roger of Salerno had re-opened some discussion with Brother Thomas on a type of spotted fever that was baffling them both in England and abroad; John took note of the keen profile, and—it might serve as a note for the Great Luke—his hand moved to his bosom. The Abbot saw, and nodded permission. John whipped out silver-point and sketch-book.

'Nay—modesty is good enough—but deliver your own opinion,' the Italian was urging the Infirmarian. Out of courtesy to the foreigner nearly all the talk was in table-Latin; more formal and more copious than monk's patter. Thomas began with his meek stammer.

'I confess myself at a loss for the cause of the fever unless—as Varro saith in his *De Re Rustica**—certain small animals which the eye cannot follow enter the body by the nose and mouth, and set up grave diseases. On the other hand, this is not in Scripture.'

Roger of Salerno hunched head and shoulders like an angry cat. 'Always *that*!' he said, and John snatched down the twist of the thin lips.

'Never at rest, John,' the Abbot smiled at the artist. 'You should break off every two hours for prayers, as we do. St Benedict* was no fool. Two hours is all that a man can carry the edge of his eye or hand.'

'For copyists—yes. Brother Martin is not sure after one hour. But when a man's work takes him, he must go on till it lets him go.'

'Yes, that is the Demon* of Socrates,' the Friar from Oxford rumbled above his cup.

'The doctrine leans toward presumption,' said the Abbot. 'Remember, "Shall mortal man be more just than his Maker?" '

'There is no danger of justice'; the Friar spoke bitterly. 'But at least Man might be suffered to go forward in his Art or his thought. Yet if Mother Church sees or hears him move anyward, what says she? "No!" Always "No." '

'But if the little animals of Varro be invisible'—this was Roger of Salerno to Thomas—'how are we any nearer to a cure?'

'By experiment'—the Friar wheeled round on them suddenly. 'By reason and experiment. The one is useless without the other. But Mother Church——'

'Ay!' Roger de Salerno dashed at the fresh bait like a pike. 'Listen, Sirs. Her bishops—our Princes—strew our roads in Italy with carcasses that they make for their pleasure or wrath. Beautiful corpses! Yet if I—if we doctors—so much as raise the skin of one of them to look at God's fabric beneath, what says Mother Church? "Sacrilege! Stick to your pigs and dogs, or you burn!" '

'And not Mother Church only!' the Friar chimed in. '*Every* way we are barred—barred by the words of some man, dead a thousand years, which are held final. Who is any son of Adam that his one say-so should close a door towards truth? I would not except even Peter Peregrinus,* my own great teacher.'

'Nor I Paul of Aegina,'*Roger of Salerno cried. 'Listen, Sirs! Here is a case to the very point. Apuleius* affirmeth, if a man eat fasting of the juice of the cut-leaved buttercup—*sceleratus* we call it, which means "rascally" '—this with a condescending nod towards John—'his soul will leave his body laughing. Now this is the lie more dangerous than truth, since truth of a sort is in it.'

'He's away!' whispered the Abbot despairingly.

'For the juice of that herb, I know by experiment, burns, blisters, and wries the mouth. I know also the rictus, or pseudo-laughter on the face of such as have perished by the strong poisons of herbs allied to this ranunculus. Certainly that spasm resembles laughter. It seems then, in my judgement, that Apuleius, having seen the body of one thus poisoned, went off at score and wrote that the man died laughing.'

'Neither staying to observe, nor to confirm observation by experiment,' added the Friar, frowning.

Stephen the Abbot cocked an eyebrow toward John.

'How think *you*?' said he.

'I'm no doctor,' John returned, 'but I'd say Apuleius in all these years might have been betrayed by his copyists. They take short-cuts to save 'emselves trouble. Put case that Apuleius wrote the soul *seems to* leave the body laughing, after this poison. There's not three copyists in five (*my* judgement) would not leave out the "seems to." For who'd question Apuleius? If it seemed so to him, so it must be. Otherwise any child knows cut-leaved buttercup.'

'Have you knowledge of herbs?' Roger of Salerno asked curtly.

'Only, that when I was a boy in convent, I've made tetters round my mouth and on my neck with buttercup-juice, to save going to prayer o' cold nights.'

'Ah!' said Roger. 'I profess no knowledge of tricks.' He turned aside, stiffly.

'No matter! Now for your own tricks, John,' the tactful Abbot broke in. 'You shall show the doctors your Magdalene and your Gadarene Swine and the devils.'

'Devils? Devils? *I* have produced devils by means of drugs; and have abolished them by the same means. Whether devils be external to mankind or immanent, I have not yet pronounced.' Roger of Salerno was still angry.

'Ye dare not,' snapped the Friar from Oxford. 'Mother Church makes Her own devils.'

'Not wholly! Our John has come back from Spain with brand-new ones.' Abbot Stephen took the vellum handed to him, and laid it tenderly on the table. They gathered to look. The Magdalene was drawn in palest, almost transparent, grisaille, against a raging, swaying background of woman-faced devils, each broke to and by her special sin, and each, one could see, frenziedly straining against the Power that compelled her.

'I've never seen the like of this grey shadow-work,' said the Abbot. 'How came you by it?'

'*Non nobis!** It came to me,' said John, not knowing he was a generation or so ahead of his time in the use of that medium.

'Why is she so pale?' the Friar demanded.

'Evil has all come out of her—she'd take any colour now.'

'Ay, like light through glass. *I* see.'

Roger of Salerno was looking in silence—his nose nearer and nearer the page. 'It is so,' he pronounced finally. 'Thus it is in epilepsy—mouth, eyes, and forehead—even to the droop of her wrist there. Every sign of it! She will need restoratives, that woman, and, afterwards, sleep natural. No poppy-juice, or she will vomit on her waking. And thereafter—but I am not in my Schools.' He drew himself up. 'Sir,' said he, 'you should be of Our calling. For, by the Snakes of Aesculapius,* you *see!*'

The two struck hands as equals.

'And how think you of the Seven Devils?' the Abbot went on.

These melted into convoluted flower- or flame-like bodies, ranging in colour from phosphorescent green to the black purple of outworn iniquity, whose hearts could be traced beating through their substance. But, for sign of hope and the sane workings of life, to be regained, the deep border was of conventionalized spring flowers and birds, all crowned by a kingfisher in haste, atilt through a clump of yellow iris.

Roger of Salerno identified the herbs and spoke largely of their virtues.

'And now, the Gadarene Swine,' said Stephen. John laid the picture on the table.

Here were devils dishoused, in dread of being abolished to the Void, huddling and hurtling together to force lodgment by every opening into the brute bodies offered. Some of the swine fought the invasion, foaming and jerking; some were surrendering to it, sleepily, as to a luxurious back-scratching; others, wholly possessed, whirled off in bucking droves for the lake beneath. In one corner the freed man stretched out his limbs all restored to his control and Our Lord, seated, looked at him as questioning what he would make of his deliverance.

'Devils indeed!' was the Friar's comment. 'But wholly a new sort.'

Some devils were mere lumps, with lobes and protuberances—a hint of a fiend's face peering through jelly-like walls. And there was a family of impatient, globular devillings who had burst open the belly of their smirking parent, and were revolving desperately toward their prey. Others patterned themselves into rods, chains, and ladders, single or conjoined, round the throat and jaws of a shrieking sow, from whose ear emerged the lashing, glassy tail of a devil that had made good his refuge. And there were granulated and conglomerate devils, mixed up with the foam and slaver where the attack was fiercest. Thence the eye carried on to the insanely active backs of the downward-racing swine, the swineherd's aghast face, and his dog's terror.

Said Roger of Salerno, 'I pronounce that these were begotten of drugs. They stand outside the rational mind.'

'Not these,' said Thomas the Infirmarian, who as a servant of the Monastery should have asked his Abbot's leave to speak. 'Not *these*—look!—in the bordure.'

The border to the picture was a diaper of irregular but balanced compartments or cellules, where sat, swam, or weltered, devils in blank, so to say—things as yet uninspired by Evil—indifferent, but lawlessly outside imagination. Their shapes resembled, again, ladders, chains, scourges, diamonds, aborted buds, or gravid phosphorescent globes—some well-nigh star-like.

Roger of Salerno compared them to the obsessions of a Churchman's mind.

'Malignant?' the Friar from Oxford questioned.

' "Count everything unknown for horrible," ' * Roger quoted with scorn.

'Not I. But they are marvellous—marvellous. I think——'

The Friar drew back. Thomas edged in to see better, and half opened his mouth.

'Speak,' said Stephen, who had been watching him. 'We are all in a sort doctors here.'

'I would say then'—Thomas rushed at it as one putting out his life's belief at the stake—'that these lower shapes in the bordure may not be so much hellish and malignant as models and patterns upon which John has tricked out and embellished his proper devils among the swine above there!'

'And that would signify?' said Roger of Salerno sharply.

'In my poor judgement, that he may have seen such shapes—without help of drugs.'

'Now who—*who*,' said John of Burgos, after a round and unregarded oath, 'has made thee so wise of a sudden, my Doubter?'

'I wise? God forbid! Only John, remember—one winter six years ago—the snow-Xakes melting on your sleeve at the cookhouse-door. You showed me them through a little crystal, that made small things larger.'

'Yes. The Moors call such a glass the Eye of Allah,' John confirmed.

'You showed me them melting—six-sided. You called them, then, your patterns.'

'True. Snow-flakes melt six-sided. I have used them for diaper-work often.'

'Melting snow-flakes as seen through a glass? By art optical?' the Friar asked.

'Art optical? *I* have never heard!' Roger of Salerno cried.

'John,' said the Abbot of St Illod's commandingly, 'was it—is it so?'

'In some sort,' John replied, 'Thomas has the right of it. Those shapes in the bordure were my workshop-patterns for the devils above. In *my* craft, Salerno, we dare not drug. It kills hand and eye. My shapes are to be seen honestly, in nature.'

The Abbot drew a bowl of rose-water towards him. 'When I was prisoner with—with the Saracens after Mansura,' he began, turning up the fold of his long sleeve, 'there were certain magicians—physicians—who could show—' he dipped his third finger delicately in the water—'all the firmament of Hell, as it were, in—' he shook off one drop from his polished nail on to the polished table—'even such a supernaculum * as this.'

'But it must be foul water—not clean,' said John.

'Show us then—all—all,' said Stephen. 'I would make sure—once more.' The Abbot's voice was official.

John drew from his bosom a stamped leather box, some six or eight inches long, wherein, bedded on faded velvet, lay what looked like silver-bound compasses* of old box-wood, with a screw at the head which opened or closed the legs to minute fractions. The legs terminated, not in points, but spoon-shapedly, one spatula pierced with a metal-lined hole less than a quarter of an inch across, the other with a half-inch hole. Into this latter John, after carefully wiping with a silk rag, slipped a metal cylinder that carried glass or crystal, it seemed, at each end.

'Ah! Art optic!' said the Friar. 'But what is that beneath it?'

It was a small swivelling sheet of polished silver no bigger than a florin, which caught the light and concentrated it on the lesser hole. John adjusted it without the Friar's proffered help.

'And now to find a drop of water,' said he, picking up a small brush.

'Come to my upper cloister. The sun is on the leads still,' said the Abbot, rising.

They followed him there. Half-way along, a drip from a gutter had made a greenish puddle in a worn stone. Very carefully, John dropped a drop of it into the smaller hole of the compass-leg, and, steadying the apparatus on a coping, worked the screw in the compass-joint, screwed the cylinder, and swung the swivel of the mirror till he was satisfied.

'Good!' He peered through the thing. 'My Shapes are all here. Now look, Father! If they do not meet your eye at first, turn this nicked edge here, left- or right-handed.'

'I have not forgotten,' said the Abbot, taking his place. 'Yes! They are here—as they were in my time—my time past. There is no end to them, I was told. . . . There *is* no end!'

'The light will go. Oh, let me look! Suffer me to see, also!' the Friar pleaded, almost shouldering Stephen from the eye-piece. The Abbot gave way. His eyes were on time past. But the Friar, instead of looking, turned the apparatus in his capable hands.

'Nay, nay,' John interrupted, for the man was already fiddling at the screws. 'Let the Doctor see.'

Roger of Salerno looked, minute after minute. John saw his blue-veined cheek-bones turn white. He stepped back at last, as though stricken.

'It is a new world—a new world and—Oh, God Unjust!—I am old!'

'And now Thomas,' Stephen ordered.

John manipulated the tube for the Infirmarian, whose hands shook, and he too looked long. 'It is Life,' he said presently in a breaking voice. 'No Hell! Life created and rejoicing—the work of the Creator. They live, even as I have dreamed. Then it was no sin for me to dream. No sin—O God—no sin!'

He flung himself on his knees and began hysterically the *Benedicite omnia Opera.* *

'And now I will see how it is actuated,' said the Friar from Oxford, thrusting forward again.

'Bring it within. The place is all eyes and ears,' said Stephen.

They walked quietly back along the leads, three English counties laid out in evening sunshine around them; church upon church, monastery upon monastery, cell after cell, and the bulk of a vast cathedral moored on the edge of the banked shoals of sunset.

When they were at the after-table once more they sat down, all except the Friar who went to the window and huddled bat-like over the thing. 'I see! I see!' he was repeating to himself.

'He'll not hurt it,' said John. But the Abbot, staring in front of him, like Roger of Salerno, did not hear. The Infirmarian's head was on the table between his shaking arms.

John reached for a cup of wine.

'It was shown to me,' the Abbot was speaking to himself, 'in Cairo, that man stands ever between two Infinities—of greatness and littleness. Therefore, there is no end—either to life—or——'

'And *I* stand on the edge of the grave,' snarled Roger of Salerno. 'Who pities *me*?'

'Hush!' said Thomas the Infirmarian. 'The little creatures shall be sanctified—sanctified to the service of His sick.'

'What need?' John of Burgos wiped his lips. 'It shows no more than the shapes of things. It gives good pictures. I had it at Granada. It was brought from the East, they told me.'

Roger of Salerno laughed with an old man's malice. 'What of Mother Church? Most Holy Mother Church? If it comes to Her ears that we have spied into Her Hell without Her leave, where do we stand?'

'At the stake,' said the Abbot of St Illod's, and, raising his voice a trifle, 'You hear that? Roger Bacon, heard you that?'

The Friar turned from the window, clutching the compasses tighter.

'No, no!' he appealed. 'Not with Falcodi—not with our English-hearted Foulkes made Pope.* He's wise—he's learned. He reads what I have put forth. Foulkes would never suffer it.'

' "Holy Pope is one thing, Holy Church another," ' Roger quoted.

'But I—*I* can bear witness it is no Art Magic,' the Friar went on. 'Nothing is it, except Art optical—wisdom after trial and experiment, mark you. I can prove it, and—my name weighs with men who dare think.'

'Find them!' croaked Roger of Salerno. 'Five or six in all the world. That makes less than fifty pounds by weight of ashes at the stake. I have watched such men—reduced.'

'I will not give this up!' The Friar's voice cracked in passion and despair. 'It would be to sin against the Light.'

'No, no! Let us—let us sanctify the little animals of Varro,' said Thomas.

Stephen leaned forward, fished his ring out of the cup, and slipped it on his finger. 'My sons,' said he, 'we have seen what we have seen.'

'That it is no magic but simple Art,' the Friar persisted.

''Avails nothing. In the eyes of Mother Church we have seen more than is permitted to man.'

'But it was Life—created and rejoicing,' said Thomas.

'To look into Hell as we shall be judged—as we shall be proved—to have looked, is for priests only.'

'Or green-sick* virgins on the road to sainthood who, for cause any mid-wife could give you——'

The Abbot's half-lifted hand checked Roger of Salerno's outpouring.

'Nor may even priests see more in Hell than Church knows to be there. John, there is respect due to Church as well as to Devils.'

'My trade's the outside of things,' said John quietly. 'I have my patterns.'

'But you may need to look again for more,' the Friar said.

'In my craft, a thing done is done with. We go on to new shapes after that.'

'And if we trespass beyond bounds, even in thought, we lie open to the judgement of the Church,' the Abbot continued.

'But thou knowest—*knowest!*' Roger of Salerno had returned to the attack. 'Here's all the world in darkness concerning the causes of things—from the fever across the lane to thy Lady's—thine own Lady's—eating malady. Think!'

'I have thought upon it, Salerno! I have thought indeed.'

Thomas the Infirmarian lifted his head again; and this time he did not stammer at all. 'As in the water, so in the blood must they rage and war with each other! I have dreamed these ten years—I thought it was a sin—but my dreams and Varro's are true! Think on it again! Here's the Light under our very hand!'

'Quench it! You'd no more stand to roasting than—any other. I'll give you the case as Church—as I myself—would frame it. Our John here returns from the Moors, and shows us a hell of devils contending in the compass of one drop of water. Magic past clearance! You can hear the faggots crackle.'

'But thou knowest! Thou hast seen it all before! For man's poor sake! For old friendship's sake—Stephen!' The Friar was trying to stuff the compasses into his bosom as he appealed.

'What Stephen de Sautré knows, you his friends know also. I would have you, now, obey the Abbot of St Illod's. Give to me!' He held out his ringed hand.

'May I—may John here—not even make a drawing of one—one screw?' said the broken Friar, in spite of himself.

'Nowise!' Stephen took it over. 'Your dagger, John. Sheathed will serve.'

He unscrewed the metal cylinder, laid it on the table, and with the dagger's hilt smashed some crystal to sparkling dust which he swept into a scooped hand and cast behind the hearth.

'It would seem,' said he, 'the choice lies between two sins. To deny the world a Light which is under our hand, or to enlighten the world before her time. What you have seen, I saw long since among the physicians at Cairo. And I know what doctrine they drew from it. Hast *thou* dreamed, Thomas? I also —with fuller knowledge. But this birth, my sons, is untimely. It will be but the mother of more death, more torture, more division, and greater darkness in this dark age.* Therefore I, who know both my world and the Church, take this Choice on my conscience. Go! It is finished.'

He thrust the wooden part of the compasses deep among the beech logs till all was burned.

THE LAST ODE*

(*Nov.* 27, BC 8)

HORACE, Ode 31, Bk. V.

As watchers couched beneath a Bantine oak,
    Hearing the dawn-wind stir,
Know that the present strength of night is broke
    Though no dawn threaten her
Till dawn's appointed hour—so Virgil died,
Aware of change at hand, and prophesied*

Change upon all the Eternal Gods had made
    And on the Gods alike—
Fated as dawn but, as the dawn, delayed
    Till the just hour should strike—

A Star new-risen above the living and dead;
    And the lost shades that were our loves restored
As lovers, and for ever. So he said;
    Having received the word . . .

Maecenas waits me on the Esquiline:
    Thither tonight go I. . . .
And shall this dawn restore us, Virgil mine,
    To dawn? Beneath what sky?

DAYSPRING MISHANDLED *

C'est moi, c'est moi, c'est moi!
Je suis la Mandragore!
La fille des beaux jours qui s'éveille à l'aurore—
Et qui chante pour toi!

C. Nodier. *

IN the days beyond compare and before the Judgements, a genius called Graydon foresaw that the advance of education and the standard of living would submerge all mind-marks in one mudrush of standardized reading-matter, and so created the Fictional Supply Syndicate to meet the demand.

Since a few days' work for him brought them more money than a week's elsewhere, he drew many young men—some now eminent—into his employ. He bade them keep their eyes on the Sixpenny Dream Book, the Army and Navy Stores Catalogue (this for backgrounds and furniture as they changed), and *The Hearthstone Friend*, a weekly publication which specialized unrivalledly in the domestic emotions. Yet, even so, youth would not be denied, and some of the collaborated love-talk in 'Passion Hath Peril', and 'Ena's Lost Lovers', and the account of the murder of the Earl in 'The Wickwire Tragedies'—to name but a few masterpieces now never mentioned for fear of blackmail—was as good as anything to which their authors signed their real names in more distinguished years.

Among the young ravens driven to roost awhile on Graydon's ark was James Andrew Manallace—a darkish, slow northerner of the type that does not ignite, but must be detonated. Given written or verbal outlines of a plot, he was useless; but, with a half-dozen pictures round which to write his tale, he could astonish.

And he adored that woman who afterwards became the mother of Vidal Benzaquen, * and who suffered and died because she loved one unworthy. There was, also, among the company a mannered, bellied person called Alured Castorley,

who talked and wrote about 'Bohemia', but was always afraid
of being 'compromised' by the weekly suppers at Neminaka's
Café in Hestern Square, where the Syndicate work was appor-
tioned, and where everyone looked out for himself. He, too,
for a time, had loved Vidal's mother, in his own way.

Now, one Saturday at Neminaka's, Graydon, who had given
Manallace a sheaf of prints—torn from an extinct children's
book called *Philippa's Queen*—on which to improvise, asked for
results. Manallace went down into his ulster-pocket, hesitated
a moment, and said the stuff had turned into poetry on his
hands.

'Bosh!'

'That's what it isn't,' the boy retorted. 'It's rather good.'

'Then it's no use to us.' Graydon laughed. 'Have you
brought back the cuts?'

Manallace handed them over. There was a castle in the
series; a knight or so in armour; an old lady in a horned
head-dress; a young ditto; a very obvious Hebrew; a clerk, with
pen and inkhorn, checking wine-barrels on a wharf; and a
Crusader. On the back of one of the prints was a note, 'If he
doesn't want to go, why can't he be captured and held to
ransom?' Graydon asked what it all meant.

'I don't know yet. A comic opera, perhaps,' said Manallace.

Graydon, who seldom wasted time, passed the cuts on to
someone else, and advanced Manallace a couple of sovereigns
to carry on with, as usual; at which Castorley was angry and
would have said something unpleasant but was suppressed.
Half-way through supper, Castorley told the company that a
relative had died and left him an independence; and that he
now withdrew from 'hackwork' to follow 'Literature'. Generally, the Syndicate rejoiced in a comrade's good fortune, but
Castorley had gifts of waking dislike. So the news was received
with a vote of thanks, and he went out before the end, and, it
was said, proposed to 'Dal Benzaquen's mother, who refused
him. He did not come back. Manallace, who had arrived a little
exalted, got so drunk before midnight that a man had to stay
and see him home. But liquor never touched him above the
belt, and when he had slept awhile, he recited to the gas-
chandelier the poetry he had made out of the pictures; said
that, on second thoughts, he would convert it into comic opera;

deplored the Upas-tree influence of Gilbert and Sullivan; sang somewhat to illustrate his point; and—after words, by the way, with a negress in yellow satin—was steered to his rooms.

In the course of a few years, Graydon's foresight and genius were rewarded. The public began to read and reason upon higher planes, and the Syndicate grew rich. Later still, people demanded of their printed matter what they expected in their clothing and furniture. So, precisely as the three guinea hand-bag is followed in three weeks by its thirteen and sevenpence ha'penny, indistinguishable sister, they enjoyed perfect synthetic substitutes for Plot, Sentiment, and Emotion. Graydon died before the Cinema-caption school came in,* but he left his widow twenty-seven thousand pounds.

Manallace made a reputation, and, more important, money for Vidal's mother when her husband ran away and the first symptoms of her paralysis showed. His line was the jocundly sentimental Wardour Street brand of adventure, told in a style that exactly met, but never exceeded, every expectation.

As he once said when urged to 'write a real book': 'I've got my label, and I'm not going to chew it off. If you save people thinking, you can do anything with 'em.' His output apart, he was genuinely a man of letters. He rented a small cottage in the country and economized on everything, except the care and charges of Vidal's mother.

Castorley flew higher. When his legacy freed him from 'hackwork', he became first a critic—in which calling he loyally scalped all his old associates as they came up—and then looked for some speciality.* Having found it (Chaucer was the prey), he consolidated his position before he occupied it, by his careful speech, his cultivated bearing, and the whispered words of his friends whom he, too, had saved the trouble of thinking. It followed that, when he published his first serious articles on Chaucer, all the world which is interested in Chaucer said: 'This is an authority.' But he was no impostor. He learned and knew his poet and his age; and in a month-long dogfight in an austere literary weekly, met and mangled a recognized Chaucer expert of the day. He also, 'for old sake's sake', as he wrote to a friend, went out of his way to review one of Manallace's books with an intimacy of unclean deduction (this was before the days of Freud) which long stood as a record. Some member of the extinct Syndicate took occasion to ask him if he would—for old sake's sake—help Vidal's mother to a new treatment. He answered that he had 'known the lady very slightly and the calls on his purse were so heavy that,' etc. The writer showed the letter to Manallace, who said he was glad Castorley hadn't interfered. Vidal's mother was then wholly paralysed. Only her eyes could move, and those always looked for the husband who had left her. She died thus in Manallace's arms in April of the first year of the War.

During the War he and Castorley worked as some sort of departmental dishwashers in the Office of Co-ordinated Super-visals. Here Manallace came to know Castorley again. Castor-ley, having a sweet tooth, cadged lumps of sugar for his tea from a typist, and when she took to giving them to a younger man, arranged that she should be reported for smoking in unauthorized apartments. Manallace possessed himself of every detail of the affair, as compensation for the review of his book. Then there came a night when, waiting for a big air-raid, the two men had talked humanly, and Manallace spoke of Vidal's mother. Castorley said something* in reply, and from that hour—as was learned several years later—Manallace's real life-work and interests began.

The War over, Castorley set about to make himself Supreme Pontiff on Chaucer by methods not far removed from the employment of poison-gas. The English Pope was silent, through private griefs, and influenza had carried off the learned Hun who claimed continental allegiance. Thus Castorley crowed unchallenged from Uppsala to Seville, while Manallace went back to his cottage with the photo of Vidal's mother over the mantelpiece. She seemed to have emptied out his life, and left him only fleeting interests in trifles. His private diversions were experiments* of uncertain outcome, which, he said, rested him after a day's gadzooking and vitalstapping. I found him, for instance, one week-end, in his toolshed-scullery, boiling a brew of slimy barks which were, if mixed with oak-galls, vitriol, and wine, to become an ink-powder. We boiled it till the Monday, and it turned into an adhesive stronger than birdlime, and entangled us both.

At other times, he would carry me off, once in a few weeks, to sit at Castorley's feet, and hear him talk about Chaucer. Castorley's voice, bad enough in youth, when it could be shouted down, had, with culture and tact, grown almost insupportable. His mannerisms, too, had multiplied and set. He minced and mouthed, postured and chewed his words throughout those terrible evenings; and poisoned not only Chaucer, but every shred of English literature which he used to embellish him. He was shameless, too, as regarded self-advertisement and 'recognition'—weaving elaborate intrigues; forming petty friendships and confederacies, to be dissolved next week in favour of more promising alliances; fawning, snubbing, lecturing, organizing, and lying as unrestingly as a politician, in chase of the Knighthood due not to him (he always called on his Maker to forbid such a thought) but as tribute to Chaucer. Yet, sometimes, he could break from his obsession and prove how a man's work will try to save the soul of him. He would tell us charmingly of copyists of the fifteenth century in England and the Low Countries, who had multiplied the Chaucer MSS, of which there remained—he gave us the exact number—and how each scribe could by him (and, he implied, by him alone) be distinguished from every other by some peculiarity of letter-formation, spacing or like trick of pen-work; and how he could fix the dates of their work within five years. Sometimes he would give us an hour of really interesting stuff and then return to his overdue 'recognition'. The changes sickened me, but Manallace defended him, as a master in his own line who had revealed Chaucer to at least one grateful soul.

This, as far as I remembered, was the autumn when Manallace holidayed in the Shetlands or the Faroes, and came back with a stone 'quern'—a hand corn-grinder. He said it interested him from the ethnological standpoint. His whim lasted till next harvest, and was followed by a religious spasm which, naturally, translated itself into literature. He showed me a battered and mutilated Vulgate of 1485, patched up the back with bits of legal parchments, which he had bought for thirty-five shillings. Some monk's attempt to rubricate chapter-initials had caught, it seemed, his forlorn fancy, and he dabbled in shells of gold and silver paint for weeks.

That also faded out, and he went to the Continent to get local colour for a love-story, about Alva* and the Dutch, and the next year I saw practically nothing of him. This released me from seeing much of Castorley, but, at intervals, I would go there to dine with him, when his wife—an unappetizing, ash-coloured woman*—made no secret that his friends wearied her almost as much as he did. But at a later meeting, not long after Manallace had finished his Low Countries' novel, I found Castorley charged to bursting-point with triumph and high information hardly withheld. He confided to me that a time was at hand when great matters would be made plain, and 'recognition' would be inevitable. I assumed, naturally, that there was fresh scandal or heresy afoot in Chaucer circles, and kept my curiosity within bounds.

In time, New York cabled that a fragment of a hitherto unknown Canterbury Tale lay safe in the steel-walled vaults of the seven-million-dollar Sunnapia Collection. It was news on an international scale—the New World exultant—the Old deploring the 'burden of British taxation which drove such treasures, etc.', and the lighter-minded journals disporting themselves according to their publics; for 'our Dan',* as one earnest Sunday editor observed, 'lies closer to the national heart than we wot of.' Common decency made me call on Castorley, who, to my surprise, had not yet descended into the arena. I found him, made young again by joy, deep in just-passed proofs.

Yes, he said, it was all true. He had, of course, been in it from the first. There had been found one hundred and seven new lines of Chaucer tacked on to an abridged end of *The Persone's Tale*, the whole the work of Abraham Mentzius, better known as Mentzel of Antwerp (1388–1438/9)—I might remember he had talked about him—whose distinguishing peculiarities were a certain Byzantine formation of his *g*'s, the use of a 'sickle-slanted' reed-pen, which cut into the vellum at certain letters; and, above all, a tendency to spell English words on Dutch lines, whereof the manuscript carried one convincing proof. For instance (he wrote it out for me), a girl praying against an undesired marriage, says:—

'Ah Jesu-Moder, pitie my oe peyne.
Daiespringe mishandeelt cometh nat agayne.'

Would I, please, note the spelling of 'mishandeelt'? Stark
Dutch and Mentzel's besetting sin! But in *his* position one took
nothing for granted. The page had been part of the stiffening
of the side of an old Bible, bought in a parcel by Dredd, the
big dealer, because it had some rubricated chapter-initials, and
by Dredd shipped, with a consignment of similar odds and
ends, to the Sunnapia Collection, where they were making a
glass-cased exhibit of the whole history of illumination and did
not care how many books they gutted for that purpose. There,
someone who noticed a crack in the back of the volume had
unearthed it. He went on: 'They didn't know what to make of
the thing at first. But they knew about *me*! They kept quiet till
I'd been consulted. You might have noticed I was out of
England for three months.

'I was over there, of course. It was what is called a "spoil"—a
page Mentzel had spoiled with his Dutch spelling—I expect he
had had the English dictated to him—then had evidently used
the vellum for trying out his reeds; and then, I suppose, had
put it away. The "spoil" had been doubled, pasted together,
and slipped in as stiffening to the old book-cover. I had it
steamed open, and analysed the wash. It gave the flour-grains
in the paste—coarse, because of the old millstone—and there
were traces of the grit itself. What? Oh, possibly a handmill of
Mentzel's own time. He may have doubled the spoilt page and
used it for part of a pad to steady wood-cuts on. It may have
knocked about his workshop for years. That, indeed, is practically certain because a beginner from the Low Countries has
tried his reed on a few lines of some monkish hymn—not a bad
lilt tho'—which must have been common form. Oh yes, the
page may have been used in other books before it was used for
the Vulgate. That doesn't matter, but *this* does. Listen! I took
a wash, for analysis, from a blot in one corner—that would be
after Mentzel had given up trying to make a possible page of
it, and had grown careless—and I got the actual *ink* of the
period! It's a practically eternal stuff compounded on—I've
forgotten his name for the minute—the scribe at Bury St
Edmunds, of course—hawthorn bark and wine. Anyhow, on

his formula. *That* wouldn't interest you either, but, taken with all the other testimony, it clinches the thing. (You'll see it all in my Statement to the Press on Monday.) Overwhelming, isn't it?'

'Overwhelming,' I said, with sincerity. 'Tell me what the tale was about, though. That's more in my line.'

'I know it; but *I* have to be equipped on all sides. The verses are relatively easy for one to pronounce on. The freshness, the fun, the humanity, the fragrance of it all, cries—no, shouts—itself as Dan's work. Why "Daiespringe mishandled" alone stamps it from Dan's mint. Plangent as doom, my dear boy—plangent as doom! It's all in my Statement. Well, substantially, the fragment deals with a girl whose parents wish her to marry an elderly suitor. The mother isn't so keen on it, but the father, an old Knight, is. The girl, of course, is in love with a younger and a poorer man. Common form? Granted. Then the father, who doesn't in the least want to, is ordered off to a Crusade and, by way of passing on the kick, as we used to say during the War, orders the girl to be kept in duresse* till his return or her consent to the old suitor. Common form, again? Quite so. That's too much for her mother. She reminds the old Knight of his age and infirmities, and the discomforts of Crusading. Are you sure I'm not boring you?'

'Not at all,' I said, though time had begun to whirl backward through my brain to a red-velvet, pomatum-scented side-room at Neminaka's and Manallace's set face intoning to the gas.

'You'll read it all in my Statement next week. The sum is that the old lady tells him of a certain Knight-adventurer on the French coast, who, for a consideration, waylays Knights who don't relish crusading and holds them to impossible ransoms till the trooping-season is over, or they are returned sick. He keeps a ship in the Channel to pick 'em up and transfers his birds to his castle ashore, where he has a reputation for doing 'em well. As the old lady points out:

> 'And if perchance thou fall into his honde
> By God how canstow ride to Holilonde?'

'You see? Modern in essence as Gilbert and Sullivan, but handled as only Dan could! And she reminds him that "Honour and olde bones" parted company long ago. He makes one splendid appeal for the spirit of chivalry:

> Lat all men change as Fortune may send,
> But Knighthood beareth service to the end,

and *then*, of course, he gives in:

> For what his woman willeth to be don
> Her manne must or wauken Hell anon.

'Then she hints that the daughter's young lover, who is in the Bordeaux wine-trade, could open negotiations for a kidnapping without compromising him. And *then* that careless brute Mentzel spoils his page and chucks it! But there's enough to show what's going to happen. You'll see it all in my Statement. Was there ever anything in literary finds to hold a candle to it? . . . And they give grocers Knighthoods for selling cheese!'

I went away before he could get into his stride on that course. I wanted to think, and to see Manallace. But I waited till Castorley's Statement came out. He had left himself no loophole. And when, a little later, his (nominally the Sunnapia people's) 'scientific' account of their analyses and tests appeared, criticism ceased, and some journals began to demand 'public recognition'. Manallace wrote me on this subject, and I went down to his cottage, where he at once asked me to sign a Memorial on Castorley's behalf. With luck, he said, we might get him a KBE * in the next Honours List. Had I read the Statement?

'I have,' I replied. 'But I want to ask you something first. Do you remember the night you got drunk at Neminaka's, and I stayed behind to look after you?'

'Oh, *that* time,' said he, pondering. 'Wait a minute! I remember Graydon advancing me two quid. He was a generous paymaster. And I remember—now, who the devil rolled me under the sofa—and what for?'

'We all did,' I replied. 'You wanted to read us what you'd written to those Chaucer cuts.'

'I don't remember that. No! I don't remember anything after the sofa-episode. . . . *You* always said that you took me home—didn't you?'

'I did, and you told Kentucky Kate outside the old Empire* that you had been faithful, Cynara, in your fashion.'*

'Did I?' said he. 'My God! Well, I suppose I have.' He stared into the fire. 'What else?'

'Before we left Neminaka's you recited me what you had made out of the cuts—the whole tale! So—you see?'

'Ye-es.' He nodded. 'What are you going to do about it?'

'What are *you*?'

'I'm going to help him get his Knighthood—first.'

'Why?'

'I'll tell you what he said about 'Dal's mother—the night there was that air-raid on the offices.' He told it.

'That's why,' he said. 'Am I justified?'

He seemed to me entirely so.

'But after he gets his Knighthood?' I went on.

'That depends. There are several things I can think of. It interests me.'

'Good Heavens! I've always imagined you a man without interests.'

'So I was. I owe my interests to Castorley. He gave me every one of 'em except the tale itself.'

'How did *that* come?'

'Something in those ghastly cuts touched off something in me—a sort of possession, I suppose. I was in love too. No wonder I got drunk that night. I'd *been* Chaucer for a week! Then I thought the notion might make a comic opera. But Gilbert and Sullivan were too strong.'

'So I remember you told me at the time.'

'I kept it by me, and it made me interested in Chaucer—philologically and so on. I worked on it on those lines for years. There wasn't a flaw in the wording even in '14. I hardly had to touch it after that.'

'Did you ever tell it to anyone except me?'

'No, only 'Dal's mother—when she could listen to anything—to put her to sleep. But when Castorley said—what he did about her, I thought I might use it. 'Twasn't difficult. *He* taught me. D'you remember my birdlime experiments, and the stuff on our hands? I'd been trying to get that ink for more than a year. Castorley told me where I'd find the formula. And your falling over the quern, too?'

'That accounted for the stone-dust under the microscope?'

'Yes. I grew the wheat in the garden here, and ground it myself. Castorley gave me Mentzel complete. He put me on to an MS in the British Museum which he said was the finest sample of his work. I copied his "Byzantine *g* 's" for months.'

'And what's a "sickle-slanted" pen?' I asked.

'You nick one edge of your reed till it drags and scratches on the curves of the letters. Castorley told me about Mentzel's spacing and margining. I only had to get the hang of his script.'

'How long did that take you?'

'On and off—some years. I was too ambitious at first—I wanted to give the whole poem. That would have been risky. Then Castorley told me about spoiled pages and I took the hint. I spelt "Dayspring mishandeelt" Mentzel's way—to make sure of him. It's not a bad couplet in itself. Did you see how he admires the "plangency" of it?'

'Never mind him. Go on!' I said.

He did. Castorley had been his unfailing guide throughout, specifying in minutest detail every trap to be set later for his own feet. The actual vellum was an Antwerp find, and its introduction into the cover of the Vulgate was begun after a long course of amateur bookbinding. At last, he bedded it under pieces of an old deed, and a printed page (1686) of Horace's *Odes*, legitimately used for repairs by different owners in the seventeenth and eighteenth centuries; and at the last moment, to meet Castorley's theory that spoiled pages were used in workshops by beginners, he had written a few Latin words in fifteenth century script—the Statement gave the exact date—across an open part of the fragment. The thing ran: '*Illa alma Mater ecca, secum afferens me acceptum. Nicolaus Atrib.*'* The disposal of the thing was easiest of all. He had merely hung about Dredd's dark bookshop of fifteen rooms, where he was well known, occasionally buying but generally browsing, till, one day, Dredd Senior showed him a case of cheap black-letter stuff, English and Continental—being packed for the Sunnapia people—into which Manallace tucked his contribution, taking care to wrench the back enough to give a lead to an earnest seeker.

'And then?' I demanded.

'After six months or so Castorley sent for me. Sunnapia had found it, and as Dredd had missed it, and there was no money-motive sticking out, they were half convinced it was genuine from the start. But they invited him over. He conferred with their experts, and suggested the scientific tests. *I* put that into his head, before he sailed. That's all. And now, will you sign our Memorial?'

I signed. Before we had finished hawking it round there was a host of influential names to help us, as well as the impetus of all the literary discussion which arose over every detail of the glorious trove. The upshot was a KBE* for Castorley in the next Honours List; and Lady Castorley, her cards duly printed, called on friends that same afternoon.

Manallace invited me to come with him, a day or so later, to convey our pleasure and satisfaction to them both. We were rewarded by the sight of a man relaxed and ungirt—not to say wallowing naked—on the crest of Success. He assured us that 'The Title' should not make any difference to our future relations, seeing it was in no sense personal, but, as he had often said, a tribute to Chaucer; 'and, after all,' he pointed out, with a glance at the mirror over the mantelpiece, 'Chaucer was the prototype of the "veray parfit gentil Knight"* of the British Empire so far as that then existed.'

On the way back, Manallace told me he was considering either an unheralded revelation in the baser Press which should bring Castorley's reputation about his own ears some breakfast-time, or a private conversation, when he would make clear to Castorley that he must now back the forgery as long as he lived, under threat of Manallace's betraying it if he flinched.

He favoured the second plan. 'If I pull the string of the shower-bath in the papers,' he said, 'Castorley might go off his veray parfit gentil nut. I want to keep his intellect.'

'What about your own position? The forgery doesn't matter so much. But if you tell this you'll kill him,' I said.

'I intend that. Oh—my position? I've been dead since—
April, Fourteen, it was.* But there's no hurry. What was it *she*
was saying to you just as we left?'

'She told me how much your sympathy and understanding
had meant to him. She said she thought that even Sir Alured
did not realize the full extent of his obligations to you.'

'She's right, but I don't like her putting it that way.'

'It's only common form—as Castorley's always saying.'

'Not with *her*. She can hear a man think.'

'She never struck me in that light.'

'*You* aren't playing against her.'

"Guilty conscience, Manallace?"

'H'm! I wonder. Mine or hers? I *wish* she hadn't said that.
"More even than *he* realizes it." I won't call again for awhile.'

He kept away till we read that Sir Alured, owing to slight
indisposition, had been unable to attend a dinner given in his
honour.

Inquiries brought word that it was but natural reaction, after
strain, which, for the moment, took the form of nervous
dyspepsia, and he would be glad to see Manallace at any time.
Manallace reported him as rather pulled and drawn, but full of
his new life and position, and proud that his efforts should have
martyred him so much. He was going to collect, collate, and
expand all his pronouncements and inferences into one
authoritative volume.

'I must make an effort of my own,' said Manallace. 'I've
collected nearly all his stuff about the Find that has appeared
in the papers, and he's promised me everything that's missing.
I'm going to help him. It will be a new interest.'

'How will you treat it?' I asked.

'I expect I shall quote his deductions on the evidence, and
parallel 'em with my experiments—the ink and the paste and
the rest of it. It ought to be rather interesting.'

'But even then there will only be your word. It's hard to catch
up with an established lie,' I said. 'Especially when you've
started it yourself.'

He laughed. 'I've arranged for that—in case anything
happens to me. Do you remember the "Monkish Hymn"?'

'Oh yes! There's quite a literature about it already.'

'Well, you write those ten words above each other, and read down the first and second letters of 'em; and see what you get.'* My Bank has the formula.'

He wrapped himself lovingly and leisurely round his new task, and Castorley was as good as his word in giving him help. The two practically collaborated, for Manallace suggested that all Castorley's strictly scientific evidence should be in one place, with his deductions and dithyrambs as appendices. He assured him that the public would prefer this arrangement, and, after grave consideration, Castorley agreed.

'That's better,' said Manallace to me. 'Now I sha'n't have so many hiatuses in my extracts. Dots always give the reader the idea you aren't dealing fairly with your man. I shall merely quote him solid, and rip him up, proof for proof, and date for date, in parallel columns. His book's taking more out of him than I like, though. He's been doubled up twice with tummy attacks since I've worked with him. And he's just the sort of flatulent beast who may go down with appendicitis.'

We learned before long that the attacks were due to gall-stones, which would necessitate an operation. Castorley bore the blow very well. He had full confidence in his surgeon, an old friend of theirs; great faith in his own constitution; a strong conviction that nothing would happen to him till the book was finished, and, above all, the Will to Live.

He dwelt on these assets with a voice at times a little out of pitch and eyes brighter than usual beside a slightly-sharpening nose.

I had only met Gleeag, the surgeon, once or twice at Castorley's house, but had always heard him spoken of as a most capable man. He told Castorley that his trouble was the price exacted, in some shape or other, from all who had served their country; and that, measured in units of strain, Castorley had practically been at the front through those three years he had served in the Office of Co-ordinated Supervisals. However, the thing had been taken betimes, and in a few weeks he would worry no more about it.

'But suppose he dies?' I suggested to Manallace.

'He won't. I've been talking to Gleeag. He says he's all right.'

'Wouldn't Gleeag's talk be common form?'

'I *wish* you hadn't said that. But, surely, Gleeag wouldn't have the face to play with me—or her.'

'Why not? I expect it's been done before.'

But Manallace insisted that, in this case, it would be impossible.

The operation was a success and, some weeks later, Castorley began to recast the arrangement and most of the material of his book. 'Let me have my way,' he said, when Manallace protested. 'They are making too much of a baby of me. I really don't need Gleeag looking in every day now.' But Lady Castorley told us that he required careful watching. His heart had felt the strain, and fret or disappointment of any kind must be avoided. 'Even,' she turned to Manallace, 'though you know ever so much better how his book should be arranged than he does himself.'

'But really,' Manallace began. 'I'm very careful not to fuss——'

She shook her finger at him playfully. 'You don't think you do; but, remember, he tells me everything that you tell him, just the same as he told me everything that he used to tell *you*. Oh, I don't mean the things that men talk about. I mean about his Chaucer.'

'I didn't realize that,' said Manallace, weakly.

'I thought you didn't. He never spares me anything; but *I* don't mind,' she replied with a laugh, and went off to Gleeag, who was paying his daily visit. Gleeag said he had no objection to Manallace working with Castorley on the book for a given time—say, twice a week—but supported Lady Castorley's demand that he should not be over-taxed in what she called 'the sacred hours'. The man grew more and more difficult to work with, and the little check he had heretofore set on his self-praise went altogether.

'He says there has never been anything in the History of Letters to compare with it,' Manallace groaned. 'He wants now to inscribe—he never dedicates, you know—inscribe it to me, as his "most valued assistant". The devil of it is that *she* backs him up in getting it out soon. Why? How much do you think she knows?'

'Why should she know anything at all?'

'You heard her say he had told her everything that he had
told me about Chaucer? (I *wish* she hadn't said that!) If she
puts two and two together, she can't help seeing that every one
of his notions and theories has been played up to. But then—
but then . . . Why is she trying to hurry publication? She talks
about me fretting him. *She's* at him, all the time, to be quick.'

Castorley must have over-worked, for, after a couple of
months, he complained of a stitch in his right side, which
Gleeag said was a slight sequel, a little incident of the operation.
It threw him back awhile, but he returned to his work
undefeated.

The book was due in the autumn. Summer was passing, and
his publisher urgent, and—he said to me, when after a longish
interval I called—Manallace had chosen this time, of all, to take
a holiday. He was not pleased with Manallace, once his
indefatigable *aide*, but now dilatory, and full of time-wasting
objections. Lady Castorley had noticed it, too.

Meantime, with Lady Castorley's help, he himself was doing
the best he could to expedite the book; but Manallace had
mislaid (did I think through jealousy?) some essential stuff
which had been dictated to him. And Lady Castorley wrote
Manallace, who had been delayed by a slight motor accident
abroad, that the fret of waiting was prejudicial to her husband's
health. Manallace, on his return from the Continent, showed
me that letter.

'He has fretted a little, I believe,' I said.

Manallace shuddered. 'If I stay abroad, I'm helping to kill
him. If I help him to hurry up the book, I'm expected to kill
him. *She* knows,' he said.

'You're mad. You've got this thing on the brain.'

'I have not! Look here! You remember that Gleeag gave me
from four to six, twice a week, to work with him. She called
them the "sacred hours". You heard her? Well, they *are*! They
are Gleeag's and hers. But she's so infernally plain, and I'm
such a fool, it took me weeks to find it out.'

'That's their affair,' I answered. 'It doesn't prove she knows
anything about the Chaucer.'

'She *does*! He told her everything that he had told me when I was pumping him, all those years. She put two and two together when the thing came out. She saw exactly how I had set my traps. I know it! She's been trying to make me admit it.'

'What did you do?'

''Didn't understand what she was driving at, of course. And then she asked Gleeag, before me, if he didn't think the delay over the book was fretting Sir Alured. He didn't think so. He said getting it out might deprive him of an interest. He had that much decency. *She's* the devil!'

'What do you suppose is her game, then?'

'If Castorley knows he's been had, it'll kill him. She's at me all the time, indirectly, to let it out. I've told you she wants to make it a sort of joke between us. Gleeag's willing to wait. He knows Castorley's a dead man. It slips out when they talk. They say "He was," not "He is." Both of 'em know it. But *she* wants him finished sooner.'

'I don't believe it. What are you going to do?'

'What can I? I'm not going to have him killed, though.'

Manlike, he invented compromises whereby Castorley might be lured up by-paths of interest, to delay publication. This was not a success. As autumn advanced Castorley fretted more, and suffered from returns of his distressing colics. At last, Gleeag told him that he thought they might be due to an overlooked gallstone working down. A second comparatively trivial operation would eliminate the bother once and for all. If Castorley cared for another opinion, Gleeag named a surgeon of eminence. 'And then,' said he, cheerily, 'the two of us can talk you over.' Castorley did not want to be talked over. He was oppressed by pains in his side, which, at first, had yielded to the liver-tonics Gleeag prescribed; but now they stayed—like a toothache—behind everything. He felt most at ease in his bedroom-study, with his proofs round him. If he had more pain than he could stand, he would consider the second operation. Meantime Manallace—'the meticulous Manallace,' he called him—agreed with him in thinking that the Mentzel page-facsimile, done by the Sunnapia Library, was not quite good enough for the great book, and the Sunnapia people were, very decently, having it re-processed. This would hold things back till early spring, which had its advantages, for he could run a fresh eye over all in the interval.

One gathered these news in the course of stray visits as the days shortened. He insisted on Manallace keeping to the 'sacred hours', and Manallace insisted on my accompanying him when possible. On these occasions he and Castorley would confer apart for half an hour or so, while I listened to an unendurable clock in the drawing-room. Then I would join them and help wear out the rest of the time, while Castorley rambled. His speech, now, was often clouded and uncertain—the result of the 'liver-tonics'; and his face came to look like old vellum.

It was a few days after Christmas—the operation had been postponed till the following Friday—that we called together. She met us with word that Sir Alured had picked up an irritating little winter cough, due to a cold wave, but we were not, therefore, to abridge our visit. We found him in steam per-fumed with Friar's Balsam. * He waved the old Sunnapia facsimile at us. We agreed that it ought to have been more worthy. He took a dose of his mixture, lay back and asked us to lock the door. There was, he whispered, something wrong somewhere. He could not lay his finger on it, but it was in the air. He felt he was being played with. He did not like it. There was something wrong all round him. Had we noticed it? Manallace and I severally and slowly denied that we had noticed anything of the sort.

With no longer break than a light fit of coughing, he fell into the hideous, helpless panic of the sick—those worse than captives who lie at the judgement and mercy of the hale for every office and hope. He wanted to go away. Would we help him to pack his Gladstone? Or, if that would attract too much attention in certain quarters, help him to dress and go out? There was an urgent matter to be set right, and now that he had The Title and knew his own mind it would all end happily and he would be well again. *Please* would we let him go out, just to speak to—he named her; he named her by her 'little' name out of the old Neminaka days? Manallace quite agreed, and recommended a pull at the 'liver-tonic' to brace him after so long in the house. He took it, and Manallace suggested that

it would be better if, after his walk, he came down to the cottage
for a week-end and brought the revise with him. They could
then re-touch the last chapter. He answered to that drug and
to some praise of his work, and presently simpered drowsily.
Yes, it *was* good—though he said it who should not. He praised
himself awhile till, with a puzzled forehead and shut eyes, he
told us that *she* had been saying lately that it was too good—the
whole thing, if we understood, was *too* good. He wished us to
get the exact shade of her meaning. She had suggested, or
rather implied, this doubt. She had said—he would let us draw
our own inferences—that the Chaucer find had 'anticipated the
wants of humanity'. Johnson, of course. No need to tell *him*
that. But what the hell was her implication? Oh God! Life had
always been one long innuendo! *And* she had said that a man
could do anything with anyone if he saved him the trouble of
thinking. What did she mean by that? *He* had never shirked
thought. He had thought sustainedly all his life. It *wasn't* too
good, was it? Manallace didn't think it was too good—did he?
But this pick-pick-picking at a man's brain and work was too
bad, wasn't it? *What* did she mean? Why did she always bring
in Manallace, who was only a friend—no scholar, but a lover
of the game—Eh?—Manallace could confirm this if he were
here, instead of loafing on the Continent just when he was most
needed.

'I've come back,' Manallace interrupted, unsteadily. 'I can
confirm every word you've said. You've nothing to worry
about. It's *your* find—*your* credit—*your* glory and—all the rest
of it.'

'Swear you'll tell her so then,' said Castorley. 'She doesn't
believe a word I say. She told me she never has since before we
were married. * Promise!'

Manallace promised, and Castorley added that he had
named him his literary executor, the proceeds of the book to
go to his wife. 'All profits without deduction,' he gasped. 'Big
sales if it's properly handled. *You* don't need money. . . .
Graydon'll trust *you* to any extent. It 'ud be a long . . .'

He coughed, and, as he caught breath, his pain broke
through all the drugs, and the outcry filled the room. Manallace
rose to fetch Gleeag, when a full, high, affected voice, unheard
for a generation, accompanied, as it seemed, the clamour of a

beast in agony, saying: 'I wish to God someone would stop that old swine howling down there! *I* can't . . . I was going to tell you fellows that it would be a dam' long time before Graydon advanced *me* two quid.'

We escaped together, and found Gleeag waiting, with Lady Castorley, on the landing. He telephoned me, next morning, that Castorley had died of bronchitis, which his weak state made it impossible for him to throw off. 'Perhaps it's just as well,' he added, in reply to the condolences I asked him to convey to the widow. 'We might have come across something we couldn't have coped with.'

Distance from that house made me bold.

'You knew all along, I suppose? What was it, really?'

'Malignant kidney-trouble—generalized at the end. 'No use worrying him about it. We let him through as easily as possible. Yes! A happy release. . . . What? . . . Oh! Cremation. Friday, at eleven.'

There, then, Manallace and I met. He told me that she had asked him whether the book need now be published; and he had told her this was more than ever necessary, in her interests as well as Castorley's.

'She is going to be known as his widow—for a while, at any rate. Did I perjure myself much with him?'

'Not explicitly,' I answered.

'Well, I have now—with *her*—explicitly,' said he, and took out his black gloves. . . .

As, on the appointed words, the coffin crawled sideways through the noiselessly-closing door-flaps, I saw Lady Castorley's eyes turn towards Gleeag.

GERTRUDE'S PRAYER

(Modernized from the 'Chaucer' of Manallace.)

That which is marred at birth Time shall not mend,
  Nor water out of bitter well make clean;
All evil thing returneth at the end,
  Or elseway walketh in our blood unseen.
Whereby the more is sorrow in certaine—
Dayspring mishandled cometh not againe.

To-bruized be that slender, sterting spray
  Out of the oake's rind that should betide
A branch of girt and goodliness, straightway
  Her spring is turnèd on herself, and wried
And knotted like some gall or veiney wen.—
Dayspring mishandled cometh not agen.

Noontide repayeth never morning-bliss—
  Sith noon to morn is incomparable;
And, so it be our dawning goth amiss,
  None other after-hour serveth well.
Ah! Jesu-Moder, pitie my oe paine—
Dayspring mishandled cometh not againe!

THE MANNER OF MEN *

'If after the manner of men I have fought with beasts.'
1 Cor. 15: 32.

HER cinnabar-tinted topsail, nicking the hot blue horizon, showed she was a Spanish wheat-boat hours before she reached Marseilles mole. There, her mainsail brailed itself, * a spritsail broke out forward, and a handy driver aft; and she threaded her way through the shipping to her berth at the quay as quietly as a veiled woman slips through a bazaar.

The blare of her horns told her name to the port. An elderly hook-nosed Inspector came aboard to see if her cargo had suffered in the run from the South, and the senior ship-cat purred round her captain's legs as the after-hatch was opened.

'If the rest is like this—' the Inspector sniffed—'you had better run out again to the mole and dump it.'

'That's nothing,' the captain replied. 'All Spanish wheat heats a little. They reap it very dry.'

''Pity you don't keep it so, then. What would you call *that*—crop or pasture?'

The Inspector pointed downwards. The grain was in bulk, and deck-leakage, combined with warm weather, had sprouted it here and there in sickly green films.

'So much the better,' said the captain brazenly. 'That makes it waterproof. Pare off the top two inches, and the rest is as sweet as a nut.'

'*I* told that lie, too, when I was your age. And how does she happen to be loaded?'

The young Spaniard flushed, but kept his temper.

'She happens to be ballasted, under my eye, on lead-pigs and bagged copper-ores.'

'I don't know that they much care for verdigris in their dole-bread * at Rome. But—you were saying?'

'I was trying to tell you that the bins happen to be grain-tight, two-inch chestnut, floored and sided with hides.'

'Meaning dressed African leathers on your private account?'

'What has that got to do with you? We discharge at Port of Rome, not here.'

'So your papers show. And what might you have stowed in the wings of her?'

'Oh, apes! Circumcised apes—just like you!'

'Young monkey! Well, if you are not above taking an old ape's advice, next time you happen to top off with wool and screw in *more bales than are good for her, get your ship under-girt* before you sail. I know it doesn't look smart coming into Port of Rome, but it'll save your decks from lifting worse than they are.'

There was no denying that the planking and waterways round the after-hatch had lifted a little. The captain lost his temper.

'I know your breed!' he stormed. 'You promenade the quays all summer at Caesar's expense, jamming your Jew-bow into everybody's business; and when the norther blows, you squat over your brazier and let us skippers hang in the wind for a week!'

'You have it! Just that sort of a man am I now,' the other answered. 'That'll do, the quarter-hatch!'

As he lifted his hand the falling sleeve showed the broad gold armlet with the triple vertical gouges which is only worn by master mariners who have used all three seas—Middle, Western, and Eastern.

'Gods!' the captain saluted. 'I thought you were——'

'A Jew, of course. Haven't you used Eastern ports long enough to know a Red Sidonian when you see one?'

'Mine the fault—yours be the pardon, my father!' said the Spaniard impetuously. 'Her topsides *are* a trifle strained. There was a three days' blow coming up. I meant to have had her undergirt off the Islands, but hawsers slow a ship so—and one hates to spoil a good run.'

'To whom do you say it?' The Inspector looked the young man over between horny sun and salt creased eyelids like a brooding pelican. 'But if you care to get up your girt-hawsers tomorrow, I can find men to put 'em overside. It's no work for open sea. Now! Main-hatch, there! . . . I thought so. She'll need another girt abaft the foremast.' He motioned to one of his staff, who hurried up the quay to where the port Guard-boat basked at her mooring-ring. She was a stoutly-built, single-banker,* eleven a side, with a short punching ram; her duty being to stop riots in harbour and piracy along the coast.

'Who commands her?' the captain asked.

'An old shipmate of mine, Sulinus—a River man. We'll get his opinion.'

In the Mediterranean (Nile keeping always her name) there is but one river—that shifty-mouthed Danube, where she works through her deltas into the Black Sea. Up went the young man's eyebrows.

'Is he any kin to a Sulinor of Tomi,* who used to be in the flesh-traffic—and a Free Trader? My uncle has told me of him. He calls him Mango.'*

'That man. He was my second in the wheat-trade my last five voyages, after the Euxine grew too hot to hold him. But he's in the Fleet now. . . . You know your ship best. Where do you think the after-girts ought to come?'

The captain was explaining, when a huge dish-faced Dacian,* in short naval cuirass, rolled up the gangplank, carefully saluting the bust of Caesar on the poop, and asked the captain's name.

'Baeticus,* for choice,' was the answer.

They all laughed, for the sea, which Rome mans with foreigners, washes out many shore-names.

'My trouble is this——' Baeticus began, and they went into committee, which lasted a full hour. At the end, he led them to the poop, where an awning had been stretched, and wines set out with fruits and sweet shore water.

They drank to the Gods of the Sea, Trade, and Good Fortune, spilling those small cups overside,* and then settled at ease.

'Girting's an all-day job, if it's done properly,' said the Inspector. 'Can you spare a real working-party by dawn tomorrow, Mango?'

'But surely—for you, Red.'

'I'm thinking of the wheat,' said Quabil curtly. He did not like nicknames so early.*

'Full meals *and* drinks,' the Spanish captain put in.

'Good! Don't return 'em too full. By the way'—Sulinor lifted a level cup—'where do you get this liquor, Spaniard?'

'From our Islands (the Balearics). Is it to your taste?'

'It is.' The big man unclasped his gorget in solemn preparation.

Their talk ran professionally, for though each end of the Mediterranean scoffs at the other, both unite to mock landward, wooden-headed Rome and her stiff-jointed officials.

Sulinor told a tale of taking the Prefect of the Port, on a breezy day, to Forum Julii, * to see a lady, and of his lamentable condition when landed.

'Yes,' Quabil sneered. 'Rome's mistress of the world—as far as the foreshore.'

'If Caesar ever came on patrol with me,' said Sulinor, 'he might understand there was such a thing as the Fleet.'

'Then he'd officer it with well-born young Romans,' said Quabil. 'Be grateful you are left alone. *You* are the last man in the world to want to see Caesar.'

'Except one,' said Sulinor, and he and Quabil laughed.

'What's the joke?' the Spaniard asked.

Sulinor explained.

'We had a passenger, our last trip together, who wanted to see Caesar. It cost us our ship and freight. That's all.'

'Was he a warlock—a wind-raiser?'

'Only a Jew philosopher. But he *had* to see Caesar. He said he had; and he piled up the *Eirene* on his way.'

'Be fair,' said Quabil. 'I don't like the Jews—they lie too close to my own hold—but it was Caesar lost me my ship.' He turned to Baeticus. 'There was a proclamation, our end of the world, two seasons back, that Caesar wished the Eastern wheat-boats to run through the winter, and he'd guarantee all loss. Did *you* get it, youngster?'

'No. Our stuff is all in by September. I wager Caesar never paid you! How late did you start?'

'I left Alexandria across the bows of the Equinox—well down in the pickle, * with Egyptian wheat—half pigeon's dung—and the usual load of Greek sutlers and their women. The second day out the sou'-wester caught me. I made across it north for the Lycian coast, and slipped into Myra* till the wind should let me get back into the regular grain-track again.'

Sailor-fashion, Quabil began to illustrate his voyage with date and olive stones from the table.

'The wind went into the north, as I knew it would, and I got under way. You remember, Mango? My anchors were apeak when a Lycian patrol threshed in with Rome's order to us to wait on a Sidon packet with prisoners and officers. Mother of Carthage, I cursed him!'

"Shouldn't swear at Rome's Fleet. 'Weatherly craft, those Lycian racers! Fast, too. I've been hunted by them! 'Never thought I'd command one,' said Sulinor, half aloud.

'And now I'm coming to the leak in *my* decks, young man,' Quabil eyed Baeticus sternly. 'Our slant north had strained her, and I should have undergirt her at Myra. Gods know why I didn't! I set up the chain-staples in the cable-tier for the prisoners. I even had the girt-hawsers on deck—which saved time later; but the thing I should have done, that I did *not*.'

'Luck of the Gods!' Sulinor laughed. 'It was because our little philosopher wanted to see Caesar in his own way at our expense.'

'Why did he want to see him?' said Baeticus.

'As far as I ever made out from him and the centurion, he wanted to argue with Caesar—about philosophy.'

'He was a prisoner, then?'

'A political suspect—with a Jew's taste for going to law,' Quabil interrupted. 'No orders for irons. Oh, a little shrimp of a man, but—but he seemed to take it for granted that he led everywhere. He messed with us.'

'And he was worth talking to, Red,' said Sulinor.

'*You* thought so; but he had the woman's trick of taking the tone and colour of whoever he talked to. Now—as I was saying . . . '

There followed another illustrated lecture on the difficulties that beset them after leaving Myra. There was always too much west in the autumn winds, and the *Eirene* tacked against it as far as Cnidus. * Then there came a northerly slant, on which she ran through the Aegean Islands, for the tail of Crete; rounded that, and began tacking up the south coast.

'Just darning the water again, as we had done from Myra to Cnidus,' said Quabil ruefully. 'I daren't stand out. There was the bone-yard of all the Gulf of Africa under my lee. But at last we worked into Fairhaven *—by that cork yonder. Late as it was, *I* should have taken her on, but I had to call a ship-council as to lying up for the winter. That Rhodian law may have suited open boats and cock-crow coasters,* but it's childish for ocean-traffic.'

'*I* never allow it in any command of mine,' Baeticus spoke quietly. 'The cowards give the order, and the captain bears the blame.'

Quabil looked at him keenly. Sulinor took advantage of the pause.

'We were in harbour, you see. So our Greeks tumbled out and voted to stay where we were. It was my business to show them that the place was open to many winds, and that if it came on to blow we should drive ashore.'

'Then I,' broke in Quabil, with a large and formidable smile, 'advised pushing on to Phenike, round the cape,* only forty miles across the bay. My mind was that, if I could get her undergirt there, I might later—er—coax them out again on a fair wind, and hit Sicily. But the undergirting came first. She was beginning to talk too much—like me now.'

Sulinor chafed a wrist with his hand.

'She was a hard-mouthed old water-bruiser in any sea,' he murmured.

'She could lie within six points of any wind,' Quabil retorted, and hurried on. 'What made Paul vote with those Greeks? He said we'd be sorry if we left harbour.'

'Every passenger says that, if a bucketful comes aboard,' Baeticus observed.

Sulinor refilled his cup, and looked at them over the brim, under brows as candid as a child's, ere he set it down.

'Not Paul. He did not know fear. He gave me a dose of my own medicine once. It was a morning watch coming down through the Islands. We had been talking about the cut of our topsail—he was right—it held too much lee wind—and then he went to wash before he prayed. I said to him: "You seem to have both ends and the bight of most things coiled down in your little head, Paul. If it's a fair question, what *is* your trade ashore?" And he said: "I've been a man-hunter—Gods forgive me; and now that I think The God has forgiven me, I am man-hunting again." Then he pulled his shirt over his head, and I saw his back. Did *you* ever see his back, Quabil?'

'I expect I did—that last morning, when we all stripped; but I don't remember.'

'*I* shan't forget it! There was good, sound lictor's work and criss-cross Jew scourgings like gratings; and a stab or two; and, besides those, old dry bites—when they get good hold and rugg you. That showed he must have dealt with the Beasts.* So, whatever he'd done, he'd paid for. I was just wondering what he *had* done, when he said: "No; not your sort of man-hunting." "It's your own affair," I said: "but *I* shouldn't care to see Caesar with a back like that. I should hear the Beasts asking for me." "I may that, too, some day," he said, and began sluicing himself, and—then—— What's brought the girls out so early? Oh, I remember!'

There was music up the quay, and a wreathed shore-boat put forth full of Arlesian women. A long-snouted three-banker was hauling from a slip till her trumpets warned the benches to take hold. As they gave way, the *hrmph-hrmph* of the oars in the oar-ports reminded Sulinor, he said, of an elephant choosing his man in the Circus.

'She has been here re-masting. They've no good rough-tree at Forum Julii,' Quabil explained to Baeticus. 'The girls are singing her out.'

The shallop ranged alongside her, and the banks held water, while a girl's voice came across the clock-calm harbour-face:

'Ah, would swift ships had never been about the seas to rove!
For then these eyes had never seen nor ever wept their love.
Over the ocean-rim he came—beyond that verge he passed,
And I who never knew his name must mourn him to the last!' *

'And you'd think they meant it,' said Baeticus, half to himself.

'That's a pretty stick,' was Quabil's comment as the man-of-war opened the island athwart the harbour. 'But she's over-masted by ten fôot. A trireme's only a bird-cage.'

''Luck of the Gods I'm not singing in one now,' Sulinor muttered. They heard the yelp of a bank being speeded up to the short sea-stroke.

'I wish there was some way to save mainmasts from racking.' Baeticus looked up at his own, bangled with copper wire.

'The more reason to undergirt, my son,' said Quabil. '*I* was going to undergirt that morning at Fairhaven. You remember, Sulinor? I'd given orders to overhaul the hawsers the night before. My fault! Never say "Tomorrow." The Gods hear you. And then the wind came out of the south, mild as milk. All we had to do was to slip round the headland to Phenike—and be safe.'

Baeticus made some small motion, which Quabil noticed, for he stopped.

'My father,' the young man spread apologetic palms, 'is not that lying wind the in-draught of Mount Ida? It comes up with the sun, but later——'

'You need not tell *me*! We rounded the cape, our decks like a fair (it was only half a day's sail), and then, out of Ida's bosom the full north-easter stamped on us! Run? What else? I needed a lee to clean up in. Clauda* was a few miles down wind; but whether the old lady would bear up when she got there, I was not so sure.'

'She did.' Sulinor rubbed his wrists again. 'We were towing our longboat half-full. I steered somewhat that day.'

'What sail were you showing?' Baeticus demanded.

'Nothing—and twice too much at that. But she came round when Sulinor asked her, and we kept her jogging in the lee of the island. I said, didn't I, that my girt-hawsers were on deck?'

Baeticus nodded. Quabil plunged into his campaign at long and large, telling every shift and device he had employed. 'It was scanting daylight,' he wound up, 'but I daren't slur the job. Then we streamed our boat alongside, baled her, sweated her up, and secured. You ought to have seen our decks!'

''Panic?' said Baeticus.

'A little. But the whips were out early. The centurion—Julius—lent us his soldiers.'

'How did your prisoners behave?' the young man went on.

Sulinor answered him. 'Even when a man is being shipped to the Beasts, he does not like drowning in irons. They tried to rive the chain-staples out of her timbers.'

'I got the main-yard on deck'—this was Quabil. 'That eased her a little. They stopped yelling after a while, didn't they?'

'They did,' Sulinor replied. 'Paul went down and told them there was no danger. And they believed him! Those scoundrels believed him! He asked me for the keys of the leg-bars to make them easier. "*I*'ve been through this sort of thing before," he said, "but they are new to it down below. Give me the keys." I told him there was no order for him to have any keys; and I recommended him to line his hold for a week in advance, because we were in the hands of the Gods. "And when are we ever out of them?" he asked. He looked at me like an old gull lounging just astern of one's taffrail in a full gale. *You* know that eye, Spaniard?'

'Well do I!'

'By that time'—Quabil took the story again—'we had drifted out of the lee of Clauda, and our one hope was to run for it and pray we weren't pooped. None the less, I could have made Sicily with luck. As a gale I have known worse, but the wind never shifted a point, d'ye see? We were flogged along like a tired ox.'

'Any sights?' Baeticus asked.

'For ten days not a blink.'

'Nearer two weeks,' Sulinor corrected. 'We cleared the decks of everything except our ground-tackle, and put six hands at the tillers. She seemed to answer her helm—sometimes. Well, it kept *me* warm for one.'

'How did your philosopher take it?'

'Like the gull I spoke of. He was there, but outside it all. *You* never got on with him, Quabil?'

'Confessed! I came to be afraid at last. It was not my office to show fear, but I was. *He* was fearless, although I knew that he knew the peril as well as I. When he saw that trying to—er—cheer me made me angry, he dropped it. 'Like a woman, again. You saw more of him, Mango?'

'Much. When I was at the rudders he would hop up to the steerage, with the lower-deck ladders lifting and lunging a foot at a time, and the timbers groaning like men beneath the Beasts. We used to talk, hanging on till the roll jerked us into the scuppers. Then we'd begin again. What about? Oh! Kings and Cities and Gods and Caesar. He was sure he'd see Caesar. I told him I had noticed that people who worried Those Up Above'—Sulinor jerked his thumb towards the awning—'were mostly sent for in a hurry.'

'Hadn't you wit to see he never wanted you for yourself, but to get something out of you?' Quabil snapped.

'Most Jews are like that—and all Sidonians!' Sulinor grinned. 'But what *could* he have hoped to get from anyone? We were doomed men all. You said it, Red.'

'Only when I was at my emptiest. Otherwise I *knew* that with any luck I could have fetched Sicily! But I broke—we broke. Yes, we got ready—you too—for the Wet Prayer.'

'How does that run with you?' Baeticus asked, for all men are curious concerning the bride-bed of Death.

'With us of the River,' Sulinor volunteered, 'we say: "I sleep; presently I row again." '

'Ah! At our end of the world we cry: "Gods, judge me not as a God, but a man whom the Ocean has broken." ' Baeticus looked at Quabil, who answered, raising his cup: 'We Sidonians say, "Mother of Carthage, I return my oar!" But it all comes to the one in the end.' He wiped his beard, which gave Sulinor his chance to cut in.

'Yes, we were on the edge of the Prayer when—do you remember, Quabil?—*he* clawed his way up the ladders and said: "No need to call on what isn't there. My God sends me sure word that I shall see Caesar. *And* he has pledged me all your lives to boot. Listen! No man will be lost." And Quabil said: "But what about my ship?" ' Sulinor grinned again.

'That's true. I had forgotten the cursed passengers,' Quabil confirmed. 'But he spoke as though my *Eirene* were a fig-basket. "Oh, she's bound to go ashore, somewhere," he said, "but not a life will be lost. Take this from me, the Servant of the One God." Mad! Mad as a magician on market-day!'

'No,' said Sulinor. 'Madmen see smooth harbours and full meals. I have had to—soothe that sort.'

'After all,' said Quabil, 'he was only saying what had been in my head for a long time. I had no way to judge our drift, but we likely might hit something somewhere. Then he went away to spread his cook-house yarn among the crew. It did no harm, or I should have stopped him.'

Sulinor coughed, and drawled:

'I don't see anyone stopping Paul from what he fancied he ought to do. But it was curious that, on the change of watch, I——'

'No—I!' said Quabil.

'Make it so, then, Red. Between us, at any rate, we felt that the sea had changed. There was a trip and a kick to her dance. *You* know, Spaniard. And then—I *will* say that, for a man half-dead, Quabil here did well.'

'I'm a bosun-captain, and not ashamed of it. I went to get a cast of the lead. (Black dark and raining marlinspikes!) The first cast warned me, and I told Sulinor to clear all aft for anchoring by the stern. The next—shoaling like a slip-way— sent me back with all hands, and we dropped both bowers and spare and the stream.'

'He'd have taken the kedge * as well, but I stopped him,' said Sulinor.

'I had to stop *her*! They nearly jerked her stern out, but they held. And everywhere I could peer or hear were breakers, or the noise of tall seas against cliffs. We were trapped! But our people had been starved, soaked, and half-stunned for ten days, and now they were close to a beach. That was enough! They must land on the instant; and was I going to let them drown within reach of safety? *Was* there panic? I spoke to Julius, and his soldiers (give Rome her due!) schooled them till I could hear my orders again. But on the kiss-of-dawn some of the crew said that Sulinor had told them to lay out the kedge in the long-boat.'

'I let 'em swing her out,' Sulinor confessed. 'I wanted 'em for warnings. But Paul told me his God had promised their lives to him along with ours, and any private sacrifice would spoil the luck. So, as soon as she touched water, I cut the rope before a man could get in. She was ashore—stove—in ten minutes.'

'Could you make out where you were by then?' Baeticus asked Quabil.

'As soon as I saw the people on the beach—yes. They are my sort—a little removed. Phoenicians by blood. It was Malta— *one* day's run from Syracuse, where I would have been safe! Yes, Malta and my wheat gruel. Good port-of-discharge, eh?'

They smiled, for Melita may mean 'mash' as well as 'Malta'.

'It puddled the sea all round us, while I was trying to get my bearings. But my lids were salt-gummed, and I hiccoughed like a drunkard.'

'And drunk you most gloriously were, Red, half an hour later!'

'Praise the Gods—and for once your pet Paul! That little man came to me on the fore-bitts, puffed like a pigeon, and pulled out a breastful of bread, and salt fish, and the wine—the good new wine. "Eat," he said, "and make all your people eat, too. Nothing will come to them except another wetting. They won't notice that, after they're full. Don't worry about *your* work either," he said. "You *can't* go wrong today. You are promised to me." And then he went off to Sulinor.'

'He did. He came to me with bread and wine and bacon—good they were! But first he said words over them, and then rubbed his hands with his wet sleeves. I asked him if he were a magician. "Gods forbid!" he said. "I am so poor a soul that I flinch from touching dead pig." As a Jew, he wouldn't like pork, naturally. Was that before or after our people broke into the store-room, Red?'

'Had *I* time to wait on them?' Quabil snorted. 'I know they gutted my stores full-hand, and a double blessing of wine atop. But we all took that—deep. Now this is how we lay.' Quabil smeared a ragged loop on the table with a wine-wet finger. 'Reefs—see, my son—and overfalls to leeward here; something that loomed like a point of land on our right there; and, ahead, the blind gut of a bay with a Cyclops surf* hammering it. How we had got in was a miracle. Beaching was our only chance, and meantime she was settling like a tired camel. Every foot I could lighten her meant that she'd take ground closer in at the last. I told Julius. He understood. "I'll keep order," he said. "Get the passengers to shift the wheat as long as you judge it's safe." '

'Did those Alexandrian achators* really work?' said Baeticus.

'*I've* never seen cargo discharged quicker. It was time. The wind was taking off in gusts, and the rain was putting down the swells. I made out a patch of beach that looked less like death than the rest of the arena, and I decided to drive in on a gust under the spitfire-sprit—and, if she answered her helm before she died on us, to humour her a shade to starboard, where the water looked better. I stayed the foremast; set the spritsail fore and aft, as though we were boarding; told Sulinor to have the rudders down directly he cut the cables; waited till a gust came; squared away the sprit, and drove.'

Sulinor carried on promptly:—

'I had two hands with axes on each cable, and one on each rudder-lift; and, believe me, when Quabil's pipe went, both blades were down and turned before the cable-ends had fizzed under! She jumped like a stung cow! She drove. She sheared. I think the swell lifted her, and overran. She came down, and struck aft. Her stern broke off under my toes, and all the guts of her at that end slid out like a man's paunched by a lion. I jumped forward, and told Quabil there was nothing but small kindlings abaft the quarter-hatch, and he shouted: "Never mind! Look how beautifully I've laid her!" '

'I had. What I took for a point of land to starboard, y'see, turned out to be almost a bridge-islet, with a swell of sea 'twixt it and the main. And that meeting-swill, d'you see, surging in as she drove, gave her four or five foot more to cushion on. I'd hit the exact instant.'

'Luck of the Gods, *I* think! Then we began to bustle our people over the bows before she went to pieces. You'll admit Paul was a help there, Red?'

'I dare say he herded the old judies well enough; but he should have lined up with his own gang.'

'He did that, too,' said Sulinor. 'Some fool of an under-officer had discovered that prisoners must be killed if they look like escaping; and he chose that time and place to put it to Julius—sword drawn. Think of hunting a hundred prisoners to death on those decks! It would have been worse than the Beasts!'

'But Julius saw—Julius saw it,' Quabil spoke testily. 'I heard him tell the man not to be a fool. They couldn't escape further than the beach.'

'And how did your philosopher take *that*?' said Baeticus.

'As usual,' said Sulinor. 'But, you see, we two had dipped our hands in the same dish for weeks; and, on the River, that makes an obligation between man and man.'

'In my country also,' said Baeticus, rather stiffly.

'So I cleared my dirk—in case I had to argue. Iron always draws iron with me. But *he* said: "Put it back. They are a little scared." I said: "Aren't *you*?" "What?" he said; "of being killed you mean? No. Nothing can touch me till I've seen Caesar." Then he carried on steadying the ironed men (some were slavering-mad) till it was time to unshackle them by fives, and give 'em their chance. The natives made a chain through the surf, and snatched them out breast-high.'

'Not a life lost! 'Like stepping off a jetty,' Quabil proclaimed.

'Not quite. But he had promised no one should drown.'

'How *could* they—the way I had laid her—gust and swell and swill together?'

'And was there any salvage?'

'Neither stick nor string, my son. We had time to look, too. We stayed on the island till the first spring ship sailed for Port of Rome. They hadn't finished Ostia breakwater that year.'

'And, of course, Caesar paid you for your ship?'

'I made no claim. I saw it would be hopeless; and Julius, who knew Rome, was against any appeal to the authorities. He said that was the mistake Paul was making. And, I suppose, because I did not trouble them, and knew a little about the sea, they offered me the Port Inspectorship here. There's no money in it—if I were a poor man. Marseilles will never be a port again. Narbo* has ruined her for good.'

'But Marseilles is far from under-Lebanon,' Baeticus suggested.

'The further the better. I lost my boy three years ago in Foul Bay, off Berenice, with the Eastern Fleet. He was rather like you about the eyes, too. You and your circumcised apes!'

'But—honoured one! My master! Admiral!—Father mine— how could I have guessed?'

The young man leaned forward to the other's knee in act to kiss it. Quabil made as though to cuff him, but his hand came to rest lightly on the bowed head.

'Nah! Sit, lad! Sit back! It's just the thing the Boy would have said himself. You didn't hear it, Sulinor?'

'I guessed it had something to do with the likeness as soon as I set eyes on him. You don't so often go out of your way to help lame ducks.'

'You can see for yourself she needs undergirting, Mango!'

'So did that Tyrian tub last month. And you told her she might bear up for Narbo or bilge for all of you! But he shall have his working-party tomorrow, Red.'

Baeticus renewed his thanks. The River man cut him short.

'Luck of the Gods,' he said. 'Five—four—years ago I might have been waiting for you anywhere in the Long Puddle with fifty River men—and no moon.'

Baeticus lifted a moist eye to the slip-hooks on his yardarm, that could hoist and drop weights at a sign.

'You might have had a pig or two of ballast through your benches coming alongside,' he said dreamily.

'And where would my overhead-nettings have been?' the other chuckled.

'Blazing—at fifty yards. What are fire-arrows for?'

'To fizzle and stink on my wet sea-weed blindages. Try again.'

They were shooting their fingers at each other, like the little boys gambling for olive-stones on the quay beside them.

'Go on—go on, my son! Don't let that pirate board,' cried Quabil.

Baeticus twirled his right hand very loosely at the wrist.

'In that case,' he countered, 'I should have fallen back on my foster-kin—my father's island horsemen.'

Sulinor threw up an open palm.

'Take the nuts,' he said. 'Tell me, is it true that those infernal Balearic slingers of yours can turn a bull by hitting him on the horns?'

'On either horn you choose. My father farms near New Carthage. They come over to us for the summer to work. There are ten in my crew now.'

Sulinor hiccoughed and folded his hands magisterially over his stomach.

'Quite proper. Piracy *must* be put down! Rome says so. I do so,' said he.

'I see,' the younger man smiled. 'But tell me, why did you leave the slave—the Euxine trade, O Strategos?'*

'That sea is too like a wine-skin. 'Only one neck. It made mine ache. So I went into the Egyptian run with Quabil here.'

'But why take service in the Fleet? Surely the Wheat pays better?'

'I intended to. But I had dysentery at Malta that winter, and Paul looked after me.'

'Too much muttering and laying-on of hands for *me*,' said Quabil; himself muttering about some Thessalian jugglery with a snake * on the island.

'*You* weren't sick, Quabil. When I was getting better, and Paul was washing me off once, he asked if my citizenship were in order. He was a citizen himself. Well, it was and it was not. As second of a wheat-ship I was *ex officio* Roman citizen—for signing bills and so forth. But on the beach, my ship perished, he said I reverted to my original shtay—status—of an extra-provinshal Dacian by a Sich—Sish—Scythian—I think she was—mother. Awkward—what? All the Middle Sea echoes like a public bath if a man is wanted.'

Sulinor reached out again and filled. The wine had touched his huge bulk at last.

'But, as I was saying, once *in* the Fleet nowadays one is a Roman with authority—no waiting twenty years for your papers. And Paul said to me: "Serve Caesar. You are not canvas I can cut to advantage at present. But if you serve Caesar you will be obeying at least some sort of law." He talked as though I were a barbarian. Weak as I was, I could have snapped his back with my bare hands. I told him so. "I don't doubt it," he said. "But that is neither here nor there. If you take refuge under Caesar at sea, you may have time to think. Then I may meet you again, and we can go on with our talks. But that is as The God wills. What concerns you *now* is that, by taking service, you will be free from the fear that has ridden you all your life." '

'Was he right?' asked Baeticus after a silence. *

'He was. I had never spoken to him of it, but he knew it. *He* knew! Fire—sword—the sea—torture even—one does not think of them too often. But not the Beasts! Aie! *Not* the Beasts! I fought two dog-wolves for the life on a sand-bar when I was a youngster. Look!'

Sulinor showed his neck and chest.

'They set the sheep-dogs on Paul at some place or other once—because of his philosophy! And he was going to see Caesar—going to see Caesar! And he—he had washed me clean after dysentery!'

'Mother of Carthage, you never told me that!' said Quabil.

'Nor should I now, had the wine been weaker.'

AT HIS EXECUTION

I am made all things to all men*—
   Hebrew, Roman, and Greek—
   In each one's tongue I speak,
Suiting to each my word,
That some may be drawn to the Lord!

I am made all things to all men—
   In City or Wilderness
   Praising the crafts they profess
That some may be drawn to the Lord—
By any means to my Lord!

Since I was overcome
   By that great Light and Word,
I have forgot or forgone
The self men call their own
(Being made all things to all men)
   So that I might save some
   At such small price, to the Lord,
As being all things to all men.

I was made all things to all men,
   But now my course is done—
   And now is my reward—
Ah, Christ, when I stand at Thy Throne
With those I have drawn to the Lord,
Restore me my self again!

'PROOFS OF HOLY WRIT'*

> *Arise, shine; for thy light is come, and the glory of the Lord is risen upon thee.*
>
> *2. For, behold, the darkness shall cover the earth, and gross darkness the people: but the Lord shall arise upon thee, and his glory shall be seen upon thee.*
>
> *3. And the Gentiles shall come to thy light, and kings to the brightness of thy rising.*
>
> *19. The sun shall be no more thy light by day; neither for brightness shall the moon give light unto thee: but the Lord shall be unto thee an everlasting light, and thy God thy glory.*
>
> *20. Thy sun shall no more go down; neither shall thy moon withdraw itself: for the Lord shall be thine everlasting light, and the days of thy mourning shall be ended.*
>
> Isaiah LX. Authorized Version.

THEY seated themselves in the heavy chairs on the pebbled floor beneath the eaves of the summer-house by the orchard. A table between them carried wine and glasses, and a packet of papers, with pen and ink. The larger man of the two, his doublet unbuttoned, his broad face blotched and scarred, puffed a little as he came to rest. The other picked an apple from the grass, bit it, and went on with the thread of the talk that they must have carried out of doors with them.

'But why waste time fighting atomies who do not come up to your belly-button, Ben?' he asked.

'It breathes me—it breathes me, between bouts! *You*'d be better for a tussle or two.'

'But not to spend mind and verse on 'em. What was Dekker* to you? Ye knew he'd strike back—and hard.'

'He and Marston had been baiting me like dogs . . . about my trade* as they called it, though it was only my cursed stepfather's. "Bricks and mortar," Dekker said, and "hodman". And he mocked my face. * 'Twas clean as curds in my youth. This humour has come on me since.'

'Ah! "Every man *and* his humour"? *But why did ye not have at Dekker in peace—over the sack, as you do at me?'

'Because I'd have drawn on him—and he's no more worth a hanging than Gabriel. * Setting aside what he wrote of me, too, the hireling dog has merit, of a sort. His *Shoemaker's Holiday*. Hey? Though my *Bartlemy Fair*, when 'tis presented, will furnish out three of it and——'

'Ride all the easier. I have suffered two readings of it already. It creaks like an overloaded hay-wain,' the other cut in. 'You give too much.'

Ben smiled loftily, and went on. 'But I'm glad I lashed him in my *Poetaster*, for all I've worked with him since. How comes it that I've never fought with thee, Will?'

'First, Behemoth,'* the other drawled, 'it needs two to engender any sort of iniquity. Second, the betterment of this present age—and the next, maybe—lies, in chief, on our four shoulders. If the Pillars of the Temple fall out, Nature, Art, and Learning come to a stand. Last, I am not yet ass enough to hawk up my private spites before the groundlings. What do the Court, citizens, or 'prentices give for thy fallings-out or fallings-in with Dekker—or the Grand Devil?'

'They should be taught, then—taught.'

'Always *that*? What's your commission to enlighten us?'

'My own learning which I have heaped up, lifelong, at my own pains. My assured knowledge, also, of my craft and art. I'll suffer no man's mock or malice on it.'

'The one sure road to mockery.'

'I deny nothing of my brain-store to my lines. I—I build up my own works throughout.'

'Yet when Dekker cries "hodman" y'are not content.'

Ben half heaved in his chair. 'I'll owe you a beating for that when I'm thinner. Meantime, here's on account. I say, *I* build upon my own foundations; devising and perfecting my own plots; adorning 'em justly as fits time, place, and action. In all of which you sin damnably. *I* set no landward principalities on sea-beaches.'*

'They pay their penny for pleasure—not learning,' Will answered above the apple-core.

'Penny or tester, you owe 'em justice. In the facture of plays—nay, listen, Will—at all points they must be dressed historically—*teres atque rotundus**—in ornament and temper. As my *Sejanus*, of which the mob was unworthy.'

Here Will made a doleful face, and echoed, 'Unworthy! I was—what did I play, Ben, in that long weariness? Some most grievous ass.'

'The part of Caius Silius,' said Ben stiffly.

Will laughed aloud. 'True. "Indeed that place *was* not my sphere." '*

It must have been a quotation, for Ben winced a little, ere he recovered himself and went on: 'Also my *Alchemist* which the world in part apprehends. The main of its learning is necessarily yet hid from 'em. To come to your works, Will——'

'I am a sinner on all sides. The drink's at your elbow.'

'Confession shall not save ye—nor bribery.' Ben filled his glass. 'Sooner than labour the right cold heat to devise your own plots you filch, botch, and clap 'em together out o' ballads, broadsheets, old wives' tales, chap-books——'

Will nodded with complete satisfaction. 'Say on,' quoth he.

''Tis so with nigh all yours. I've known honester jackdaws. And whom among the learned do ye deceive? Reckoning up those—forty, is it?—your plays you've misbegot, there's not six which have not plots common as Moorditch.'

'Ye're out, Ben. There's not one. My *Love's Labour* (how I came to write it, I know not) is nearest to lawful issue. My *Tempest* (how I came to write *that*,* I know) is, in some part, my own stuff. Of the rest, I stand guilty. Bastards all!'

'And no shame.'

'None! Our business must be fitted with parts hot and hot—and the boys are more trouble than the men. Give me the bones of any stuff, I'll cover 'em as quickly as any. But to hatch new plots is to waste God's unreturning time like a—'—he chuckled—'like a hen.'

'Yet see what ye miss! Invention next to Knowledge, whence it proceeds, being the chief glory of Art——'

'Miss, say you? Dick Burbage—in my *Hamlet* that I botched for him when he had staled of our Kings? (Nobly he played it.) Was *he* a miss?'

Ere Ben could speak Will overbore him.

'And when poor Dick was at odds with the world in general and womenkind in special, I clapped him up my *Lear* for a vomit.'

'An hotch-potch of passion, outrunning reason,' was the verdict.

'Not altogether. Cast in a mould too large for any boards to bear. (My fault!) Yet Dick evened it. And when he'd come out of his whoremongering aftermaths of repentance, I served him my *Macbeth* to toughen him. Was that a miss?'

'I grant you your *Macbeth* as nearest in spirit to my *Sejanus*; showing for example: "How fortune plies her sports when she begins To practise 'em." * We'll see which of the two lives longest.'

'Amen! I'll bear no malice among the worms.'

A liveried serving-man, booted and spurred, led a saddle-horse through the gate into the orchard. At a sign from Will he tethered the beast to a tree, lurched aside, and stretched on the grass. Ben, curious as a lizard, for all his bulk, wanted to know what it meant.

'There's a nosing Justice of the Peace lost in thee,' Will returned. 'Yon's a business I've neglected all this day for thy fat sake—and he by so much the drunker. . . . Patience! It's all set out on the table. Have a care with the ink!'

Ben reached unsteadily for the packet of papers and read the superscription: ' "To William Shakespeare, Gentleman, at his house of New Place in the town of Stratford, these—with diligence from M. S." Why does the fellow withhold his name? Or is it one of your women? I'll look.'

Muzzy as he was, he opened and unfolded a mass of printed papers expertly enough.

'From the most learned divine, Miles Smith * of Brazen Nose College,' Will explained. 'You know this business as well as I. The King has set all the scholars of England to make one Bible, which the Church shall be bound to, out of all the Bibles that men use.'

'*I* knew,' Ben could not lift his eyes from the printed page. 'I'm more about Court than you think. The learning of Oxford and Cambridge—"most noble and most equal", as I have said—and Westminster, to sit upon a clutch of Bibles. Those 'ud be Geneva (my mother read to me out of it at her knee),

Douai, Rheims, Coverdale, Matthew's, the Bishops', the Great,* and so forth.'

'They are all set down on the page there—text against text. And you call me a botcher of old clothes?'

'Justly. But what's your concern with this botchery? To keep peace among the Divines? There's fifty of 'em at it as I've heard.'

'I deal with but one. He came to know me when we played at Oxford—when the plague was too hot in London.'

'I remember this Miles Smith now. Son of a butcher? Hey?' Ben grunted.

'Is it so?' was the quiet answer. 'He was moved, he said, with some lines of mine in Dick's part. He said they were, to his godly apprehension, a parable, as it might be, of his reverend self, going down darkling to his tomb 'twixt cliffs of ice and iron.'

'What lines? I know none of thine of that power. But in my *Sejanus*——'

'These were in my *Macbeth*. They lost nothing at Dick's mouth:—

> "Tomorrow, and tomorrow, and tomorrow
> Creeps in this petty pace from day to day
> To the last syllable of recorded time,
> And all our yesterdays have lighted fools
> The way to dusty death——"

or something in that sort. Condell* writes 'em out fair for him, and tells him I am Justice of the Peace (wherein he lied) and *armiger*,* which brings me within the pale of God's creatures and the Church. Little and little, then, this very reverend Miles Smith opens his mind to me. He and a half-score others, his cloth, are cast to furbish up the Prophets—Isaiah to Malachi. In his opinion by what he'd heard, I had some skill in words, and he'd condescend——'

'How?' Ben barked. 'Condescend?'

'Why not? He'd condescend to inquire o' me privily, when direct illumination lacked, for a tricking-out of his words or the turn of some figure. For example'—Will pointed to the papers—'here be the first three verses of the Sixtieth of Isaiah, and the nineteenth and twentieth of that same. Miles has been at a stand over 'em a week or more.'

'They never called on *me*.' Ben caressed lovingly the hand-pressed proofs on their lavish linen paper. 'Here's the Latin atop and'—his thick forefinger ran down the slip—'some three—four—Englishings out of the other Bibles. They spare 'emselves nothing. Let's to it together. Will you have the Latin first?'

'Could I choke ye from that, Holofernes?'*

Ben rolled forth, richly: ' "*Surge, illumare, Jerusalem, quia venit lumen tuum, et gloria Domini super te orta est. Quia ecce tenebrae operient terram et caligo populos. Super te autem orietur Dominus, et gloria ejus in te videbitur. Et ambulabunt gentes in lumine tuo, et reges in splendore ortus tui*". Er-hum? Think you to better that?'

'How have Smith's crew gone about it?'

'Thus.' Ben read from the paper. ' "Get thee up, O Jerusalem, and be bright, for thy light is at hand, and the glory of God has risen up upon thee." '

'Up-pup-up!' Will stuttered profanely.

Ben held on. ' "See how darkness is upon the earth and the peoples thereof." '

'That's no great stuff to put into Isaiah's mouth. And further, Ben?'

' "But on thee God shall shew light and on——" or "in", is it?' (Ben held the proof closer to the deep furrow at the bridge of his nose.) ' "On thee shall His glory be manifest. So that all peoples shall walk in thy light and the Kings in the glory of thy morning." '

'It may be mended. Read me the Coverdale of it now. 'Tis on the same sheet—to the right, Ben.'

'Umm—umm! Coverdale saith, "And therefore get thee up betimes, for thy light cometh, and the glory of the Lord shall rise up upon thee. For lo! while the darkness and cloud covereth the earth and the people, the Lord shall shew thee light, and His glory shall be seen in thee. The Gentiles shall come to thy light, and kings to the brightness that springeth forth upon thee." But "gentes" is, for the most part, "peoples",' Ben concluded.

'Eh?' said Will indifferently. 'Art sure?'

This loosed an avalanche of instances from Ovid, Quintilian, Terence, Columella, Seneca, and others. Will took no heed till the rush ceased, but stared into the orchard, through the September haze. 'Now give me the Douai and Geneva for this "Get thee up, O Jerusalem," ' said he at last. 'They'll be all there.'

Ben referred to the proofs. ' 'Tis "arise" in both,' said he. ' "Arise and be bright" in Geneva. In the Douai 'tis "Arise and be illuminated." '

'So? Give me the paper now.' Will took it from his companion, rose, and paced towards a tree in the orchard, turning again, when he had reached it, by a well-worn track through the grass. Ben leaned forward in his chair. The other's free hand went up warningly.

'Quiet, man!' said he. 'I wait on my Demon!' * He fell into the stage-stride of his art at that time, speaking to the air.

'How shall this open? "Arise?" No! "Rise!" Yes. And we'll have no weak coupling. 'Tis a call to a City! "Rise—shine" . . . Nor yet any schoolmaster's "because"—because Isaiah is not Holofernes. *"Rise—shine; for thy light is come, and——!"* ' He refreshed himself from the apple and the proofs as he strode. ' "And—and the glory of God!"—No! "God" 's over short. We need the long roll here. *"And the glory of the Lord is risen on thee."* (Isaiah speaks the part. We'll have it from his own lips.) What's next in Smith's stuff? . . . "See how?" Oh, vile—vile! . . . And Geneva hath "Lo"? (Still, Ben! Still!) "Lo" is better by all odds: but to match the long roll of "the Lord" we'll have it "Behold". How goes it now? *"For, behold, darkness clokes the earth and—* and——"* What's the colour and use of this cursed *caligo*, Ben?—*"Et caligo populos."* '

' "Mistiness" or, as in Pliny, "blindness". And further——'

'No—o . . . Maybe, though, *caligo* will piece out *tenebrae*. *"Quia ecce tenebrae operient terram et caligo populos."* Nay! "Shadow" and "mist" are not men enough for this work. . . . Blindness, did ye say, Ben? . . . The blackness of blindness atop of mere darkness? . . . By God, I've used it in my own stuff many times! "Gross" searches it to the hilts! "Darkness covers"—no—"clokes" (short always). *"Darkness clokes the earth, and gross—gross darkness the people!"* (But Isaiah's prophesying, with the storm behind him. Can ye not *feel* it, Ben?

It must be "shall")— *"Shall cloke the earth"* . . . The rest comes clearer. . . . "But on thee God shall arise" . . . (Nay, that's sacrificing the Creator to the Creature!) *"But the Lord shall arise on thee"*, and—yes, we'll sound that "thee" again—"and on thee shall"—No! . . . *"And His glory shall be seen on thee."* Good!' He walked his beat a little in silence, mumbling the two verses before he mouthed them.

'I have it! Heark, Ben! *"Rise—shine; for thy light is come, and the glory of the Lord is risen on thee. For, behold, darkness shall cloke the earth, and gross darkness the people. But the Lord shall arise on thee, and His glory shall be seen upon thee."* '

'There's something not all amiss there,' Ben conceded.

'My Demon never betrayed me yet, while I trusted him. Now for the verse that runs to the blast of rams'-horns. * *"Et ambulabunt gentes in lumine tuo, et reges in splendore ortus tui."* How goes that in the Smithy? "The Gentiles shall come to thy light, and kings to the brightness that springs forth upon thee?" The same in Coverdale and the Bishops'—eh? We'll keep "Gentiles", Ben, for the sake of the indraught of the last syllable. But it might be "And the Gentiles shall draw." No! The plainer the better! "The Gentiles shall come to thy light, and kings to the splendour of——" (Smith's out here! We'll need something that shall lift the trumpet anew.) "Kings shall—shall—Kings to——" (Listen, Ben, but on your life speak not!) "Gentiles shall come to thy light, and kings to thy brightness"—No! "Kings to the brightness that springeth——" Serves not! . . . One trumpet must answer another. And the blast of a trumpet is always *ai-ai*. "The brightness of"— *"Ortus"* signifies "rising", Ben—or what?'

'Ay, or "birth", or the East in general.'

'Ass! 'Tis the one word that answers to "light". "Kings to the brightness of thy rising." Look! The thing shines now within and without. God! That so much should lie on a word!' He repeated the verse—' *"And the Gentiles shall come to thy light, and kings to the brightness of thy rising."* '

He walked to the table and wrote rapidly on the proof margin all three verses as he had spoken them. 'If they hold by this,' said he, raising his head, 'they'll not go far astray. Now for the nineteenth and twentieth verses. On the other sheet, Ben. What? What? Smith says he has held back his rendering till he hath seen mine? Then we'll botch 'em as they stand. Read me first the Latin; next the Coverdale, and last the Bishops'. There's a contagion of sleep in the air.' He handed back the proofs, yawned, and took up his walk.

Obedient, Ben began: ' *"Non erit tibi amplius Sol ad lucendum per diem, nec splendor Lunae illuminabit te."* Which Coverdale rendereth, "The Sun shall never be thy day light, and the light of the Moon shall never shine unto thee." The Bishops read: "Thy sun shall never be thy daylight and the light of the moon shall never shine on thee." '

'Coverdale is the better,' said Will, and, wrinkling his nose a little, 'The Bishops put out their lights clumsily. Have at it, Ben.'

Ben pursed his lips and knit his brow. 'The two verses are in the same mode, changing a hand's-breadth in the second. By so much, therefore, the more difficult.'

'Ye see *that*, then?' said the other, staring past him, and muttering as he paced, concerning suns and moons. Presently he took back the proof, chose him another apple, and grunted. 'Umm-umm! "Thy Sun shall never be———" No! Flat as a split viol. *"Non erit tibi amplius Sol———"* That *amplius* must give tongue. Ah! . . . "Thy Sun shall not—shall not—shall no more be thy light by day" . . . A fair entry. "Nor?"—No! Not on the heels of "day". "Neither" it must be—"Neither the Moon"— but here's *splendor* and the rams'-horns again. (Therefore— *ai—ai!*) "Neither for brightness shall the Moon—" (Pest! It is the Lord who is taking the Moon's place over Israel. It must be "thy Moon".) "Neither for brightness shall thy Moon light—give—make—give light unto thee." Ah! . . . Listen here! . . . *"The Sun shall no more by thy light by day: neither for brightness shall thy Moon give light unto thee."* That serves, and more, for the first entry. What next, Ben?'

Ben nodded magisterially as Will neared him, reached out his hand for the proofs, and read: ' *"Sed erit tibi Dominus in lucem sempiternam et Deus tuus in gloriam tuam."* Here is a jewel of Coverdale's that the Bishops have wisely stolen whole. Hear! *"But* the Lord Himself shall be thy everlasting light, and thy God shall be thy glory." ' Ben paused. 'There's a hand's-breadth of splendour for a simple man to gather!'

'Both hands rather. He's swept the strings as divinely as David before Saul,' Will assented. 'We'll convey it whole, too. . . . What's amiss now, Holofernes?'

For Ben was regarding him with a scholar's cold pity. 'Both hands! Will, hast thou *ever* troubled to master *any* shape or sort of prosody—the mere names of the measures and pulses of strung words?'

'I beget some such stuff and send it to you to christen. What's your wisdomhood in labour of?'

'Naught. Naught. But not to know the names of the tools of his trade!' Ben half muttered and pronounced some Greek word * or other which conveyed nothing to the listener, who replied: 'Pardon, then, for whatever sin it was. I do but know words for my need of 'em, Ben. Hold still awhile!'

He went back to his pacings and mutterings. ' "For the Lord Himself shall be thy—or thine?—everlasting light." Yes. We'll convey that.' He repeated it twice. 'Nay! Can be bettered. Hark ye, Ben. Here is the Sun going up to over-run and possess all Heaven for evermore. *There*fore (Still, man!) we'll harness the horses of the dawn. Hear their hooves? "The Lord Himself shall be unto thee thy everlasting light, and——" Hold again! After that climbing thunder must be some smooth check—like great wings gliding. *There*fore we'll not have "shall be thy glory," but "*And* thy God thy glory!" Ay—even as an eagle alighteth! Good—good! Now again, the sun and moon of that twentieth verse, Ben.'

Ben read: ' "*Non occidet ultra Sol tuus et Luna tua non minuetur: quia erit tibi Dominus in lucem sempiternam et complebuntur dies luctus tui.*" '

Will snatched the paper and read aloud from the Coverdale version. ' "Thy Sun shall never go down, and thy Moon shall not be taken away. . . ." What a plague's Coverdale doing with his blocking *ets* and *urs*, Ben? What's *minuetur*? . . . I'll have it all anon.'

'Minish—make less—appease—abate, as in——'

'So?' . . . Will threw the proofs back. 'Then "wane" should serve. "Neither shall thy moon wane" . . . "Wane" is good, but over-weak for place next to "moon" ' . . . He swore softly. 'Isaiah hath abolished both earthly sun and moon. *Exeunt ambo*. Aha! I begin to see! . . . Sol, the man, goes down—down stairs

or trap—as needs be. Therefore "Go down" shall stand. "Set"
would have been better—as a sword sent home in the scab-
bard—but it jars—it jars. Now Luna must retire herself in some
simple fashion. . . . Which? Ass that I be! 'Tis common talk in
all the plays. . . . "Withdrawn" . . . "Favour withdrawn" . . .
"Countenance withdrawn". "The Queen withdraws herself" . . . "Withdraw", it shall be! "Neither shall thy moon
withdraw herself." (Hear her silver train rasp the boards, Ben?)
*Thy sun shall no more go down—neither shall thy moon withdraw
herself. For the Lord . . ."*—ay, the Lord, simple of Himself—
"shall be thine"—yes, "thine" here—*"everlasting light, and"* . . .
How goes the ending, Ben?'

' *"Et complebuntur dies luctus tui."* ' Ben read. ' "And thy
sorrowful days shall be rewarded thee," says Coverdale.'

'And the Bishops?'

' "And thy sorrowful days shall be ended." '

'By no means. And Douai?'

' "Thy sorrow shall be ended." '

'And Geneva?'

' "And the days of thy mourning shall be ended." '

'The Switzers have it! Lay the tail of Geneva to the head of
Coverdale and the last is without flaw.' He began to thump
Ben on the shoulder. 'We have it! I have it all, Boanerges!*
Blessed be my Demon! Hear! *"The sun shall no more be thy light
by day, neither for brightness the moon by night. But the Lord
Himself shall be unto thee thy everlasting light, and thy God thy
glory."* ' He drew a deep breath and went on. ' *"Thy sun shall
no more go down; neither shall thy moon withdraw herself, for the
Lord shall be thine everlasting light, and the days of thy mourning
shall be ended."* ' The rain of triumphant blows began again. 'If
those other seven devils in London let it stand on this sort, it
serves. But God knows what they can *not* turn upsee-dejee!'*

Ben wriggled. 'Let be!' he protested. 'Ye are more moved by
this jugglery than if the Globe were burned.'*

'Thatch—old thatch! And full of fleas! . . . But, Ben, ye
should have heard my Ezekiel making mock of fallen Tyrus in
his twenty-seventh chapter. Miles sent me the whole, for, he
said, some small touches. I took it to the Bank—four o'clock
of a summer morn; stretched out in one of our wherries—and
watched London, Port and Town, up and down the river,

waking all arrayed to heap more upon evident excess. Ay! "A merchant for the peoples of many isles" . . . "The ships of Tarshish did sing of thee in thy markets"?* Yes! I saw all Tyre before me neighing her pride against lifted heaven. . . . But what will they let stand of all mine at long last? Which? I'll never know.'

He had set himself neatly and quickly to refolding and cording the packet while he talked. 'That's secret enough,' he said at the finish.

'He'll lose it by the way.' Ben pointed to the sleeper beneath the tree. 'He's owl-drunk.'

'But not his horse,' said Will. He crossed the orchard, roused the man; slid the packet into an holster which he carefully rebuckled; saw him out of the gate, and returned to his chair.

'Who will know we had part in it?' Ben asked.

'God, maybe—if He ever lay ear to earth. I've gained and lost enough—lost enough.' He lay back and sighed. There was long silence till he spoke half aloud. 'And Kit* that was my master in the beginning, he died when all the world was young.'

'Knifed on a tavern reckoning—not even for a wench!' Ben nodded.

'Ay. But if he'd lived he'd have breathed me! 'Fore God, he'd have breathed me!'

'Was Marlowe, or any man, *ever* thy master, Will?'

'He alone. Very he. I envied Kit. Ye do not know that envy, Ben?'

'Not as touching my own works. When the mob is led to prefer a baser Muse, I have felt the hurt, and paid home. Ye know that—as ye know my doctrine of play-writing.'

'Nay—not wholly—tell it at large,' said Will, relaxing in his seat, for virtue had gone out of him. He put a few drowsy questions. In three minutes Ben had launched full-flood on the decayed state of the drama, which he was born to correct; on cabals and intrigues against him which he had fought without cease; and on the inveterate muddle-headedness of the mob unless duly scourged into approbation by his magisterial hand.

It was very still in the orchard now that the horse had gone. The heat of the day held though the sun sloped, and the wine had done its work. Presently, Ben's discourse was broken by a snort from the other chair.

'I was listening, Ben! Missed not a word—missed not a word.' Will sat up and rubbed his eyes. 'Ye held me throughout.' His head dropped again before he had done speaking.

Ben looked at him with a chuckle and quoted from one of his own plays:—

> ' "Mine earnest vehement botcher
> And deacon also, Will, I cannot dispute with you." ' *

He drew out flint, steel and tinder, pipe and tobacco-bag from somewhere round his waist, lit and puffed against the midges till he, too, dozed.

'TEEM'

A TREASURE-HUNTER*

There's a gentleman of France—better met by choice than chance,
  Where there's time to turn aside and space to flee—
He is born and bred and made for the cattle-droving trade,
  And they call him Monsieur Bouvier de Brie.
'What—Brie?' Yes, Brie. 'Where those funny cheeses come
    from?' Oui! Oui! Oui!
But his name is great through Gaul as the wisest dog of all,
  And France pays high for Bouvier de Brie.
'De Brie?' C'est lui. And, if you read my story, you will see*
  What one loyal little heart thought of Life and Love and Art,
And notably of Bouvier de Brie—
  'My friend the Vicomte Bouvier de Brie.'

NOTHING could prevent my adored Mother from demanding at once the piece of sugar which was her just reward for every Truffle she found. My revered Father, on the other hand, contented himself with the strict practice of his Art. So soon as that Pierre, our Master, stooped to dig at the spot indicated, my Father moved on to fresh triumphs.

From my Father I inherit my nose, and, perhaps, a touch of genius. From my Mother a practical philosophy without which even Genius is but a bird of one wing.

In appearance? My Parents come of a race built up from remote times on the Gifted of various strains. The fine flower of it today is small—of a rich gold, touched with red; pricked and open ears; a broad and receptive brow; eyes of intense but affable outlook, and a Nose in itself an inspiration and unerring guide. Is it any wonder, then, that my Parents stood apart from the generality? Yet I would not make light of those worthy artisans who have to be trained by Persons to the pursuit of Truffles. They are of many stocks and possess many virtues, but not the Nose—that gift which is incommunicable.

Myself? I am not large. At birth, indeed, I was known as The Dwarf; but my achievements early won me the title of The Abbé. It was easy. I do not recall that I was ever trained by any Person. I watched, imitated, and, at need, improved upon, the technique of my Parents among the little thin oaks of my country where the best Truffles are found; and that which to the world seemed a chain of miracles was, for me, as easy as to roll in the dust.

My small feet could walk the sun up and down across the stony hill-crests where we worked. My well-set coat turned wet, wind, and cold, and my size enabled me to be carried, on occasion, in my Master's useful outside pocket.

My companions of those days? At first Pluton and Dis—the solemn, dewlapped, black, mated pair who drew the little wooden cart whence my Master dispensed our Truffles at the white Château near our village, and to certain shopkeepers in the Street of the Fountain where the women talk. Those Two of Us were peasants in grain. They made clear to me the significance of the flat round white Pieces, and the Thin Papers, which my Master and his Mate buried beneath the stone by their fireplace. Not only Truffles but all other things, Pluton told me, turn into Pieces or Thin Papers at last.

But my friend of friends; my preceptor, my protector, my lifelong admiration; was Monsieur le Vicomte Bouvier de Brie—a Marshal of Bulls whom he controlled in the stony pastures near the cottage. There were many sheep also, with whom neither the Vicomte nor I was concerned. Mutton is bad for the Nose, and, as I have reason to know, for the disposition.

He was of race, too—'born'* as I was—and so accepted me when, with the rash abandon of puppyhood, I attached myself to his ear. In place of abolishing me, which he could have done with one of his fore-paws, he lowered me gently between both of them, so that I lay blinking up the gaunt cliff of his chest into his unfathomable eyes, and 'Little bad one!' he said. 'But I prophesy thou wilt go far!'

Here, fenced by those paws, I would repair for my slumbers, to avoid my enemies or to plague him with questions. And, when he went to the Railway Station to receive or despatch more Bulls, I would march beneath his belly, hurling infantile insults at the craven doggerie of the Street of the Fountain.

After I was expert in my Art, he would talk to me of his own, breaking off with some thunder of command to a young Bull who presumed to venture too near the woods where our Truffles grow, or descending upon him like hail across walls which his feet scorned to touch.

His strength, his audacity, overwhelmed me. He, on his side, was frankly bewildered by my attainments. 'But how—*how*, little one, is it done, your business?' I could not convey to him, nor he to me, the mystery of our several Arts. Yet always unweariedly he gave me the fruits of his experience and philosophy.

I recall a day when I had chased a chicken which, for the moment, represented to me a sufficiently gross Bull of Salers. * There seemed a possibility of chastisement at the hands of the owner, and I refuged me beneath my friend's neck where he watched in the sun. He listened to my foolish tale, and said, as to himself, 'These Bulls of mine are but beef fitted with noses and tails by which one regulates them. But these black hidden lumps of yours which only such as you can unearth—*that* is a business beyond me! I should like to add it to my repertoire.'

'And I,' I cried (my second teeth were just pushing), 'I will be a Driver of Bulls!'

'Little one,' he responded with infinite tenderness, 'here is one thing for us both to remember. Outside his Art, an Artist must never dream.'

About my fifteenth month I found myself brother to four who wearied me. At the same time there was a change in my Master's behaviour. Never having had any regard for him, I was the quicker to notice his lack of attention. My Mother, as always, said, 'If it is not something, it is sure to be something else.' My Father simply, 'At all hazards follow your Art. That can never lead to a false scent.'

There came a Person of abominable odours to our cottage, not once but many times. One day my Master worked me in his presence. I demonstrated, through a long day of changing airs, with faultless precision. After supper, my Master's Mate said to him, 'We are sure of at least two good workers for next season—and with a dwarf one never knows. It is far off, that England the man talks of. Finish the affair, Pierril.'

Some Thin Papers passed from hand to hand. The Person then thrust me into his coat-pocket (Ours is not a breed to be shown to all) and there followed for me alternations of light and dark in stink-carts: a period when my world rose and rolled till I was sick; a silence beside lapping water under stars; transfer to another Person whose scent and speech were unintelligible; another flight by stink-cart; a burst of sunrise between hedges; a scent of sheep; violent outcries and rockings: finally, a dissolution of the universe which projected me through a hedge from which I saw my captor lying beneath the stink-cart where a large black-and-white She bit him with devotion.

A ditch led me to the shelter of a culvert. I composed myself within till the light was suddenly blocked out by the head of that very She, who abused me savagely in *Lingua canina*.* (My Father often recommended me never to reply to a strange She.) I was glad when her Master's voice recalled this one to her duties, and I heard the clickety of her flock's feet above my head.

In due time I issued forth to acquaint myself with this world into which I had been launched. It was new in odour and aspect, but with points of likeness to my old one. Clumps of trees fringed close woods and smooth green pastures; and, at the bottom of a shallow basin crowned with woodland, stood a white Château even larger than the one to which Pluton and Dis used to pull their cart.

I kept me among the trees and was congratulating my Nose on its recovery from the outrageous assaults it had suffered during my journeys, when there came to it the unmistakable aroma of Truffles—not, indeed, the strawberry-scented* ones of my lost world, but like enough to throw me into my working-pose.

I took wind, and followed up my line. I was not deceived. There were Truffles of different sorts in their proper places under those thick trees. My Mother's maxim had proved its truth. This was evidently the 'something else' of which she had spoken; and I felt myself again my own equal. As I worked amid the almost familiar odours it seemed to me that all that had overtaken me had not happened, and that at any moment I should meet Pluton and Dis with our cart. But they came not. Though I called they did not come.

A far-off voice interrupted me, with menace. I recognized it for that of the boisterous She of my culvert, and was still.

After cautious circuits I heard the sound of a spade, and in a wooded hollow saw a Person flattening earth round a pile of wood, heaped to make charcoal.* It was a business I had seen often.

My Nose assured me that the Person was authentically a peasant and (I recalled the memory later) had not handled One of Us within the time that such a scent would hang on him. My Nose, further, recorded that he was imbued with the aromas proper to his work and was, also, kind, gentle, and equable in temperament. (You Persons wonder that All of Us know your moods before you yourselves realize them? Be well sure that every shade of his or her character, habit, or feeling cries itself aloud in a Person's scent. No more than We All can deceive Each Other can You Persons deceive Us—though We pretend—We pretend—to believe!)

His coat lay on a bank. When he drew from it bread and cheese, I produced myself. But I had been so long at gaze that my shoulder, bruised in transit through the hedge, made me fall. He was upon me at once and, with strength equal to his gentleness, located my trouble. Evidently—though the knowledge even then displeased me—he knew how We should be handled.

I submitted to his care, ate the food he offered, and, reposing in the crook of his mighty arm, was borne to a small cottage where he bathed my hurt, set water beside me and returned to his charcoal. I slept, lulled by the cadence of his spade and the bouquet of natural scents in the cottage, which included all those I was used to, except garlic and, strangely, Truffles.

I was roused by the entry of a She-Person who moved slowly and coughed. There was on her (I speak now as We speak) the Taint of *the* Fear—of that Black Fear which bids Us throw up our noses and lament. She laid out food. The Person of the Spade entered. I fled to his knee. He showed me to the Girl-Person's dull eyes. She caressed my head, but the chill of her hand increased the Fear. He set me on his knees, and they talked in the twilight.

Presently, their talk nosed round hidden flat Pieces and Thin Papers. The tone was so exactly that of my Master and his Mate that I expected they would lift up the hearthstone. But *theirs* was in the chimney, whence the Person drew several white Pieces, which he gave to the Girl. I argued from this they had admitted me to their utmost intimacy and—I confess it—I danced like a puppy. My reward was their mirth—his specially. When the Girl laughed she coughed. But *his* voice warmed and possessed me before I knew it.

After night was well fallen, they went out and prepared a bed on a cot in the open,* sheltered only by a large faggot-stack. The Girl disposed herself to sleep there, which astonished me. (In my lost world out-sleeping is not done, except when Persons wish to avoid Forest Guards.) The Person of the Spade then set a jug of water by the bed and, turning to re-enter the house, delivered a long whistle. It was answered across the woods by the unforgettable voice of the old She of my culvert. I inserted myself at once between, and a little beneath, some of the more robust faggots.

On her silent arrival the She greeted the Girl with extravagant affection and fawned beneath her hand, till the coughings closed in uneasy slumber. Then, with no more noise than the moths of the night, she quested for me in order, she said, to tear out my throat. 'Ma Tante,' I replied placidly from within my fortress, 'I do not doubt you could save yourself the trouble by swallowing me alive. But, first, tell me what I have done.' 'That there is *My* Bone,' was the reply. It was enough! (Once in my life I had seen poor honest Pluton stand like a raging wolf between his Pierril, whom he loved, and a Forest Guard.) *We* use that word seldom and never lightly. Therefore, I answered, 'I assure you she is not mine. She gives me the Black Fear.'

You know how We cannot deceive Each Other? The She accepted my statement; at the same time reviling me for my lack of appreciation—a crookedness of mind not uncommon among elderly Shes.

To distract her, I invited her to tell me her history. It appeared that the Girl had nursed her through some early distemper. Since then, the She had divided her life between her duties among sheep by day and watching, from the First Star till Break of Light, over the Girl, who, she said, also suffered from a slight distemper. This had been her existence, her joy and her devotion long before I was born. Demanding nothing more, she was prepared to back her single demand by slaughter.

Once, in my second month, when I would have run away from a very fierce frog, my friend the Vicomte told me that, at crises, it is best to go forward. On a sudden impulse I emerged from my shelter and sat beside her. There was a pause of life and death during which I had leisure to contemplate all her teeth. Fortunately, the Girl waked to drink. The She crawled to caress the hand that set down the jug, and waited till the breathing resumed. She came back to me—I had not stirred—with blazing eyes. 'How can you *dare* this?' she said. 'But why not?' I answered. 'If it is not something, it is sure to be something else.' Her fire and fury passed. 'To whom do you say it!' she assented. 'There is always something else to fear—not for myself but for My Bone yonder.'

Then began a conversation unique, I should imagine, even among Ourselves. My old, unlovely, savage Aunt, as I shall henceforth call her, was eaten alive with fears for the Girl—not so much on account of her distemper, but because of Two She-Persons-Enemies—whom she described to me minutely by Eye and Nose—one like a Ferret, the other like a Goose.

These, she said, meditated some evil to the Girl against which my Aunt and the Girl's Father, the Person of the Spade, were helpless. The Two Enemies carried about with them certain papers, * by virtue of which the Girl could be taken away from the cottage and my Aunt's care, precisely as she had seen sheep taken out of her pasture by Persons with papers, and driven none knew whither.

The Enemies would come at intervals to the cottage in daytime (when my Aunt's duty held her with the sheep) and always they left behind them the Taint of misery and anxiety. It was not that she feared the Enemies personally. She feared nothing except a certain Monsieur The-Law who, I understood later, cowed even her.

Naturally I sympathized. I did not know this *gentilhommier** de Loire, but I knew Fear. Also, the Girl was of the same stock as He who had fed and welcomed me and Whose voice had reassured. My Aunt suddenly demanded if I purposed to take up my residence with them. I would have detailed to her my adventures. She was acutely uninterested in them all except so far as they served her purposes, which she explained. She would allow me to live on condition that I reported to her, nightly beside the faggot-stack, all I had seen or heard or suspected of every action and mood of the Girl during the day; any arrival of the Enemies, as she called them; and whatever I might gather from their gestures and tones. In other words I was to spy for her as Those of Us who accompany the Forest Guards spy for their detestable Masters.

I was not disturbed. (I had had experience of the Forest Guard.) Still there remained my dignity and something which I suddenly felt was even more precious to me. 'Ma Tante,' I said, 'what I do depends not on you but on *My* Bone in the cottage there.' She understood. 'What is there on *Him*,' she said, 'to draw you?' 'Such things are like Truffles,' was my answer. 'They are there or they are not there.' 'I do not know what "Truffles" may be,' she snapped. 'He has nothing useful to me except that He, too, fears for my Girl. At any rate your infatuation for Him makes you more useful as an aid to my plans.' 'We shall see,' said I. 'But—to talk of affairs of import-ance—do you seriously mean that you have no knowledge of Truffles?' She was convinced that I mocked her. 'Is it,' she demanded, 'some lapdog's trick?' She said this of Truffles—of my Truffles!

The impasse was total. Outside of the Girl on the cot and her sheep (for I can testify that, with them, she was an Artist) the square box of my Aunt's head held not one single thought. My patience forsook me, but not my politeness. 'Cheer up, old one!' I said. 'An honest heart outweighs many disadvantages of ignorance and low birth.' . . .

And She? I thought she would have devoured me in my hair! When she could speak, she made clear that she was 'born'—entirely so—of a breed mated and trained since the days of the First Shepherd. In return I explained that I was a specialist in the discovery of delicacies which the genius of my ancestors had revealed to Persons since the First Person first scratched in the first dirt.

She did not believe me—nor do I pretend that I had been entirely accurate in my genealogy—but she addressed me henceforth as 'My Nephew'.

Thus that wonderful night passed, with the moths, the bats, the owls, the sinking moon, and the varied respirations of the Girl. At sunrise a call broke out from beyond the woods. My Aunt vanished to her day's office. I went into the house and found Him lacing one gigantic boot. Its companion lay beside the hearth. I brought it to Him (I had seen my Father do as much for that Pierrounet my Master).

He was loudly pleased. He patted my head, and when the Girl entered, told her of my exploit. She called me to be caressed, and, though the Black Taint upon her made me cringe, I came. She belonged to Him—as at that moment I realized that I did.

Here began my new life. By day I accompanied Him to His charcoal—sole guardian of His coat and the bread and cheese on the bank, or, remembering my Aunt's infatuation, fluctuated between the charcoal-mound and the house to spy upon the Girl, when she was not with Him. He was all that I desired—in the sound of His solid tread; His deep but gentle voice; the sympathetic texture and scent of His clothes; the safe hold of His hand when He would slide me into His great outer pocket and carry me through the far woods where He dealt secretly with rabbits. Like peasants, who are alone more than most Persons, He talked aloud to himself, and presently to me, asking my opinion of the height of a wire from the ground.

My devotion He accepted and repaid from the first. My Art he could by no means comprehend. For, naturally, I followed my Art as every Artist must, even when it is misunderstood. If not, he comes to preoccupy himself mournfully with his proper fleas.

My new surroundings; the larger size and closer spacing of the oaks; the heavier nature of the soils; the habits of the lazy wet winds—a hundred considerations which the expert takes into account—demanded changes and adjustments of my technique. . . . My reward? I found and brought Him Truffles of the best. I nosed them into His hand. I laid them on the threshold of the cottage and they filled it with their fragrance. He and the Girl thought that I amused myself, and would throw—throw!—them for me to retrieve, as though they had been stones and I a puppy! What more could I do? The scent over that ground was lost.

But the rest was happiness, tempered with vivid fears when we were apart lest, if the wind blew beyond moderation, a tree might fall and crush Him; lest when He worked late He might disappear into one of those terrible river-pits so common in the world whence I had come, and be lost without trace. There was no peril I did not imagine for Him till I could hear His feet walking securely on sound earth long before the Girl had even suspected. Thus my heart was light in spite of the nightly conferences with my formidable Aunt, who linked her own dismal apprehensions to every account that I rendered of the Girl's day-life and actions. For some cause or other, the Two Enemies had not appeared since my Aunt had warned me against them, and there was less of Fear in the house. Perhaps, as I once hinted to my Aunt, owing to my presence.

It was an unfortunate remark. I should have remembered her gender. She attacked me, that night, on a new scent, bidding me observe that she herself was decorated with a Collar of Office which established her position before all the world. I was about to compliment her, when she observed, in the low even tone of detachment peculiar to Shes of age, that, unless I were so decorated, not only was I outside the Law (that Person of whom, I might remember, she had often spoken) but could not be formally accepted into any household.

How, then, I demanded, might I come by this protection? In her own case, she said, the Collar was hers by right as a Preceptress of Sheep. To procure a Collar for me would be a matter of Pieces or even of Thin Papers, from His chimney. (I recalled poor Pluton's warning that everything changes at last into such things.) If He chose to give of His Pieces for my Collar, my civil status would be impregnable. Otherwise, having no business or occupation, I lived, said my Aunt, like the rabbits—by favour and accident.

'But, ma Tante,' I cried, 'I have the secret of an Art beyond all others.'

'That is not understood in these parts,' she replied. 'You have told me of it many times, but I do not believe. What a pity it is not rabbits! You are small enough to creep down their burrows. But these precious things of yours under the ground which no one but you can find—it is absurd.'

'It is an absurdity, then, which fills Persons' chimney-places with Pieces and Thin Papers. Listen, ma Tante!' I all but howled. 'The world I came from was stuffed with things underground which all Persons desired. This world here is also rich in them, but I—I alone—can bring them to light!'

She repeated acridly, 'Here is not there. It should have been rabbits.'

I turned to go. I was at the end of my forces.

'You talk too much of the world whence you came,' my Aunt sneered. 'Where is that world?'

'I do not know,' I answered miserably and crawled under my faggots. As a matter of routine, when my report had been made to my Aunt, I would take post on the foot of His bed where I should be available in case of bandits. But my Aunt's words had barred that ever-open door.

My suspicions worked like worms in my system. If He chose, He could kick me off on to the floor—beyond sound of His desired voice—into the rabid procession of fears and flights whence He had delivered me. Whither, then, should I go? . . . There remained only my lost world where Persons knew the value of Truffles and of Those of Us who could find them. I would seek that world!

With this intention, and a bitterness in my belly as though I had mouthed a toad, I came out after dawn and fled to the edge of the woods through which He and I had wandered so often. They were bounded by a tall stone wall, along which I quested for an opening. I found none till I reached a small house beside shut gates. Here an officious One of Us advanced upon me with threats. I was in no case to argue or even to expostulate. I hastened away and attacked the wall again at another point.

But after a while, I found myself back at the house of the Officious One. I recommenced my circuit, but—there was no end to that Wall. I remembered crying aloud to it in hope it might fall down and pass me through. I remember appealing to the Vicomte to come to my aid. I remember a Xight of big black birds, calling the very name of my lost world—'Aa—or'*—above my head. But soon they scattered in all directions. Only the Wall continued to continue, and I blindly at its foot. Once a She-Person stretched out her hand towards me. I fled—as I fled from an amazed rabbit who, like myself, existed by favour and accident.

Another Person coming upon me threw stones. This turned me away from the Wall and so broke its attraction. I subsided into an aimless limp of hours, until some woods that seemed familiar received me into their shades. . . .

I found me at the back of the large white Château in the hollow, which I had seen only once, far off, on the first day of my arrival in this world. I looked down through bushes on to ground divided by strips of still water and stone. Here were birds, bigger than turkeys, with enormous voices and tails which they raised one against the other, while a white-haired She-Person dispensed them food from a pan she held between sparkling hands. My Nose told me that she was unquestionably of race—descended from champion strains. I would have crawled nearer, but the greedy birds forbade. I retreated uphill into the woods, and, moved by I know not what agonies of frustration and bewilderment, threw up my head and lamented.

The harsh imperative call of my Aunt cut through my self-pity. I found her on duty in pastures still bounded by that Wall which encircled my world. She charged me at once with having some disreputable affair, and, for its sake, deserting my post with the Girl. I could but pant. Seeing, at last, my distress, she said, 'Have you been seeking that lost world of yours?' Shame closed my mouth. She continued, in softer tones, 'Except when it concerns My Bone, do not take all that I say at full-fang. There are others as foolish as you. Wait my return.'

She left me with an affectation, almost a coquetry, of extreme fatigue. To her charge had been added a new detachment of sheep who wished to escape. They had scattered into separate crowds, each with a different objective and a different speed. My Aunt, keeping the high ground, allowed them to disperse, till her terrible voice, thrice lifted, brought them to halt. Then, in one long loop of flight, my Aunt, a dumb fury lying wide on their flank, swept down with a certainty, a speed, and a calculation which almost reminded me of my friend the Vicomte. Those diffuse and errant imbeciles reunited and inclined away from her in a mob of mixed smells and outcries—to find themselves exquisitely penned in an angle of the fence, my Aunt, laid flat at full length, facing them! One after another their heads dropped and they resumed their eternal business of mutton-making.

My Aunt came back, her affectation of decrepitude heightened to heighten her performance. And who was I, an Artist also, to mock her?

'You wonder why my temper is not of the bluntest?' she said. '*You* could not have done that.'

'But at least I can appreciate it,' I cried. 'It was superb! It was unequalled! It was faultless! You did not even nip one of them.'

'With sheep that is to confess failure,' she said. 'Do *you*, then, gnaw your Truffles?' It was the first time that she had ever admitted their existence! My genuine admiration, none the worse for a little flattery, opened her heart. She spoke of her youthful triumphs at sheep-herding expositions; of rescues of lost lambs, or incapable mothers found reversed in ditches. Oh, she was all an Artist, my thin-flanked, haggard-eyed Aunt by enforced adoption. She even let me talk of the Vicomte!

Suddenly (the shadows had stretched) she leaped, with a grace I should never have suspected, on to a stone wall and stood long at far gaze. 'Enough of this nonsense,' she said brutally. 'You are rested now. Get to your work. If you could see, my Nephew, you would observe the Ferret and the Goose walking there, three fields distant. They have come again for My Bone. They will keep to the path made for Persons. Go at once to the cottage before they arrive and—do what you can to harass them. Run—run—mountebank of a yellow imbecile that you are!'

I turned on my tail, as We say, and took the direct line through my well-known woods at my utmost speed since her orders dispatched me without loss of dignity towards my heart's one desire. And I was received by Him, and by the Girl with unfeigned rapture. They passed me from one to the other like the rarest of Truffles; rebuked me, not too severely, for my long absence; felt me for possible injuries from traps; brought me bread and milk, which I sorely needed; and by a hundred delicate attentions showed me the secure place I occupied in their hearts. I gave my dignity to the cats, and it is not too much to say that we were all engaged in a veritable *pas de trois* when a shadow fell across our threshold and the Two Enemies most rudely entered!

I conceived, and gave vent to, instant detestation which, for a while, delayed their attack. When it came, He and the Girl accepted it as yoked oxen receive the lash across the eyes—with the piteous dignity which Earth, having so little to give them, bestows upon her humbles. Like oxen, too, they backed side by side and pressed closer together. I renewed my commina-tions* from every angle as I saw how these distracted my adversaries. They then pointed passionately to me and my pan of bread and milk which joy had prevented me from altogether emptying. Their tongues, I felt, were foul with reproach.

At last He spoke. He mentioned my name more than once, but always (I could tell) in my defence. The Girl backed His point. I assisted with—and it was something—all that I had ever heard in my lost world from the *sans-kennailerie** of the Street of the Fountain. The Enemies renewed the charge. Evidently my Aunt was right. Their plan was to take the Girl away in exchange for pieces of paper. I saw the Ferret wave a paper beneath His nose. He shook His head and launched that peasant's 'No', which is one in all languages.

Here I applauded vehemently, continuously, monotonously, on a key which, also, I had learned in the Street of the Fountain. Nothing could have lived against it. The Enemies threatened, I could feel, some prodigious action or another; but at last they marched out of our presence. I escorted them to the charcoal-heap—the limit of our private domain—in a silence charged with possibilities for their thick ankles.

I returned to find my Two sunk in distress, but upon my account. I think they feared I might run away again, for they shut the door. They frequently and tenderly repeated my name, which, with them, was '*Teem*'. Finally He took a Thin Paper from the chimney-piece, slid me into His outside pocket and walked swiftly to the Village, which I had never smelt before.

In a place where a She-Person was caged behind bars, He exchanged the Thin Paper for one which He laid under my nose, saying 'Teem! Look! This is Licence-and-Law all-right!' In yet another place, I was set down before a Person who exhaled a grateful flavour of dried skins.* My neck was then encircled by a Collar bearing a bright badge of office. All

Persons round me expressed admiration and said 'Lor!' many times. On our return through the Village I stretched my decorated neck out of His pocket, like one of the gaudy birds at the Château to impress Those of Us who might be abroad that I was now under full protection of Monsieur Le Law (whoever he might be), and thus the equal of my exacting Aunt.

That night, by the Girl's bed, my Aunt was at her most difficult. She cut short my history of my campaign, and cross-examined me coldly as to what had actually passed. Her interpretations were not cheering. She prophesied our Enemies would return, more savage for having been checked. She said that when they mentioned my name (as I have told you) it was to rebuke Him for feeding me, a vagabond, on good bread and milk, when I did not, according to Monsieur Le Law, belong to Him. (She herself, she added, had often been shocked by His extravagance in this regard.) I pointed out that my Collar now disposed of inconvenient questions. So much she un-graciously conceded, but—I had described the scene to her—argued that He had taken the Thin Paper out of its hiding-place because I had cajoled Him with my 'lapdog's tricks', and that, in default of that Paper, He would go without food, as well as without what he burned under His nose, which to Him would be equally serious.

I was aghast. 'But, ma Tante,' I pleaded, 'show me—make me any way to teach Him that the earth on which He walks so loftily can fill His chimneys with Thin Papers, and I promise you that *She* shall eat chicken!' My evident sincerity—perhaps, too, the finesse of my final appeal—shook her. She mouthed a paw in thought.

'You have shown Him those wonderful underground-things of yours?' she resumed.

'But often. And to your Girl also. They thought they were stones to throw. It is because of my size that I am not taken seriously.' I would have lamented, but she struck me down. Her Girl was coughing.

'Be silent, unlucky that you are! Have you shown your Truffles, as you call them, to anyone else?'

'Those Two are all I have ever met in this world, my Aunt.'

'That was true till yesterday,' she replied. 'But at the back of the Château—this afternoon—eh?' (My friend the Vicomte was right when he warned me that all elderly Shes have six ears and ten noses. And the older the more!)

'I saw that Person only from a distance. You know her, then, my Aunt?'

'If I know Her! She met me once when I was lamed by thorns under my left heel-pad. She stopped me. She took them out. She also put her hand on my head.'

'Alas, *I* have not your charms!' I riposted.

'Listen, before my temper snaps, my Nephew. She has returned to her Château. Lay one of those things that you say you find, at her feet. *I* do not credit your tales about them, but it is possible that *She* may. She is of race. She knows all. She may make you that way for which you ask so loudly. It is only a chance. But, if it succeeds, and My Bone does *not* eat the chickens you have promised her, I will, for sure, tear out your throat.'

'My Aunt,' I replied, 'I am infinitely obliged. You have, at least, shown me a way. What a pity you were born with so many thorns under your tongue!' And I fled to take post at the foot of His bed, where I slept vigorously—for I had lived that day!—till time to bring Him His morning boots.

We then went to our charcoal. As official Guardian of the Coat I permitted myself no excursions till He was busied stopping the vents of little flames on the flanks of the mound. Then I moved towards a patch of ground which I had noted long ago. On my way, a chance of the air told me that the Born One of the Château was walking on the verge of the wood. I fled to my patch, which was even more fruitful than I had thought. I had unearthed several Truffles when the sound of her tread hardened on the bare ground beneath the trees. Selecting my largest and ripest, I bore it reverently towards her, dropped it in her path, and took a pose of humble devotion. Her Nose informed her before her eyes. I saw it wrinkle and sniff deliciously. She stooped and with sparkling hands lifted my gift to smell. Her sympathetic appreciation emboldened me to pull the fringe of her clothes in the direction of my little store exposed beneath the oak. She knelt and, rapturously inhaling their aroma, transferred them to a small basket on her arm. (All Born Ones bear such baskets when they walk upon their own earths.)

Here He called my name. I replied at once that I was coming, but that matters of the utmost importance held me for the moment. We moved on together, the Born One and I, and found Him beside His coat setting apart for me my own bread and cheese. We lived, we two, each always in the other's life!

I had often seen that Pierrounet my Master, who delivered me to strangers, uncover and bend at the side-door of the Château in my lost world over yonder. At no time was he beautiful. But He—My Own Bone to me!—though He too was uncovered, stood beautifully erect and as a peasant of race should bear himself when He and His are not being tortured by Ferrets or Geese. For a short time, He and the Born One did not concern themselves with me. They were obviously of old acquaintance. She spoke; she waved her sparkling hands; she laughed. He responded gravely, at dignified ease, like my friend the Vicomte. Then I heard my name many times. I fancy He may have told her something of my appearance in this world. (We peasants do not tell all to *any* one.) To prove to her my character, as He conceived it, He threw a stone. With as much emphasis as my love for Him allowed, I signified that this game of lapdogs was not mine. She commanded us to return to the woods. There He said to me as though it were some question of His magnificent boots, 'Seek, Teem! Find, Teem!' and waved His arms at random. He did not know! Even then, My Bone did not know!

But I—I was equal to the occasion! Without unnecessary gesture; stifling the squeaks of rapture that rose in my throat; coldly, almost, as my Father, I made point after point, picked up my lines and worked them (His attendant spade saving me the trouble of digging) till the basket was full. At this juncture the Girl—they were seldom far apart—appeared with all the old miseries on her face, and behind her (I had been too occupied with my Art, or I should have yelled on their scent) walked the Two Enemies!

They had not spied us up there among the trees, for they rated her all the way to the charcoal-heap. Our Born One descended upon them softly as a mist through which shine the stars, and greeted them in the voice of a dove out of summer foliage. I held me still. She needed no aid, that one! They grew louder and more loud; she increasingly more suave. They flourished at her one of their detestable papers which she received as though it had been all the Truffles in the world. They talked of Monsieur Le Law. From her renewed smiles I understood that he, too, had the honour of her friendship. They continued to talk of him. . . . Then . . . she abolished them! How? Speaking with the utmost reverence of both, she reminded me of my friend the Vicomte disentangling an agglomeration of distracted, and therefore dangerous, beefs at the Railway Station. There was the same sage turn of the head, the same almost invisible stiffening of the shoulders, the very same small voice out of the side of the mouth, saying, '*I* charge myself with this.' And then—and then—those insupportable offspring of a jumped-up *gentilhommier**** were transformed into amiable and impressed members of their proper class, giving ground slowly at first, but finally evaporating—yes, evaporating—like bad smells—in the direction of the world whence they had intruded.

During the relief that followed, the Girl wept and wept and wept. Our Born One led her to the cottage and consoled. We showed her our bed beside the faggots and all our other small dispositions, including a bottle out of which the Girl was used to drink. (I tasted once some that had been spilt. It was like unfresh fish—fit only for cats.) She saw, she heard, she considered all. Calm came at her every word. She would have given Him some Pieces, in exchange, I suppose, for her filled basket. He pointed to me to show that it was my work. She repeated most of the words she had employed before—my name among them—because one must explain many times to a peasant who desires *not* to comprehend. At last He took the Pieces.

Then my Born One stooped down to me beside His foot and said, in the language of my lost world, 'Knowest thou, Teem, that this is all *thy* work? Without thee we can do nothing. Knowest thou, my little dear Teem?' If I knew! Had He listened to me at the first the situation would have been regularized half a season before. Now I could fill his chimney-places as my Father had filled that of that disgusting Pierrounet. Logically, of course, I should have begun a fresh demonstration of my Art in proof of my zeal for the interests of my famille. But I did not. Instead, I ran—I rolled—I leaped—I cried aloud—I fawned at their knees! What would you? It was hairless, toothless sentiment, but it had the success of a hurricane! They accepted me as though I had been a Person—and He more unreservedly than any of them. It was my supreme moment!

I have at last reduced my famille to the Routine which is indispensable to the right-minded among Us. For example: At intervals He and I descend to the Château with our basket of Truffles for our Born One. If she is there she caresses me. If elsewhere, her basket pursues her in a stink-cart. So does, also, her Chef, a well-scented Person and, I can testify, an Artist. This, I understand, is our exchange for the right to exploit for ourselves all other Truffles that I may find inside the Great Wall. These we dispense to another stink-cart, filled with delightful comestibles, which waits for us regularly on the stink-cart-road by the House of the Gate where the Officious One pursued me. We are paid into the hand (trust us peasants!) in Pieces or Papers, while I stand guard against bandits.

As a result, the Girl has now a wooden-roofed house of her own—open at one side and capable of being turned round against winds by His strong one hand. Here she arranges the bottles from which she drinks, and here comes—but less and less often—a dry Person of mixed odours, who applies his ear at the end of a stick, to her thin back. Thus, and owing to the chickens which, as I promised my Aunt, she eats, the Taint of her distemper diminishes. My Aunt denies that it ever existed, but her infatuation—have I told you?—has no bounds! She has been given honourable demission from her duties with sheep and has frankly installed herself in the Girl's outside bed-house, which she does not encourage me to enter. I can support that. I too have My Bone. . . .

Only it comes to me, as it does to most of Us who live so swiftly, to dream in my sleep. Then I return to my lost world—to the whistling, dry-leaved, thin oaks that are not these giant ones—to the stony little hillsides and treacherous river-pits that are not these secure pastures—to the sharp scents that are not these scents—to the companionship of poor Pluton and Dis—to the Street of the Fountain up which marches to meet me, as when I was a rude little puppy, my friend, my protector, my earliest adoration, Monsieur le Vicomte Bouvier de Brie.

At this point always, I wake; and not till I feel His foot beneath the bedderie, and hear His comfortable breathing, does my lost world cease to bite. . . .

Oh, wise and well-beloved guardian and playmate of my youth—it is true—it is true, as thou didst warn me—Outside his Art an Artist must never dream!

THE END

EXPLANATORY NOTES

THE following abbreviations are in general use in these notes:

CK   C. E. Carrington's notes from Mrs Kipling's diaries.
DV   *Rudyard Kipling's Verse: Definitive Edition*, Hodder & Stoughton.
KJ   The Kipling Journal, published quarterly by the Kipling Society.
KP   Kipling Papers, University of Sussex Library.
SOM   *Something of Myself* (page numbers as Uniform edn.).
SB   Sussex and Burwash editions.

For other abbreviations, see headnotes to the individual stories. Where references are given without publication details, see Select Bibliography. For dates of Kipling's major publications, see Chronology.

3   MRS BATHURST: written in South Africa Jan.–Feb. 1904 (CK). First published *Windsor Magazine* (*WM*) and *Metropolitan*, Sept. 1904, and collected in *Traffics and Discoveries*. The *Windsor* text is bowdlerized, blurring (for instance) any references to sex. The character of Pyecroft appears in three earlier stories in *Traffics*: 'The Bonds of Discipline', 'Their Lawful Occasions', and 'Steam Tactics'.

From Lyden's 'Irenius': this was later partly incorporated into *Gow's Watch* (see DV), a pastiche Jacobean play on which he worked for many years but which was never finished.

versary: from Latin 'versare', to turn.

Simpliciter: (Latin) simply, naturally.

coneycatch: cheat (from 'coney', rabbit).

4   *gerb*: from French 'gerbe', sheaf or spray (used of fireworks).

5   *Simon's Bay*: an indentation on the west side of False Bay, south of Cape Town. A British naval base until 1957.

Greeks: many Greeks owned cafés and stores in South Africa.

6   *the voices . . . picnickers*: not in *WM*.

he felt . . . waistcoat-pocket: not in *WM*.

6 *boiler-seatings*: bed-plates of boilers, difficult of access, and therefore liable to corrode.

7 *verbatim*: word for word (not 'in so many words'). Malapropism and hyperbole have been established in the earlier Pyecroft stories as characteristic of his speech.

purr . . . ex officio: *per mare per terram* (by land and by sea), motto of the Royal Marines. Latin 'ex officio': by virtue of his office.

Barnado: 'Barnato' in *WM*, confounding Dr Barnardo, founder of charity homes for orphans, and Barnato the diamond magnate.

8 *a farm*: in *WM*, '. . . a quarter. What was it, Pye?' 'Section of one hundred and sixty acres of land if we applied for it.'

steerin'-flat: compartment housing the steering-gear.

Buncrana: on Lough Swilly, Co. Donegal.

9 *Mormonastic*: a pun on 'Mormons', who were polygamous, and 'monastic'.

copper: copper sheathing to protect the hull.

P. and O.: Peninsular and Orient Line. See poem 'The Exiles' Line' (DV).

ammunition: left there by the naval brigades sent to support the army during the Boer War.

10 *casus belli*: (Latin) cause of war (not 'case').

'. . . 'Ence, "Click." ': follows in *WM*: ' "Mr Vickery was 'is Number One name." '

status quo: (Latin) existing condition (not 'seat' or 'stern').

11 *commission*: period at sea; normally three years at this time.

12 *Slits*: the American beer Schlitz.

13 *she never . . . scorpion*: Kipling said that this sentence, overheard in a train, inspired the story (SOM, p. 101).

14 *Phyllis's Circus*: Fillis's Circus, based at Johannesburg.

Tickey: note in *WM*: 'Threepenny'.

peeris: peri, a Persian fairy.

15 *submerged flat*: compartment for underwater torpedo tubes.

16 *spirit*: see 'The Bonds of Discipline'.

17 *Scripture says*: see Gen. 1: 5.

17   *his hand . . . waistcoat-pocket*: not in *WM*.

19   *epicycloidal*: a type of gear-wheel.

   war: the Boer War, 1899–1902.

20   *silence*: *Hamlet*, v. ii.

   'The Honeysuckle and the Bee': song by Albert H. Fitz.

   kapje: bonnet.

21   *curve*: after this in *WM*, 'It's all black, boggy soil'.

   charcoal: thought to be based on a real incident (*KJ*, Sept. 1937, p. 74). But Kipling's description of a man killed by lightning is unlikely.

   mate: some readers take the second tramp to be Mrs Bathurst, but 'mate' is more usually interpreted as a male companion.

23   *'WIRELESS'*: begun in 1899, completed 1901 (CK). First published *Scribner's Magazine* (*SM*), Aug. 1902. Collected in *Traffics and Discoveries*. The inventor Marconi visited Kipling at Rottingdean in 1899 and described to him the workings of early radio.

   (From . . . Stagnelius.): collected in DV as 'Butterflies'. Stagnelius did not write this poem. Kipling is parodying a series of verse translations that appeared in *Aunt Judy's Magazine* during his childhood.

   Psyche: can mean both soul (or spirit) and butterfly.

24   *pole*: aerial.

   Poole: one of the Marconi Company's first radio stations.

25   *Apothecaries' Hall*: headquarters of the Society of Apothecaries, founded 1617. The Apothecaries Act of 1815 gave it the right to hold examinations and award diplomas.

   Pharmaceutical Formulary: the British Pharmacopoeia.

   Culpepper: Nicholas Culpep(p)er published an English translation of the *Pharmacopoeia* in 1649 and was the author of *The English Physician Enlarged, or the Herbal* (1653). See 'A Doctor of Medicine', *Rewards and Fairies*.

   job-master: one who hires out horses and vehicles.

   New Commercial Plants: Thomas Christy, *New Commercial Plants, with directions how to grow them to the best advantage*, nos. 1–11, 1878–89.

26 *Paris-diamond*: French artificial jewellery has been famous since
    the 18th century.

    glass jars: a chemist's window traditionally held two or three
    outsize flasks containing coloured liquids.

    Rosamond: see 'The Purple Jar' by Maria Edgeworth, in *Early
    Lessons* (1801), and *The Purple Jar &c. &c.* (1856).

28 *cubeb*: dried berry used in medicine.

    danger-signals: coughing up blood is a symptom of advanced
    tuberculosis, then incurable.

34 *breast*: see Keats' 'Eve of St Agnes', l. 218.

    chromo: chromolithograph, a cheap coloured reproduction.

    birds—: see 'Eve of St Agnes', ll. 1–3. Echoes of this and other
    Keats quotations in the story can be found in the descriptions
    of Shaynor, the shop, and its environs.

    portrait—: see 'Eve of St Agnes', ll. 7–9.

35 *mould*: see 'Eve of St Agnes', ll. 14–18.

    environment: Keats was apprenticed to an apothecary-surgeon
    and was licensed by the Society of Apothecaries in 1816. He later
    developed tuberculosis; after his first haemorrhage he diagnosed
    the 'arterial blood' as his 'death-warrant'. He was in love with a
    young woman called Fanny Brawne.

37 *dreams:* see 'Eve of St Agnes', ll. 255–6.

    Lebanon: 'Eve of St Agnes', ll. 265–70.

38 *wind-blown sleet*: see 'Eve of St Agnes', ll. 324–5.

    a perilous sea: see Keats' 'Ode to a Nightingale', ll. 69–71.

39 *demon lover*: Coleridge, 'Kubla Khan', ll. 14–16.

42 'THEY': written in South Africa, Feb.–Mar. 1904 (CK). First
    published *Scribner's Magazine* (*SM*), Aug. 1904. Collected in
    Traffics and Discoveries. Many small changes in the book version
    mostly replace a word or image by a more striking one.

43 *wheels*: the car Kipling owned at this time was an open Lan-
    chester. Unlike his narrator, he did not drive but employed a
    chauffeur.

    traffic: e.g. taking guns from Sussex iron foundries to the
    Channel ports. (See 'Hal o' the Draft', *Puck of Pook's Hill*.) The

discovery of coal-mines in the north and Wales meant the
decline of iron-working in the south-east.

43 *Temple*: the 12th-century church at Shipley in Sussex is said to
have been built by the Knights Templar.

Down: Chanctonbury Ring.

51 *Colours*: Kipling's sister later claimed to have 'seen' these
phenomena as described. She was a well-known psychic and
medium, under the pseudonym of Mrs Holland.

52 *Egg*: several ancient peoples (including the Egyptians, Hindus,
and Japanese) believed that the world was egg-shaped and had
been hatched by the creator—the 'mundane' or 'Orphic' egg.

54 *Jericho*: see Josh. 6: 20.

appointed: see Church of England Catechism, 'to do my duty in
that state of life to which it shall please God to call me'. See also
'Chant-Pagan' (DV), 4th verse.

55 *Æsculapius*: Greek Asklepius; the Hippocratic oath, binding a
doctor to observe medical ethics.

Borzois: Russian wolfhounds.

tonneau: rear passenger compartment.

57 *insure:* the baby's life could only have been insured against the
usual funeral expenses. Since the Gambling Act of 1774, it has
been illegal to insure another person's life for more money than
the insurer will lose by that person's death ('insurable interest').

evergreen: this word not in *SM*.

(Men . . . in it.): this sentence not in *SM*.

58 *And all . . . call*: this sentence not in *SM*.

fifth line: of E. B. Browning's 'The Lost Bower': 'Listen,
gentle—aye, and simple! listen, children on the knee!'

59 *'seen her'*: 'seen Evie' (*SM*).

61 *cake*: oil-cake, a manufactured cattle-food.

62 *Then . . . screen*: instead of this sentence, *SM* has 'It was a
curiously mottled piece of birch, the layers of bark grilled by the
heat.'

'I understand—now': not in *SM*. See Chronology for the death
of Kipling's daughter Josephine.

63   *iron*: see 'Cold Iron', *Rewards and Fairies*; iron was supposed to drive spirits away, or prevent them from entering a dwelling.

   'I didn't . . . jealous': not in *SM*.

65   THE EDGE OF THE EVENING: written Nov. 1912 (CK). First published in *Pall Mall Magazine* (*PM*) and *Metropolitan*, Dec. 1913. Collected in *A Diversity of Creatures*. When the story was written, the strategic importance of aircraft was already being realized, but the British had fallen behind France and Germany in development and training. The Royal Flying Corps was formed in May 1912. That August, a competition for national and international aircraft designers was held on Salisbury Plain; the specifications for entries include some of the features shown by Kipling's machine, but there is also an element of science fiction in the story.

   time: first two stanzas of 'The Benefactors' (DV, p. 340).

   years ago: (author's note) ' "The Captive", *Traffics and Discoveries*.'

66   *Silencer*: aircraft engines have never had silences.

68   *Joshua*: Sir Joshua Reynolds (1723–92).

   principles: (author's note) ' "The Captive", *Traffics and Discoveries*.'

   Venetian point: a type of lace.

69   *"Honey swore"*: 'Honi soit qui mal y pense' (evil be to him who evil thinks).

   "Tria juncta": motto of the Order of the Bath, 'Tria juncta in uno' (three things in one).

   "For Valurr": the Victoria Cross.

   Handley Cross: novel by R. S. Surtees.

70   *Punkin-eater*: the nursery rhyme 'Peter, Peter, Pumpkin-Eater' was first recorded in *Mother Goose Quarto* (1825).

71   *Ellis Island*: in New York harbour, used until 1954 as a reception station for immigrants to the US.

   coon-can: a card game.

72   *Lundie*: (author's note) ' "The Puzzler", *Actions and Reactions*.'

   Debrett: *Debrett's Peerage and Baronetage*.

73   *twenty or thirty rod*: approximately 100–150 metres.

74 *Aldershot or Salisbury*: the first squadrons of the Royal Flying Corps were stationed at Farnborough, near Aldershot, and at Salisbury Plain Aerodrome (Larkhill). Two pilots of the earlier Air Battalion who went absent on training flights were suspected of landing on purpose near hospitable country houses.

75 *Cain*: see Gen. 4.

77 *The Wrecker*: the novel by Robert Louis Stevenson and Lloyd Osbourne unravels a series of swindles and misfortunes that have led to the murder of a ship's crew and her destruction by wreck and fire.

78 *Jenkins' ear*: in 1739 England declared war on Spain after a merchant captain called Jenkins claimed that Spanish customs officers had cut off his ear.

   Mason and Slidell: during the American Civil War these two emissaries of the Confederates were travelling to England on the British vessel *Trent*, when a Federal warship stopped her and took them off, causing an uproar between the US and UK.

   ex-officio: by virtue of his office.

   Big Claus and Little Claus: eponymous characters in the story by Hans Andersen.

80 *to the air*: Church of England prayer for burials at sea—'We therefore commit his/her body to the deep.' It is unlikely that the aircraft would have taken off unpiloted in the manner described.

83 THE DOG HERVEY: date of writing not recorded in CK, but Kipling was correcting the proofs in Feb. 1914. First published in *Century Magazine*, Apr., and *Nash's* (*NM*), May 1914, where the name in the title is spelt 'HARVEY'. Collected in *A Diversity of Creatures*.

   squints: is cross-eyed.

   'But . . . countenance': not in *NM*.

   Dick's hatband: proverbially 'went nine times round and wouldn't meet'. Said to refer to Richard Cromwell, unworthy successor of his father Oliver, his hatband being the crown.

84 *heavily*: *NM* 'heavily in his own favour'.

   Little Bingo: see Barham, *The Ingoldsby Legends*, introduction to 'The Lay of St Genulphus'. 'Little Bingo' is a dog whose name is similarly spelled out in the refrain to the first verse.

88 *man's*: one reader suggested that Hervey is possessed by the ghost of Dr Sichliffe (*KJ*, June 1977, p. 6). Others assume that Shend (a character who appears later in the story) is looking through the dog's eyes.

  Moses: see Num. 12: 3.

89 *Jean Ingelow's*: 'Sailing beyond Seas' (slightly misquoted).

  tritomas: kniphofias or red-hot pokers.

  waited . . . end: *NM* 'waited until it had conscientiously reached the end'.

91 *'I have . . . income'*: *NM* ' "I have five thousand seven hundred pounds a year." '

92 *Svengali's*: villain of George du Maurier's novel *Trilby*; his hypnotic power is such that the heroine is overcome by seeing his eyes in a photograph.

93 *break-down*: Afro-American dance.

94 *'It's . . . here'*: Mark 9: 5; Luke 9: 33.

95 *Thou . . . man*: 2 Sam. 12: 7.

  ewe-lamb: 2 Sam. 12: 3.

  dead-lights: cabin shutters.

96 *'They've . . . since'*: not in *NM*. Perhaps a reference to the Children Act of 1908, which made it a crime for paid minders of children to insure their charges' lives. But even before this Act, the doctor would not have had an insurable interest in an under-age patient whom he had 'let out into the world again'.

97 *Drummond Castle*: a passenger liner which in 1896 struck a rock and sank in minutes, with only three survivors.

  letter or halve it: a Masonic reference.

98 *gold*: see Thomas Moore, 'Let Erin Remember': 'When Malachi wore the collar of gold'. Here probably a leather collar with polished brass studs and name-plate.

  Demosthenes: Athenian orator, 385–322 BC.

100 *He was . . . love him*: the passage quoted occurs in Boswell's account of Johnson's first coming to London in 1737. Hervey entertained Johnson and introduced him to 'genteel company'.

103 MARY POSTGATE: written Feb. 1915 (CK). First published *Nash's-Pall Mall* (*NPM*), Sept. 1915. Collected in *A Diversity of*

Creatures. See Chronology for the death of Kipling's son, just after publication of the story.

104 *Flying Corps*: the Royal Flying Corps of the British Army.

105 *dowey*: (Scots) dismal.

Taubes . . . Zeppelins: the Taube was a German monoplane; the British flew French Farman aircraft at the beginning of the war; Zeppelins were German airships.

'rolling' . . . own: Mary has misunderstood the jargon: the usual progression was from 'rolling' or 'taxi-ing' on the ground, to flying with an instructor and finally solo. Aircraft were in short supply; it is unlikely that Wynn would have been allocated a personal machine.

106 *glanced at her*: NPM 'glanced at her from under eyebrows which had refused to whiten all these years'.

107 *Contrexeville*: French mineral water.

108 *Salisbury*: the Central Flying School was then at Netheravon, Wilts., on the edge of Salisbury Plain.

110 *Hentys . . . Garvices*: the authors named wrote stories popular with boys of the period.

111 *OTC*: Officers' Training Corps at school (now STC).

Brooklands: first motor racing track in Britain.

112 *'A bomb'*: *The Times* of 20 Jan. 1915 reported Zeppelin raids in which a youth was killed and his small sister injured. In a later report (22 Feb. 1915), a single bomb dropped by a plane over Colchester partly wrecked the room in which a baby lay asleep, also destroying a garden shed. The bombs of the period were small enough to be carried on the pilot's person and dropped by hand.

shut off its engines: again Mary gets it wrong. Few aircraft at that time had self-starters, so a pilot would be unlikely to switch off in mid-air; but if the engine (there would only be one) failed, to jettison his bombs would improve his chances of surviving the ensuing crash. This would have made comparatively little noise, the airframes of the period being made of wire, canvas, and wood.

114 *she heard*: 'it seemed to her that she heard' (*NPM*).

115 *'Cassée. . . . Le médicin!'*: 'Broken. . . . I surrender. Doctor!' (French, with guttural accent).

115   *'Nein! . . . gesehn.'*: 'No! . . . I have seen the dead child.' (Very ungrammatical German.) A contemporary propaganda poster (reproduced Gross (1972), plate 66) suggested that German nurses refused help to wounded British prisoners.

116   *help*: during a Naval Air Service raid on Friedrichshafen in Nov. 1914, a British pilot who had been shot down was injured by angry citizens. He was taken to hospital by the German military and given every care.

119   REGULUS: written May 1911 (CK). First published *Nash's-Pall Mall* (*NPM*), also in *Metropolitan*, Apr. 1917. Collected in *A Diversity of Creatures*, where 1908 is given as the date of composition; also in *The Complete Stalky & Co.* (1929); and with *Stalky & Co.* in SB. In *SOM* (p. 32) Kipling connected the character of King in this story with his old teacher William Crofts. In the original *Stalky & Co.* the character had been less sympathetically treated. The school is a fictional version of the United Services College (see Chronology). For another account see 'An English School', *Land and Sea Tales*.

    Horace: Roman poet, 65–8 BC.

    Cras . . . aequor: Horace Bk. I, Ode 7, last line: 'Tomorrow we set out across the boundless sea.'

    viva-voce: oral.

120   *Milesne Crassi*: the Roman General Crassus invaded Parthia in 54 BC, to be defeated at Carrhae, where 10,000 of his soldiers were captured. They were later settled at Merv in Central Asia.

    quantity: length or shortness of a syllable.

121   *delubris*: a more accurate rendering than Winton's would be, 'I have seen our standards fastened to Carthaginian shrines.'

122   *Flagitio . . . damnum*: a quotation from the Ode they are translating, 'to disgrace you are adding loss'.

    much-enduring man: Odysseus is thus described in the *Odyssey*, trans. Butcher and Lang.

123   *hic . . . inscius*: 'He, since he knew not how to win his life . . .'.

    O . . . ruinis: 'Oh mighty Carthage, exalted higher by Italy's shameful ruins!'.

124   *He . . . ground*: 'He is said to have put away from him, as one whose rights were lost, the lips of his chaste wife, and his little

children, and to have sternly fixed upon the ground his manly face.'

124 *Until . . . alias*: 'until by his influence he made resolute the wavering senators with counsel given at no other time'.

125 *Conington*: Conington's thin 12mo edition (1903) of the *Odes* in Latin and English, with its soft cover, could easily be hidden by cheating schoolboys.

crib: a pun on Isa. 1: 3: 'The ox knoweth his owner, and the ass his master's crib.'

As . . . bay: from Conington's version, last verse.

126 *Non . . . latus*: (author's note) ' "This side will not always be patient of rain and waiting on the threshold." '

128 *Persians*: 'which altereth not':Dan. 6: 8.

130 *ghost*: Browning's 'The Statue and the Bust' continues, 'Is—the unlit lamp and the ungirt loin . . .'.

Mantuan: Virgil was born at Mantua.

131 *Tu . . . superbos*: Virgil, *Aeneid*, vi. 851–3: 'O Roman, to rule the nations in thine empire: this shall be thine art, to lay down the law of peace, to be merciful to the conquered and to beat the haughty down'.

135 *Hypatia*: novel by Charles Kingsley.

139 *Epsom salts*: a mild laxative.

KCB: Knight Commander of the Order of the Bath.

141 *Horace . . . Ode 3*: there is no Bk. V of Horace's Odes. This is the first of a number of Horace imitations that Kipling was to publish, see Carrington, *Kipling's Horace* (1980 edn. privately printed for the Kipling Society).

Pindar: 4th century BC Greek lyric poet, whose odes inspired later writers.

142 THE WISH HOUSE: written Feb. 1924 (CK). First published *MacLean's Magazine*, Oct. 1924, *Hearst's and Nash's* (NM) Dec. 1924. Collected in *Debits and Credits*. The dialect in the story comes mainly from Kipling's Sussex neighbours (SOM, pp. 183–4), but also from Parish's *Dictionary of Sussex Dialect* (Lewes, Farncombe, 1875), of which he owned a copy.

144 *wash-poles*: radio aerials.

146   *'Takes . . . fire'*: this sentence not in *NM*.

148   *stubbin' hens*: cleaning off feather-ends after the carcass has been
plucked (Sussex dialect).

Bert Mockler's son!: 'Arry's father is of the same generation as
Grace and Liz; if he were older they would call him 'Mr Mockler'
(*KJ*, Sept. 1982, p. 24).

150   *rugg*: tug violently, tear.

vittles: victuals, food.

151   *Token*: apparition (Sussex dialect).

152   *hoppin'*: (author's note) 'Hop-picking'.

153   *over him*: in the days before antibiotics, an infection by *staphylo-
coccus aureus* would produce these symptoms; if the bone became
infected, the resulting condition could become chronic, even
fatal.

156   *weepin' boil*: a varicose ulcer.

158   *turned*: perhaps due to her mistreatment of it.

160   RAHERE: a courtier of King Henry I (sometimes said to have been
his jester—see 'The Tree of Justice', *Rewards and Fairies*), who
founded St Bartholomew's Hospital. According to legend, he
did so after seeing a family of lepers in a London street.

Gilbert: Gilbertus Anglicus, author of *Compendium Medicinae*
(approx. 1240), which includes a section on leprosy.

Wanhope: despair.

162   THE BULL THAT THOUGHT: written May 1924 (CK), first published in *Cosmopolitan*, Dec. 1924, *Nash's-Pall Mall*, Jan. 1925
(*NPM*). Collected in *Debits and Credits*. The Kiplings had met
a French wine millionaire, a Monsieur Viollet, at Vernet-les-
Bains in spring 1914.

road: the N 113 between Salon-de-Provence and Arles answers
this description.

Blue de Luxe: a fast train and ferry service from London to Paris.

level crossing: railway crossing.

Legion of Honour: French order of chivalry established by
Napoleon in 1902.

Annam and Tonquin: regions of north Vietnam.

162 *woodcutters*: 15,000 coolies were recruited by the British as the Chinese Auxiliary Force.

163 *tisanes*: herbal teas; also used of light, sweet champagnes.

165 *Carpentier*: Frenchman who was world middleweight boxing champion in 1920.

166 *Apis*: name of an Egyptian bull-god.

167 *farceur*: comedian, practical joker.

168 *circuses*: 'panem et circenses', Juvenal, *Satires*, x. 81. The south-eastern part of France was known in the Roman Empire as Provincia.

   Republic: the Third Republic, 1871–1940.

   Soult . . . Beresford: the first was one of Napoleon's Marshals, and the second a British General attached to the Portuguese army; they fought each other at the battle of Albuera, during the Peninsular War.

169 *douros*: Spanish pesetas.

   Berre . . . Saintes Maries: from east to west of the Camargue.

170 *Comédie Française*: French state theatre, founded 1680.

171 *Seventy-fives*: 75 mm. French gun.

172 *Foch*: Marshal Foch, French leader of the Allied armies in 1918.

173 *Cyrano*: Cyrano de Bergerac, 1619–55, French soldier and writer; eponymous subject of the play by E. Rostand (1897).

   Molière: 1622–73, satirical playwright: author of *Le Misanthrope*, *Le Bourgeois gentilhomme*, etc.

174 *elder Dumas*: Alexandre Dumas, author of historical adventure stories, *The Three Musketeers* (1844), etc.

175 *toril*: (Spanish) bull-pen.

176 *Mother*: the Camargue.

177 *Alnaschar*: a character in the *Arabian Nights* who, dreaming of wealth, knocks over and breaks the glassware he had hoped to sell in order to make his fortune.

   Lobengula: last king of the Ndebele, in what is now Zimbabwe. After his death the British began to move into the area; Kipling visited Bulawayo in 1898, a few years later.

177 *Mithras*: Persian deity, worshipped by many Roman soldiers (see 'A Hymn to Mithras', *Puck of Pook's Hill*). Bulls were sacrificed as part of Mithraic rites.

179 THE GARDENER: written in France in Mar. 1925 (CK). First published in *McCall's Magazine*, Apr. 1925, and *Strand Magazine* (*SM*), May 1925. Collected in *Debits and Credits*. Kipling was a member of the War Graves Commission. His own account of a visit he and his wife paid to the cemeteries in northern France, and his subsequent beginning of this story, can be found in the typescript 'Rudyard Kipling's Motor Tours' (KP).

stone away: see Matt. 28: 2.

180 *explained*: in a house with resident servants the secret could not be kept.

182 *OTC*: Officer Training Corps (now STC).

Army red: instead of the newer khaki uniforms.

K.: Field Marshal Lord Kitchener, Secretary of State for War.

distant service: 'Eastern service' (*SM*).

183 *organizations*: the Red Cross tried to find out what had happened to Kipling's son, missing at the battle of Loos.

184 *Hagenzeele*: a fictitious name, compounded from German 'Hag' (hedge, but with poetic meaning grove or enclosure) and 'Seele' (soul). Unlike Michael's, John Kipling's body was never found.

185 *ASC*: Army Service Corps.

189 *gardener*: see John 20: 15.

190 *Magdalene*: traditionally identified with the woman in Luke 7: 37–50, 'a sinner' who was forgiven 'for she loved much'.

191 THE EYE OF ALLAH: written July 1924 (CK). First published *Strand Magazine*, *McCall's Magazine*, Sept. 1926. Collected *Debits and Credits*. Kipling got information on medical history from his friend Sir William Osler, Regius Professor of Medicine at Oxford, whose student Charles Singer would compile a standard work on the subject. In 1914 Osler ran a celebration of the 700th anniversary of Roger Bacon, of which Kipling requested the proceedings (KJ, June 1983). Another source for the story is Abbot Gasquet, *English Monastic Life* (Methuen, 1904) (G), of which there is a copy in Kipling's study. Other details correspond

with Matthew Paris's *Historia Anglorum* (*English History 1235–1273*, trans. Bohn, 1852) (MP).

192 *Cantor*: was responsible for training an abbey's choir, also head librarian and archivist; the Sub-Cantor was his assistant (G).

Magnificat: Luke 1: 46–55.

193 *Cathedral*: the Cathedral at Burgos, Spain, was founded in 1221 and built over several centuries.

Granada: remained under Moorish rule until 1492.

clergy: more usually 'benefit of clergy', who could not be tried for certain offences except by ecclesiastical courts.

Infirmarian: in charge of the hospital. G says the holder of this office should be 'gentle . . . and good-tempered, kind, compassionate to the sick . . .'.

night-boots: made of cloth lined with fur, and worn by monks both for warmth and to muffle footsteps on stone during the Great Silence from Compline to Prime (G).

Mansura: St Louis of France was defeated and captured in this battle in 1250. A number of lesser prisoners were taken to Cairo and only ransomed many months later (MP).

194 *Abana and Pharpar*: see 2 Kgs 5: 12.

de Sanford: the de San(d)fords included a bishop; a preceptor of the Templars; Nicholas, 'second to no knight in England for bravery'; and his sister, governess to a royal princess (MP).

Magdalene: Luke 8: 2.

196 *cornelian*: according to a book on gems in Kipling's possession, wearing red stones was thought to check bleeding, while the cornelian also had power to relieve the pains of childbirth and 'banish all dark forebodings'.

197 *De Virtutibus Herbarum*: by St Albertus Magnus.

gloomy Cistercians: as opposed to the Benedictines, who encouraged music and the arts.

198 *Torre*: an Abbey on the Devon coast.

pulled his hair: G says that in some monasteries the Cantor was forbidden to pull choirboys' hair, the schoolmaster being the only person allowed to do so.

199 *Roger*: Rogerius Salernitanus, author of *Chirurgia*. The school of Salerno pioneered the study of anatomy and surgery.

physicus . . . sacerdos: scientist before priest.

friar: Roger Bacon taught at Oxford and Paris. He became a Franciscan friar in about 1254.

Didymus: St Thomas the Apostle was 'called Didymus', also Doubting Thomas (see John 21: 24–8).

200 *Bernard*: Bernard of Morlaix (or of Cluny), author of *De Contemptu Mundi*, in which he denounced wealthy clerics like Stephen who kept mistresses and entertained lavishly.

De Contemptu Mundi: (author's note) 'Hymn No. 226, A. and M., "The world is very evil." ' The hymn (by J. M. Neale) renders the rest of this passage:

> The times are waxing late;
> Be sober and keep vigil,
> The Judge is at the gate;
> The Judge who comes in mercy,
> The Judge who comes with might,
> Who comes to end the evil,
> Who comes to crown the right.

201 *. . . immedicabile cancer*: Ovid, *Metamorphoses*, ii. 825: 'the disease of an incurable cancer is wont to spread in all directions . . .'.

De Re Rustica: 1st century BC; see part XII, 'The Site of the Farmhouse'.

202 *St Benedict*: in the 6th century he laid down a rule for religious life, dividing the day into periods totalling 4 hours in prayer, 4 hours reading, and 6 hours manual work.

Demon: usually 'daemon' or 'daimon', a spirit half-way between gods and men. See also *SOM*, p. 208.

Peregrinus: Peter Peregrinus de Maricourt, described as the ideal scholar in Bacon's *Opus Tertium*.

Aegina: a Greek surgeon in 7th-century Alexandria, author of *Epitomae Medicae*.

Apuleius: refers to the *Herbarium* of Apuleius Platonicus, re-written for Christian readers, with additions from other sources; its text was much corrupted. Also known as Pseudo-Apuleius.

204 *Non nobis*: 'not unto us [the glory]'. Ps. 115: 1.

Snakes of Aesculapius: as wound round the caduceus that is the doctor's badge.

205 . . . *unknown for horrible*: possibly adapted from Tacitus, *Agricola*, 30, 'omne ignotum pro magnifico est', everything unknown is accounted glorious.

206 *supernaculum*: drop small enough to stand on the thumbnail.

207 *compasses*: the description that follows is of an 18th-century compass microscope with a lieberkuhn mirror; no such thing existed in the 13th century, although Arab scholars such as Alhazen had studied lenses and mirrors.

208 *Opera*: from Church of England Matins, 'Oh all ye works of the Lord, bless ye the Lord . . .'.

209 *Pope*: Cardinal Falcodi became Pope Clement IV in 1265. In 1266 he sent for a copy of Roger Bacon's works, but after his death in 1268 Bacon was imprisoned for teaching 'suspected novelties'. From this remark the dinner-party can be dated as either 1266 or 1267.

green-sick: green-sickness or chlorosis is a form of anaemia attacking girls between 15 and 25 years of age; it was known to the ancients as 'the disease of virgins'.

211 *dark age*: in England, Henry III had been fighting with his barons, whose leader Simon de Montfort was killed at the battle of Evesham in 1265. In Italy the Pope and the Emperor had been at war; the Holy Office had recently been founded at Rome to combat heresy. It was about ten years since the French had bloodily put down the Albigensian heretics. Some forty years before, Eastern Europe had been devastated by the Mongols under Gengis Khan.

212 THE LAST ODE: another of Kipling's Horace imitations. The poet is writing on his deathbed, a few days after the death of his friend and patron Maecenas.

prophesied: Virgil's fourth Eclogue foretells the birth of a child who will bring about a new golden age. This was interpreted by Christians as a prophecy of the coming of Christ.

213 DAYSPRING MISHANDLED: written Dec. 1926–Jan. 1927 (CK), partly in Paris. First published in *Strand Magazine* (*SM*), July 1928. Collected in *Limits and Renewals*.

213   *C. Nodier:* the fairy's song from 'La Fée aux Miettes':

> It's me! It's me! It's me!
> I am the mandrake!
> Daughter of fine days who wakes at dawn,
> And who sings for you!

Nodier's narrator visits a lunatic asylum and in the garden meets the fairy's 'husband', searching a bed of mandrakes for the one that sings her song; he believes that unless he finds it she must die. He describes her as an old dwarf beggar-woman who, after he passed the ordeals she set him, revealed herself as the eternally beautiful Belkiss, Queen of Sheba and widow of King Solomon (see 'The Butterfly that Stamped', *Just So Stories*). The mandrake, a poisonous plant of the potato family, is a dangerous emetic and subject of many legends; sedative and aphrodisiac qualities were once attributed to it. It was said to grow from the seed of a dead murderer, and to scream when pulled from the ground.

Vidal Benzaquen: (author's note) ' "The Village that voted the Earth was Flat," *A Diversity of Creatures*' (where the name is spelt Benzaguen).

215   *came in:* 'came in, when doubtless he would have led the new dawn' (*SM*).

speciality: 'speciality which would not lay him open to too much criticism' (*SM*).

216   *something:* Angus Wilson (1977, pp. 336–7) suggests that Castorley, who hated her for turning him down, declared that her paralysis was due to 'syphilis contracted by whoring'. But she could have caught it innocently from her 'unworthy' husband.

experiments: Kipling's daughter (Carrington, 1955, p. 516) says that her father made a hobby of 'forging' old documents. See also the illustration 'Manie Mouths of Amazons River' with 'The Beginning of the Armadilloes' (*Just So Stories*).

218   *Alva:* Commander of the army of Phillip II of Spain and conqueror of the Netherlands.

woman: 'woman with one side of her face out of drawing' (*SM*).

Dan: properly a title of respect, as in 'Dan Chaucer, well of English undefiled' (Spenser).

220   *duresse:* strict confinement.

221 *KBE*: Knight[hood] of the Order of the British Empire.

222 *Empire*: a music-hall in Leicester Square, where the Promenade was famous as a resort of prostitutes.

fashion: see Ernest Dowson, 'Non sum qualis eram sub regno Cynarae.'

223 *Atrib.*: 'Here is kind Mother Church [ecca = ecclesia], bringing me [i.e. the text he is copying] with her as a welcome [gift]. Nicolaus of Artois [Atrebensis].' 'Alma Mater Ecclesia' are the first words of a number of Latin hymns.

224 *KBE*: (author's note) 'Officially it was on account of his good work in the Department of Co-ordinated Supervisals, but all true lovers of literature knew the real reason, and told the papers so.'

Knight: see Chaucer, *Canterbury Tales*, Prologue, l. 72.

225 *it was*: 'it was—going on for twelve years now' (*SM*).

226 *get*: (author's note)

> 'Illa
> alma
> Mater
> ecca
> secum
> afferens
> me
> acceptum
> Nicolaus
> Atrib.'

The first two letters spell 'Iames A Manallace fecit' ('James A. Manallace made [or did] it').

230 *Friar's Balsam*: a patent medicine which, when mixed with boiling water, produced a pungent steam, inhaled to relieve respiratory congestion.

231 *since . . . married*: this phrase not in *SM*.

234 THE MANNER OF MEN: written either July 1927 or June 1928 (CK). First published *London Magazine* (*LM*), Sept. 1930. Collected in *Limits and Renewals*.

brailed itself: was hauled in.

dole-bread: official allowance of flour or grain to the poor of Rome.

235 *screw in*: the cargo was covered by a layer of wool, then forced
down by a system of screws operating a ram. This practice
strained the timbers and caused leaks, especially if the wool got
wet.

undergirt: a hawser was passed under and round the hull and
strained taut, to keep the planks above the hold from opening.

236 *single-banker*: powered by one bank of oars.

Tomi: a Black Sea port in Scythia.

Mango: (Latin) slave-trader.

Dacian: from an area between the Danube and the Carpathians,
now mostly in Romania.

Baeticus: from Baetica, the southern province of Roman Spain.

overside: as a libation to the gods.

He did . . . early: this sentence not in *LM*.

237 *Forum Julii*: modern Fréjus.

pickle: brine; i.e. he was low in the water.

Myra: now called Demre, a village between Finike and Kaş in
south-west Turkey; then a busy port.

238 *Cnidus*: on the Reşadiye peninsula, near Datça.

Fairhaven: Kaloi Limenes, on the south coast of Crete. For this
and the following events, see Acts 27 and 28.

239 *coasters*: (author's note) 'Quabil meant the coasters who worked
their way by listening to the cocks crowing on the beaches they
passed. The insult is nearly as old as sail.'

Phenike . . . cape: Phenike is now Matala on the Bay of Mesara;
Cape Lithinon.

240 *scourgings . . . Beasts*: see 2 Cor. 11: 24–5; 1 Cor. 15: 32.

the last!: echoes have been found in this verse both from the
nurse's speech at the opening of Euripides' *Medea*, and from
Callimachus (285–247 BC), *Epigrams*, XIX.

241 *Clauda*: now Gavdos, an island south of Crete.

244 *bowers . . . kedge*: 'bowers' are bow anchors, 'stream' is a small
stern anchor, and 'kedge' the smallest anchor, which could be
used in a ship's boat.

245 *surf*: see *Odyssey*, ix. 482–5.

245 *achators*: sutlers or caterers.

247 *Narbo*: Narbonne.

248 *Strategos*: (Greek) general, governor, or high-ranking official.

249 *snake*: see Acts 28: 3–6. Thessaly was famous for witchcraft.

     after a silence: these words not in *LM*.

250 *I . . . men*: 1 Cor. 9: 22.

251 'PROOFS OF HOLY WRIT': title from *Othello*, III. iii. Written Feb.
     1932–Aug. 1933 (CK). First published *Strand Magazine*, Apr.
     1934. Collected only in *Uncollected Prose*, SB. John Buchan is
     said to have given Kipling the idea for this story at a dining-club;
     the critic George Saintsbury helped with details (see *SOM* p. 86
     and *KJ*, Dec. 1989, pp. 18–27). Kipling had also seen a team of
     Catholic priests at work on biblical texts while visiting Cardinal
     Gasquet at Rome in 1917 (letter to Mrs Kipling and Elsie, 7 May
     1917, KP.) The story takes place in approximately 1611, at
     Shakespeare's home near Stratford-upon-Avon.

     Dekker: this quarrel is known as the War of the Theatres,
     1599–1601, in which John Marston, Thomas Dekker, and Ben
     Jonson lampooned each other in their plays.

     trade: see Dekker, *Satiromastix* (1601), IV. iii. 157–9. Jonson's
     stepfather was a master-bricklayer who had tried unsuccessfully
     to make the boy follow his trade.

252 *face*: *Satiromastix*, IV. iii. 92–4.

     humour: Jonson's first success was *Every Man in his Humour*
     (1597). *Every Man out of his Humour* (1599) included two
     characters satirizing Dekker and Marston.

     Gabriel: Jonson killed Gabriel Spencer in a duel in 1598. He was
     tried, escaped hanging by pleading benefit of clergy, and was
     branded instead.

     Behemoth: described in Job 40: 15 (said to be a hippopotamus).

     sea-beaches: see *The Winter's Tale*, III. iii.

253 *teres atque rotundus*: smooth and round.

     . . . sphere: *The Fall of Sejanus* (1603), I. l. 3: '*Silius*: Indeed, this
     place is not our sphere.' Shakespeare acted in the play, but it is
     not known which part he played.

     write that: see poem 'The Coiner' (*Limits and Renewals*); also
     'Shakespeare and the Tempest', *The Spectator*, 2 July 1898,

Uncollected Prose, SB. Kipling's theory was that Shakespeare met some drunken sailors in a tavern, who were newly returned from the voyage described in Jourdan, *A Discovery of the Barmudas* (1610).

254   *How . . . practise 'em*: *Sejanus*, v. xx. 878–9.

      Miles Smith: was appointed, with Thomas Bilson, to make a final revision of the text of the Old Testament for the King James Bible, first published in 1611. Later Bishop of Gloucester.

255   *Geneva . . . Great*: translations of the Bible into English: Coverdale's (1535), Matthews's (1537), the Great Bible (1539–41), the Genevan (1560), the Bishops' (1568), the Rheims (1582), the Douai (1609–10). Matthews's, the Great, and the Bishops' were used by the Church of England. The Rheims, produced by Jesuits, was illegal under Queen Elizabeth I.

      Condell: an actor and shareholder in Shakespeare's company who (with Heminge) edited the plays for publication in 1623 (the First Folio).

      armiger: one entitled to bear heraldic arms. Shakespeare's father received a grant of Arms in 1596, later borne by Shakespeare himself.

256   *Holofernes*: comic character in *Love's Labour's Lost*, fond of using Latin tags.

257   *Demon*: inspiration; see note to p. 202, also Introduction, p. xii–xiii.

258   *rams'-horns*: see Josh. 6: 4.

260   *Greek word*: it is not clear what Kipling means here. The word might be '*amphibrachys*' ('both ends short'), a metrical foot stressed short–long–short, detected by Saintsbury in the words 'shall be thy'. ' "Both hands" ' may suggest to Jonson that Shakespeare has confused the last two syllables with Greek *brachion* (arm). In 'To the Memory of My Beloved, the Author, Mr William Shakespeare' (1623) Jonson wrote 'thou hadst small Latin, and less Greek.'

261   *Boanerges*: loud-voiced preacher (see Mark 3: 17).

      upsee-dejee: combines 'upsee-Dutch', a drinking term used by Jonson in *The Alchemist*, with 'ajee' = askew.

      burned: the Globe theatre would burn down in 1613.

262   *markets?*: Ezek. 27: 3 and 25 (slightly misquoted).

262 *Kit*: Christopher Marlowe was killed in a tavern brawl in 1593.

263 '. . . *with you.*': see *The Alchemist*, v. v. 104–5.

264 'TEEM'—A TREASURE-HUNTER: begun Jan. 1935 (CK). First published *Strand Magazine*, Jan. 1936. Collected in *Thy Servant a Dog and other Dog Stories* and *Uncollected Prose* (SB). In Mar. 1935 Kipling had corresponded with a Pierre Menanteau at Evreux in France, who sent him particulars of the training of truffle-dogs, and with other unnamed sources at Cahors-en-Quercy (*KJ*, Dec. 1967, pp. 5–7). Parallels have been noticed (*KJ*, Sept. 1937, p. 75 ff.) between Teem's life and Kipling's. Bodelsen (1967, pp. 79–80) compares Teem's art with the writer's. However Kipling's daughter insisted that it was simply a story about a dog (*KJ*, Dec. 1967, p. 5). Many expressions are taken from the French, for example the formation 'clickety' from 'cliquetis', rattle or clicking.

C'est lui: that's him.

265 '*born*': a 'chien de race' is a pedigree dog. 'Born' = 'né', of noble or illustrious birth.

266 *Salers*: district of Auvergne, noted for a breed of strong and enduring draught cattle.

267 *Lingua canina*: dog-language, with an echo of *lingua franca*.

strawberry-scented: Perigord truffles are said to smell of strawberries.

268 *charcoal*: a pile of wood with air vents at base and centre was covered with turf or wet earth and fired from below. Skill was required to ensure the right temperature to produce charcoal.

269 *in the open*: once a standard treatment for tubercular patients.

270 *papers*: the Ferret and the Goose appear to be emissaries of a welfare organization, anxious to confine the girl in an isolation hospital; but some readers have seen them as debt collectors.

gentilhommier: (French) gentlemanly. This does not seem to be a correct usage.

274 '*Aa—or*': (author's note) 'Cahors?' (see headnote).

277 *comminations*: threats.

sans-kennailerie: compounded from 'sansculotte' (literally 'without breeches', member of a French revolutionary mob), 'canaille' (French for rabble) and 'kennel'.

277 *dried skins*: the local saddler, who would make, repair, and sell leather articles.

281 *gentilhommier*: again Kipling seems to have used this word incorrectly—it is an adjective, not a noun. It does not normally mean an upstart; he may have been thinking of *gentilhommière* (a gentleman's country home) or *gentilhommerie* (gentry), both of which have, or had, a pejorative sense implying pretension.

THE WORLD'S CLASSICS

A Select List

SERGEI AKSAKOV: A Russian Gentleman
Translated by J. D. Duff
Edited by Edward Crankshaw

HANS ANDERSEN: Fairy Tales
Translated by L. W. Kingsland
Introduction by Naomi Lewis
Illustrated by Vilhelm Pedersen and Lorenz Frølich

JANE AUSTEN: Emma
Edited by James Kinsley and David Lodge

Mansfield Park
Edited by James Kinsley and John Lucas

ROBERT BAGE: Hermsprong
Edited by Peter Faulkner

WILLIAM BECKFORD: Vathek
Edited by Roger Lonsdale

CHARLOTTE BRONTË: Jane Eyre
Edited by Margaret Smith

THOMAS CARLYLE: The French Revolution
Edited by K. J. Fielding and David Sorensen

LEWIS CARROLL: Alice's Adventures in Wonderland
and Through the Looking Glass
Edited by Roger Lancelyn Green
Illustrated by John Tenniel

GEOFFREY CHAUCER: The Canterbury Tales
Translated by David Wright

ANTON CHEKHOV: The Russian Master and Other Stories
Translated by Ronald Hingley

JOSEPH CONRAD: Victory
Edited by John Batchelor
Introduction by Tony Tanner

CHARLES DICKENS: Christmas Books
Edited by Ruth Glancy

ANTHONY TROLLOPE: The American Senator
Edited by John Halperin

Dr. Wortle's School
Edited by John Halperin

Orley Farm
Edited by David Skilton

VILLIERS DE L'ISLE-ADAM: Cruel Tales
Translated by Robert Baldick
Edited by A. W. Raitt

VIRGIL: The Aeneid
Translated by C. Day Lewis
Edited by Jasper Griffin

HORACE WALPOLE : The Castle of Otranto
Edited by W. S. Lewis

IZAAK WALTON and CHARLES COTTON:
The Compleat Angler
Edited by John Buxton
Introduction by John Buchan

OSCAR WILDE: Complete Shorter Fiction
Edited by Isobel Murray

The Picture of Dorian Gray
Edited by Isobel Murray

ÉMILE ZOLA:
The Attack on the Mill and other stories
Translated by Douglas Parmeé

A complete list of Oxford Paperbacks, including The World's Classics, OPUS, Past Masters, Oxford Authors, Oxford Shakespeare, and Oxford Paperback Reference, is available in the UK from the Arts and Reference Publicity Department (RS), Oxford University Press, Walton Street, Oxford OX2 6DP.

In the USA, complete lists are available from the Paperbacks Marketing Manager, Oxford University Press, 200 Madison Avenue, New York, NY 10016.

Oxford Paperbacks are available from all good bookshops. In case of difficulty, customers in the UK can order direct from Oxford University Press Bookshop, Freepost, 116 High Street, Oxford, OX1 4BR, enclosing full payment. Please add 10 per cent of published price for postage and packing.